BRENDA NOVAK

TRUST Me

MIRA®

MIRA®

Recycling programs
for this product may
not exist in your area.

ISBN-13: 978-0-7783-2903-9

TRUST ME

Copyright © 2008 by Brenda Novak.

For questions and comments about the quality of this book please contact us
at Customer_eCare@Harlequin.ca.

www.MIRABooks.com

Printed in U.S.A.

To the editors, agents, authors,
fans and friends who've come together to help me
raise hundreds of thousands of dollars for
diabetes research. Your generosity is an
inspiration. May all that positive energy
return in the form of blessings to your own life.

Together, we can make a difference!

Dear Reader,

Welcome to my new series! I generally like to write about small towns (if you've read my Stillwater trilogy you've probably guessed this), but I'm setting this story in my *home*town. Sacramento is a bit of a paradox. The metropolitan area contains more than two million people (the fourth largest urban area in California), yet it feels like a small farming community. Located in the Central Valley, we're surrounded by dairy farms, rice fields, almond orchards and places like Sutter's Fort and Coloma—relics of the Gold Rush. The heroine of this particular novel lives in the San Joaquin River delta. Sacramento's delta is a place with its own peculiarities—including towns that consist of no more than four corners, myriad waterways, bridges and wetlands.

It seemed appropriate to begin this series in Sacramento because the genesis of The Last Stand is my online auction for diabetes research—another charitable organization that started in this city. I simply translated the passion, drive and determination I feel about fighting the illness my youngest son has into the passion, drive and determination Skye Kellerman feels about protecting the victims of violent crime. The cases she handles are varied and certainly challenging, but you'll soon see that the most frightening case she faces is her own.

In *Stop Me* and *Watch Me,* you'll learn more about Skye's two friends, Jasmine and Sheridan, both of whom are partners in The Last Stand. They have their own reasons for getting involved—and those reasons are every bit as compelling as Skye's.

Please visit www.brendanovak.com, where you can take a virtual tour of The Last Stand office, read a prologue to this story that doesn't appear anywhere else, download a free screen saver just for signing up on my mailing list, enter my monthly drawings for prizes—and more. You can also check out the items in the annual Online Auction for Diabetes Research. I love to hear from my readers, so feel free to drop me a note. (If you don't have e-mail access, please write to P.O. Box 3781, Citrus Heights, CA 95611.)

Here's wishing you many hours of reading pleasure!

Brenda Novak

Hell is empty and all the devils are here.

The Tempest
—William Shakespeare

1

"You already heard, right?"

David Willis glanced up at the man leaning into the cubicle surrounding his cluttered desk. Detective "Tiny" Wyman, his best friend on the force and a damn good cop, was even larger than he was, with skin like burnished copper and a ready smile that always seemed at odds with the depth of sadness in his brown eyes. He took his crime-fighting seriously; he also wasted few words. When he talked, most people listened. Including David.

"Heard what? That I'm behind on my paperwork again?" he joked.

Tiny shoved giant hands into the pockets of his khaki pants, but the casual pose didn't make him look any more comfortable in his clothes. Tiny just wasn't the kind of man who was meant to wear slacks and a sports jacket, let alone a tie. "You're always behind on your paperwork," he grumbled with a crooked grin. "You think I'd waste my valuable time pointin' that out?"

When his smile didn't linger, David knew he

hadn't stopped by to spar with him. "No," he said. "What's up?"

Tiny yanked at his tie as if it were choking him. "'Member that guy we put away for attackin' that little blond woman in the middle of the night?"

David had handled enough cases over his thirteen years with the Sacramento PD that, with such a sketchy description, he might not have instantly recalled this particular assault. But Tiny's mention of "that little blond woman" brought the details immediately to mind. Probably because those details hadn't been that deeply buried to begin with. He hadn't talked to Skye in a few months, but she was never far from his thoughts. "Yeah, I remember. Burke got eight to ten."

"Turns out it'll be closer to three."

Rocking back in his chair, David tossed his pen on the stack of paperwork he'd been forcing himself to complete. "I knew he was coming up for his first parole hearing. But last I heard, there wasn't a snowball's chance in hell he was going to get it."

"He shouldn't have gotten it," Tiny responded. "Burke is dangerous. But..." He gave up fiddling with his tie, his attitude one of surrender to another day at the office. "I guess he ratted out a fellow inmate, which meant San Francisco PD could close two previously unsolved homicides. They recommended him to the parole board."

David shot to his feet. "Didn't anyone read my damn letter? Why didn't they call us first? Check this guy out?"

"Apparently they contacted Chief Jordan several weeks ago."

"Did he tell them the body count along the river stopped once our friendly dentist went to prison?"

"Of course. And they said it could just as easily be a coincidence." Tiny finally cracked his usual broad smile. "*I* say they can bank on our intuition. But they want more."

More. That was why the chief had questioned him about the unsolved cases, wanting to know if he was any closer to developing a solid connection to Oliver Burke. Jordan had been looking for something tangible to contest San Francisco's opinions. And David hadn't been able to give it to him. But their meeting hadn't concerned him too much. He hadn't realized what was on the line. He'd figured he'd have at least two more years to uncover the missing link.

"This is bullshit." David nudged his friend aside as he squeezed through the opening of his cubicle, intent on finding Jordan. But Tiny grabbed his arm.

"Save your breath, man. There's nothing he can do. The decision's been made. Dr. Burke walks next week."

"Next *week?* Doesn't anyone care what he might do?" Two other detectives in the violent crime unit stuck their heads out into the hall. David used a pointed stare to encourage them to mind their own business and shifted his attention back to Tiny.

"Seems that San Francisco cares more about closing old cases," Tiny said. "By rewarding Burke, they give others an incentive to step forward. There're some gangbangers in there who know a lot of shit. I think the SFPD would've fought this all the way to the governor, trying to get a pardon if they had to."

Obviously, it hadn't been necessary to go that far. Burke's early release had been far easier to accomplish than David would've believed possible. "But if he attacks again, he'll know better than to leave his victim alive to testify against him. He made that mistake once and it landed him in prison."

"Which was Chief Jordan's argument."

"And?"

"He was told we can't take every 'might' into account or we'd never be able to do our jobs."

"Skye Kellerman is a 'might' that should matter!"

Tiny ran a hand over his bald head. "She matters to *you,* right?"

As usual, Tiny's voice was a low rumble, but David couldn't help noticing the subtle inflection. He ignored it, as well as the memory of Tiny warning him that he was getting too emotionally involved with Skye. Then, as now, he'd been trying to reconcile with his ex-wife.

"I wouldn't put it past Burke to seek her out—to take what he couldn't get from her, along with an extra measure of revenge." The image created by his own words made him sick.

Tiny's gaze remained steady. "Neither would I."

"We have to do something."

"What? Unless we find the proof we're missing on those old murders, or he commits another crime, there's nothin' we can do." He released a long, laborious sigh. "You want me to call her?"

David wished he could let Tiny deliver the news. Or someone else. This was the last thing he wanted to tell Skye. But he refused to take the easy way out. It had to be him. "No, I'll do it."

"You're sure?"

"I'm sure." With a curse, he smacked the divider as Tiny left. Tiny didn't bother to look back. He knew David too well, shared his frustration. But several heads popped into the hall again.

"What are you staring at?" David growled.

Everyone disappeared, but intimidating his coworkers didn't make him feel any better. How was he going to tell Skye that the fear she faced daily—after surviving Burke's attack—was about to get a lot worse?

Skye Kellerman's shoulder blades tensed as she heard tires in her gravel drive. It was a cold morning in early January, not dark, but a thick blanket of fog made her feel completely isolated. Cut off from the rest of the world.

Vulnerable...

Hurrying to the antique secretary she'd inherited, along with the house, when her mother passed away a year earlier, she selected her Kel-Tec P-3AT semiautomatic handgun over her Sig P232—because it was lighter, thinner and easier to conceal. Carrying it with her, she ran to get a T-shirt from her bedroom. She wanted to cover the cleavage and stomach revealed by the jogging bra and Lycra shorts she wore while working out. She was self-conscious about her breast size, which drew more attention than she felt comfortable with.

A car door slammed and footsteps approached the house. Heavy footsteps. The footsteps of a man.

Pulling on a baggy T-shirt that said The Last Stand: Where Victims Fight Back, she went to peek through the wooden shutters of her front windows, then the peephole she'd drilled in the door. But the fog was too thick, the morning shadows too murky to make out more than a large, dark shape coming toward her.

Shit.

The metallic taste of fear rose in her throat and soured her stomach. This was probably just someone who was lost and needed directions. Sherman Island, which only had 175 residents, sat in the heart of the Sacramento River Delta. Few outsiders were familiar with the sloughs, natural waterways, drawbridges and levees that made the wetlands so unique. But she would no longer assume that strangers were safe. Not since she'd been startled awake in the middle of the night by a man wearing a hood and wielding a knife.

Burke was now in prison—thank God—but because of The Last Stand, the victim's support organization she'd started with her friends Sheridan Kohl and Jasmine Stratford two years ago, she'd made a lot of enemies. This could easily be Tamara Lind's husband, a wife-beater who blamed Skye for Tamara's recent desertion. Last week, he'd threatened to bomb The Last Stand. Or it could be Kevin Sheppard. Kevin had appeared at their offices after a flurry of newspaper articles praising TLS for financially backing an investigator who'd uncovered new evidence on a high-profile murder. Kevin had wanted to help out as a volunteer, but Skye turned him away when a background check revealed accusations of stalking, at which point he'd grown unreasonably angry and stormed out. No one had seen him since.

The doorbell sounded, followed almost immediately by a sharp rap.

She imagined turning off the alarm and opening the door as far as the chain allowed, only to have it kicked wide—and felt her palm begin to sweat on the butt of her gun. *Calm down.*

She had damn good aim. But nerves could wreak

havoc on the best marksman in the world. So she wouldn't open the door. She'd pretend to be gone and hope he'd go on his way.

Holding her breath, she pressed her spine more firmly to the wall, wondering what the students from her various shooting classes would think if they could see her now—sweating and shaking over some fog and an unexpected visitor. Most viewed her as indestructible when she had a gun in her hand. They acted like their own guns made them invincible, too. But they didn't understand what it was really like in a desperate standoff, didn't fully grasp that a woman could own a million firearms and *still* be vulnerable. Unless she was prepared to pull the trigger.

Was she willing to kill Kevin Sheppard? Or Tamara's estranged husband?

If she had to…

She hadn't made a move or a sound, but her visitor didn't seem to be buying that she wasn't at home. He rang the doorbell again. Knocked. Then his body blocked the window as he tried to see in.

"Skye? Skye, are you there? It's me, Detective Willis."

Exhaling slowly, she consciously released the pressure of her fingers on the gun. David… She wasn't in mortal danger. But knowing *he* was standing on her front step certainly didn't slow her heart rate.

"Your car's in the drive," he yelled. "You gonna answer?"

Taking another steadying breath, she flipped the safety on her gun, dropped it in the pocket of her coat, which hung on the hall tree by the door, and dashed a hand across her moist upper lip.

"Skye?"

"Coming." After shutting off the alarm system, she slid the chain aside, turned the dead bolt and opened the door.

He was wearing a green shirt and tie and looked good—too good. His tie was a little dressy for his shirt, but his style was as unique as it was appealing. Sort of James Dean "cool" mixed with Johnny Depp "different." Briefly, she remembered the time, nearly a year ago, when he'd brushed his lips against hers, then kissed her more deeply, pushing her up against the wall. In that moment, their volatile attraction had overcome reason and common sense.

"Hi." She smiled, hoping to appear unaffected, but their relationship was so complex, she couldn't take any encounter with him in stride. Especially an unexpected encounter. "What brings you out to the delta?"

His manner suggested this wasn't a social call. She almost wondered if he'd forgotten the night he'd come by to help her move and they'd nearly made love. "I need to talk to you. Can I come in for a minute?"

He was being so formal, so aloof. And he hadn't called. He'd shown up at her door. What was going on?

Stepping aside, she beckoned him past her, telling herself there was no reason for the knot in her stomach. The worst was behind her. No matter what happened from here on, she'd never have to go through the same hell again. And that was all that mattered. "Can I get you a cup of green tea?"

"Green tea?" he echoed, arching a dark eyebrow.

"Sorry. I don't have any coffee. I don't drink it anymore."

"I'll pass on the tea. I'm afraid my body wouldn't know what to do with something that healthy." His light green eyes seemed to take in every detail of her face and figure—which, in turn, made her far too aware of him. But he didn't indicate whether or not he liked what he saw. He kept whatever he was thinking locked behind an implacable expression. And a second later, he shifted his attention to his surroundings.

For the first time in a long while, Skye saw the inside of her house from someone else's perspective. In the living room, she'd removed her mother's dated "for company" couch, the walnut veneer side tables, the curio cabinets and vases filled with silk flowers—given them all to Jennifer and Brenna, her two stepsisters, who lived in southern California near their father. She'd replaced the furniture with free weights, an exercise bike, a treadmill, an aerobics step and a mat for yoga. Only a slice of kitchen could be seen from their vantage point, but it showed the small indoor garden where she grew herbs and wheat grass.

"Wow, I like what you've done to the place," he said.

His sardonic smile let her know he didn't consider it an improvement. She knew that in his view it served as further proof that her past was taking control of her life, which was something they'd argued about the last time they'd talked.

"Thanks. Seemed a pity to waste so much space."

"Forever practical."

She hadn't been practical at all. Until the early-morning hours of July 11th nearly four years ago, breaking a freshly manicured nail had been classified as a catastrophe. "Having to stab a rapist tends to change a person."

The muscle that twitched in his jaw revealed his displeasure. Evidently, she'd just reminded him of the purpose of his visit—if the scar on her cheek had ever let him forget it in the first place.

"Maybe you should sit down," he said.

"Why would I need to do that?"

He cleared his throat, clearly uncomfortable. "I have bad news."

You and your ex-wife have reconciled for good? She cringed at her thoughts, knowing that if it was true, she should be happy. David's eight-year-old son deserved the kind of family David was so determined to give him.

"I'm fine where I am." When she stubbornly raised her chin, the hard line of his mouth softened. "What's the matter?" she asked. "Can't you find any evidence that it was Burke who killed those other women?"

"No. Not yet."

The grudging sound of those words told her that the failure ate at him. David didn't like losing. Somehow it had become personal with Burke, more than just a job to David. But she couldn't help being disappointed. She'd been praying he'd finally prove that Burke was every bit as evil as she claimed. She didn't care what Burke's lawyers had argued at his trial—that it had been his first offense; that he had no history of violence; that his wife, the person who knew him best, swore he'd never even raised his voice to her; that he was a high-functioning, churchgoing, productive member of the community. Skye had been there that night. She'd *felt* his deadly intent.

"Have you changed your mind?" she asked. "Do you think it was someone else?"

He thrust his hands in his pockets. "No. It's him.

Same pattern of behavior, similar victims. The shoe imprint we found at one of the scenes fits his size feet, which are unusually small for a man."

"That's not enough?"

"There were no discernible characteristics, other than size, that we could point to in order to bring charges."

"I take it there've been no more bodies."

"Nothing similar to the other three."

So why was he here? Worried that Willis's determination was waning, she grabbed his arm—and felt him tense the moment she touched him. She couldn't tell if that was because he resented the contact or welcomed it, but she couldn't lose her only police support. Almost everyone else on the force resented The Last Stand because of the publicity it brought to unsolved or mishandled cases. "It's not too late," she told him. "We've got time. We have to figure out a way to keep Burke behind bars."

Visibly wincing, he pulled out of her grasp, and that was when the real terror set in. *"What?"* she said. "He's not free, is he? He's still in prison. They gave him eight to ten. You said that would most likely mean eight."

"I'm sorry, Skye," he muttered from between clenched teeth.

She couldn't catch her breath, couldn't slow her pulse. *"What are you saying?"*

"They're letting him go next week."

2

"What's wrong?"

Sheridan's voice sounded tinny as it came through the phone. Backing up to her kitchen counter, Skye pressed the handset more tightly to her ear, hoping it'd help her stop shaking. At least she'd managed to hold herself together until David left. She wouldn't have wanted him to see her fall apart. He felt as if he'd let her down, even though he'd done everything he could. "He…he's getting out," she whispered.

"Who's getting out?"

Her friend's words came in a rush, confusion as evident as concern. They'd dealt with so many victims of violent crime since they'd started The Last Stand that Skye could've been referring to a dozen different men. "Burke."

The shocked silence indicated that Sheridan recognized the name. "How?"

"The police have never been able to connect him to any other crime. Apparently he's done the prison system a great service by providing free dental work for the past three years. And he didn't actually get away with what he wanted to do to me before I stabbed him with the scissors I'd been using for my cross-stitch."

"But he got eight to ten. Most inmates in California serve at least half their time."

"Doesn't matter. He's getting out after only three. They're putting him on parole."

"No!"

"Yes," Skye said, but she still couldn't fully believe it. The guy had held a knife to her throat while stripping off her T-shirt and pajama bottoms. He'd touched her in cruel and intrusive ways, the memory of which made her nauseous.

"But…what about those murders?" Sheridan went on. "The three young women in the university area?"

Skye slid down the side of the cabinet to the floor. The fog was beginning to lift, as it usually did around noon, but the light trickling through the window above her kitchen sink only made her feel exposed. "Burke was good at covering his tracks. You know that. Our own investigators couldn't come up with any more than David already had." If David couldn't do it, no one could….

Normally, Sheridan would've jumped on Skye's inadvertent use of David's first name. But she was obviously too engrossed in the conversation to notice. "He's well-educated, smart," she said about Burke.

"And without a conscience," Skye added. "He's far from what he appears to be. I had a roommate. He must've spent time stalking me to know my habits, where my bedroom was, when I'd be alone. He targeted me, *planned* the attack. If it wasn't for the cross-stitch stuff I'd left on my nightstand, I would've been no different than those other girls who are now corpses, their cases unsolved."

"My God," Sheridan muttered.

A flashback of stabbing Burke caused Skye's muscles to cramp and ache. It had required much more strength than she would've guessed. She'd had to strike once, twice, three times before she could do enough damage to stop him, and he'd *still* gotten away. But not before his blood had burned like fire on her cold hands and spilled onto her sheets….

"What do I do?" she whispered. "I testified against him. The way he glared at me when they read the sentence…I don't think he'll forget that I'm the reason."

"Maybe you should go into hiding," Sheridan said.

Skye jerked up her head. "What happened to not letting fear rule our lives?"

"Just for a little while, until we see where he's going to settle, what he's going to do."

"He'll probably move back in with his family."

"Does he still have a family?"

It was Burke's wife who'd taken him to the emergency room the morning after Skye had stabbed him. The doctors had found his wounds so odd they'd contacted the police, which was how Burke had been caught and arrested. But Jane had supported her husband all through the trial. Skye could still hear her weeping uncontrollably when the verdict came in. "Probably. His wife insisted that he was innocent."

"I don't want to risk losing you, Skye. And you know what Jasmine would say. We're her only family now. After what happened to her sister, I'm sure she'd rather you played it safe."

Sighing, Skye rubbed her eyes. She had no business dragging Sheridan—or Jasmine for that matter—through this with her. They faced enough of their own demons. The three of them had first met at a victims' support group, where they'd become fast friends over innumerable cups of coffee—time spent trying to come to terms with the violent incidents that had transformed their lives.

"When we started TLS, we decided to be fearless, remember? We decided to take power away from the people who'd hurt us." Maybe she hadn't completely accomplished that. But she was trying. She couldn't just give up.

"But the man who frightens me most probably still lives across the country. I can't even imagine how difficult it would be to function when you could easily stumble upon the person who tried to kill you, walking in the street or shopping in the mall."

What was her alternative?

Skye imagined running, hiding, maybe relocating closer to her stepfather. But if Burke was truly bent on finding her, he'd be able to do so sooner or later because she refused to cut all ties with the people and places she loved, refused to let him cost her any more than he already had. Besides, she didn't feel that close to her stepfather. He'd moved in with her mother when Skye was nine and moved out again when she was thirteen. Although her own father had died in a skiing accident when she was two, and Joe was all she'd ever really had as a replacement, they'd lived together for barely four years.

In any case, she couldn't leave Sheridan and Jasmine to run The Last Stand alone. They were a small army fighting for the victims of senseless violence. That was the only way they could make sense of what had happened to them.

"It'll be okay." She straightened her spine. "It just… threw me for a minute." What had she been thinking? She didn't have the luxury of crumpling beneath this news. Maybe they'd failed to uncover a connection between Burke and those three murders. But they had to keep trying, especially now. Before he attacked someone else. One of the lives she saved could be her own.

"At least sell the house and buy a gated condo here in town," Sheridan was saying. She'd been urging Skye to do that for ages, but Skye couldn't let go of the delta house. She'd moved back home after the stabbing and spent those last years with her mother. This was all she had left of her only parent, all she had left of her childhood—that period of time when she'd been so innocent, so unaware of evil in the world. It wasn't as if a condo was safe, anyway. When she was attacked, she'd been sharing an apartment off American River Drive and Howe Avenue with a woman who'd since moved to a small town in Utah.

"Even that's too much of a concession. I'm going to live life on my own terms, not his." Or come as close as she could, one day at a time.

"I understand and yet…"

"And yet you're worried. Don't be. If Burke comes after me again, he'll get more than a pair of scissors in his chest."

She heard Sheridan's sigh. "Are you coming in today? A journalist from *River City Magazine* would like to speak to one of us. He's interested in doing an article. I thought we could use it to push ticket sales for our summer barbecue, since the issue comes out in May."

"Can't Jasmine do it?" Skye was scheduled to teach a new shooting class at the range, something she did on the side, after which she'd planned to take some flyers to Sacramento State University in hopes of recruiting more volunteers to work on future fund-raisers for TLS. But, after David's visit, she wasn't sure she could concentrate on either.

"Jasmine won't be available for a few days."

"Why not?"

"She got a call from Ft. Bragg. A little girl's gone missing up there. They're hoping for some help in locating her."

"Who's looking for help—the parents?" Skye asked, perplexed that Jasmine's notoriety had spread to a coastal town six hours away.

"No, the FBI."

"No kidding? I have yet to meet a detective who's friendly to the idea of using a psychic." Even David seemed resistant to the possibility that Jasmine possessed certain gifts.

"I'm guessing they're desperate, willing to try anything, but they didn't mention her psychic abilities when they called. They asked her to profile the kidnapper."

"The FBI has its own profilers. That's what they've always told her in the past. How many times has she been turned away?"

"A lot of things are changing now that she helped solve the Ubaldi case. I think the FBI is beginning to realize she's as good as any of theirs, maybe better."

"We could've told them that," Skye said. "So what's happening with the missing child?"

"I haven't heard. Jasmine couldn't have reached Ft. Bragg more than an hour ago." There was a brief pause. "Can you handle the journalist, Skye?"

Skye glanced at the clock. She was still rattled, afraid to step foot out of the house but, at the same time, determined to make sure Burke didn't hurt anyone else. She couldn't miss an opportunity to gain public support for those who felt lost or violated. "Of course. I'll reschedule my class for next Monday or Tuesday and be there as soon as possible."

Although it seemed to David as if the inverted delta where Skye lived, with its myriad natural and man-made channels, belonged in a world all its own, it was only an hour southwest of Sacramento, where she'd lived when she was attacked. Sherman Island was almost as close to the city of San Quentin, where one of the most famous prisons in the world existed in shocking contrast to the picturesque shores of San Francisco Bay and the affluent area surrounding it.

Burke was locked away in San Quentin, along with more than 5,000 other men, behind stone walls that were over a century and a half old. Notorious for its menacing appearance, as well as its green gas chamber, this prison provided a home for the worst of the worst. And David knew its bloody reputation was well-earned. Even death row was crowded. San Quentin housed around 600 condemned inmates. The rest of its population consisted of lifers and a lower percentage of men who, like Burke, were in for less time and a lesser crime.

As the police-issue sedan bumped against yet another drawbridge, David frowned at the prospect of seeing Burke again. He'd worked tough cases in the past, but he'd somehow managed to crack most of the big ones. Sometimes he got lucky and the right piece of evidence fell into his lap; other times it was sheer determination and hard work, his refusal to leave any stone unturned, that made the difference. Occasionally it was intuition. But nothing had brought him the answers he needed on the three young women who'd been murdered in homes along the American River, and the frustration was beginning to wear on him. Particularly now that Burke was getting out.

Calling ahead to make sure he could arrange a visitation, he turned off River Road onto 4 West. He wasn't sure why he felt compelled to speak to Burke face-to-face. He hadn't seen him since court, but he suspected Skye's attacker would be unlikely to share anything new. In the intervening years, David had tried to communicate with him more than once. Burke had refused to meet with him but accepted a handful of telephone calls. In each conversation, he'd played innocent, as if he could fool David as easily as he did everyone else.

But futile though it seemed, David couldn't let Burke disappear into society without one last attempt to engage him, to see if he could gain some scrap of information that might finally crack the difficult cases, now long cold, in Sacramento.

For Skye. For the others.

David hit the brakes and barely kept his coffee from tipping over as he ran into the bumper-to-bumper traffic clogging the San Rafael Bridge. The Bay Area was almost always congested. He preferred the slower pace of life in Sacramento. Although his parents and older sister—who'd recently divorced *again* and moved home—still lived in San Jose, he'd left two years after graduating from San Jose State with a B.S. in Forensic Science. He'd planned on becoming a scientist, but eighteen months of working on fiber analysis as an intern had turned out to be too tedious for him. That was why he'd changed his aspirations and become a police officer instead. He needed a job that allowed him to move around, change his days, talk to people—and he enjoyed the constant challenge.

Just as he reached the other side of the bridge, the fog cleared enough to show the prison, sitting off to one side, seemingly as benign as a college campus.

But the electrified perimeter fence, topped with barbed and razor wire, and the forbidding machine-gun towers, gave the reality of the place away as he drew closer. The somber air that pervaded the grounds hung over him far more densely than any fog as he drove into visitor parking, located a space and got out of his car.

There was something singularly hopeless about San Quentin. It had the state's only gas chamber and nearly twice as many inmates as the prison was originally designed to accommodate. Then there was the presence of so many notorious cold-blooded killers—Kevin Cooper, convicted and sentenced to death for the hatchet-and-knife massacre of the Ryen Family; Richard Allen Davis, who'd kidnapped and murdered Polly Klaas; Charles Ng, who'd tortured and murdered eleven people; Richard Ramirez, "The Night Stalker." Cary Stayner, Brandon Wilson, Scott

Peterson. The list went on and on, setting this place apart from any other on Earth. Sprawling over 435 acres, San Quentin was a contained city of the dammed, complete with its own zip code. According to anyone who'd been there, that was Hell, California 94964.

While he passed through the outer gate, the inner gate and the security checkpoints, David considered how living in such a place might affect a man like Burke. No doubt it'd fill him with indignation and rage. He'd thought he was too good to get caught. And once he'd been hauled in to stand trial, he'd expected to outmaneuver the system so he wouldn't have to pay for his crimes.

After David had firmly established his identity and the purpose for his visit, a female corrections officer showed him into a small visitor's booth. "Just a minute," she said and disappeared, probably to follow up with whoever had been ordered to bring Burke out of his cell.

As David waited on a hard metal chair in the cold, windowless room, he wondered if Burke would refuse to see him—but doubted it. Oliver would be too eager to let David know that he'd slipped beneath the net.

Sure enough, a door opened on the other side of the thick glass that divided the room, and Burke strode in. About five foot nine, with a medium build and sandy-blond hair, he looked thinner but more muscular than when David had seen him in the courtroom. He wasn't wearing handcuffs or shackles. With only six days until his release, he'd be a fool to break any of the rules and everyone recognized the unlikelihood of that happening.

It wasn't here that Burke would misbehave—it was out there, after he'd set up the veneer of normalcy that shrouded his sick intentions.

With a polite nod, he sat down and picked up the phone that would enable them to communicate. "Guess you heard the good news, eh?"

He was gloating, just as David had predicted. "I did," he said, holding a handset to his own ear.

"That's what playing by the rules will get you."

"Or snitching on a fellow inmate," David said mildly.

A dark cloud passed over Burke's even features. With his ice-blue eyes and delicate, almost feminine features, he seemed younger than his thirty-six years, more like a harmless yuppie than a convict. His non-threatening appearance definitely worked in his favor; at least it had with the jurors at his trial, who'd deliberated for hours before reaching a verdict. Even with a solid DNA profile proving it was Burke's blood on Skye's sheets, his family—the whole community—couldn't accept that a successful dentist with a loving wife and daughter and hundreds of devoted patients was capable of such a heinous crime.

"Johnny and I weren't friends," Burke said of the inmate he'd used. "I didn't even like him."

"Did *he* know that?" David asked.

Burke ignored the question. "The San Francisco police needed my help. They were grateful for it."

"Help that coincided nicely with your parole hearing, I might add. Congratulations on timing it so perfectly."

David expected a small smile or some other sign of acknowledgment. But Burke simply persisted in creating the image he was hoping to sell. "They know I'm not like the others in here."

Irritated, David couldn't resist pressing him a little

harder. "Do you think the families of the women you murdered believe you're any different?"

Silence. Then Burke chuckled in what David interpreted as mock sadness. "I'll never be able to convince you, will I?"

"You expect me to believe that bullshit you told the jury?"

"It's true."

"No, it's not." But Burke was such a skilled liar that some members of the jury had viewed rock-solid evidence with skepticism. As far as David was concerned, even the San Francisco police had been conned by this crafty man or they wouldn't have recommended him for parole no matter how many inmates he ratted out.

"Believe what you want." Burke waved his free hand. "It's over. It doesn't matter anymore."

"It matters to me." Withdrawing the pictures he'd brought, pictures of Meredith Connelly, Amber Farello and Patty Poindexter—the three girls murdered near the American River—David used his shoulder to support the phone and held them to the glass. "This is why."

As Burke's eyes moved from one photograph to the next, they flickered with recognition but not remorse. "I've told you already. I've never seen those girls before in my life. It's not as if they were my patients or anything."

Because he was too intelligent for that. He'd chosen random victims, victims in an area other than the one in which he lived, victims with no apparent tie to him. He thought he was smarter than the police, and it galled David no end that so far that seemed to be true.

"I won't give up, you know," David said. "Ever."

Burke held the phone casually, toying with the hem of his prison-issue jeans. "Then you'll be wasting your time."

David put the pictures back in his shirt pocket. "What will you do for a living when you get out?" The dental board had revoked Burke's license when he was convicted, so he couldn't establish a new practice in California. And if he tried to go elsewhere, a background check would reveal his criminal record.

For a moment, the congenial facade slipped and David glimpsed what he saw as the real Oliver Burke. Sullen. Full of self-pity. "Thanks to you, I've lost a vocation that required six years of schooling and several more years to develop into the success it was. My wife had to sell my practice for pennies on the dollar just to survive."

"Thanks to *me?*" David echoed. "*I'm* not the one who attacked a woman with a knife."

Their eyes locked. "She attacked *me*."

"You cut her."

"In self-defense."

David had the fleeting desire to feel his hands around Burke's neck, to choke the truth out of him if there was no other way. But he knew it was the anger and frustration that goaded him. He had to watch those negative emotions, remain in control. "The evidence doesn't support your story."

"It doesn't support hers, either. If I put a knife to her throat, where is it?"

At the challenge in Burke's voice, David tightened his grip on the phone. He'd get this little son of a bitch if it was the last thing he did. "That's what I'd like to know."

"There was never any knife." Burke stared at the

fingers of his left hand as he drummed them on the table. "We were making out, feeling each other up, when she suddenly freaked out and stabbed me with her sewing scissors. Then we started fighting over them."

More lies. Skye's injuries weren't consistent with the kind of puncture wounds she would've obtained had he used her scissors against her. There'd been a knife.

"All I did wrong was go home with her," he said. "And I've been through more than enough to pay for *that*. What man has never been tempted to stray?"

"Why'd you pick her?" David asked.

"She wanted me to pick her."

"You're dreaming again."

Burke shrugged. "You weren't there that night. You didn't see the way she smiled at me, the way she went for my zipper."

David arranged his features in a calm mask. Burke was on a fishing trip, trying to provoke him and, as much as David's heart pounded at the images Burke created, he refused to give him the upper hand. "You're quite a ladies' man, Oliver."

"A guy knows when a woman's coming on to him, especially when she wants him that bad."

"Didn't you ever think about your wife, your daughter, when you were planning your attacks on innocent women?"

"I didn't attack anyone. But if I *was* the type, I can't imagine I'd be thinking of my wife. What do *you* imagine when you look at a nude woman in *Playboy?*" He'd asked as if he sincerely wanted to know, but it was a rhetorical question he answered himself. "You dream of getting it on with someone like that, don't you? And let's be honest, Skye's as hot as any centerfold."

When David didn't respond, Oliver finally seemed to grow self-conscious. "Don't you agree?"

"Quit trying to play me."

Burke leaned forward, eyes gleaming. "I saw how you looked at her in that courtroom."

David twisted his mouth into a cocky smirk. He could act as well as this asshole. "That's the best you can do?"

With a sniff, Burke lost the smile and moved the phone to his other ear. "I know you want her. Any man would want to ride her."

"Like you wanted to?"

"Sure," he said flippantly. "Why else would I have gone home with her?"

"She doesn't remember ever seeing you before you broke in."

"She remembers."

"No, she doesn't. If anything, she tossed you a polite, vacant smile and continued on her way." That type of interaction happened between total strangers all the time. It had no meaning. Except to Oliver.

"That's what she says now."

"Where was it?" David persisted. "The grocery store? The movies? Driving along on the highway? Or did you see her while you were out biking? Is that how you picked your victims?"

Burke slowly rocked back. "I've tried to be nice to you, but it doesn't make any difference. You still badger me regardless."

"You and I are not friends," David pointed out. "We will never be friends. Just answer the question."

"I already did. In court." He'd claimed he found her pulled over on the side of the road, lost and in need of directions. He'd said she invited him to her house.

Which was total bullshit, of course.

"Why not repeat the lies now?" David said. "Afraid you'll get tangled up in them?"

"Maybe if you didn't get a hard-on every time you think of Skye, you'd be able to see that I got the worst of the encounter. I lost a lot of blood that night. I lost my dental practice, my house and most of my belongings. My family was publicly humiliated. And I've spent the last three *years* living in a four-by-ten cage, sleeping on a steel bed with a two-inch mattress. When I get to go outside, I spend my time ambling around a crowded cement yard between a cinder-block wall and a scaffold filled with guards holding rifles. And you know what I do? I count the holes made by the bullets that've been fired into the yard while trying to avoid any altercation that'll start the bullets raining down again." He folded his arms. "It's not safe in here."

David laughed. "That's a bit dramatic even for you. They use rubber bullets."

"They didn't used to. Anyway, have you ever been shot with a rubber bullet?"

"You look healthy enough to me."

"It's not safe," he repeated. "Why else would I ask my wife not to visit?"

The sudden mention of Jane took David by surprise. Oliver had never wanted to talk about his wife before. Why was she on his mind today? "Hasn't she been coming?"

"I haven't seen her since the first three months." He studied his nails, which were neatly clipped, as always. "I don't want her here if they're going to hassle her."

David decided to play along, let him talk. "Why would they hassle her?"

He pursed his lips. "You know the rules. She can't wear any denim-colored clothing so she won't get mistaken for an inmate. No shorts that show more than two inches of her thigh, no shirts that reveal her figure—no underwire bra, for Pete's sake. What woman doesn't wear an underwire bra these days? Jane's busty—like Skye."

Like Skye? The allusion bothered David, but he fought the impulse to clench his teeth.

"She needs the extra lift it gives her," Oliver continued. "But she doesn't want to explain that to a dirty old prison guard."

"Your wife can't make a few minor clothing adjustments?" David asked.

Staring morosely at his feet, Burke didn't answer.

David rested his elbows on the narrow ledge in front of him. "Or is there more to the story?"

"Being together but not being able to be together is more painful than not seeing her," he said after a long pause. "You want to touch but you can't. Not really." His chest rose as he took a deep breath. "Anyway, they subjected her to a degrading search every time she came. And they purposely frightened her by warning her that if she was taken hostage while she was here they wouldn't bargain for her release." He propped the phone against one shoulder and threaded his thin, milk-white fingers around one knee. "Of course, after that, a woman wouldn't want to come back. How do you think that would make the mother of a young child feel, to hear she could be taken hostage by one of the animals in this place and no one would care?"

He consistently separated himself from regular criminals, which confirmed what David had known all along—he saw a skewed version of reality, one so tainted by his own perspective he couldn't recognize the truth. "Any other policy would put visitors in even more danger."

Growing restless, Burke shifted in his seat. "But if something were to happen to her, who'd take care of our daughter?"

"Jane's waiting for you, then? You're still together?"

A small furrow formed in his wide forehead, and it occurred to David that he looked every bit as unlikely a killer as Scott Peterson. "Of course. I told you, she doesn't come because it's too hard. And too embarrassing. She's never even known a convict before. And now her husband's in prison?"

"There's only one person to blame for that."

A muscle twitched in Burke's cheek. "It's not who you think."

"You brought this on yourself."

"I don't want to talk about the past." Burke cleared his throat. "My wife knows Skye's a liar. Jane believes in me."

It was all David could do not to shake his head at the tremendous denial that kind of faith would require. Didn't Jane Burke realize how dangerous living with someone like Oliver could be? Didn't she want to do all she could to protect their daughter from future heartache if not physical harm?

"You'd be crazy to abuse that trust," he muttered.

"I'm not going to abuse it." He sounded so resolute that David almost believed him. It was that harmless-looking face, that "I'm no different from you" attitude.

It convinced practically everyone he was harmless. But David was finished with The Oliver Burke Show. This interview wasn't getting him anywhere.

Bringing an abrupt end to the meeting, he told Oliver he'd be watching him and hung up. But Oliver got him to grab the phone again by tapping on the glass.

"How is Skye, by the way?" he asked, as if truly concerned. "Has she recovered?"

"She's fine. Completely over it," David replied, but he knew it was a lie. If she was over it, she'd quit chasing ghosts, quit running herself ragged trying to help every victim in Sacramento.

"Good. And how does she like her new home?"

David's nerves tingled with heightened alert. Skye had only relocated a year ago. "What gives you the idea she moved?"

"I can't imagine she'd stay where she was."

That was no answer. Some people did stay, for whatever reason. "Skye has nothing to do with you. If you're as smart as you think you are, you'll leave her entirely alone."

"It's not as if she's been keeping a low profile," he said, raising an indignant hand to his unimpressive chest. "I've seen her on talk shows, advocating tougher sentences for 'monsters' like me. She's been in the papers, too. As a matter of fact, there was an article just a few weeks ago about that organization of hers. What's the name of it? The Last Stand?" He chuckled. "Give me a break. She doesn't know what a real monster can do. But that's like her, isn't it? To go charging after a cause?"

David's muscles bunched at the affectionate way he spoke of the woman he'd terrorized. "You don't even know her."

"What do you mean? I know her better than anyone else. Including you," he said. Then he hung up and knocked on the door to be taken away.

David didn't respond when the corrections officer opened a door on his own side of the room. He was too busy trying to process Oliver Burke's final words, the way he'd said Skye's name.

"Detective Willis?" the corrections officer prompted.

Blinking, David set the handset in its base and walked on leaden feet toward the exit.

3

The Last Stand was located on Watt Avenue in a flat-roofed white building constructed in the early seventies, when architecture—at least in Skye's opinion—had hit an all-time low. Made of cinder block and painted white, with red lava rocks on the roof, it wasn't pretentious, but it was conveniently located, only ten minutes from downtown toward the eastern suburbs, with excellent freeway access to both Interstate 80 and Highway 50. It was also on the ground floor. And the rent was affordable. They leased three thousand square feet for only $2,000 a month. They each had a private office. There was a small kitchen in back, two meeting rooms and a large classroom, in which they offered self-defense courses or gathered with the professionals they sometimes hired to assist their clients—bodyguards, private investigators, attorneys, psychologists.

As Skye found the right key to let herself in—the door was always locked because they accepted only pre-arranged appointments—she noticed a new flyer taped to the inside of the glass door. *Missing: Sean Brady Regan, D.O.B. March 2, 1964; Last seen: New Year's Day.* Below the words was a picture of a pleasant-looking man Skye had met at the office three weeks earlier. And underneath that was a single typed sentence. *Last known whereabouts: Del Paso Heights, Sacramento, California.*

Sheridan must've spotted her standing there, stunned, because she came from inside to open the door. "I'm sorry. I didn't want to tell you when you called this morning. I knew it'd upset you and…and you'd already suffered a shock."

Skye didn't answer. She pointed to the flyer. "When did you get this?"

"The police dropped it off this morning."

"She did it," Skye said simply. "His wife killed him."

"Why? For the insurance money?"

"No, Sean didn't have any life insurance. It was one of the first things I asked him. But he told me he was afraid of her. He thought she was seeing another man and wanted a divorce but didn't want the custody battle that would go with it."

Sheridan tucked her long dark hair behind one ear. She wasn't wearing any makeup, but with her bone structure, wide periwinkle-blue eyes fringed by thick black lashes, and flawless skin, she turned heads everywhere she went, especially male heads. "We can't do it all, Skye. It's nearly the weekend. Let the police handle this one."

Skye gaped at her. "How can you say that? According to the flyer, it's been seven days. We need to get Jonathan Stivers on this right away. He's good. He can find practically anyone."

"He's also expensive, and we're running low on funds." Sheridan reached out to touch her arm. "We've got to be careful, Skye, reserve our assets so we can keep our doors open."

The fact Sheridan would say such a thing meant they were already in trouble. But Skye couldn't deal with that yet. She was too busy thinking about Sean. Thanks to his wife, the mechanic-turned–jewelry salesman who'd come to her for help could be rotting in a gully somewhere.

"I told him to leave her, to get away." Skye drew a deep breath, attempting to regroup. Again.

"He wouldn't?"

"He refused to abandon his kids. And he doubted his own fears. He said his family laughed at him when he told them he thought Tasha was dangerous."

Sheridan gave her shoulder a reassuring squeeze. "The police are doing what they can, Skye."

But it never seemed to be enough. David was the most dedicated cop she knew and even he hadn't been able to put Burke away forever. There were other problems—people falling through the cracks, the system breaking down. That was why she, Sheridan and Jasmine spent almost every minute of every day helping one victim after another. For some, they provided a private investigator to assist prosecutors. For others, it was a better attorney, a place to stay, medical help, even physical therapy and counseling. They tried to fill in wherever necessary. But that required a lot of resources, and although they took home just enough to cover their own basic needs, there was never enough money to do it all.

Fortunately, now that they'd proven they were completely committed to what they'd started three years ago, they were beginning to gain the attention of local and state officials. A state senator had promised to attend a fund-raising event at the Hyatt next weekend, bolstering Skye's hopes for more generous contributions.

"I feel an obligation to do *something*, Sher. When we met, he asked if we help men. He seemed…embarrassed, as if it was emasculating in some way. I told him we try to help as many people as we can, regardless of gender, age or ethnicity."

"So what did you promise him?"

"An appointment with Jonathan. I thought we should find out if his suspicions about his wife had any foundation in fact, but then he never came back. I called him several times, trying to touch base, but it was right before Christmas and, when I didn't hear from him, I assumed he was out of town with his family. Then…this." She bit her lip, terrified that another life had been lost—a life she might have been able to save. "I should've been more diligent, should've driven over to his place—"

"Skye, what you assumed was perfectly reasonable. We still don't know what happened. Maybe he left because he found some sort of proof that he wasn't safe."

"No. He would've taken the kids if the situation had become that desperate."

"Okay, we'll see what Jonathan can do to track him down." Sheridan tried to follow this statement with a smile, but Skye could sense the effort behind it, the worry. She hadn't seen her friend so concerned about TLS since those rocky months after they'd first launched the charity. That they were overextended wasn't a big surprise, given the number of cases they'd taken on after the last newspaper article had heightened public awareness of their existence. She should've been more sensitive to their limitations. But it was always difficult to choose whom to help. And she wasn't especially in tune with their financial situation to begin with. Sheridan handled the accounting; Skye oversaw or taught the classes they offered in self-defense, self-esteem, trauma recovery, and, as an adjunct, gun safety and target shooting. Jasmine worked with investigators to find evidence, people, anything that had gone missing. Beyond that, they each spearheaded different cases, acting as a sort of director by determining what was needed, what was available and how to mesh the two.

"Our next fund-raiser is a week from tomorrow, right?"

"That's right. Saturday evening."

"I have a few bucks left over in my account this month." Because she had bills that would now have to wait, but she wasn't about to admit that to Sheridan. "I'll pay Jonathan."

Closing her eyes, Sheridan shook her head. "Skye—"

Skye nudged her. "The organization can pay me back if the fund-raiser is as good as we hope. Okay?"

Sheridan sighed but nodded. "Okay. Let's get out of the cold. It's starting to rain."

She turned to go inside, but Skye caught her long enough to give her a quick hug. "Thanks for understanding."

"Of course I understand. That's what we do. That's why we're here." She held the door. "By the way…"

Skye dropped her keys in her purse. "What is it?"

"Have you got a date for the fund-raiser?"

"Not yet. It doesn't make sense to me. Why do we need an escort?" she asked as they moved down the hall.

"I told you. It's all about public perception. The majority of our financial backers are businessmen, bankers, farmers, ranchers, dairymen. You know, conservatives who favor law and order."

"So what?"

They reached the reception desk, which was unstaffed until the volunteers began to arrive later in the day, and Sheridan sat down to sort through the mail. "So the senator who's agreed to come is also very conservative. When his aide called, he hinted that they have to be very careful about whom they appear to support."

Skye rested her elbows on the counter and watched to see if anything had come in for her. "What's wrong with supporting people who help the victims of violent crime? Who've been victims themselves? What could be unpopular about that?"

"We're not exactly friends with local law enforcement, for one thing. That makes us seem like a bit of a gamble. And we've gotten so engrossed in our work that we've let our private lives go."

They'd talked about this before. They discussed it more often as they wandered further and further from what others would term "a normal life." But Skye wasn't in the mood to address the subject again. Not when she was giving up her grocery money to hire an investigator. "He said that?"

"No. But…"

"What?" Skye said, growing impatient.

Sheridan set two letters aside for Jasmine, threw out some junk mail and handed what looked like a card to Skye. "He hinted that he wanted to avoid any speculation about our sexual orientation."

That immediately diverted Skye's attention from her mail. "No way!"

"I wouldn't make that up."

"I hope you told him to go to hell."

"No, I assured him that associating with us wouldn't threaten the support of the people who got the senator elected."

"I would've told him to go to hell."

"No, you wouldn't. You would've realized that it's a small sacrifice for the cause."

Skye sighed and checked the return address on her envelope. It was from Joanna Lintz, a woman she'd helped when The Last Stand first opened. "Maybe," she admitted. "But it really galls me to let someone else direct what I do with my personal life." Opening the card, she glanced through it. Joanna wrote that she was happy and doing better than ever. But even that news wasn't enough to counteract everything else that had happened today. "What does speculation about our sexual orientation have to do with fighting crime?" she asked Sheridan.

"We spend a lot of time together. We don't go out very often. We have no men in our lives." Sheridan grimaced. "Well, at least, no one who isn't on our 'needs help' list. Even Jasmine hasn't been with a man since God knows when. You don't see anything wrong with that picture?"

Skye put the card in her bag and tossed the tail of her knitted scarf over one shoulder. "Nothing that should concern anyone else! Besides, Jasmine's been married."

"That doesn't mean anything and you know it."

"It's just…annoying."

"I agree, but this fund-raiser *has* to work."

No kidding. Skye wouldn't have running water and electricity if it didn't. "Fine. I'll find someone to drag along on Saturday," she grumbled. "Anything else for me?"

"Not today." Sheridan set the rest of the mail aside.

"And make sure it's someone who cleans up well," she added. "It's formal, and we want to make a good impression. This is our chance to network with people who have serious money and to make contacts in the political world."

Skye started toward her own office but turned back at the door. "Getting a guy who makes a good impression isn't as easy as it sounds. Remember Charlie Fox at the Christmas party?"

"I told you not to ask him." Sheridan stood and slid the chair back under the desk. "He's still crying in his beer over the divorce."

"You didn't say that, Sher. You said your neighbor was lonely. That it might be nice for him to get out and circulate."

Sheridan wouldn't look her in the eye. "I'm pretty sure I warned you," she said as she made her way to the office directly across from the reception area.

"No, you didn't. You said he was sweet, harmless."

"Which is true."

"True? That sweet, harmless man drank so much he reduced himself to a blithering idiot before the evening was half over. By the time I drove him home, he was snoring in the passenger seat and I could hardly get him to wake up."

Sheridan pushed her door open. Skye suspected she was hiding a smile. "I'm sorry it didn't work out. Maybe this time you should ask someone you might actually be interested in."

"Oh, no, you don't," Skye called after her. "There is no one."

Her friend pivoted to face her. "Yes, there is."

Skye waved an irritated hand. "He's married."

"He's *divorced*."

"Doesn't matter. He'll get back with her. He always does. He stays with her as long as he can take the tension, then he leaves. But he sees divorce as an admission of failure, and he's too stubborn to let himself fail."

"There is that," Sheridan agreed.

"And she's got the one thing he really cares about," Skye said.

Sheridan's expression grew serious. "He cares about you, Skye."

Skye stepped into her office. "Not as much as he cares about his son."

"It's Oliver!" Noah Burke snapped, his blue eyes revealing his dismay.

Knowing her husband was on the phone made Jane's limbs go heavy and cold. She'd just spent an hour making love to his older brother and was lying naked in bed. Whenever her mother-in-law took Kate for the weekend, Noah dropped by. He always came under the guise of fixing a leaky faucet or mowing her lawn—so his wife wouldn't suspect—but it still wasn't good that Oliver had caught him at the house.

"Yes, I'll accept the charges," she heard him say, then he raked his fingers through his thick sandy hair.

"He never calls on Saturday mornings," she whispered apologetically. The cloud of euphoria that had engulfed her moments before disappeared as she sat up. Noah hadn't intended to answer the phone. He'd been hoping to find a pizza place that was open now that it was nearly noon—only to be surprised by an operator, who had Oliver on the line and promptly announced what Jane had heard hundreds of times herself: *This recorded call is from an inmate at a California state correctional facility.*

What lousy timing. According to Oliver, there was one telephone per tier at San Quentin, which meant fifty-four guys were constantly vying for a turn. But he always managed to contact her when she least wanted to speak with him....

Of course, lately she hardly ever wanted to speak with him. He acted as if she should be excited about his parole, but what made him think he deserved a happy homecoming after everything he'd put her through? Maybe he wasn't guilty of attempted rape, but he'd broken their marriage vows long before she had. And that had led to the biggest heartache Jane could imagine. She'd lost everything and her dignity, too. No one else in her circle of acquaintances had to live with the shame of having a spouse in prison. It would've been bad enough had he been accused of embezzling or some other white-collar crime. But attempted *rape* reflected on her as much as it did him. The experts claimed it was about power, not sex—God, how many times had she heard that?—but it still held a stigma, made her seem incapable of satisfying her man. *If he's getting what he needs at home, why does he have to look elsewhere?* No one had actually asked her that, but she could tell by the way they watched her that they wondered.

She wished they could see her with Noah. Much taller than his brother, Noah had a construction business that kept him in great physical shape, and he couldn't wait to get his hands on her.

Not that she felt good about what they were doing. Her zealously religious aunt, who'd finished raising her when her own parents were killed in an automobile accident, was probably rolling over in her grave. Besides, Jane loved her sister-in-law and Oliver's parents, all of whom would be hurt if they knew.

Covering the mouthpiece, Noah motioned to her, as if to ask, *What the hell am I going to tell him?*

Desperate for an immediate response, she resorted to the excuse she'd given her mother-in-law when Betty Burke had visited unexpectedly last week and found Noah standing in the kitchen. "Tell him my toilet's stopped up and you came over to take care of it," she murmured. "He knows you help me occasionally. He's grateful."

He rolled his eyes at "grateful," and hung his head, which tempted her to take the phone. Sometimes Noah's guilt weighed on him even more heavily than Jane's weighed on her. She feared it might drag the truth out of him someday. But Oliver had no doubt heard Noah's voice. It'd seem odd if he didn't say a few words before putting her on the line.

Sending her a helpless glance, Noah rubbed his left temple as he spoke into the receiver. "Yes…that's right, it's me. How are you?…Fine. What's been happening down there since my last visit?…No kidding? I'm glad you're getting out…Sorry I didn't come more often this past year…I know. Business has been crazy…Still, I should've found the time…."

Jane got up and crossed the room to sit at Noah's feet, oddly tempted to moan or make some other noise that would give them away. Oliver deserved the pain that knowing about their involvement would bring. If he hadn't allowed Skye Kellerman to lure him to her house, they wouldn't be where they were now.

But Jane knew she'd never tell him or anyone else about Noah. She couldn't. Letting that secret out would destroy too many relationships, impact too many lives—including her daughter's. Then there was Wendy. Jane didn't want to repay her sister-in-law's many kindnesses by revealing such a betrayal.

"So you'll have a parole officer for a few years?" Noah was saying. "What'll that be like?"

Jane imagined her and Noah in the room from a bird's-eye perspective and was sickened by what she saw. She, who'd once been a model wife and mother, was having sex with her husband's older brother. She was a terrible person....

"Mom and Dad are looking forward to seeing you, too." Noah gave her a sad smile. Maybe that was why she was so addicted to him. He treated her as if she was important, a priority. As if her feelings mattered. Besides, the affair wasn't *all* her fault. She wouldn't have fallen in love with Noah if he hadn't come over so often, trying to help her with the house and with Kate. Oliver had left her drowning in a sea of pain and loss, and she'd been grabbing for something, anything to cling to until she could right her world.

"Too bad about the dental practice. You'll find something else, though," he said as he played with a few strands of her hair. "You bet. We'll get together as soon as you're home. Okay, here's Jane."

Relinquishing the phone, he covered his face with his hands and dropped his head back.

Jane couldn't find her voice. She had to say hello twice to get it to sound right.

"Hi, babe," Oliver said. "How are you?"

Bringing her knees up, she hugged them to her chest and stared at her lacquered toenails while she talked. "Fine."

"What's Noah doing there?"

"Just—" she cleared her throat "—fixing a few things. You know, helping me get the house ready for when you come home."

"That's nice of him."

She felt her heart break a little, because she'd no longer have Noah once Oliver returned. She wished their affair didn't have to end, knew the coming months would be easier if he was there to support her. But they couldn't risk continuing the relationship.

"He knows I want it to be nice for you. He and your parents have been so good to me." Feeling Noah's hand on her head, she let her forehead rest against his knee.

"They *should* be good to you. You're my wife," Oliver said.

That was something she wasn't likely to forget. Her tie to him had humiliated her in the worst possible way. And yet he was the father of her daughter, the man she'd once loved, someone who could *never* have committed the crimes Skye Kellerman claimed.

"You still getting out on Friday?" she asked.

"Yeah. Just six more days. I can't believe it, can you?"

"No."

"Once I'm home, we'll forget about the past and move on. We'll buy a big house, like we had before. My folks will help us if we need them to."

Betty and Maurice had told her the same thing. They knew, just as Jane did, that Oliver wasn't a violent criminal. Sure, there'd been a desperate struggle between him and Skye Kellerman. Oliver had come home pretty carved up that fateful night, so badly injured Jane had been forced to take him to the emergency room. But it was Skye who'd freaked out and attacked him. She must've been on drugs, just like he said.

"Jane?" Noah whispered. He knew she was dying inside, but she couldn't look at him. It was too hard.

Raising a hand to indicate that he should wait until she'd dealt with Oliver, she walked over to the window to gaze out at the postage-stamp yard behind her cheap rental. She hated living here. The neighbors went on drunken binges and fought half the night. Teens loitered in the empty lots, smoking pot, or they ran around vandalizing property. And the schools were nothing like the one Kate should've been attending. Jane had to get out of here. But she wasn't going to do that cutting hair at a low-end beauty salon. She needed Oliver. They had to re-establish what they used to have, forget everything that had happened since—Skye, prison, Noah, the anger, the hurt, the resentment. Even the guilt.

Suddenly cold, she wrapped both arms around herself. "Skye was on television again last week," she told Oliver.

"I know," he responded. "Don't worry about her. She's a pathological liar."

"She was raising money to help other *victims*."

"Hopefully, they're real victims, not like her."

"She's capitalizing on what she did to you, using it to launch a whole new career. I mean, look at all the publicity and sympathy she got because of her lies." It made

Jane want to write her another letter. She'd sent a few over the years, telling Skye what she thought of her. But they'd all gone unanswered. And any more she sent would probably go unanswered, too.

"I'll bet she's taking a hefty salary from that nonprofit, too," he said.

While Jane was cutting hair eight hours a day just to pay the rent on a dump like this…

"But it doesn't matter what she does. That's all behind us," he went on.

Could it be true? Jane ached with the mere hope of it.

Noah came up and kissed the back of her neck, and she let the enjoyable sensations he evoked force Skye from her mind. She wouldn't think about the past. The past brought such rage. "We'll start over, build a new life," she said into the phone, repeating what Oliver had told her so often.

"Exactly."

"Just like the one we had before."

"Just like the one we had before," he echoed.

She leaned into Noah, drawing strength from him while she could. "Sounds great. See you Friday morning."

"Leave Kate with my mom and bring enough money for a hotel. We deserve a night alone in San Francisco, don't you think?"

"I guess so."

"Aren't you excited?" Oliver asked.

She wasn't sure. She'd loved him once. Would that feeling return after he came home? She hoped so—for her sake, for Kate's sake, for everyone's. "Of course."

4

"You're late."

David stood on the stoop of his ex-wife's two-story home—his old home—and managed what he hoped was a pleasant smile. "Nice to see you, too, Lynnette."

"Where've you been?" she asked. "I've been trying to reach you."

He'd silenced his phone so he wouldn't have to listen to it ring. Hearing her bitch at him as he fought the Monday-evening commute wasn't going to bring him home—to *her* house—any sooner. He refused to let her badger him. "Bad day at the office."

"They're all bad." She walked away, leaving the door open, her irritation dissolving into an attitude of bored indifference. "Jeremy's been asking for you. He was afraid you'd cancel again."

It was David's turn to be irritated. "What are you talking about? I hardly ever cancel. Only when work gets in the way."

"Yeah, well, you do love your work."

As a phlebotomist at a local lab, her hours were fixed—nine to three, five days a week, which was perfect because it coincided with Jeremy's school day.

But the regularity of her schedule certainly didn't make her more understanding of the spontaneity and extra hours required in police work. "You know I can't always quit at five, Lynnette." His job was demanding, but not nearly as demanding as *she'd* been when they were together. Highly emotional, she was quick to laugh when she was in a good mood and quick to anger when she wasn't.

"Spare me." She pulled on her shoes and grabbed a coat. Then she motioned at the closet, partially jammed with his jackets, hats, umbrellas, ski equipment. "You still have stuff in here."

"I know." Was she asking him to remove it? So far, she'd been careful not to go that far. And he'd purposely ignored the fact that he'd left some things behind. Since Lynnette had been diagnosed with Multiple Sclerosis, which was discovered after their second divorce became final, he didn't feel he could just walk away. What kind of man would abandon the mother of his child when she was facing a lifelong battle with a disease like that? "I'll get it soon," he said with a shrug.

"No, you won't. You'll let it sit here till it rots or I throw it in the street."

Because he didn't have a choice. It wasn't as if she had any reliable family to turn to. His family had become her family, and they'd decided to stand by her, for her sake *and* Jeremy's. A phlebotomist didn't make that much, and it probably wouldn't be long before she couldn't work anymore. He'd already seen significant changes in her, including an even more volatile temper.

But they used to love each other. They had ten years invested in the relationship. Surely, with enough effort and persistence, they could make it work. If only he could forget about Skye…

"I won't be home until midnight," she said.

Why so late? He spent every Monday with Jeremy while she attended an art class over at American River College. But she'd never come home past ten. Had she met someone else?

If so, he couldn't believe it would last, couldn't believe she'd find a new husband who'd be willing to take care of her when her health began to deteriorate. He wasn't sure he wanted Jeremy to have a stepfather, anyway. That invited a whole slew of additional problems. This was *his* family; he'd take care of them. "Have fun," he said.

She eyed him skeptically. "Aren't you going to ask me where I'm going after class?"

"Should I?"

A pained expression crossed her face. "No, I guess not. Jeremy's here. He's all you care about."

"Lynn."

She didn't look up. Taking her keys off the counter, she started for the door.

"Lynn," he said again, catching her arm.

When she lifted her eyelashes, he could see tears glistening in her eyes.

"What is it?" he asked.

"You think you're coming back," she said. "You tell me you want things to work out between us. That you won't leave me to deal with this disease alone."

"I won't."

"But only because you feel obligated. You don't love me anymore."

He didn't know what to say or what to make of her erratic behavior. Although they never argued in front of Jeremy—as far as David was concerned, that was an unbreakable rule—half the time she acted as if she could barely contain her animosity toward him. The other half, she was so frightened by what was happening to her and so clingy he couldn't breathe. "I care about you. I want you to be happy."

"You want Jeremy to be happy."

"That, too."

"But I can tell…"

He filled the gap so she wouldn't find the words she was looking for. It would just be more of the same complaints he'd been hearing for the past five years. "We don't have to be miserable if we're together," he said. "We'll get more counseling—"

"We've had enough counseling, David!"

Her voice was shrill as the tears spilled over her lashes, and David worried that Jeremy would hear her and be confronted with an upsetting scene. "Come on." He tried to take her in his arms, to calm her down, but she shoved him away.

"No! Don't you understand? This is killing me! I have to get over you. You'll never love me the way you used to."

David couldn't contradict her. What he'd felt was dead and gone long before the diagnosis. All the hushed arguments and complaints and accusations had killed it and, hard as he tried, he couldn't resurrect it. But there were other elements in a marriage. Trust. Stability. Companionship. As time went on, those things often became more important than the head-over-heels, I-can't-stop-thinking-about-you devotion she craved. At least she'd have someone to lean on and Jeremy could be sure his mother would be well taken care of. "I'm not a quitter. I'll always be there for you, support you as much as I can, be true to you—"

"In other words, you'll soldier on," she interrupted bitterly. "That's not enough. I love Jeremy, too. He's the reason I've hung on. But I can't be a good mother when I'm this miserable." Dashing a hand across her cheeks, she seemed to rally. "I have a date tonight. You might want to sleep here because I'll be late. Maybe I'll even stay the night with him." This last comment she tossed over her shoulder as she turned toward the door again.

"Lynnette." She paused at the sharp way he'd said her name. "If you don't know this guy very well, be careful."

"That's all you've got to say? Be *careful?*"

"Don't do anything rash just to get back at me."

"I wouldn't be doing it to get back at anyone," she retaliated. "I want to make love, I want to be loved, I want to feel good about myself again! You bring out the worst in me. *I* don't even like me when you're around!"

David told himself to stop her, to say the words she wanted to hear, to take her to her room and make love to her. But Jeremy came to the top of the stairs and looked down at them uncertainly. "Dad? Mom? What's wrong?"

Glancing between his ex-wife and his son, David almost breathed a sigh of relief. "Nothing, bud," he said, and climbed the stairs to reassure his son.

The front door opened and closed. Then Lynnette's car started and she drove off. Listening to her engine fade into the distance, David felt more of the old self-recrimination. What the hell was the matter with him?

Lynnette had a debilitating disease. Why couldn't he give her what she needed?

He just couldn't. He couldn't make love to her and pretend she was the one he wanted. Not today. Not after seeing Skye this morning.

"Dad?"

"What?" he said.

"You're still moving home, right?"

David winced as he stared into his son's tortured eyes. Somehow he had to stop the pain. For all of them.

"Dad? You said you were moving home."

"I will, bud."

"When?"

David clenched his jaw. "Soon."

Grinning widely, Jeremy threw his little arms around David and gave him a big hug. "Yay!"

Rain always made Skye a little uneasy, but tonight the hollow, echoing patter on her roof unnerved her more than usual and drove her from her bed. Sometimes, if it was a big storm, the sloughs would overflow their banks, break through the levees and wash out the roads. It was fairly common in winter, part of life in the delta—the excitement of which she'd loved as a child. But knowing Oliver Burke would soon be back in Sacramento, free to roam wherever he wished, transformed the anticipation she'd once felt into raw anxiety. It wasn't a good time to be worrying about getting cut off from the rest of civilization.

God, if she was this unsettled *before* he got out of prison, what would she be like afterward? She'd been this way all weekend.

Fixing herself a cup of tea, she turned on the television and tried to focus on the news. But when the immaculately groomed anchorman launched into a story on the disappearance of a "Del Paso Heights man in his early forties," she turned it off. Sean Regan. She hadn't rescued him in time.

But she was doing what she could, right? Jonathan had started on the case last Friday. He'd find Sean eventually.

Unfortunately, that didn't make her feel a whole lot better. Sean was out there somewhere, in the storm, like so many other victims....

Using exercise to work off her excess energy, she did fifty push-ups, two hundred stomach crunches and a half hour of yoga but still couldn't relax.

After making another cup of tea, she settled at the kitchen table to call Jasmine. They'd spoken briefly over the weekend—Jasmine had called the second she heard Burke was about to be paroled, but she'd been with an FBI agent at the time so they hadn't been able to discuss the situation in Ft. Bragg. Skye hoped Jas was in her hotel room now. She needed to talk to someone, and she was eager to hear how Jasmine had been received by the small, conservative police force that had requested her help.

"Hello?"

Skye winced at Jasmine's raspy, exhausted voice. She was in her room, all right, and had probably been fast asleep before the jangle of the phone. "Did I wake you?"

"Skye?"

"Yeah."

"I haven't been in bed long. Are you okay?"

"I'm worried about you."

"Why me? I'm fine. I guess," she added.

It had been on the tip of Skye's tongue to tell Jasmine to go back to sleep, that they'd talk tomorrow, but the concern she felt over the "I guess" overcame the concern generated by the fatigue in her voice. "You don't sound too sure."

"This isn't going to be easy." Skye could hear the bedclothes rustle as Jasmine moved. "I have an especially hard time whenever a child's involved."

Most people had a more difficult time working a case that involved an endangered child. But Jasmine's qualms went deeper than that. One hot August day fifteen years ago, when she was only twelve years old, her own sister had been taken from their home and never found. To this day, Jasmine had no idea what'd happened to her. She could use her psychic abilities to find others but drew a complete blank when it came to her own sister. She'd been to hypnotists, counselors and other psychics, all in an attempt to break through the mental block. But she couldn't even help a sketch artist come up with a good likeness. The trauma she'd experienced back then—and since—had been too much. Which was probably why she embraced each abduction case.

If it turned out that the Ft. Bragg girl had already been killed, how would Jasmine react? Would she feel responsible? Have a breakdown like the one she'd had ten years ago? As it was, she blamed herself for the fact that they'd never been able to recover Kimberly. She'd seen the man who took her sister, had even spoken to him, but her inability to recall enough details to identify him still devastated her.

"How old is the girl you're looking for?" Skye purposely used the present tense. She refused to believe they'd already lost the child when they were doing everything they could to recover her.

"Only three."

So young… That meant they couldn't rely on any help from her. At that age, she wouldn't know her own telephone number or even 911. "Are you sure she didn't wander off?"

"I'm sure."

"How do you know?"

There was an audible sigh on the other end of the line. "I just do."

In other words, she could "feel" it. She didn't like saying so because she knew it sounded hokey and unbelievable. Jasmine explained her gift as a sort of sixth sense about certain people. She was the first to admit she couldn't read minds or envision the past or future. Neither could she lead police directly to a kidnap victim or perpetrator. Rather than crystal-clear answers, she received impressions, which often resulted from touching something that had belonged to the kidnapper or victim, or being in their homes, cars or workplaces.

Combined with all the study she'd done on criminal behavior and psychology, these impressions had been enough to save more than a few victims. And Jasmine seemed to be getting better as she learned to trust her intuition. A few of her cases had even garnered national attention. In the Ubaldi case, a child had been stolen from a school playground and Jasmine had assisted authorities in tracking down the middle-aged woman who'd taken her. She'd known the woman lived near the school, had been adamant that they continue to check the houses on the same block.

"This was a crime of opportunity," she was saying. "It was someone who either lives close by or has been visiting the area."

"Have you canvassed the neighborhood?"

"There isn't really a neighborhood to canvass. The mom's single but living with her boyfriend in an older home set off in the woods."

"Do the police have any suspects?"

"They believe the mother is covering for the boyfriend."

"You don't?"

"No."

The rain pounded harder, but Skye ignored it. *Block it out. It won't flood. She'd be able to drive away anytime she wanted.* "What's her story?"

"Six days ago, the mother put the child down for a nap and lay down herself. When she woke up, Lily was gone."

"Where was the boyfriend?"

"He claims he loaded their Christmas tree in the back of his truck and went to get rid of it."

"No one can confirm his whereabouts during that time?"

"He took police to where he dumped the tree, but there's no way of telling how long he was gone."

"No one saw him?"

"He purposely avoided being seen. He didn't want to get fined for dumping the tree on private property."

Crossing the room, Skye tried to lower the blind at the window but couldn't get the knot out of the cord. She'd tied it earlier, when she'd been trying to get the damn thing to stay up. "No evidence of an intruder at the house?"

"No forced entry. But the doors weren't locked, so anyone could've walked in. The only clue is an odd-size footprint in the mud near the front walkway."

Skye glared at the water-streaked window with the broken blind. She wanted that blind down. It felt like someone was out there, watching her. But she knew she was just letting the old fear get to her again. Burke's release was hitting her hard, making her regress. *It's a kitchen window. A lot of people don't even put blinds on a kitchen window.* "What's odd about the size of the footprint?"

"It's too small for the boyfriend and too big for the mother."

"What about a serviceman, the postman, the meter reader?"

"The mother says there hasn't been anyone else at the house for days, yet it's a fresh print."

"That *is* strange."

"They're taking impressions. We'll see if we can find a match."

Skye's call-waiting beeped, and she frowned in surprise. It was after midnight on a Monday night. Who would be calling so late? She would've checked the caller ID, but it didn't register a second caller's number when she was already on the phone.

Assuming it was one of her stepsisters, she asked Jasmine to hold for a minute and switched over. "Hello?"

There was a long pause.

"Hello?" she said again.

"Skye Kellerman?"

The deep voice wasn't one she recognized. "Yes?"

"When I get out, I'm going to slit your throat."

Skye sat perfectly still as the memory of Burke's attack intruded. He was straddling her, holding her down as she fought him. His blade, aimed at her eye, cut her cheek instead because she was twisting and turning beneath him, trying to free herself. Then there was pain, more panic, and the blood that poured from the cut, smearing everywhere, blinding her as she fought like a mad-woman....

"Who is this?" she asked, but the phone clicked and the caller was gone.

Her focus returned to the window. It couldn't be Burke, she told herself. He didn't have unmonitored access to a phone. Not yet, anyway. Had he put someone else up to it? He must have. The caller didn't say something general like, "I'm watching you" or "I'm going to kill you." He'd said, *"When I get out—"*

"Skye? Are you back?"

Jasmine.

Answer. Taking a deep breath, she cleared her throat. "Yeah, I'm here."

"Who was it?"

She shivered as the words ran through her mind again. Whoever had spoken them didn't sound like a young boy trying to frighten strangers. It had been a man.

But she was unlisted. How did he get her number? "I don't know."

"What do you mean?"

Skye stood and slipped out of the kitchen, hiding from whoever might be on the other side of that large, square window, looking in at her. "Someone who knows that

Burke is about to be released just threatened me." *With a knife…*

"What did he say exactly?"

"When I get out, I'm going to—" she swallowed hard, trying to stem the onslaught of fresh fear "—to slit your throat."

"Call the police!" Jasmine nearly shouted. "Make sure they haven't let Burke out early."

Skye leaned against the wall in the entryway. "I don't think they have. David would've warned me. Besides, it doesn't have to be Burke who's behind it. We've all talked to the press about our past encounters with criminal violence."

"Maybe a lot of people know how you were attacked. But how many know Burke is being paroled?"

Again Skye tried to convince herself that it could be more people than she realized. "That depends on who he's told, who they've told—"

"Still, you have to go to the police."

Outside, the rain fell harder, hitting her porch like pebbles, and Skye imagined the water in the sloughs rising steadily, cutting off her escape…. "I can't. If they respond at all, they'll take their time about it. They've warned me on several occasions that I'm making myself a target, hinted that I'll be putting myself at risk if I continue to get involved in potentially dangerous situations."

"Call them anyway. And do it now. Then make sure your doors and windows are locked. I'll get hold of Sheridan and have her come out and stay with you. I'm too far away or I'd come myself."

"Don't call Sheridan. I have what I need to take care of myself." She withdrew the gun she'd stuffed in the pocket of her coat on Friday, when David dropped by. Still loaded. Ready to shoot.

"But you'd rest better if someone was with you," Jasmine argued. "You don't get much sleep as it is."

It wasn't for lack of trying. Skye couldn't let her guard down long enough to sleep. Bad things happened when she closed her eyes....

"I can't expect Sheridan to get up in the middle of the night and drive an hour in the pouring rain just to hold my hand."

"Yes, you can. On Friday you learned that the man who attacked you is getting out of prison, for crying out loud. Sheridan won't mind."

"Don't bother her. She was exhausted when we left the office." Skye held the side of the gun to her chest, reassured by the weight of it, the fit of the handle, the cool metal against her skin. After Burke, she was more terrified of knives than any other weapon, but a gun could outdo a knife any day. As long as she saw him coming. "I'll be fine."

Jasmine hesitated, but finally relented. "I'll back off because he's not out yet. But only if you promise to call the police and ask them to do a drive-by."

"It'd have to be the sheriff. I'm outside the city limits."

"Whoever. Have someone walk the perimeter of your property."

"Okay."

"Let me know if you get another call. I mean it. I don't care what time it is."

"I will." Skye disconnected, then went around the house to make extra-sure she'd locked the doors and windows. She performed the same routine every evening—once, twice, three times. Occasionally she got up in the wee hours of the morning just to check them again or to sit at a window and peek through the blinds and the iron bars she'd paid a contractor to attach, watching for the worst.

Tonight was one of those nights. She wouldn't call the police. She wouldn't call anyone. If Burke or someone like him came after her, she'd terminate the threat—right here.

The vibration of the cell phone in his pocket woke David long before dawn. Blinking to clear his vision, he squinted at the furnishings in the room, trying to figure out where he was. He was sleeping in a twin bed. There were two large beanbag chairs and some shelves that contained...

Jeremy's toys and books. He was in the guest room at his old house. He must've fallen asleep before Lynnette came home.

Rubbing his face, he yawned and got up, intending to see if his ex-wife was in her bed. He had a lot to do in the morning and wanted to go home so he wouldn't have to wake to the kind of tedious rehashing that usually followed one of her emotional outbursts. He'd spent most of the weekend and all day Monday working on those old murder cases, going over the autopsy reports, studying the crime-scene pictures, rereading the statements of those who'd last seen each victim alive. He had to find *something* that would put Burke back in prison before anyone else got hurt. Especially Skye.

He started for the door, but when his cell phone vibrated, he remembered that was what had awakened him in the first place.

Pulling it from his pocket, he snapped it open. "'Lo?"

"Detective Willis?"

"Yes?"

"This is Sergeant Blazer at the Marysville Boulevard station."

David tensed at the possibility that he was about to be directed to a new crime scene. The worst calls always came in the middle of the night or in the early morning hours. Just a few weeks ago, he'd helped process a house in Oak Park where a man had shot his wife and two children before turning the gun on himself. "Yes?"

"Jasmine Stratford from The Last Stand called here a few minutes ago."

A knot immediately formed in David's stomach. Why would they be hearing from Jasmine? "Was she looking for me?"

"Not specifically. She wanted to make a report."

David's blood ran cold as he imagined the criminals Skye, Jasmine and Sheridan angered on a daily basis, and the revenge they might seek. "On what?"

"I guess her partner in that victims' group got a threatening phone call last night."

"Which partner?" he asked, but he already knew.

"Skye Kellerman."

His grip tightened on the phone. "Did Jasmine give you any details?"

"Some guy called and said, 'When I get out, I'm gonna slit your throat.'" The sergeant's voice assumed a note of self-importance. "I told Ms. Stratford it was probably a pervert who gets his kicks out of scaring women. But she and her friends have more enemies than I can count on two hands, and a lot of those enemies are pretty damn dangerous. That's why I thought you might want to know about this, in case it wasn't a prank."

"You did the right thing, Sergeant. I appreciate the courtesy." Except for the part about getting out, David might've been able to believe it was someone who'd heard about the attack on Skye and was using it to terrorize her in retaliation for the assistance she'd given a wife or lover. But the mention of a knife, together with getting out… How many people could know about Burke's impending release? It wasn't as if the papers had picked it up. Hell, *he'd* just learned last Friday. "If anything else that has to do with TLS or the three women involved in it comes in, please get in touch right away."

"Will do."

David hit the Off button, but he didn't pocket his phone. He shut the door so Lynnette couldn't hear him if she was home and dialed Skye's number. This was a business call; he didn't plan on saying anything particularly private. But he felt guilty whenever he contacted Skye.

"Hello?"

He doubted she'd been sleeping because she'd answered on the first ring.

"It's me," he said. "I heard about your caller."

"Jasmine told you?"

"She called the Marysville Boulevard station."

"Why? I told her I'm not within the city limits anymore."

"Does that mean you reported it to the sheriff?"

There was a long pause that told him what he'd already guessed. She thought she could handle it on her own. But that was crazy and reckless. She might overestimate her own strength and judgment, and the idea terrified him.

Shaking his head, he pictured Skye as he'd first seen her, in the hospital with forty stitches below her left eye. She'd also had several deep cuts on her hands and forearms from trying to defend herself against Burke's knife. Just the memory of her injuries, and the disillusionment, was enough to strengthen his commitment to putting Burke away. She'd been so shaken, so fragile.

But she wasn't fragile anymore. The cut below her eye had healed into a thin scar, and the others were even less noticeable. Her body had gone through a sort of metamorphosis since the attack, too. She'd toned up, trading her soft curves for well-defined muscle. Now she was a convert to the gospel of health and fitness. But, as hard as she worked to make herself tough, there was still that sensitive core. David wanted to protect that, to vanquish the haunted look he saw in her eyes.

"Why didn't you call me?" he asked, angry that he wouldn't have heard about the incident if Jasmine hadn't reported it. "When something like this happens, you need to let me know."

"Why?"

He remembered the way Burke had said her name. *I know her better than anyone. Including you.* He was still obsessed with her. "So I know what's going on!"

Her voice dropped. "Would you have come over?"

He knew better than to spend much time alone with Skye. If he went over there now, he wouldn't be able to resist taking what he so desperately wanted—taking what she'd willingly offer. And then he wouldn't be able to make a life with Lynnette, would never be satisfied with what his conscience dictated he had to do. "If it meant protecting you," he told her gruffly.

"I can protect myself," she said and hung up.

Frowning, David hit the redial button.

She let it ring several times, but finally answered. "What is it?"

"Call me the minute anything like that happens again. Do you understand?"

"Because…"

"Because I'm worried about you, damn it!"

"Be careful, Detective. That sounds like you're beginning to care." Except for that one kiss, and the time he'd nearly spent the night, he'd been circumspect, kept her at arm's length. But she knew how he felt. She *had* to know. He couldn't look at her without wanting her.

"I've cared from the beginning," he snapped. "Sometimes you're all I can think about."

He hadn't made an actual admission before, but those words didn't seem to improve the situation. Maybe because they'd been spoken so grudgingly.

"You'd change that if you could," she said, the statement an accusation.

He didn't deny it. Surely it would be easier to fulfill his obligations to Lynnette and his promises to Jeremy if he didn't dream of making love to Skye. "Yes."

"And I'm supposed to be satisfied with that?"

He shoved a frustrated hand through his hair. "It's all I can give."

Click.

David nearly called her again. He wanted—needed—*something*. Closure. Understanding. Acceptance of his limitations. Concurrence that he was doing the right thing. But it wouldn't be enough, because what he really wanted was her.

Tossing his phone away to remove the temptation, he cursed under his breath. He had to let go, forget her if he was ever going to rebuild his family. But now that Burke was getting out, he *couldn't* forget Skye—or she could wind up dead.

5

What was he missing?

David had left his ex-wife's house the moment he discovered she was safe in her bed, and was now in his home office, actually the third bedroom of his Midtown apartment. Sunlight crept across his desk as the sun rose, making the lamp he'd turned on unnecessary. But he didn't bother to turn it off. He was too engrossed in the files he'd spread out. He'd already gone through them over the weekend, but he was studying every piece of paper and every photograph yet again. There had to be something here, some piece of evidence that tied Burke to the three young women who were murdered in their homes. What was it?

He went over it all in his mind, trying to recap what he knew and see what he might be missing. All three, Meredith Connelly, Amber Farello and Patty Poindexter, were between the ages of eighteen and twenty-five....

Burke's question came back to him as he studied their pictures: *What do you imagine when you look at a nude woman in* Playboy? Like Skye, these victims were all exceptionally attractive—and big-breasted. At the prison, Burke had mentioned that his own wife was "busty," which led David to believe Burke might have a fetish for that part of a woman's body.

David wasn't sure what that told him. Most guys liked a woman's breasts. But he tucked the information away in case it connected with something else later on, some way of determining how and where Burke had chosen his victims. Considering what he'd said about the women he saw in magazines, David was beginning to wonder if he'd been attacked those young women in an attempt to obtain what he idolized. Had he been spurned by someone in the past? Someone especially pretty who thought she was too good for him?

It was worth checking out. Making a quick note, David moved on.

Amber and Patty were single and lived with their parents. Meredith had been sharing a rental home with a boyfriend. Amber's mom and dad were in their bedroom during the attack but heard nothing, which made the situation particularly heart-wrenching for them.

Although Patty and Meredith had died in the evening around 8:00 p.m., Amber had been killed between 2:00 and 4:00 a.m. A bicycle enthusiast, Oliver had ridden to work every day and sometimes didn't come home until well after dark, when he used a headlight to make his way back up the bike trail from downtown, where he'd worked, to Granite Bay, where he'd lived. That created the opportunity for the evening attacks.

What about the attacks on Amber and Skye? At first David hadn't been able to figure out how Oliver had managed to leave home in the middle of the night without waking Jane.

Fortunately, he'd solved that riddle by researching

Jane's medical history, which revealed that shortly after she'd had Kate she'd suffered from postpartum depression and insomnia and had relied heavily on sedatives in order to sleep.

David still wondered where Oliver had put his bloody clothes after each murder, and how he'd cleaned up before returning home. Of course, two years had passed by the time Burke became a suspect and they'd inspected his house. They hadn't found any trace of Amber's blood in the drains or on any of Oliver's shoes or clothes. His vehicles were clean, too.

Rubbing his lip, David decided to reinterview Oliver's friends and neighbors. When the story broke, Burke had pretended to be such a martyr—telling any reporter who'd listen that Skye had attacked him while she was on drugs. As a result, almost everyone who knew him had rallied to his defense. David had received letters that said, "How can you let the lies of one woman break up a loving family?" The mayor's daughter, one of Burke's patients at the time, had even testified as a character witness.

David wished Burke had come up with the "Skye on drugs" scenario when they could've tested to disprove it. But he'd wisely kept his mouth shut, offering nothing as he conferred privately with his lawyers. It was weeks before he claimed he'd gone to Skye's place for consensual sex, at which point *she'd* attacked *him.* No one could prove anything one way or the other. There was no evidence to suggest Skye had ever taken drugs. But earlier that night she'd gone out with some new friends from work to a party where Ecstasy had been available. According to Skye, she'd left early because of it and gone home alone, but since her roommate was in Tahoe that weekend, it came down to her word against Burke's. Finding Oliver's DNA in Skye's bedroom merely established that he'd been there, not that he'd been there *uninvited,* especially because they couldn't figure out how he'd gotten in. Unlike the murders along the river, there was no cut screen. The police found the front door unlocked when they arrived, but Skye claimed she'd locked it when she went to bed. David guessed Burke had seen her use a hide-a-key sometime before that and helped himself. He must've put it right back, though. When they checked, the key was where she always put it.

Fortunately, Skye was a strong witness and they got the conviction, but it wasn't as easy as it should've been.

Skye… Frustrated that he couldn't think of her with the same emotional detachment he could put between himself and the other people he met through his work, he used his son's words as a talisman—*You're still moving home, right?*—and tried again to concentrate.

All three girls lived in single-family homes located in the Campus Commons area along the American River. One worked at the Pavilions, an upscale shopping center in an affluent area. The other two attended Sacramento State University, which was basically a commuter school.

The crime-scene photos drew his eye. So many of Burke's patients had been concerned about his family. But look what *he'd* done to these other families.

Knowing that Skye might've been in a similar photo if she hadn't managed to stab him, David cursed. The thought of Burke touching Skye, even *looking* at her, turned his stomach.

He took a sip of the now-cold coffee he'd bought on his way home this morning and held the photographs closer, studying them for new clues. There had to be something here, he told himself again, something he hadn't previously spotted or surmised. But he'd already done everything he could with the facts he had. So he started making a list of what he knew so far:

—*Considers himself normal but is sexually sadistic.* The extra stab wounds and excessive bruising told him that.

—*Raped and sodomized victims, but no evidence of necrophilia.*

—*Wore gloves.* There was no fingerprint evidence at any of the murder scenes, even on the windows.

—*Wore a hood.* Skye had confirmed this.

—*Most likely shaved his genital area.* There hadn't been any pubic hair at the murder scenes.

—*No footprints in the bushes near point of entry.* Had he covered his feet with those cotton booties doctors wore over their shoes? *Possibly,* David wrote. But there'd been that one print near the front walkway of Patty Poindexter's house, so maybe he didn't use them all the time.

—*Must have used a condom, which he took away from the scene.* The girls' bodies yielded no semen samples, although it was clear they'd been forcefully penetrated.

—*Was comfortable using a knife.* Possibly from having experience with a scalpel?

—*Probably wasn't over six feet tall.* Because the perpetrator had come through a bedroom window at least twice, he couldn't be very big. The bigger the guy, the harder it'd be to use that mode of entry.

—*Stalked his victims, was familiar with their routines.* This killer knew when the girls were alone in their bedrooms, even though they all lived with others. Was that part of the fun for him? Probably, or he would've chosen easier targets. *Likes the chase,* David added.

—*Brazen.* He dared to intrude, even when one girl's parents were home, so it followed that he liked flirting with the threat of capture. David guessed it gave him as big a rush as showing women that they weren't safe in their own homes, that *he* held the power.

—*Disciplined.* Or he would've left some evidence behind.

—*Probably watches a lot of crime shows on TV in an effort to figure out how to avoid detection.* Many violent criminals were fascinated with police, and Burke was no different. When David searched his home, he found no souvenirs taken from the victims, no bloody clothing, no knife, which was the hard evidence he'd been hoping to recover. But he did find bookcases full of true-crime books, many of them detailed accounts of slayings by serial killers.

Sitting back, David reread what he'd written. *Every* item fit the man who was already in prison. Equally compelling was the fact that there'd been no similar attacks since he'd been put behind bars. A dentist would be more comfortable cutting a person than someone who'd never sliced human flesh, he reasoned. A dentist would know how to make the most efficient incision and wouldn't be afraid of blood. Burke definitely considered himself "normal." He was smart, short and had a slight build.

But even David had to admit these points could apply

to a lot of men. It was his own gut feeling that convinced him more than anything else, that and the strange look Oliver Burke had given him during the initial interrogation—as if he was tempted to confess…

A gut feeling and an expression were tough to sell to a prosecutor. Or a jury, for that matter. He needed more.

With a sigh, he closed the files. There was nothing else here. He'd been through all of this before. He had to come up with some fresh information or these cases would never be solved.

And, in order to do that, he had to appeal to the people who knew Burke best.

When I get out, I'm going to slit your throat….

Skye sat at her desk, staring into space. She hadn't been able to work all morning. Whether that call had come from Oliver Burke or not, she still believed he'd want revenge against her for testifying in court. He'd come after her….

"Hello, this is Peter Vaughn, a volunteer with The Last Stand. We're a nonprofit organization dedicated to supporting the victims of violent crime…."

From the other room, Skye could hear the telephone soliciting that went on for three hours a day as volunteers helped raise the funds to keep their doors open. Volunteers came and went. It was difficult to sustain people's motivation when they weren't being paid. But there were a few who stuck around, usually those who knew someone who'd been killed or raped, and Peter was one of them. He'd lost an older brother to a drive-by shooting and, although only eighteen, he was a pro on the phone.

As distracted as she was, Skye could easily sit and

listen to Peter all morning. But she had her own work to do. She had a list of current cases to follow up on and several messages to return. One was from Jonathan, who'd learned that Sean Regan's wife sometimes met a certain heavyset but wealthy stranger for lunch. Another was from a client who'd gone back to the man who was abusing her, always a worry. Skye also needed to find a dress for the fund-raiser, as well as a date. And she wanted to draft a new press release with the details of Burke's release, emphasizing the importance of continued support for charities like TLS.

She began the press release first, hoping it'd ease her mind to be taking some action to defend herself, but it wasn't as cathartic as she'd hoped. She kept stopping and staring at the phone, waiting for word from David. Their earlier conversation hadn't ended well, but she was so tired of hoping for something she wasn't going to get. She needed to permanently relegate David to the realm of platonic friends. But what she felt for him wasn't an emotion she could switch on and off. They'd both fought it from the beginning. And now Burke was getting out, and the whole thing seemed to be starting over. The contact. The worry. The desire. The fear.

She told herself to stop thinking about David *and* Burke, but it was no good. She felt as if she'd gone back four years. Burke was still a threat. David was still trying to help her. She was more in love with him than ever. And he was still trying to get back with his ex-wife. Why hadn't anything changed?

She couldn't stay on guard for the rest of her life....

Shoving away from her computer, she massaged her temples. She had to do more than send out another flurry of press releases. David wouldn't like it, but maybe she needed to be aggressive rather than sitting and waiting and hoping for the best. Maybe she needed to become more familiar with Burke and his lifestyle.

Maybe it was time to fight fire with fire.

After standing for more than five hours, Jane's feet ached. She needed a break, and there finally seemed to be enough of a lull to take one. Sitting in her own salon chair, she lit a cigarette and gazed out the large front window advertising haircuts for ten bucks. The kind of cheapskates who wanted a ten-dollar haircut rarely remembered to tip. The last guy had handed her a fistful of change, which he said equaled ten dollars, but by the time she finished counting up all the pennies, he was gone and she was a dollar short.

"Jerk," she muttered. She'd even worn a low-cut shirt. It increased her tip average. The men liked a good view, and she didn't see how that hurt anything. A woman had to get by. But this last loser had leered, then stiffed her anyway.

"Hey!" Danielle, a fellow stylist, wagged a finger at her. "You can't smoke in here. The State of California doesn't allow it."

"Screw the State of California. Nobody's in here but you, and you smoke more in a day than I do."

"The boss will smell it," she warned. "And you'll get yourself fired."

"Who's she going to replace me with? No one else will work so hard for so little."

"That's where you're wrong. There's a line of hopefuls right behind you, sugar."

Jane didn't want to hear it. "So? I won't be needing

this job much longer." Oliver was getting out on Friday, and he was an educated man. Before their lives had gone to hell, he'd been making over a quarter million a year and they'd lived in a home that was the envy of all their friends. They'd regain what they'd lost. It was just a matter of time.

"You're quittin' then?"

Disgruntled that she couldn't even smoke a damn cigarette in peace, Jane finally stubbed it out. "Happy?"

Danielle gave her a dirty look. "I didn't make the law. Besides, you have to sweep up the hair around your chair before you take a break."

Getting up, Jane grudgingly swept and straightened her station, then went out next to the smelly Dumpster in back, which was their designated "smoking area," and lit up again. But she'd barely taken her first drag when Danielle stuck her head out the door. "Someone's here to see ya."

"Is he cute?" she asked.

"I'd go home with him."

"That's not saying much."

Danielle scowled. "Shut up! You're in such a crappy mood today."

"You know I'm kidding," Jane said, although she hadn't been kidding at all.

"Doesn't matter, anyway. Neither one of us could get this guy," she responded with a shrug.

Jane studied her coworker. "He's that hot?"

"We're talking two hundred pounds of lean muscle, the tightest ass I've ever seen and the kind of lips that could keep a woman on her back for weeks." With that, the door closed.

Choosing between her desire to smoke and her avid curiosity, Jane put out her second cigarette and followed Danielle inside. Then she wished she'd asked for a name. The guy was gorgeous, all right. With close-cropped dark hair, so dark it was almost black, light-green eyes and a rugged, well-sculpted face, he definitely made an impression.

Too bad he was the detective who'd put her husband away.

"What do *you* want?" she asked.

Danielle glanced up at her waspish tone.

"This guy's a cop," Jane told her.

"Must've heard you were smoking in the shop." Danielle sent him a smile that showed her dimples, but also revealed her crooked teeth. "I hope he brought his handcuffs."

Detective Willis's eyebrows went up, but the grin he wore said he wasn't uncomfortable with the compliment.

"Danielle's getting desperate," Jane grumbled. "The extra weight's affecting her love life."

Looking more surprised by her insult than Danielle's shameless flirting, Willis didn't comment on either. "Will you step outside with me for a minute?"

"Are you taking volunteers?" Danielle asked.

Giving her a more practiced smile, the kind of smile meant to be polite while maintaining a certain distance, he flashed a wedding band, the sight of which surprised Jane. Last she'd heard, the detective was divorced.

"Damn," Danielle muttered. "The good ones are always taken."

"Don't let him fool you," Jane said. "My husband could tell you a thing or two about the great detective."

Willis's intriguing eyes focused on her. "Do you really want to talk about your husband in here?"

His sober tone made Jane nervous. Did he have bad news? She knew he thought Oliver had murdered three women. She already battled nightmares featuring a policeman knocking at her door to tell her it was true. If this turned out to be that visit, Jane didn't think she could cope. Not with the stress of ending her relationship with Noah while hanging in there for Kate.

"I can't leave right now," she said uncertainly. "You took away the breadwinner in my family, and now I've got bills to pay." *You've brought me enough grief. Please, God, make him go away.*

But her prayers went unanswered.

"How long does it take you to do a haircut?" he asked.

"Twenty, thirty minutes."

He handed her a twenty. "I just bought a half hour of your time. Would you prefer I sit in your chair, or can we go for a walk?"

She made a show of tucking the money into her bra, but his eyes didn't lower to her cleavage. Danielle was right. She couldn't get Detective Willis even if she wanted him. At forty-two, she was older, and the years were beginning to show. She had more years on him than she did on Oliver. Would her husband find her unattractive when he came home?

If he came home, she corrected herself. She wasn't sure of anything now that the detective was standing in the salon.

Wrapping her long purple sweater tightly around her, she went outside with him. "Mind if I smoke?"

"Not if it makes you more comfortable."

She lit up and inhaled deeply. It was a nasty habit, one her old friends would've frowned upon. But it got her through the day. "What is it?" she asked, bracing for the worst.

"Are you still taking sleeping pills?"

She gave him a dirty look. Thanks to him, the D.A. had made a big deal out of that at the trial, claiming Oliver could've done anything while she was unconscious and she never would've known. But she didn't feel he was bullying her. He really wanted to know. "No. For the most part, I can get to sleep on my own now."

"That's good. Have you discovered anything since your husband went to prison, maybe in the move, that might indicate Oliver knew Meredith Connelly, Patty Poindexter or Amber Farello?"

"You think I'd tell you if I did?"

"It's been three years," he countered. "I'm hoping you've had some time to consider the possibilities."

Jane breathed a little easier. So he had nothing new, just more of the same. Maybe she could handle this. "Determined, aren't you?"

She realized his friendly expression was calculated to charm her—yet it still worked. With broad shoulders and the kind of muscles you saw in men determined to stay in top physical shape, the detective was rugged, cocky, intense. In her mentally fragile state, he posed a real threat to her defenses. "What was I supposed to find?" she asked.

"An article of clothing. A piece of jewelry. A knife."

"Why is it so hard for you to believe that my husband isn't what you think? Skye Kellerman was on drugs. She stabbed Oliver with her scissors, for crying out loud."

His thick dark lashes created the perfect frame for his green eyes. "Skye wasn't on drugs."

"You don't know that. You just can't imagine such a beautiful woman being the one at fault—can you?"

If he heard the hint of jealousy in her voice, he ignored it. "I'm talking about trophies. Some rapists and murderers like to collect them, treasure them, use them to relive their crimes."

Rapists and murderers... She scowled at him. "You're not going to answer my question?"

"Skye's beauty has nothing to do with my reason for being here."

"Yes, it does," she said. "It has everything to do with me being here, too."

"Did you ever wake up to find your husband gone? Or maybe washing up in the bathroom?"

He was so eager to move on she wondered if she could've misread some of the heated looks he and Skye Kellerman had exchanged during the trial. Was it just the emotion of the moment? A common cause and genuine sympathy, however misplaced? Or something deeper? "He was a busy man. He came home late some evenings, got up early most mornings."

"Were there days when he got up so early you had no idea what time he actually left the house?"

"Of course. But that doesn't mean anything. A lot of wives could say the same. I generally slept later than he did, whether I'd taken a sleeping pill the night before or not. I didn't expect him to clock in and out." She frowned. "But that was in the good old days..."

"Were they all good?"

"What do you mean?"

"Oliver never behaved distantly, strangely? Nothing happened that made you wonder if he was the man you thought he was?"

Jane immediately recalled the weekend she'd avoided talking about—when Oliver had wanted to experiment with Viagra right after it hit the market. A few days later, he'd brought home something he said would charge *her* up, make her hungry for sex. So she'd agreed to take it. She hadn't wanted her husband to think she was boring just because she was a few years older. But it'd turned out to be the strangest experience. Oliver claimed they'd made love several times. He had scratches on his body to prove she'd gotten a little out of control. But she couldn't remember ever touching him, and none of those women had been murdered at that time. It was probably nothing….

"Jane?" the detective prompted, and she realized she'd stopped walking.

"He was perfectly normal," she replied and started moving again.

Willis stared at the ground as he kept pace with her. "Remaining silent could be dangerous, Jane."

She was tired of the questions, the constant assault on what she believed.

Or was it only what she *wanted* to believe? Rubbing her eyes with her free hand, she sighed. "Will you stop?"

Hooking his thumbs in the pockets of his well-worn jeans, he stepped in front of her, blocking her forward progress. The T-shirt beneath his leather jacket stretched across his chest, revealing the contours of his pectoral muscles, which was definitely distracting and made it more difficult to remember that he was her enemy.

"Think about what could happen if you're wrong," he said.

He was trying to undermine her confidence, frighten her. And it was working. "I'm not taking sleeping pills, so I'll be more aware."

"You figure that'll stop him?"

"You're worried about nothing," she insisted, but she wasn't as positive as she'd once been. That weekend when Oliver had behaved so strangely had always troubled her, but it troubled her even more now. Still, no one had been hurt that weekend. "You searched my house and you found *nothing,* remember?"

Rubbing the beard growth that was just beginning to shadow his chin, Willis switched tactics. "At trial, you said you met Oliver at a pizza parlor when you were already working as a hairstylist. He was only a junior in high school, but you were attracted to each other right away, went out that night and became exclusive shortly after."

She laughed bitterly. "And I was worried about the age difference. I never guessed I'd have to deal with anything like what's happened since." She stared at the handsome detective through the smoke curling from her cigarette. "You can't imagine what it's been like for me, having the father of my child, my *husband,* convicted of attempted rape."

Willis seemed genuinely sympathetic. "It's a wonder you've hung on through all of this."

"I've hung on because he didn't do it," she said matter-of-factly, but the suspicion she'd denied for so long was reasserting itself. *What if?* her mind kept asking. Did she know Oliver as well as she thought she did?

"Tell me about some of the girls he used to date—or wanted to date or simply admired."

"Back in high school?" She dropped her hand. Where was Willis going with this? Maybe she was disillusioned, exhausted, confused, but she had to be on her toes constantly. Protect what she had left.

"Anytime."

"Why? None of the girls Oliver knew back then have been raped or killed. A couple even came forward as character witnesses at his trial."

"Was there a particular girl he might've wanted who didn't return his interest? Someone he had a crush on?"

She didn't bother to search her memory. She knew the safe answer. "No. I'm the only woman he's ever loved."

"I'm not asking about love."

"We all meet people we'd like to get with. They come and go. My friend at the salon's interested in you, right?" Jane suspected most women would have difficulty remaining immune to Willis's raw sexuality but she liked pretending she wasn't one of them.

"This wouldn't be someone who merely turned his head. This would be someone who stood out. A fixation with the prom queen, the captain of the cheer squad, someone he talked about a lot."

"The captain of the cheer squad *was* the prom queen, at least in his senior year. I went to the football game with him and watched the crowning ceremony. If I remember right, she wasn't that attractive. Certainly nothing remarkable."

"Who was the prettiest girl in school?"

Jane was about to say she had no idea. But then she remembered Oliver staring at a slim redhead who sat on the float next to the prom queen, wearing a stunning evening gown that showed off her incredible figure. He'd been so mesmerized by this homecoming "princess" that Jane had caught him hours later trying to talk her into dancing with him. The girl couldn't be persuaded, and her refusal had bothered Oliver so much he'd been agitated for the rest of the evening.

Jane hadn't felt jealous of many girls. Being older was a good thing back then, an advantage, and she wasn't bad-looking herself. But jealousy had struck hard and fast that night. "Miranda Dodge," she said, almost automatically.

"Who was she?"

She took another drag on her cigarette. "The girl all the guys wanted." She blew out the smoke. "The kind you'd probably like. And get."

"Who'd she end up with?"

"I don't know. She went on to become a model, though. Last I heard she had a big spread in *Playboy*."

"Playboy?" Willis repeated the name of the magazine as if he wanted to be sure he'd heard right.

"Yeah, *Playboy*." Shortly after Jane had married Oliver, she'd discovered that particular issue in Oliver's desk drawer. Which had also bothered her. "Why?"

Willis didn't respond.

"Detective?" His manner made Jane nervous, and she wondered if she'd given away more than she'd intended by mentioning a pretty girl from Oliver's past. "He hasn't had any contact with her. It doesn't mean anything."

"Do you know anyone who might still be in contact with Miranda?"

She waved the hand with the cigarette. "I have no

idea why I even remember her name." Except for those few hours of intense jealousy and that damn magazine in her husband's drawer, which had been so dog-eared she'd known he'd spent a great deal of time admiring Miranda's pictures.

"The age difference between you and Oliver didn't—"

"Age has nothing to do with attraction," she said, her words curt.

"You were twenty-two when you started dating. He was barely sixteen. Some parents would worry about him finishing school, getting an education."

"I was able to put him through school because I had a job," she said. "They should be damn grateful to me."

"Are they?"

"I guess they are, now."

"And then?"

"Until he graduated, we didn't tell them how old I was. They thought I was going to a high school across town." She glanced at her watch, wanting to get back to work before she said something that would really cause repercussions. "My break is over."

He lifted a finger, indicating that he needed just one more minute. "Do you think Oliver ever cheated on you before the incident with Skye?"

This was the question that had gnawed at Jane ever since she'd first heard about Skye Kellerman. Granted, Skye was exceptionally pretty. But if Oliver could succumb to temptation that easily, there had to be other indiscretions, didn't there? Jane had even wondered if he'd messed around with some of his patients or dental assistants, people she knew and socialized with. Had she given one of her husband's lovers a Christmas bonus? Had *he?*

Considering what she'd done since, she couldn't get too indignant. Still… "You're wasting your time asking *me*. I'm the last person he'd tell, for obvious reasons."

"You might be the last person he'd tell, but I'm betting you'd be the first to guess."

She took a final drag on her cigarette, which had burned all the way to the filter. "I suspect he did, okay? What wife wouldn't question his fidelity after what I've been through?"

"Did he ever come home late, receive unexplained e-mails or phone calls, act in an evasive manner?"

He was asking her the same question *again,* going at it from a different angle, one that might slip beneath her defenses. "Not specifically." Tossing the butt of her cigarette onto the oil-stained blacktop, she crushed it beneath the toe of her high-heeled shoe. "Sometimes when we were out together, he'd stop in the middle of the street to watch a pretty woman walk by. But a lot of men do that."

"What about his sexual habits?"

"What about them?"

"Would you say he was normal in that regard?"

She already craved another cigarette. "What's normal? Everyone's different." Except that she was pretty sure the detective didn't have trouble performing on demand. Sometimes Oliver couldn't get a hard-on. His occasional impotence had been a source of frustration to them both, especially because Oliver always blamed her for any failed attempts to make love. Usually he said she wasn't exciting enough.

"Was he addicted to sex?"

"How do you define an addiction?" she asked flippantly. "Almost every man I know is addicted to sex."

"Enjoying sex and being addicted to it aren't the same thing. Did he want it once a day, twice a day, more? Did he talk about it excessively?"

If anything, Oliver had the opposite problem. More often than not, he'd preferred to take care of his own needs. She figured he used Miranda's photos to help him with that, which really bothered her. But she supposed that wasn't so unusual. Plenty of men fantasized with girlie magazines. "No."

"Once a week?"

Reluctant to say it was only once a month or so, for fear the detective would wonder if she was lacking in some way, she looked over her shoulder at the shop—and saw Danielle standing at the door, ostensibly smoking but watching them curiously. "That kind of stuff is none of your business. I've gotta go," she said, but Willis's next question held her as surely as if he'd reached out to grab her.

"How often did he shave his genital area?"

Pivoting, Jane lowered her voice. "Wh-what?"

Willis seemed to notice Danielle, too. Turning his back to her, he leaned closer to Jane. "You heard me. Come on, Jane. I'm only asking for the truth."

"You're twisting the truth to destroy an innocent man!" she whispered harshly. "And you're destroying me along with him!"

"Are you *sure* he's innocent?" It wasn't a question he expected her to answer. But the way he was looking at her, as if he could read every doubt, made even her teeth ache.

"Leave me alone."

"How often did he shave himself?"

"A lot of men shave. He was a cyclist."

"Cyclists shave their *arms* and *legs*."

She twisted her fingers together so tightly they hurt. "It's popular to do more than that these days."

"Then what harm could it do to tell me?"

Little warning bells were going off inside Jane's head. But they couldn't retry Oliver on the Kellerman attack. That was double jeopardy….

"Help me out," he said.

When he used that line, Jane figured just about any woman would sell her soul to give him what he wanted. And she wasn't as different as she would've liked. "Every now and then," she admitted.

"Did he refuse to let the hair grow back? Or was there a regular pattern—like shaving every other day or every weekend?"

She considered lighting another cigarette, decided against it. The nicotine calmed her. But she didn't want the detective to interpret the action as an invitation to stay longer. She was beginning to feel as if he was her friend, and that was very dangerous indeed. "He didn't shave all the time. There was no pattern."

Folding his arms, Willis glanced away and cleared his throat. "Did he want you to…you know, shave the same area?"

Jane found his obvious regret at having to ask such a personal question as unexpected as it was appealing. Not only was Willis sexy as hell, he came off like a decent guy, and that decency was at odds with the blame Jane laid at his feet. "No. Whether Oliver shaved or not, or when he shaved, didn't seem to have anything to do with me. He did it just like he was…I don't know, clipping his nails. Why?"

Willis didn't answer. He withdrew a card from his pocket. "Call me if you notice anything unusual. Particularly if he's shaved the same day."

She laughed in disbelief and exasperation. "You're convinced my husband is a murderer!"

"Completely," he said and handed her his card.

6

"Some of you have probably been told that guns are not for women." Fighting the fatigue that plagued her after another sleepless night, Skye stood before fifteen students in the small classroom at the shooting range. For many of these women, today would be the first time they'd ever held a gun, so she always started by dispelling the myths that surrounded their use. "You've heard that women are too timid or frightened to handle a gun. Women don't have the upper-body strength to become efficient marksmen. Women don't have the 'guts' to manage such a powerful weapon." She paused, made eye contact with each person. "Raise your hand if you've ever heard something like this."

Several hands went up.

"Don't believe it. I won't discuss the sexism inherent in this kind of talk, but I will address the only one of those statements that is, at least partially, true. Women often lack upper-body strength, which can put them at a disadvantage when handling a gun. Most of our strength comes from our legs. But with the right technique, almost any woman, no matter how small, can learn to shoot and do it well."

Turning away to cover a yawn of exhaustion, she

moved closer to a diagram she'd drawn on the board. "First, it's important to get the correct-size gun for your hand. Make sure it fits comfortably and that you have a good grip. In this picture, the gun is too big. See how the line of the wrist has to be broken for the finger to reach the trigger? You don't want that. You want the backstrap to fit perfectly in the web of your hand so that it lines up with the bones in your forearm, like this." She pointed at the ideal fit in the second diagram. "It's easier to use a gun that's too small than one that's too large." She circled a third picture showing a tiny gun held by a large woman. "You'll just have to be careful not to put too much of your finger on the trigger while you're firing."

She approached a table where she'd placed a variety of unloaded handguns. "Now, let's look at the differences between pistols and semiautomatics, and why one might work better than the other in certain circumstances."

A hand went up.

Skye motioned for the woman to ask her question.

"How long have you been shooting?"

"Four years."

The brunette in the third row raised her hand.

"Yes?"

"Did it take a while to become good at it?"

Skye hid a sigh. She hadn't prefaced her lecture with her usual bio because she wanted to get through the material as quickly as possible. Her mind wasn't on teaching. It was on the threatening call she'd received, on Burke's impending release, which was getting closer and closer, Sean Regan's sudden disappearance, Jasmine and the child she was searching for in Ft. Bragg and the financial difficulties they were facing at The Last Stand. The list was getting long….

But she should've given more of her background. Apparently "My name is Skye Kellerman. I'll be your gun instructor today," wasn't enough. "No," she replied, "but I was determined to learn fast, and I've spent a great deal of time practicing. Now—"

"Are you a policewoman?" another woman interrupted.

They wouldn't stop until they had the whole story. "No. I was the victim of an attempted rape."

A collective murmur went through the room.

"I decided to prepare myself in case such an attack ever happens again," she explained.

"Did they catch the guy?" the bone-thin woman in the front row wanted to know.

"Yes, the police tracked him down and put him in prison." But that didn't relieve the fear she felt as a result of her experience. *Nothing* relieved the fear. They wouldn't understand that, though, not unless they'd been through a similar trauma.

"How many years did he get?" It was the woman sitting next to the thin lady.

"Eight to ten. But the reality is three. He'll be out on parole this weekend."

The voices grew loud as they responded with alarm, but she didn't believe in minimizing what had happened to her. The public needed to know. *Women* needed to know. *It could happen to you* was her message. They had to be prepared.

"Are you the person who started that victim's organization I've read about?" a middle-aged woman with salt-and-pepper hair asked.

"I'm one of them," she clarified. Then several hands shot up, but she shook her head. "I'm happy to tell you all about The Last Stand, what we do and what we're about. Maybe you'd even like to get involved. But let's finish our class first, okay?"

The class quieted and she returned to the blackboard just as someone at the very back spoke up. The voice startled her because it was a man's. "How many guns do you own?"

Turning, Skye saw that Detective Willis had slipped into the room. Where he'd come from or why he was there, she had no idea. But he was scowling.

"I have several, Detective," she said. "I have a 9mm pistol, but I generally prefer the Kel-Tec P-3AT semi-automatic—although I wouldn't recommend it to a novice—or the P232 Sig Sauer."

"And do they help you sleep better at night?"

"I wouldn't want to be without them," she retorted.

He said nothing more, but the disapproval on his face bothered her. After his remarks in the past, she could imagine what he was thinking: *What, no machine gun? No grenade launcher?* He wasn't happy that she hadn't called him last night; he thought she was trying to do too much on her own.

Skye continued her class as if he wasn't there and, a few minutes later, he stalked out. His attitude made her angry, and she wanted him to know. But she had fifteen people in the room, who were all there to learn about self-defense. She discussed caliber in relation to gun size, had each woman try the various guns for fit and distributed a pamphlet on gun safety that she told them they had to read and sign. Then she put in a plug for TLS, promised to bring a sign-up sheet for volunteers to their next class and smiled as they filed out.

But even after it was over, she was angry. What did David think he was doing, showing up and making his views—his negative views—so obvious? He told her to rely on him but he wouldn't rely on her. Acted like he cared but didn't *really* care. Wanted her but not enough to take what she had to offer.

When everyone had left, Skye marched out of the building and down the front steps, planning to call him the minute she reached her car. But she didn't need to. He was waiting for her. She'd barely stepped onto the ground when he shoved away from the building and intercepted her. "Hey."

"What did you think you were doing in there?" she demanded.

His eyebrows knitted. "You're getting carried away, Skye."

"What does it matter to you?"

"It matters."

She remembered the way he sat with her in the hospital, hour after hour. How gently he'd tried to question her, to pull everything she could possibly remember about Burke from her mind. The way he'd held her when those dark memories were too ugly to face. He'd been there for her through the darkest period of her life. But as soon as she'd begun to recover, he'd begun to back away.

"Then ignore it," she said. "You're good at ignoring things." She'd thought she wanted to talk to him, but she didn't. What was there to say? They'd only disagree. She tried to pass him, but he blocked her from going around him.

"Can't you see yourself?" he asked. "You didn't call the sheriff's department last night because you think you've got it covered, with your guns and your training and your 'been there, done that' tough bullshit. Are you trying to become some sort of female Rambo? If so, that's foolish. Reckless."

"Says you!"

"Yeah, says me! It's already Tuesday. Burke is getting out in three days. Do you really want to shut me out right now, when we most need to work together?"

She didn't. That was the problem. She wanted his help professionally, but working with him left her emotionally vulnerable. She couldn't separate the two, not as easily as he seemed to do.

She wished they could go back to the early days, when their feelings were first developing, when everything was still so innocent and unexpected that it took them both unawares. Now that David knew he had to guard against personal involvement, nothing was the same, which was why she'd changed, too—grown defensive. "And where will you be when Burke comes after me again?" she asked. "Sleeping with your ex-wife?"

He blanched but didn't respond to the verbal jab. "I'm hoping to find something that will enable me to arrest him again before that can happen. And I could use a little cooperation."

"I'm handling the situation the best way I know how."

He glared at her for a moment, then sighed as if he realized it was his other feelings—the frustration and confusion he felt with her—that had him so worked up. "I talked with Jane this morning," he said, obviously trying to control his emotions.

Skye caught her breath, curious in spite of the need to put distance between them. "Jane Burke?"

"Yes."

"How's she getting by without her husband?"

"She's making it, I guess. She cuts hair for a living at a small salon off Greenback and Van Maren."

"Is she still with Oliver?"

"Evidently. But she's beginning to wonder about him. Depending on how well they get along when he's released, she might become an ally before this is over."

"That's what you came to tell me?"

He shoved his hands in his pockets. "I was hoping it might make his imminent parole a bit easier for you—the fact that some of the people who were once so loyal to him might be having second thoughts."

"How'd you know I'd be here?" she asked.

"Sheridan told me." He touched her arm. "There's more, Skye."

Struggling to shore up her anger against the unrequited longing she always felt in David's presence, Skye tightened the ponytail that held her hair back. "What is it?"

"I checked with the phone company. That call the other night came from a pay phone in Oak Park."

Oak Park was a rough section of Sacramento, about as rough as California's capital got. But it wasn't San Quentin. "So it couldn't have been Oliver."

"No, but we already knew that."

"Thanks for checking." She started to move off again, but he closed the distance between them.

"Skye."

Stopping, she turned. "What?"

He said nothing. She could tell it was just more of the same old attraction. And the same old refusal to act on that attraction.

"It'd probably be best if you called when you need to talk to me," she said.

"You don't want to see me?" He said it as if he knew it was a lie.

"Not particularly."

She walked off again, and he caught her arm, only this time when she turned he didn't say anything. Pulling her to him, he slid his hand into her hair and glared down at her. The conflict inside him made his eyes darker than usual, gave his features a slightly harsh edge.

She parted her lips, determined to tell him to release her. But then his mouth found hers.

Skye had wanted this for so long she didn't hesitate. Closing her eyes, she clung to him, greedily accepting what he offered. His tongue moved over hers, tasting, touching, giving—as his kiss said everything he never would.

It wasn't until another car entered the parking lot that they finally broke apart.

"God, you make me crazy," he muttered.

Winded, she gazed up at him. "Is that really so bad?"

He raked a hand through his hair. "Yes!"

"Why?"

"Because it's turning me into someone I'd rather not be."

"*Human,* David? Is it so bad to want someone?"

"When that desire means giving in to the easy thing, the most selfish thing, yes."

She pressed her fingers to both temples. She knew she

should continue to her car, but that kiss had brought hope roaring back to life. "I need a date for Saturday night."

"You're asking me out?" The strain in his face eased into a half-hearted grin. "That kiss must've been even better than I thought."

"I'm not exactly weak in the knees," she lied. "Anyway, it's not an invitation to stay the night. It's business."

The grin disappeared. "What kind of business?"

"A fund-raiser for The Last Stand."

He shook his head. "Leave me out of it. In my opinion, you're already too involved. Someone called you last night to say he's going to slit your throat. Do you think I want you out there making more enemies?"

"I'm helping the little guy. If that makes enemies, so be it."

"*So be it?* Listen to yourself! You're making it impossible for me to protect you!"

"I'm ready for anyone who comes after me."

He stepped closer but didn't touch her. "Then God forbid you ever shoot someone you don't mean to kill."

"Maybe you don't like what I'm doing, but what's my other choice?" she said. "Should I sit back and do nothing? Call you every time I get scared? Leave the battle to others? We *have* to fight back."

"That's what I do every day. That's what police are for!"

She didn't want to say they were falling short, not when he worked so hard. But they *were* falling short. Look at Sean Regan. Before class, she'd contacted the detective assigned to his case, a guy by the name of Fitzer. She'd told him of her experience with Sean and her suspicions about Tasha Regan, but he didn't seem concerned. He'd brushed her off, said, "I'm checking into it," but gave her the impression that he was either so overworked or so incompetent he hadn't done in the entire past week what he should've done the first day.

It was a good thing she'd hired Jonathan. He'd already reported that Sean's wife was likely seeing someone else, as Sean had said. And she'd gone on a spending spree, as if she was celebrating something. Those were hardly the actions of a traumatized wife.

Briefly covering her eyes with her hand, Skye struggled to rein in her emotions, to put the situation in perspective. She almost wished she didn't feel so passionate about everything—especially David. "It's just dinner and dancing, okay? All you have to do is smile and shake a few hands."

"Skye—"

She cut him off before he could argue any more. "It'd really help to have some police presence there, the appearance of support. I can't imagine it'd be bad for the department, either. We're both on the victim's side, right? We should act friendly even if we're not."

"I just want to keep you *safe*."

"Then make sure I'm safe on Saturday."

With a heavy sigh, he shifted his gaze and stared off toward the shooting range, from which they could hear the "crack" and "pop" of gunfire. "I have Jeremy this weekend."

That was the one excuse she couldn't contest, which frustrated her more than ever. "Fine." Pivoting, she hurried across the parking lot, but when she reached her car, he called after her.

"I'll find a babysitter. What time do I pick you up?"

Pulling out her keys, she unlocked her door.

"Are you going to answer me?"

She told herself to put an end to the tug-of-war between them. To tell him to forget it and never contact her again. But, in the end, she couldn't do it. "Six."

"I'll be there."

"One more thing," she said.

"What's that?"

"It's formal."

"Formal?" His tone was a complaint, but she didn't give him the chance to back out. Getting in her car, she drove away.

The address in the phone book for Jane Burke corresponded to a rental off Sunrise. Tonight that rental was dark and quiet and had been since ten. Skye knew because she'd been sitting across the street in her 1998 Volvo sedan for two hours. This late, there wasn't much to see. But it was still creepy to be here, to know Burke's wife and daughter were so close and that he'd be joining them in just three days.

Tilting her seat back, Skye took a deep breath and narrowed her eyes at the building with its peeling paint and the child's swing hanging from a tree in the front yard. She wanted to leave and not look back, to go on as if what had happened with Burke would never happen again. David would be furious if he knew what she was doing tonight. But she *couldn't* leave. Every time she closed her eyes, she saw Burke glaring at her as they read the verdict. He planned to come after her. Maybe not right away, but eventually. And how many others would he hurt in the meantime?

She knew what he was. Couldn't ignore it. Which meant she had to stay one step ahead of him, anticipate his movements, act before he could. If she was lucky, she'd uncover enough evidence to put him away for life. If she wasn't…

Burke's blade flashed in her mind's eye, so real she almost lifted her arms to protect herself. *When I get out, I'm going to slit your throat….* He couldn't have made that call himself. But someone else could've made it for him.

Alone on the dark street, frightened by her own thoughts, she grew even more uneasy when a pair of headlights swung around the corner. Ducking so the driver couldn't see her, she listened for the hum of the motor. But the car didn't pass as quickly as she expected it to. It decelerated as it drew near, then sped up again and continued down the street.

Why had it slowed? Raising her head long enough to check the rearview mirror, she noted that it was a midsize Lexus, which wouldn't draw stares in a middle- or upper-class neighborhood but didn't fit here. This neighborhood was cluttered with dented trucks, economy cars and a few pimped-out sports cars.

Still, she didn't think much of it until five minutes later, when the same car made another pass.

Again she slid down, listening. This time the Lexus moved at a crawl when it reached her, and she got the uneasy feeling the driver was trying to peer into her windows.

Obviously, she'd caught someone's interest. Jane's? There'd been a porch light on when Skye arrived, which had since gone off, but perhaps Jane had left a babysitter in charge of Kate.

Afraid that whoever it was would come by again—and that this time he or she would park and approach the car—Skye waited until the taillights of the Lexus disappeared around the corner. Then she grabbed her flashlight and gun, shoved them into the pocket of her heavy coat, and crept out the passenger side, which fronted a duplex that looked every bit as drab as Jane Burke's house.

Circling to avoid the light shed by the street lamps, she cut across to Jane's side yard, where she made a soft clicking sound at the gate to see if Jane had a dog.

No barking, growling, whining or pawing. Nothing.

Lifting the latch, Skye slipped inside.

It didn't take long to realize that Jane was home. There was a light glowing in back that couldn't be seen from the street because the garage hid everything except the narrow walkway that approached the front door. Skye could see Oliver's wife through the living room window, pacing in the kitchen, appearing and then disappearing as she walked back and forth, talking on the phone.

Fortunately, the kitchen blinds were drawn, making it possible for Skye to move close enough to hear her voice.

"I'm telling you that car's been parked out there all night… I saw someone in it—" Skye couldn't decipher the next few words. "…Do you think it could be the police? That detective came by the shop earlier…. Can't you check again? For *me?*"

Going back to the gate, Skye squatted to peer through a gap in the fence boards, watching for the Lexus—which came rolling down the street for the third time. She couldn't see the driver—it was too dark inside the vehicle—but the brake lights flashed as whoever it was stopped in front of her Volvo.

A car door opened, then shut. The driver must have been looking inside her car. As the Lexus pulled away a moment later, the phone rang in the house and, through the window, Skye saw Jane pick up. She took her time returning to the back—she didn't want to bump into anything in her haste—so she missed the first part of Jane's side of the conversation.

"…It's just that, well, you know how awful it's been," Jane was saying. "I know you weren't planning to stop, but can't you come in?… Just tell her I was frightened, that I needed you to check the windows and doors. That'll give us a few minutes…." Jane must've turned away or lowered her head, because Skye could make out only a few more words—"waiting," "quick," and "I love you"—before the conversation ended.

Who was Jane talking to? David had said she was still with Oliver, but this made Skye wonder.

Circling to the side again, she watched the Lexus pull up to the curb. A man, about six feet tall, wearing jeans and a heavy jacket, exited the car.

The living room light went on as Jane answered the door, forcing Skye to back away from the window. She was so busy making sure she was out of sight, she didn't get a good glimpse of Jane's visitor until Jane had let him in. Then Skye could see him easily enough from her vantage point beside the window—and immediately recognized him. He was Oliver's brother. Along with the rest of Oliver's family, he'd attended almost every day of the trial.

Jane had spotted the Volvo across the street and called her brother-in-law to check it out.

Feeling a little guilty for frightening her, Skye pressed her back to the rough stucco wall of the house and stopped watching. Jane was a victim of what Oliver had done, too. She just didn't understand who she should blame judging by the hate letters she'd sent Skye.

But a final glance inside the house, to ensure that it was safe to let herself out of the yard, left Skye rooted to the grassless earth. Jane was kissing Oliver's brother—and not the way one would typically kiss a brother-in-law. He had his tongue in her mouth and his hand inside her robe.

Tell her I was frightened... That'll give us a few minutes.... Tell who? His wife? Was Jane having an affair with *her brother-in-law?*

If so, Skye didn't want to know about it. Oliver was being released in three days. What would he do if he found out? Would he kill his wife—his brother, too? And what would happen to the young girl, Kate, if she lost her mother?

Obviously, Jane had no clue how dangerous her husband was. She'd never faced the sharp point of his knife. But that could change. Especially now.

Closing her eyes, Skye sank to the ground and didn't get up until long after Oliver's brother had left and the house was completely dark. It was safer to wait. And yet, even after all that time, she couldn't decide what to do. She wanted to warn Jane. After fighting Oliver for her own life, Skye *knew* what he was capable of. But what were the chances that Jane would listen to her?

Skye could only hope that Oliver never found out....

Eager to put some distance between herself and this place, she opened the gate. Jane's garbage can stood next to her in all its stinking glory, and it hadn't been emptied in a while. Maybe it contained letters from Oliver, something that might tell Skye about the Burkes' future plans.

Returning to her car, she drove to the closest convenience store, bought some plastic bags and rubber gloves and went back to claim what Jane Burke was throwing away.

7

"I can't believe you brought that into my house," Sheridan grumbled, shying away from the smelly heap Skye had dumped on an old sheet in the middle of her kitchen floor.

"You're the one who called me up and insisted I come over." Skye sat down and began picking through the trash. "I told you I was investigating a case, that I had some garbage with me."

"I was worried when I couldn't reach you at home." She leaned against the opening to the kitchen, watching in obvious repugnance. "Did Detective Willis ever get hold of you?"

"He confronted me at the shooting range, right in front of my class. Thank you for that, by the way."

Sheridan bristled at the sarcasm. "Now I can't tell him where to find you?"

Skye wasn't sure. She'd spent all afternoon trying not to think of that kiss in the parking lot. "I don't know."

"That's some clear direction."

With a shrug, Skye kept digging.

"You're going to stay here tonight, aren't you?" Using her foot, Sheridan pushed a crumpled sack farther onto the blanket. "I mean, if I have to smell this, it should be for a good reason."

"If you want me to."

"Wow, that was easy." She smiled in relief. "So, whose garbage is this? Don't tell me you took it from Sean Regan's house."

"No. I'm trusting Jonathan to do what needs to be done there." She had to. She had too much going on in her own life.

"What case are you working on?"

"My own."

A suspicious silence met this response. Bending, Sheridan plucked an envelope out of the garbage. "Jane A. Burke," she read aloud. Then her jaw dropped and her eyes went round. "You've got to be kidding me."

Skye kept sifting and tossing. An empty cookie package. An empty potato chip bag…

"Have you lost your mind?" Sheridan demanded.

"No." Skye refused to look up.

"You get angry at Detective Willis for saying you're asking for trouble. But what do you call *this?*"

Skye finally met her friend's agitated gaze. "For your information, he thinks we're all asking for trouble. And if Burke really killed those women, he's a serial rapist and murderer, Sheridan. That kind of person doesn't stop. He has to *be* stopped. I know how coldly calculating Burke is, how much pleasure he derives from hurting women."

"That's the problem. It's possible he's still obsessed with you. If he finds out you were at his house, it'll be like…like pulling the tail of a rabid dog! He'll come after you. You know he will."

Skye suspected he'd come after her anyway. "His wife is having an affair with his brother."

As expected, that statement stole the fire from Sheridan's anger. *"What?"*

"I saw them together. Tonight."

Her eyebrows went up. "Not doing…"

"Kissing passionately. Definitely a precursor."

"Not only were you stealing Jane Burke's trash, you were peeking in her windows?"

Skye wrinkled her nose at a soggy napkin. "It's a long story. Bottom line, I was trying to become familiar with Burke's situation before he gets home."

"So you can do what?"

"Keep an eye on him. Put him away when he acts out again."

Sheridan shook her head. "That's not your job."

"Yes, it is. I've made it my job, and you've done the same, on other cases for other people."

"Those other people aren't so close to me. This scares me. It's bad enough that he's getting out. Now you're surveilling his place?"

"I've gotta do what I've gotta do. I can't just run scared."

Sheridan straightened. "How do you think he'll react when he finds out that his wife is sleeping with his brother?"

"The same way you think he'll react."

Placing both hands on her head, Sheridan said, "Oh, boy. She's in trouble."

"And she doesn't even know it." With a heavy sigh, Skye went back to work.

Sheridan sank to her knees. "Do we warn her?"

"I can't decide." Skye found a note from Burke's

daughter's school. Kate was misbehaving, so the teacher requested a parent-teacher conference.

As Skye set the note aside, she tried not to feel any empathy for Jane. Jane certainly wouldn't thank her for it. But Burke's wife was struggling; she could tell.

"What'd you find?" Sheridan asked.

"Another small bit of Jane's life."

Sheridan stared at the note. "Should we call her?"

"And say what? If all the testimony she heard in that trial didn't make her wonder if her husband could be dangerous, nothing *I* say will convince her."

"What a mess."

Skye didn't know if she was talking literally or figuratively, but the comment fit regardless.

Shoving the sleeves of her sweatshirt up to her elbows, Sheridan sat crossed-legged on the floor and joined in. "What are we looking for?"

"Anything that'll give us an idea where they plan to live, what they plan to do. Someone has to keep very close tabs on him."

Sheridan fished out an empty wine bottle. "Hey, this is expensive stuff."

Skye studied the label. "A quiet evening alone," she said, her mind on what she'd witnessed earlier.

"Tell me Oliver's brother doesn't have a wife."

"I'm pretty sure he does."

Sheridan cursed under her breath. "And it gets uglier."

"There might be kids involved, too. Besides poor Kate, I mean."

Sheridan held up a wet Post-it note. Although the ink was running, Oliver's name was still legible, as well as an address someone had jotted down. "What about this?"

"Doesn't have a city or zip," Skye mused.

"That means it's probably local. But there might not be any real connection between Oliver and the address. Jane might've been doodling."

"It's worth checking."

Sheridan relinquished the yellow note into Skye's hand. "Do you think Oliver's wife ever wonders if you're telling the truth about what happened?"

"Going by the letters she sent me a few years ago, she seems convinced I lied about the whole thing."

"Maybe she's in denial. Maybe she can't face that she has a child with a man who's capable of doing what Burke's done." Sheridan tossed a torn shoebox at the discard pile. "Or maybe she doesn't care whether he's innocent or not."

"She cares." The level of passion in the letters Skye had received clearly revealed that. So did the way Jane had behaved at trial.

"But you'd have to question your own beliefs at some point, wouldn't you? Can you imagine what her life's been like?"

"She needs to take her little girl and move on, go somewhere Burke will never find her."

Sheridan stacked a few letters, mostly junk mail, off to one side. "Why didn't you call me before you went to Burke's house?" She looked slightly wounded. "I would've gone with you."

"You would've tried to talk me out of it."

"Of course. I'm your friend. But then I would've given in."

For the same reason. Skye responded with a tired smile. "I know. I just didn't have the energy to deal with the initial resistance." The fatigue that ebbed and flowed, depending on the amount of adrenaline in Skye's system, was making a determined resurgence. She was glad she'd come to Sheridan's condo. Maybe she'd actually be able to forgo her compulsive checking of doors and windows and get some sleep.

"What about Detective Willis?" Sheridan asked.

Skye remembered his mouth on hers, their bodies pressed tightly together in that parking lot—and wanted more. It was crazy to be so desperate for physical contact, but the heightened emotions of the past few days only made her desire to be with him that much stronger. "What about him?"

"Are you going to tell him you went over to Burke's?"

Skye grimaced as she opened a plastic bag that held rotting meat. "Ugh, not good." Quickly closing it, she carried the bag outside to dispose of it. She was pretty sure it held steak scraps—more evidence of a romantic dinner.

"You didn't answer me," Sheridan said when Skye returned.

Skye plopped onto the floor. "Because I haven't thought it through. He won't be happy to know I was over there. But I need his help to protect Jane. So…yeah, I'll probably tell him. When I get a minute."

"Then you'll be done, right? You'll turn whatever you find here over to him and quit nosing around?"

"How can I be done when Burke will still be on the loose?"

Sheridan frowned as she gathered up all the trash that had no possible value to them. "Because Detective Willis will take over and eventually put him away."

Eventually was the key word. Skye knew David was a good detective. But David had to play by the rules and Burke didn't. Burke had gotten away with murder. "This isn't David's only case, Sheridan. He has new stuff coming at him all the time. He needs whatever help we can give him."

"Then we'll hire Jonathan."

"Jonathan's busy."

"It wouldn't matter," Sheridan said. "You're caught up in this. You won't back off until…" She didn't finish.

"It's personal," Skye admitted.

Sheridan worked in silence for a few minutes. When she spoke again, the tone of her voice had changed. "Do you ever think we're getting carried away?"

Reluctant to address that question, Skye kept her hand down. "I have to know where he is, what he's doing."

"I'm not talking about Burke—not exclusively, anyway. I'm talking about living our lives the way we do."

Skye was about to throw out a sour cream container but hesitated in midmotion. She didn't see what they did at The Last Stand as getting carried away; she saw it as survival. Each case meant a lot to someone—health, safety, life and limb. She nearly said, "At what point do we decide a life is too much trouble to save?" But Sheridan's tortured expression quelled the impulse.

"Is it too much for you, Sher?" she asked. "Are you having second thoughts about The Last Stand? The sacrifice and risks involved?"

Sheridan didn't deny it as quickly as Skye had expected. She actually seemed to consider the question.

"Sometimes." A spark of defiance brought her chin

up. "I know we're providing an important service. I believe in our cause. But I'd be lying if I said I don't wish I could be as oblivious as all the people out there who've never been touched by violence, who don't have the kind of memories we do, or…"

Skye tossed the sour cream container in the bag. "Or who simply don't care?"

"Exactly."

Understanding what was at the root of Sheridan's comments, Skye offered her a sympathetic frown. "Sher, you have to quit torturing yourself." Skye had to live with the consequences of Burke's actions—and now, his imminent release—but at least she didn't have to live with the belief that she was somehow responsible for an attack that had cost the life of a friend and nearly killed her, too. "We've talked about this before, millions of times. What happened to Jason wasn't your fault."

"He wouldn't have been there without me." There was no detectable emotion in her voice—but, obviously, the tragedy still weighed heavily on her heart. Sheridan always came back to the same issue. She couldn't get beyond it.

"You were just talking to him, getting to know him," Skye said. "It was completely innocent."

"*Innocent?* I was trying to make his older brother jealous. Cain was the one I really wanted, Skye. Instead, I cost him his only sibling and he hasn't spoken to me since."

"*You* didn't cost him anything! You were barely sixteen, Sher! You meant no harm. You were playing normal boy-girl games when a man showed up with a gun, opened the door of the truck and shot you both. Out of the blue. For no reason. It was senseless and random and could've happened to anyone."

"Jason wouldn't have been there without me!"

"Sher—" Helpless in the face of her friend's pain, Skye didn't know what more she could say. Their pasts intruded again and again. It was their reality, the kind of reality they wanted to help others avoid.

With a sniff, Sheridan sat straighter. "I'm sorry. I'm okay." She'd gone pale talking about it, but she was moving again, cleaning up Jane Burke's garbage. "I'm tired, that's all. I don't think about Jason unless I'm tired."

It was a lie. Skye knew Sheridan thought about him all the time. Usually, she just covered it better. "Let's get rid of this so we can go to bed."

Sheridan nodded, but when Skye came back from taking out the garbage, she found her friend sitting in the same spot, staring into space.

"Sher?"

She blinked, then focused as if she hadn't realized Skye had ever left.

"Don't you want to spray some sanitizer?"

"Of course. It's under the sink." She stood to get it, but even after they'd finished cleaning, Sheridan wasn't herself. Skye was so worried about her she brought up the one subject she really didn't want to talk about, only because she knew it might cheer up her friend.

"I have a date for the fund-raiser."

An expectant smile curved Sheridan's lips. "Who?"

"Guess."

"You asked Detective Willis?"

Skye could see the ghosts of Sheridan's past being

forced back into the shadows of her mind and felt a measure of relief. "Yes."

"He's not back with his wife, then?"

"I'm sure he isn't or he wouldn't have agreed to go with me."

"What's happening with his ex?"

The question dimmed Skye's excitement. David wasn't in love with Lynnette—Skye was positive of that. He hadn't been for a long time. But neither could he seem to let her go. "We don't talk about her." They hadn't talked much at all, not since he'd gone back to Lynnette after the first divorce.

"Maybe there's nothing to say. Maybe she's history."

"I doubt it." Skye knew it couldn't be that simple or David would've come over last night. She could tell he'd wanted to. "So who's going to be your companion for the evening?"

A little color returned to Sheridan's cheeks as she laughed and threw up her hands. "I'm determined to come up with someone, but I haven't figured out who. The only men in my life are the ones I'm trying to help other women escape. I might have to hire a paid escort!"

"Maybe you should ask your divorced neighbor," Skye teased. "He provided me with such a wonderful time at the Christmas party."

"No way. Charlie drops by often enough as it is."

"Maybe you should suggest him to Jasmine."

"I don't think she'll be back by Saturday."

Skye sobered instantly. "Things aren't going well in Ft. Bragg?"

Sheridan's brief flash of happiness disappeared. "They found the girl's dress."

A knot formed in the pit of Skye's stomach. "Anything else?"

"Not so far."

"How's Jasmine managing?"

"Jasmine's convinced she's dead."

That said it all. "So…not well."

Sheridan's mouth formed a straight line. "No different than us, I guess."

Oliver Burke waited patiently for Victor Romey to make his way through the fifty or sixty men who were playing basketball, lifting weights or milling around in the yard. He didn't like Romey, but during the past three years they'd done a fair amount of business together. How else was he going to manage in a prison so violent it had been nicknamed The Arena? And Romey had contacts, could get things Oliver couldn't. Extra paper. Pens. Chocolate. Information. It was the information Oliver craved most. It made him feel powerful despite his incarceration. But he had to pay handsomely for every tidbit.

"You find it yet?" He glanced up at the elevated catwalk bolted to the outside wall, where several guards watched all the inmates, rifles at the ready. "The badges," as the other inmates called them, had to be particularly vigilant in the yard. If there was trouble, it was usually here. Because of the potential for violence, Oliver preferred the library or the small office in which he performed dental work for the other prisoners. That was the reason he'd been sent to San Quentin instead of somewhere else. He only came out to the yard if he needed to talk to Vic.

Vic spat at the ground. "I'm still working on it."

It didn't sound as if he was trying very hard. "What's going on? I paid you for the information two months ago."

"It's not easy. She's not listed, and she uses a post office box for her mail."

"I thought you had ways of getting around that."

"Takes time. I can give you her office address, if that helps."

Oliver rolled his eyes. "I can get that through directory assistance. Why would I pay you?"

"As long as you can find her, why do you need her home address?"

"Because I do. What is this, twenty questions? What happened to discretion?"

Victor chuckled softly. "Discretion. That's a good one."

"So you'll get it?"

"When I can."

Fighting the hatred that suddenly washed over him, Oliver gritted his teeth. He'd already paid Vic. "Are you stalling?"

Vic's eyes narrowed and Oliver nervously stepped back. He had to watch himself. Avoid making enemies. Especially now.

"Did you just call me a liar, *Ollie?*" Vic breathed.

"No...no, of course not," Oliver said, but the placating words tasted bitter in his mouth. *Ollie?* He was better than Vic, better than all the rest of the prisoners and even the guards. He'd graduated from dental school, had established a successful practice. These guys were losers—dope addicts and thugs. Most had never even been able to hold down a job.

But he'd get back at Vic later. If a man had enough patience, there were ways. He always evened the score.

"I'm anxious to get what I paid for, that's all." Oliver's gaze roved over the crowd as he tried to determine whether Vic had any friends close by who might spring at him with a homemade weapon. "I'm out in two days."

"And you're still worried about her damn address? Shit, man, she must be pretty important to you."

She was important. Extremely important. Skye had cost him everything. He wouldn't forget that. "I owe her…some money."

"Right." Vic laughed again, then quickly sobered. "Tell you what, Ollie. I'll get you her address—as soon as you give me a little something in return."

Oliver eyed him warily. "I've already paid."

"I'm afraid it's gonna cost you more than we originally agreed."

Standing with his back to the cinder-block wall, Oliver studied the men around him even more carefully.

"Not money," Vic went on. "That's not good enough this time."

"What, then?" Oliver asked. "Smokes?"

Vic leaned in close and whispered, "Get me a boulder."

Oliver stiffened in surprise. "Crack? You want me to get you *drugs?*"

Vic's eyes remained hard and glittery. "Don't sound so shocked."

"But…I *am* shocked. I'm not involved in the drug trafficking that goes on in here. I never have been, and you know it. Why are you asking me?"

"No one's really watching you right now. You're a

short-timer, eh? Anyway, it's the only way you can redeem yourself, *snitch*."

"Snitch" made Oliver's pulse race. How did Victor know about his deal with the San Francisco police? The detectives had promised they wouldn't say a word or make a move until he was free. Informing on someone, especially while he was on the inside, could get him killed.

Or was that the point?

Oliver couldn't trust anyone not to turn on him. Except Jane.

"I don't know what you're talking about," he said, feigning bewilderment.

Victor's mouth twitched. "Right. You're walkin' outta here on Friday 'cause they like you."

"I'm getting out on parole." But he wouldn't be going *anywhere,* even to work in the prison dental office, if they caught him with drugs. They'd revoke his parole, maybe send him to the Adjustment Center on a rule violation, and he'd rot there for as long as they wanted.

He couldn't let that happen. San Quentin was killing him a day at a time. The stench of the place already seemed to seep from his pores. He wondered if he'd ever wake without the memory of it.

Victor scuffed the dirt, spat again. "See that smoke-stack over there?"

Oliver glanced at the green pipe protruding from the roof of North Block. He knew it originated from the infamous gas chamber. Everyone did. "What about it?"

"That's the only way I'm gettin' outta here."

"You're not condemned."

"I will be. They're bringing new charges against me. And these will stick."

Oliver didn't care. The sooner they killed Vic, the better. As far as he was concerned it'd save him the trouble. "They don't gas people anymore," he said, unmoved. "They use lethal injection."

"What's the difference, smart guy? They gonna kill me, right? I got nothin' to lose."

Oliver was smaller than Vic, smaller than most guys. He shrank back to make Vic believe he was frightened of him. "We've always had a good relationship. I've paid you a lot over the years."

"So? Now someone else is paying me more." He kicked a pebble that hit Oliver's shin. "Get me what I want."

The stinging pain spread through Oliver's body. As he watched the rock roll to one side, he almost didn't notice that Vic was walking away. "I can't," he called after him. "I don't even know how."

"You'll figure it out."

But that would risk everything! "I don't understand. Why are you turning on me?"

"Turning on *you?*" He laughed without mirth. "Who turned on who, Ollie? Wasn't Johnny Pew your friend? Didn't he trust you when he told you what he done?" He made a *tsking* sound. "It's a damned shame you have no loyalty, that's what it is, a damned shame."

Oliver's mind stumbled over itself, searching for a solution. Vic was setting him up. If he got the drugs, someone would tip off the guards, he'd be caught and his parole would be suspended. If he didn't get the drugs, someone would stab him before he could walk out the front gates. "This isn't right," he yelled after Vic. "I didn't snitch on anyone."

"Just be sure you don't snitch on me, or the only way *you're* gettin' out of here is in a body bag."

8

Miranda Dodge had a Web site.

David skipped lunch with Tiny and one of the other detectives to view the photos she had posted, most of which were taken years earlier, while she was at the height of her modeling career. Tall, with auburn hair, Ms. Dodge had a face and figure reminiscent of Marilyn Monroe's. Very curvy. Big-busted. A build that hadn't always been an asset. She'd been trying to break into modeling during the nineties, when Kate Moss set the standard and women were starving themselves to achieve the "waif" look.

She hadn't gotten as far as she would've liked. The spread in *Playboy* was extensive—five pages of her in various stages of undress, standing beneath a waterfall, swimming in a tropical pond, lying on the beach covered only in sand. But she hadn't appeared in any other major publications. David guessed she kept her *Playboy* pictures on her site, despite the fact that they were rather dated, simply to build demand for what she was doing now—selling a workout video and diet plan with her own label.

He read through her guest book, which contained

entries from the visitors to her site. Most were men, drooling over the nude pictures. One comment came from a teenage girl interested in being introduced to Hugh Hefner and getting her own "start in the biz."

Ms. Dodge had a blog, too, which she used to promote her weight-loss products. She wrote about the number of calories burned in her daily workouts, what she did during each session, even listed the foods she ate.

The photos in this section weren't as revealing as the ones in *Playboy,* but she was obviously using her body to motivate others to buy her video and diet products. She posed in skimpy outfits to show how particular exercises had tightened her abs or toned her behind. There was related information, too—various low-calorie recipes, clothing suggestions, hair- and skin-care tips.

David wondered how often Oliver Burke had frequented this site. He checked the guest book for past entries, but it didn't go back far enough—

"Whoa, now I know why you told Tiny you had to work. I'd rather spend my lunch hour with her, too."

David twisted to the side to see Mike Fitzer standing at the entrance to his cubicle, looking at his monitor.

"She's involved in one of my cases," David explained.

"If you have to bring her in, I'll pay you fifty bucks to let me frisk her."

David wished Mike would mind his own business. He was the laziest detective on the force. It was difficult to believe someone could accomplish so little and still manage to hang on to a job.

"Hate to disappoint you, but I'll be lucky to speak with her. She's only peripherally involved."

"Too bad."

Mike didn't move on, so David rolled away from his desk. "Something I can do for you, Mike?"

"Actually, there is. You know the woman who started The Last Stand?"

"I know the three women."

"I'm talking about the one who's been getting so much press lately. Skye Something."

"Kellerman."

"That's her."

No surprise there. This was the second time in two days someone on the force had mentioned Skye to him. But ever since she and her friends had started TLS, hearing her name at the station wasn't all that uncommon. "What about her?"

"She's a major pain in the ass."

"What's she done?"

"She's hired a private investigator to look into one of my cases, and he's majorly pissing me off."

David momentarily lost interest in Miranda's Web site. "Because…?"

"He keeps getting in my face, telling me how things should be done. He thinks he knows more about running an investigation than I do."

David thought he probably did. "Which case is this?"

"Sean Regan's."

"The man who went missing on New Year's Day?" David had read about Regan in the paper, heard about him at the office.

"That's the one. Skye's convinced his wife had him killed, so this private investigator of hers is badgering me to run a few license plates and get other information."

"Is there any chance the wife did it?"

"Not in my opinion."

"What do the *facts* suggest?"

"There's no life insurance to speak of, so she had nothing to gain financially from his death. She's a good mother, someone with no criminal history. Why would she all of a sudden decide to kill her husband?"

"Why does Skye think she did it?"

"She claims Mr. Regan thought his wife was having an affair, that Mrs. Regan wanted to get rid of him so she wouldn't have to fight him for custody of their kids. But chances are greater it was *Sean* who was cheating, and now he's run off to avoid his family responsibilities. His boss told me Sean missed a lot of work in the weeks right before he went missing. Said he was acting strange."

So Mike had done *some* legwork…. "Strange in what way?"

"Whispering on the phone while he huddled in the corner. Coming back very late from lunch. Making stupid mistakes."

"You think he'd up and leave his kids?"

"For the right woman? Hell, yeah. He wouldn't be the first father to do it."

The enthusiasm in that statement made David a little uncomfortable. What would he do for the right woman? Forget his own responsibilities?

He understood that temptation better than most. "I'll talk to Skye," he said.

"Tell her to stay out of my business before she really pisses me off," Mike grumbled. Another detective called his name and, nodding at David, he crossed the room.

Muttering a curse, David turned back to his desk, clicked on the *E-mail Me* button and sent Miranda Dodge a message telling her he had a few questions about Oliver Burke. Then he signed off. He had some appointments this afternoon and needed to be on his way. One was with the hygienist who'd worked for Burke before he was forced to close his doors.

Skye easily located the address written on the slip of paper she'd salvaged from Jane Burke's garbage. It happened to be only a few blocks away from Jane's current residence. Initially, she'd thought Jane and Oliver might be planning to move, but the place wasn't for sale or rent, so she looked up the phone number in a crisscross directory, and called to ask if anyone at that location had any connection to the Burkes. The woman at the other end of the line said her daughter was a playmate of Kate's—then asked why she wanted to know and Skye hung up.

So much for the extra effort….

Disappointed that her garbage foray hadn't netted more, she threw the note away and used Google and the fee-based online resources of LexisNexis, ChoicePoint and Merlin Data to search for anything connected to Oliver or Jane Burke.

Prior to Burke's attack, Skye had been an account executive for a carpet company, completely ignorant of how the criminal justice system worked. But since then, thanks to her efforts with The Last Stand, she'd learned a lot about running an investigation.

She found the Burkes' marriage certificate, which held no surprises. The birth certificate for their daughter, Kate. Bankruptcy and foreclosure papers from when Jane lost the house after Oliver went to prison. Quite a few newspaper articles about the trial surfaced on the

Internet, too. Normally, an attempted rape would rate a one on a scale of one to ten compared to the more sensational topics, such as arson, murder and terrorism, which received the majority of media attention. But Oliver had been such an unlikely rapist, and so well-known in the community, that prosecuting him had drawn fierce battle lines between the believers and unbelievers—the kind of controversy that sold papers.

For the heck of it, Skye tracked down the name of Burke's brother and ran a few searches on him, too. Now that she knew he was having an affair with Jane, she was curious to learn more about him.

Noah was definitely married, with three kids ages ten, eight and five. He lived in Orangevale and ran what appeared to be a successful construction business: NSL Construction. He had excellent credit, coached Little League, seemed to be a pretty upstanding guy. Except with regard to Jane.

Skye wondered if his wife had any idea what was going on. Then she decided she was too emotionally spent to imagine the heartbreak and put it from her mind. She had to focus, keep working, find something that would give her an advantage over Burke....

Besides all the newspaper stuff and magazine articles, Oliver's name came up on some civil litigation—two lawsuits, both initiated by people who'd once lived on the same street as the Burkes. The first dated back ten years and was filed by a man named Markum. He claimed that Oliver had killed his dog. In the second, a Mr. and Mrs. Harold Simmons had sued the Burkes for throwing acid on their lawn.

Skye wasn't sure whether the information she'd managed to dig up would mean anything in the end. David had probably found it already and discarded it as too old or inconsequential. But, at the very least, she had the names of two neighbors who might be willing to share what they knew about Oliver Burke.

Planning to visit both households, she jotted down the house numbers. But before she could grab her purse and set off, the phone rang.

"Any more threats?" It was Jasmine. She sounded tired, depressed and worried—and she didn't even know about their financial predicament at The Last Stand or that Sheridan was struggling with her past again.

"No more threats," she responded. "But then, I haven't been home. I spent the night with Sher."

"Smart move. I don't like you living all the way out in the boondocks."

"Don't start." Skye's nerves were frayed enough. The minutes seemed to be marching past her, indifferent to her growing anxiety, carrying her forward, ever closer to Burke's release.

Would he come after her right away? Part of her wished he would. Better to get it over with than spend God knows how long looking over her shoulder, afraid to sleep or even breathe in case she missed some sign.

"A place in town would be safer," Jasmine said.

"Not necessarily. That would only prolong the inevitable."

"Don't be so fatalistic. It doesn't *have* to end that way."

A gut sense told Skye it could end no other way, but she didn't attempt to explain the unexplainable. "Maybe, maybe not," she said to avoid an argument. Then she got up and closed her office door because she could scarcely hear above the solicitations going on over the phone in the lobby. "How's it going in Ft. Bragg?"

"Not good."

Skye returned to her seat. "You haven't found her?"

The quality of Jasmine's voice changed. "They found what was left of her."

"Oh, Jasmine. I'm so sorry."

Silence, followed by a muffled sniffle, let Skye know Jasmine was crying. She waited, giving her friend time to grieve.

Finally Jasmine spoke. "They found her in a trash bag, tossed onto a rocky section of beach from the highway above. Can you believe it?"

Unfortunately, Skye could. "When was this?"

"Just after dawn."

"Will you be okay, Jas? Should I come get you?"

"No, I can drive. I wouldn't want to leave my car behind. Anyway, how long have we been doing this? I'm getting used to the worst possible outcomes. But the hardest thing, the thing I will never get over, is the sense-lessness. *Why?* Why would *anyone* do this to a child?"

"That's the age-old question," Skye said. "Do you know who did it?"

"Not yet. But I've finished the profile. It's up to the FBI and the local police now. I might as well go home. I've got work to do."

"It can wait if you need the time."

"It can't wait. It's all so…critical."

And that was why working at The Last Stand was draining, heartbreaking, thrilling and rewarding. The emotional pendulum swung so wide. "Maybe you should take a break."

"I prefer the distraction." There was another lengthy silence while Jasmine tried to control her emotions. "I'll call you when I get back."

"Okay, do."

"See you soon."

Jasmine hung up, and Skye sat at her desk staring at the wall, which held the photographs of several famous serial killers—Ted Bundy, Son of Sam, Leonard Lake. They all looked so ordinary. That was why she'd hung them there, to remind her that their appearances masked the monsters they were.

Reaching into her drawer, she took out the picture she couldn't bear to put on her wall—the picture some reporter had wangled out of a family member of Oliver's and published the day after the trial. It showed him as a ten-year-old boy, scrubbed and polished in a suit and tie with his hair slicked back. He'd been a small kid for his age, a cute kid, which was the reason Skye had clipped his photo from the paper. He, more than any of the others, reminded her that predators could come in all shapes and sizes, that even little boys with good parents could turn out to be conscienceless criminals who destroyed anyone and everyone they could.

"You won't win," she whispered, staring into his black, grainy eyes. But she shivered when she glanced at her calendar.

It was Wednesday afternoon. Oliver would be released on Friday.

Oliver lay in his bunk, staring at the ceiling while listening to the snores of his cellmate below. The tap of footsteps on concrete, an occasional moan, even the echo of various conversations ebbed and flowed in a constant hum. But the noise, the cold and the drafty air that smelled heavily of body odor wouldn't be part of his life much longer. It was nearly Thursday. One more day and he'd be born again, out of the bowels of hell....

He couldn't believe the torturous wait was nearly over. All he had to do was continue avoiding Vic. And, now that it was down to a matter of hours, Oliver felt confident he could do that. He would simply remain in his cell until Friday morning. Then Jane would pick him up and off they'd go.

Vic could go to hell. Vic wouldn't be able to hurt him.

Closing his eyes, he pictured his wife's eager greeting. Three years was a long time to wait for a man. But Jane was an incredible woman. Maybe Skye had cost him a lot, but she hadn't cost him Jane—or Kate, who'd just turned seven.

Oliver retrieved his flashlight—prisoners who weren't a behavioral problem and performed as many services as he did were allowed more possessions than the average inmate—and pulled the blanket over his head so he could study the notes he'd made in ciphertext. He'd gotten so good at forward substitution that he no longer needed the key he'd created; he knew it by heart.

His cellmate snorted and rolled over. "Damn, Ollie, go to sleep. What are you doing up there? Jerking off again?"

Oliver ignored him. He had a right to jerk off if he wanted to. It was certainly better than his other options at the moment. His small size and soft-spoken manner had proved to be a real attraction to the men in prison, but homosexual encounters left him more disgusted than satisfied. Except for Larry. He'd met Larry in the library one day. They'd had a lot in common—liked the same books and music. Larry was gentle and quiet, and he knew how to make Oliver feel like somebody. But in the end he'd turned out to be a big disappointment. Sometimes Oliver regretted what he'd had to do to Larry. Sometimes he missed Larry more than Jane.

Putting Larry from his mind, he flipped back several pages and read over what he'd written, quickly translating it into plaintext. He'd created his method of encryption years ago so he could put his thoughts on paper without worrying that someone might get hold of his notebooks and read them. He remembered doing it when he was as young as ten. But the simple alphabet substitutions he'd started with had grown into a much more elaborate cipher system that included numbers and even geometric symbols. He doubted there were many people, in San Quentin, anyway, who'd be able to crack it. Jane had certainly never managed to figure it out. And, just in case, he was careful to use initials and never full names when referring to people who had the dubious honor of being mentioned. People such as Detective Willis, Mrs. Grady, the teacher who was giving Jane so much trouble over Kate's recent behavior and, at the front of the book, Miranda Dodge. He'd never properly thanked her for the rejection that still ate at him.

But that was because he'd been so undecided about her. What punishment would be best? He still wanted to be with her. If she'd give him half a chance, he'd show her what a good friend and passionate lover he could be. He'd always felt they were meant to be together, since that first day when she'd walked into his fifth-grade class with her auburn hair pulled back in those pretty purple barrettes.

He could definitely forgive Miranda. If she'd let him.

But not Skye. He hated Skye more than anyone, because no one had wronged him as badly as she had. She'd gone to the police, testified against him and cried in happiness and relief when they led him off to prison. The way she kept appearing in public, talking about what he'd done, was an embarrassment, and he doubted it'd end anytime soon. She was making a calling out of their little skirmish.

At least she'd given him plenty to think about in prison. Closing his eyes, he eagerly relived the heart-pounding excitement of peering in her windows and watching as she moved from room to room…. Pictured her talking on the phone, laughing, lifting her long hair off her neck. Imagined getting the key he'd seen her use, silently opening the door and stepping inside.

Scarcely able to breathe, he slipped his hand into his shorts, feeling the tension, fear and excitement coalesce until his nerves vibrated with power and exhilaration. He had to have Skye; he had to *hurt* her.

He smiled as he imagined using his knife to hold her still while he touched her. The whites of her eyes showed clearly in the dark room and her lips moved, begging him to stop. Her helplessness was the best part. It fed some need he couldn't understand or deny. He wanted to punish her, pinch her, claw her, even bite her.

Skye…Skye…Skye, his mind chanted. But it wasn't until he heard her cry out in pain and anguish, completely broken, that his body finally shuddered in release.

"Your wife doesn't care?" his cellmate asked when it was all over.

Oliver had been so caught up in his memories of Skye he hadn't realized T.J. hadn't gone back to sleep. Lying perfectly still, he tried to recover while wondering how to respond.

"Every guy has his fantasies," he said at last.

"Yours is a freakin' obsession. You pant the name *Skye* almost every night."

"No, I don't." But the knowledge that he'd soon be able to even the score had made tonight's fantasy more visceral than ever. "We have unfinished business."

T.J. chuckled low in his throat. "You attack her again, you'll get a life sentence."

They wouldn't catch him. He'd see to that. If not for those damn scissors, they wouldn't have caught him the last time. Willis suspected him of killing those other women—young women who wouldn't have had to die if only they'd been decent to him. Oliver felt bad about Meredith. But the detective hadn't been able to do a damn thing about it because he hadn't left any evidence. "I'm not going to touch her."

"Sure you won't."

Oliver didn't respond. He wanted T.J. to go back to sleep and leave him alone. But that didn't happen. T.J.'s bedding rustled as he rolled onto his back, and his tone grew friendlier.

"Hey, Oliver."

"What?" he said, hating T.J. almost as much as Vic.

"All that moanin' turned me on, man. Why don't you help me take care of the problem? We could call it a going-away present."

Oliver found his pen. He knew what "taking care of the problem" entailed. As T.J.'s "bitch," he'd had to perform sexual favors for him before. It was the only way he could ensure he had a protector. And he needed T.J. more than ever now.

But it enraged him to feel so powerless, so cornered. "Caused me to perform in prison," he wrote next to T.J.'s name. It wasn't the first time he'd recorded this offense, but writing it down siphoned off some of the rage. He liked keeping count. Then, when he settled the score, he'd be able to cross off each entry, which would make his victory even more meaningful.

"Come on," T.J. snapped.

"Will you keep Vic and his friends away from me till I get out of here?" Oliver asked, knowing he had little choice regardless.

"Make it the best I've ever had and Vic won't touch you."

Setting his precious book aside, Oliver got up and cleaned himself with a few pieces of the cheap thin toilet paper provided by the state. Then he glanced through the bars at the upper gun rail opposite the bank of cages. The guards stationed there were supposed to watch for any sexual activity. Theoretically, they were also supposed to stop it. But enforcing that rule wasn't very practical. If they watched too closely, just about every guy in the place would end up being sent to solitary, and they didn't have the facilities. Unless someone cried rape, they mostly turned a blind eye.

But it didn't always require brute force to rape a person.

The guard on duty didn't seem to notice that Oliver was out of bed. Or he didn't care. As he paced the length of the gun rail, he paused to adjust his machine gun. Then he pivoted and started walking in the other direction.

Confident there'd be no intervention, Oliver knelt by T.J.'s bed.

What got him from one minute to the next in here didn't matter. The wait was almost over....

9

An e-mail from Miranda Dodge came Thursday morning. David had just climbed out of bed, grabbed a quick cup of coffee and a piece of toast and fired up his in-home computer when he received it. It was later on the East Coast, so she'd probably been up for at least three hours.

Of course I remember Oliver Burke. When we were in high school, the little weasel would call me incessantly and beg me to go out with him. The moment I refused, he'd hang up on me. But then he'd call back and apologize. It was weird. He did other stuff, too. One time, I caught him outside my bedroom window spying on me. I told my parents, and my father called his father, but his father shrugged it off, saying any red-blooded American boy would like to see a girl undress. That made my father really mad. He said it was almost as if Mr. Burke *applauded* the behavior.

Anyway, it's early in Sacramento. I'll call you later. I'm not sure I know anything that can help with your investigation, but when I heard Oliver went to prison for rape, I was probably the only person on the planet who wasn't surprised.

Miranda Dodge

David drummed his fingers on the desk. Was this where it had all started? With Miranda? He'd spoken to Burke's hygienist yesterday. She still claimed she'd never worked for a finer man. But she was a member of Burke's church. It was entirely possible that he treated her differently because of the connection, or that loyalty caused her to look more kindly on his indiscretions. It was also possible that she wasn't attractive enough to warrant Burke's attention. With a triple chin and straggly blond hair, she hardly fit the profile of his other victims.

The phone rang, interrupting his thoughts. "Hello?"

"Will you meet me for lunch today?"

Lynnette. "You're up already?"

"I have to go to work early. Anyway, I couldn't sleep."

"Why not? Did you have a setback?" She was on medication intended to slow, if not arrest, the progress of the disease, but it didn't seem to be doing much. Her MS manifested itself in weakness and fatigue. Her balance had been affected, and she was losing some of the dexterity in her hands, which was a constant worry, considering the kind of work she did.

"It wasn't that. I've been thinking."

"About…"

"I'd rather discuss it over lunch. Can you make it?"

"You can leave the lab?" She got off midafternoon, so she generally took a sack lunch and clocked out for less than thirty minutes, just long enough to sit outside on the grass and eat.

"I'm off at one today. That's why I'm going in early."

David wasn't excited about the prospect of another emotional encounter, especially in the middle of his workday. As much as he wanted Lynnette to be happy, he couldn't seem to stop being the cause of her unhappiness. And with Burke's imminent release, it was difficult to concentrate on anything else.

But now he felt guilty about his reaction last night and the fact that he didn't really want to see her. Maybe making her more of a priority in his life would be a good thing. Maybe it would help him keep his head on straight when it came to Skye. "Where?"

"Pyramid House."

They'd gone there to celebrate the last time they'd officially reunited. Was that significant? Or was it simply a restaurant she liked and they were both familiar with? "Sure."

"I'll see you there right after I get off work," she said and hung up.

David frowned as he set the handset back in its cradle. He didn't know what lunch was all about, but he was almost afraid to find out.

Skye smiled brightly when a completely bald man in his late fifties or early sixties opened the door. "Mr. Markum?"

"Yes?" Wearing a jogging suit, he had several expensive-looking rings on his fingers and a medallion at his neck, reminding Skye of a Hollywood producer.

"My name is Skye Kellerman. I'm with The Last Stand."

"The Last What?"

"The Last Stand. We're a victims' assistance charity."

He pointed to a little sign next to the doorbell that said *No Soliciting*. "This is a gated community. How'd you get in here?"

"I waited until someone else came through and followed him in. And I'm not soliciting funds. I'm here to talk to you about Oliver Burke."

The expression on his face changed from annoyance to interest. "Burke went to prison for attempting to rape some woman."

Skye shoved the strap of her purse higher on her shoulder and took a deep breath. "I'm that woman."

His eyes widened. "No kidding? You stabbed him, right? With a pair of scissors?"

She tried not to wince, but mention of the incident always evoked a visceral response. "It was the only thing I could do."

"How'd you happen to have a pair handy?"

"They were on my nightstand. I'd been doing some cross-stitch before bed."

"Good for you! You're a survivor!" Grinning widely, he reached out to shake her hand.

"How well did you know Oliver?" she asked.

A small dog, some kind of spaniel, kept trying to escape between his legs. Using one foot to hold back his pet, he stepped onto the porch and shut the door. "Why?"

"He's being released tomorrow."

The dog barked from behind the door, but he ignored it. "That didn't take long." He whistled. "What's it been…two, three years? Must make you sick, eh?"

Worse than sick… "I'm concerned because I think he's still dangerous."

"He *is* dangerous. To animals as well as humans. That bastard killed one of my dogs."

Skye didn't want to reveal that she already knew about the lawsuit. Many people didn't realize how public most records were, and it made them uncomfortable to learn that someone had been snooping around. So she remained vague. "How do you know it was him?"

"It happened a few days after we had a run-in. My daughter and son-in-law had parked their RV out on the street. He didn't like that it blocked the curbside view of his house from a certain angle. I guess he figured people on this street had nothing better to do than admire his home. I told him I wasn't about to have them move it. It was fine where it was. They were leaving to go home in another week."

"He didn't like that response?"

"You would've thought I'd done something really terrible. His face turned red and he stomped out of here. But that was it—until two days later. We left the dogs in the backyard while we went out for the day. We were showing the kids around, hoping they'd consider moving closer to us, you know, but they like it where they are. Anyway, when we returned, we let Bonnie and Clyde into the house and about an hour later, Bonnie started shaking and heaving. I couldn't figure out what was wrong with her, but I knew it was serious. So my wife and I rushed her over to the vet clinic, where she died later that night." Furrows formed between his eyebrows—evidence that losing his pet had been painful for him. "The vet eventually concluded that someone had fed her a piece of poisoned meat."

"Someone?"

"Oliver Burke. It had to be him. I didn't have another enemy in the whole neighborhood. Still don't."

"You don't have proof that it was him, do you?"

"No, but the neighbors on this side over here—" he pointed to the left "—can verify he was at home that day, which wasn't all that common. He was usually at his dental office."

"Nothing happened to Clyde?"

"He got sick, too, but Bonnie got the worst of it. That's Clyde in there." Markum tapped the door and the dog barked again.

"I'm sorry to hear about Bonnie. It must've been horrible."

"It was. I called the police, but they said there wasn't enough proof to do anything about it. They suggested I file a civil suit, that I might have a better chance of winning. But it was a bust. Burke put on such a good act, the judge fell for it."

"Yeah, he's good at playing the martyr."

"No kidding. It was pretty damn frustrating. I told the detective who came by here just after they charged him with attacking you, too, hoping it might help establish a history of violence, but…"

"He probably told you the same thing."

"He did. Without proof, it didn't mean much."

"Did you approach Oliver about what happened *before* you went to court?"

"I did. I told him he must not have a heart if he could hurt such an innocent creature."

"How did he respond?"

"Shocked. Dismayed. Pretended it wasn't him. But I

could tell that deep down he was happy about the misery he'd caused me."

That reminded Skye of how Burke had behaved when she'd accused him of attacking her.

"He's a convincing liar, I have to hand him that," Markum added.

"When was the last time you saw Oliver?"

"I don't know.... A few days before they arrested him, I guess. I wanted to attend some of the trial, but my wife teaches music in Italy once a year, and we were in Europe. I was glad when I heard the outcome, though. It was as if Bonnie got a little justice that day, too."

"Have you ever met Oliver's brother?"

"A few times. Every once in a while, Noah and his wife would visit next door. They were pleasant enough. Especially Wendy, Noah's wife. Why?"

"Just curious about his family situation. How did Oliver treat his daughter?"

"Hard to tell. She wasn't much more than a toddler then and he worked a lot. We saw her with Jane more often than with him."

"Did he ever come and go late at night?" Skye knew David would've asked every neighbor this question already, back when he was building a case against Burke, back when he'd probably heard about the dog. But she wanted to hear Mr. Markum's answer for herself.

"Not by car. I would've noticed. And the computer at the gatehouse keeps track of every time the gate's opened."

"So you think he left on foot?"

"Or bicycle. He fancied himself quite a cyclist. Used to shave his legs and all that. I never did understand why. I can't imagine it'd really help with wind shear, but he took it quite seriously. Rode to work almost every day."

"Even in the winter?"

"Even in the winter. Used a battery-powered nightlight that was nearly as powerful as a car's headlights."

Skye remembered David saying Burke had spent a lot of time on the bike trail. They didn't know how he'd stalked her, or how he'd gotten into her house, but during the trial the district attorney had suggested he used a bike. A bike provided a quiet mode of transportation, freedom of movement and an excuse to be gone for long periods of time—alone. The other attacks had happened near the bike trail, too.

"Did you like his wife?"

"She wasn't the nicest person in the world. Sort of pretentious, if you ask me. But she was sure singing a different tune once Oliver went to prison. Then I had to feel sorry for her, especially when she lost the house. She didn't get much for his practice after all that bad publicity."

Skye knew he'd feel even worse for Jane Burke if he saw where she was living now. "I'm convinced Oliver is responsible for murdering three other women, women he met before he attacked me."

He whistled. "Is that why you're here?"

"Partly. If you remember anything else, will you contact me?"

He accepted the card she handed him. "Definitely."

"Thanks." She walked three houses down to the Simmons residence, which sat at the top of a small hill. There, she heard a similar story about how a conflict over some trees had provoked Oliver into ruining their front lawn. Like Markum, they had more suspicion than proof, though, and had lost their suit.

On her way to the car, Skye stopped to stare at the house where Oliver and his family had been living when he'd tried to rape her. It looked just as normal as every other house on the block, better than most people's version of normal. Back then he'd been part of a privileged elite and had lived behind a gate by choice.

On a sudden impulse, Skye approached the house. A van sat in the front drive, and there were toys scattered all around—a football, a trike, some skates. She wasn't sure what she was hoping to achieve by introducing herself to the current owners. Chances were that they didn't even know the Burkes. And yet this home retained a certain mystique for her. Oliver had not only lived here, he'd prided himself on his ability to afford such a lovely place, had allegedly killed his neighbor's dog over an RV that blocked other people's view of it.

Maybe, in this house that meant so much to him, he'd left something of himself behind.

David sat across from Lynnette in the same corner where they'd had a romantic dinner two years ago. He suspected she'd requested this particular booth. She was also wearing his favorite dress. Both of which made him inexplicably uncomfortable. He knew his son needed him, knew Lynnette needed him, too. He also knew that the best way he could be there for them both was to keep the family together. But the prospect of returning to the same situation was becoming more and more difficult to face.

"How was work?" he asked.

"Fine."

He loosened his tie and unfastened the top button of his shirt. "You look like you're feeling better today."

"I have good days and bad days. This is a good day." She took a sip of the ice water the waitress had brought before they'd ordered and studied him.

"What?" he said, arching his eyebrows at the intense scrutiny.

Her gaze dropped to her glass, which she began to turn around and around on the table. "I had sex with my date the other night."

He hadn't asked because he didn't want to acknowledge his own ambivalence. "And?"

"I didn't like it." She shook her head, still staring at her glass. "It was…meaningless. Empty."

"I'm sorry."

Her eyes lifted. "You wish it had been better?"

"I'm sorry you're so miserable. How well did you know him?"

"Not well enough. It was a desperate attempt to make my life feel real again. That was all." She scratched her forehead in a gesture that revealed frustration at the same time it suggested she was thoughtfully selecting her next words. "I wanted it to be you every second, David, which made me realize something."

He drank some of his own water, wishing he could put her on pause until he could overcome his growing reluctance. "What's that?"

"I'm not over you. I don't want to call it quits in spite of everything we've been through."

David took a deep breath. At least her confession proved she was willing to work on their relationship. That was positive, wasn't it? But it brought him no relief. It only made the metaphorical handcuffs chafe that much more: *Till death do us part.* "So you're ready to try again?"

"Are you?" she asked hopefully.

Thinking of Jeremy, he wanted to jump at the chance. He'd promised it often enough. He wanted to make Lynnette happy, too. She'd been young, just twenty-one, when he promised her forever. With her improved attitude, maybe they could make it work. But when he thought of Skye, he longed to put as much emotional distance as possible between him and his ex-wife, regardless of her condition. How selfish was that? "It's worth considering."

She sat back, obviously shocked by his less than enthusiastic response. He was the one who'd decided to move out, both times, but all the complaints had come from her. He wasn't giving enough to the relationship. She deserved more than she was getting. He didn't love her anymore.

He feared she was right about the third one....

"Worth *considering?*" she echoed.

The waitress refilled their glasses and told them their meals would be out in a minute. David waited until they were alone again to respond. "We have to do things differently so it'll work this time, Lynn."

"Not a lot," she said. "It's your job. If you'd find something else, we'd be fine."

His *job?* "And what would you have me do?"

"Become a P.I. Lots of cops become private investigators. You'd make more money, set your own hours, have less stress."

"How would my being a P.I. help us?"

"Are you kidding?" Her expression grew intense. "It'd

keep you from being called out in the middle of the night to some gruesome murder scene, for one thing. There's going to come a time when I might need you to be home all night. And maybe, if you were working in a better environment, you'd be around the house more often and wouldn't get so consumed with your job."

He had a feeling Lynnette would be jealous of any pursuit that took his attention away from her. But his cell phone rang before he could say so. Using the distraction to give him a few extra seconds to formulate a response that might avoid starting an argument, he checked the caller ID—and promptly put the phone back in his pocket. It was Skye. He didn't want to talk to her in front of Lynnette, and since she was calling from The Last Stand, there'd be numerous people around her, so he was sure she was okay. At least for now.

"Aren't you going to answer that?" she asked.

"No."

Her eyes narrowed. "If it was work-related you would've taken the call."

Maybe, maybe not. But she was resentful enough to make that generalization. In his opinion, it was her inflexibility that had destroyed their marriage, not his job. "It can wait."

For a moment, David thought his refusal to explain would put an end to their peace-making lunch. But she rallied.

"So what do you say? Are you willing to make a few changes? Try again?"

A few changes made it sound as if she wasn't asking for much of a sacrifice. But giving up his position on the force could hardly be classified as minor.

"You're always telling me you want to get back together," she went on. "That you want to be a family for Jeremy."

It had nothing to do with *want*. "I haven't forgotten."

"But you don't want that badly enough to do something else for a living?"

Police work wasn't just a job to him. It was a calling. She didn't understand. Or maybe she did. Maybe that was why she was so jealous of his commitment to the force. "I like what I do, Lynn. I don't see what you're suggesting as a viable solution. But…give me a while to think about it." He'd address it later. Maybe he could beat his stubborn resistance into submission. Then moving back in with her wouldn't seem like such a miserable option.

"How long?" she asked.

When his phone rang again, she rolled her eyes and motioned for him to take the call.

He didn't apologize, despite her obvious annoyance. He was a detective; he needed to be available at all times. And the number on his caller ID indicated it was the station. "Excuse me."

"And you wonder why I hate your job," she grumbled under her breath.

He knew he hadn't managed to bury his irritation as deeply as he'd intended when he heard the impatience in his voice. "That doesn't mean I'm willing to let you choose my occupation."

Her mouth opened, but he answered his phone before she could respond. "Willis here."

"Detective, this is Sergeant Burns."

"Yes?"

"I just ran across a note that says we're supposed to notify you immediately if anything comes in on Skye Kellerman or The Last Stand."

David straightened in his seat. "That's true."

"Ms. Kellerman is looking for you. I thought you might like to know."

"Did she sound upset?"

"No."

The waitress came with Lynnette's pasta and his steak sandwich as he brought the call to a close.

"Okay, I'll take care of it." When he hung up, he could tell from the expression on Lynnette's face that he'd had the volume turned up too high. Although he'd held the phone pressed tight to his ear, she'd overheard Officer Burns relay his message.

"Is that who called you a minute ago?" she asked. "Skye Kellerman?"

Lynnette didn't know how he felt about Skye, but she suspected something was going on. She still asked about Skye periodically, even though it had been three years since the investigation. *She's pretty, don't you think?…So how's that woman who was attacked by the dentist? Do you ever talk to her?…I saw there was another article about The Last Stand in the paper today.…*

"Her case is heating up again." He took a bite of his sandwich, but Lynnette didn't start on her meal.

"How could it be heating up again, David? The trial's been over for three years." Her voice dropped. "Unless there's something I don't know about."

Ignoring the not-so-subtle inflection in her voice, he swallowed his food. "Burke's getting out of prison tomorrow. If Skye can help me tie him to those murders near the American River, it might save other women's lives. There's also a good chance he could come after her again. She testified against him, as you know."

Lynnette folded her arms. "If the situation was that dire, why didn't you take her call?"

"He's not out yet."

"But I'll bet you would've been more than happy to hear from her if I wasn't here." Laughing bitterly, she picked up her purse.

"Where are you going?" he asked.

"I'm not hungry anymore."

David watched her walk out on him. Then he pushed a thumb and finger against his closed eyelids. What was he going to do with his personal life? He couldn't get too angry with Lynnette. She was only reacting to the knowledge that he didn't feel what she wanted him to feel. And she still hadn't fully adjusted to the disease that was affecting her central nervous system.

"Is your lady friend coming back?" the waitress asked.

Lowering his hand, he managed a smile. "No, you can box up her meal, if you don't mind."

"No problem." Her own smile was a bit too bright for mere courtesy. He recognized the romantic interest. But he didn't return it. No one could tempt him away from Lynnette and Jeremy.

Except Skye.

After finishing his own meal, he responded to the message Sergeant Burns said Skye had left at the station.

"We have a problem," Skye said as soon as David had her on the line.

They had more than one. Not the least of which was

the fact that he was looking forward to taking her to the fund-raiser on Saturday, despite what had just happened with Lynnette. That might even be why their lunch had gone so badly.

"You've received another threatening call?"

"No."

"Good." David accepted his change and the receipt for his meal from the waitress and gathered the take-out boxes. "What then?"

"Jane Burke."

"How is she a problem?"

"She's having an affair with Oliver's brother."

David froze halfway to the door, torn between two responses: shock and dismay over the affair, and the realization that this information probably shouldn't be coming from Skye.

Concern over Skye's involvement won out. "And how would you know something so personal about Jane Burke?"

"I saw them together."

"Where?"

She didn't answer right away.

"I just asked you a question, Skye."

"Don't freak out, but…"

"But?"

"It was through the window. Last night."

"What window?"

"Jane's window."

"You were surveilling Jane's *house?*" He shook his head. This was the woman who kept him from reconciling with Lynnette? How could he let himself get any more involved with her? She didn't even know when to avoid a dangerous situation, one that risked her own safety and that of anyone associated with her—which could include his son. "Did anyone recognize you?"

"I don't think so."

"You don't sound too sure."

"Jane and her brother-in-law saw my car."

People in the nearest booth were staring at him, so David walked outside but stood under the eaves because it had begun to rain. "When you say they *saw* your car... You didn't do anything to draw attention to yourself, did you? Your Volvo was just one car among many," he said.

No response.

"Please tell me I'm right, Skye. We don't need this to get back to the psychopath who'll be living there in a few days."

"There weren't a lot of other cars on the street last night. My Volvo might've stood out a little. But it was so late I expected Jane and everyone else to be asleep." Her voice fell. "I just wanted to get a glimpse of the place, check out the situation."

"But Jane wasn't asleep."

"No."

"Great," he said with a sigh, too preoccupied to cross the puddle-filled lot.

"It's okay. Once they saw each other, Jane and Noah weren't interested in anyone else."

He pinched the bridge of his nose. "Maybe I should start by reiterating that I believe Burke *murdered* three women."

"I haven't forgotten."

"Then would it do me any good to tell you to stay the hell away?"

"None."

"Just as I thought." He breathed in the rain-scented air. "You're flirting with danger, Skye."

"Consider me warned."

"Those weapons of yours will only help if you see him coming."

"Scaring me won't make any difference. That's why I own those weapons. That's why I went to his house in the first place."

"So what do I do?"

"You listen, okay? Just listen. I've found something else you should know about."

He muttered a curse. "I'm almost afraid to hear it."

"I visited Oliver's former residence, too."

He shoved his free hand inside the warm pocket of his jacket, intrigued in spite of his anger and concern. "And?"

"I had a nice visit with the Griffins, the people who bought the house from the bank after Jane lost it."

"I've already been there, talked to them. Do you think I'm not doing my job?"

"This is one of those chance timing issues."

"What does that mean?"

"It means, when Mr. Griffin put away the Christmas decorations a few weeks ago, he decided to have some lighting installed in the attic. He was tired of trying to organize stuff with a flashlight. So he hired an electrician, who spotted something shoved into a crack near a beam at the far corner."

David's heart began to pound. Two years ago, just after they'd moved in, he'd asked the Griffins to search every nook and cranny of their house hoping they'd find the knife or another object that might have been missed during the police search. Oliver had been living in that house when he was carted off to prison. It stood to reason that if he'd hidden something, it would be there. But the Griffins had insisted the house was empty.

Thank God for Christmas storage. Skye was right—this was about timing. "Jewelry? Clothing?" He stepped back as a car drove by and nearly splashed his shoes. "The knife?"

"No. A spiral notebook."

That wasn't what he'd been expecting. "Tell me it contains a signed confession."

"It might. I don't know. It's in some sort of code."

Encryption? That could prove interesting. Provided the notebook had belonged to Burke. And provided they could break the code.

"It's written in a very meticulous hand, a neat hand—I think it's Oliver's," she added.

It was tough to be too upset with Skye when she came up with possible evidence like this. He'd pretty much given up on finding anything at Burke's former house. "Does it look complicated?"

"Complicated enough. I've been fiddling with it for a while and I think I know the character for *e* because it shows up the most often, but that's it."

"Mr. Griffin should've called me the minute his electrician handed that over."

"He wasn't sure it meant anything. The Burkes weren't the first people to own the house so, as far as he was concerned, it didn't necessarily belong to them. And it's very strange. Not only are the letters scrambled, there's a few geometric shapes mixed in. He would've thrown it out if not for the drawings in the back."

"What kind of drawings?"

"Skulls, knives."

Gooseflesh rose on David's arms. "I'd bet my soul it belonged to Burke."

"I would, too." She paused for a moment. "And guess what? There are even dates in here. For whatever reason, he didn't bother putting numbers in code. There's one with each entry."

"When's the last entry?"

"June of 2004. Several months before he broke into my house."

David fished in his pocket for his keys. "You have the notebook with you?"

"Yes."

"Can you bring it to the station? I want it checked for prints, among other things."

"Can we get prints after so long?"

"It's actually a good surface. The amino acids left behind by a human hand often seep down into the paper fibers. Fingerprints on paper can last up to forty years if it hasn't been exposed to water."

"I don't think it has been."

"It might be more beneficial to break the code first. That could reveal the author *and* his thoughts."

"There's enough here to do both at once, believe me."

"Okay, I'll have some specialists look at it," he said.

"How long do you suppose it'll take to break the code?"

"With a computer, maybe an hour or so. Unless he's a whole lot smarter than I think he is."

There was a slight pause on the other end of the line. "Let's hope it tells us what we need to know."

"Skye?" he said before she could hang up.

"What?"

"Detective Fitzer isn't enjoying the input of the private investigator you hired to search for Sean Regan."

"He said something to you?"

"Yes."

"Well, I don't care," she said. "Fitzer isn't doing his job. *Someone* needs to help Sean."

"How do you know Fitzer isn't doing his job?"

"He refuses to listen or cooperate."

"He's lead detective on this, Skye, not you. Your guy's pushing too hard."

"I just talked to Jonathan. He's discovered some very interesting stuff."

"Like…"

"There's a four-door sedan that keeps showing up at Tasha Regan's house late at night."

"You think she's having an affair?"

"I think the consistency and timing are suspicious, don't you?"

David considered the information in light of Mike Fitzer's complaint, and ultimately had to agree with Skye. "It is suspicious. The license plate you want Fitzer to run—does it belong to the sedan?"

"Yes. But Fitzer won't help. He won't even entertain the possibility that Tasha Regan could be responsible. You know why?"

"Why?"

"He thinks she's hot."

Remembering Mike's comment about Miranda Dodge, David cringed. "How do you know?"

"He's been showing up at her place a little more often

than you might expect. If he ends up solving this thing, it'll be because he stumbled into this other guy and finally got serious about uncovering the truth."

"Doesn't Jonathon have a contact at the DMV who can handle this?"

"That's illegal, remember?" she retorted.

"It happens." David scowled at the bleak weather—and the fact that he was about to get involved in something he was better off avoiding. "Fine," he said at length. "What's the plate number?"

"I'll drop it off with the notebook."

"You do that."

"Thanks, David," she said.

He heard the smile in her voice and hung up before he could ask about seeing her tonight. Maybe she had too many emotional scars from Burke's attack and was too obsessed with weapons to be an ideal mother for Jeremy, but he knew she'd be one hell of a lover. She was passionate about everything. He wanted to experience her intensity skin to skin, feel her arms around his neck as she offered him what he'd craved since he'd come to know her four years ago. Especially now, when every second seemed so precious.

He was going to be in trouble Saturday night....

Sheltering his phone beneath his jacket so it wouldn't get wet, he ducked into the rain. Lynnette had slept with her date. That gave him license, didn't it?

No. It wouldn't be the same. If he ever made love with Skye, there'd be no going back. At least not to the life he'd known with his ex. Not for the sake of Lynnette's health. Not for Jeremy's sake. Not for anyone's sake.

10

"You've known for almost a week and you didn't call me?"

Wincing at the hurt in Jennifer's voice, Skye adjusted the earpiece that let her use her cell phone in the car as she brought her Volvo to a stop at the intersection of Sunrise and Madison Avenue. The light had barely turned yellow—she could've made it through—but she wanted a few seconds to concentrate on the conversation instead of driving. She'd been meaning to call her family. Every morning since she'd heard the news about Burke, she'd gotten out of bed planning to contact them. But she always managed to find some excuse to put it off another day.

The main problem was that she didn't really want to talk to her former stepfather. Although there'd never been any kind of impropriety or falling out, she felt uncomfortable around Joe Rumsey, as if they should mean more to each other than they did. How had they gone from being father and daughter to being…nothing? Or maybe "nothing" wasn't the best way to describe the relationship. They were cordial. Casual friends. But *friends* seemed an odd label for the man she'd once called Daddy.

"I've been crazy busy," she said. Which was true. Right now she was on her way to NSL Construction. She knew she'd be smarter to stay away, but since she'd started The Last Stand, keeping a low profile wasn't on the agenda.

"Too busy to tell us about Burke?"

More or less. David had run the license plate number she'd given him and called her with information about the driver, which she'd passed to Jonathan. It was registered to a woman, but when Jonathan followed up he'd learned that the woman was the live-in lover of Sean's boss at the jewelry store. More and more it seemed that Sean had been right all along—Tasha was having an affair. But there was still no sign of Sean himself.

"That news must've hit you hard, Skye," Jennifer was saying. "You weren't expecting him to get out for another five to seven *years*."

The news *had* hit hard. She was still trying to grasp that he'd be circulating in Sacramento—her city—by tomorrow night. But she couldn't admit her worries to Jennifer. That would only trigger an obligatory call from Skye's former stepfather, who worked about twenty minutes from where Jennifer shared an apartment with two friends. Joe felt bad that Skye's mother had died, leaving her virtually alone in the world, and occasionally attempted to include her. He'd invited her down for Christmas last month. But, regardless of his good intentions, he already had Jennifer and Brenna and a couple of younger children with his new wife. There wasn't any room in his life for her. Skye appreciated his attempt to be generous, but she was also afraid to love him as a father for fear the gestures he made were merely that—gestures.

"It's just the way things are," she said, trying to sound matter-of-fact about the situation.

"Why do you always withdraw when something bad happens?" Jennifer asked.

"I'm not withdrawing. I've been busy, like I said."

She was relieved when Jennifer didn't pursue the accusation. It was an old argument, one she definitely didn't want to rehash. "Is he coming back to Sacramento?" her stepsister asked instead.

The light turned green. Reluctant to arrive at the construction office before she could finish her conversation with Jennifer, Skye started out slowly enough to receive an impatient honk from the car behind her. "I'm going, I'm going," she muttered.

"What'd you say?"

"Burke can't practice dentistry anymore. But his wife still lives here, as well as the rest of his family."

"Won't he be too embarrassed to face them? If I were him, I'd rather crawl under a rock than go back home after being in prison for that kind of crime."

"He's not like you. For starters, he's not taking responsibility for what he did. He insists he's innocent, and there are people who believe him. We've had several incidents of vandalism at TLS, all aimed at me for what I supposedly did to a 'good family man.'"

"His wife's probably behind them."

It was possible. Jane had sent enough nasty letters.

"I don't know how she can believe in him," Jennifer went on. "My God, he—"

She caught herself before she finished, and Skye was grateful. She didn't need a reminder of what he'd done. She still had nightmares in which she felt Burke's blade slicing into her neck. Nightmares in which she struggled beneath his weight only to wake and find that she'd been battling the covers. He must've eaten a mint immediately prior to the attack because she still associated the smell of peppermint with him. To this day she couldn't even look at a candy cane. "He can go anywhere he wants," she said. "He'll be a free man."

"Will you be able to find out where he settles?"

"He's supposed to register as a sex offender, so anyone can keep track of him." But whether he actually did was another story. Sacramento had only two detectives to follow up on more than 2,500 sex offenders.

"Just what you want to do, eh? Check the Megan's Law Web site every morning while you pour yourself a cup of tea."

"Thank goodness there *is* a registry. Imagine how helpless past victims have felt."

"Why not move closer to us, escape the memories *and* the threat? Now that she's going back for her master's, Brenna's pretty wrapped up in her life at San Diego State, but she comes to visit probably once a month. And Dad's close by."

Distance from Sacramento was no escape, just the illusion of escape. "I don't want to move, Jen."

"Why not? There's plenty of violent crime down here. This is L.A., remember? You could open up an expansion office."

Skye liked living in the house where she'd grown up. Besides, Sheridan and Jasmine needed her. And, although she didn't want to acknowledge it, even to herself, Detective Willis was here…. "Maybe someday."

This answer was met with silence.

"Jennifer?"

"I don't know what to say," her stepsister admitted. "I'm scared, so I know you must be, too. Only I don't want to tell you I'm scared in case I make this harder on you."

Skye turned onto Greenback Lane. "I'll be okay."

"*How* will you be okay? What'll you do if he comes after you again?"

"I'll kill him."

"I wish there'd been some hesitation before you said that. It gave me chills."

It was pointless to try and explain the desperation that created such resolve. Skye decided it was better to get off the phone. "I've got to go."

"Are you mad at me?"

"No, I have an appointment."

"Will you call me later?"

Skye turned into the driveway that led to Noah's office. His car wasn't in the front lot, but she could see a truck—with an NSL Construction logo on the door— when she peered down the alley.

"Skye?" Jennifer prompted.

"Sure, in an hour or two," she said, parking off to the side where she couldn't immediately be spotted through the large window. It wouldn't be a big deal if he did see her car. She was about to speak to him, in any case. But this way, he'd have less time to prepare.

David was pretty sure the journal Skye had dropped by the station was Burke's, especially now that he could read it. Using letter statistics and letter positions, it had taken the cryptographer to whom David had copied and faxed just three pages less than two hours to break what turned out to be a basic transposition cipher. The notebook contained a list of initials that corresponded with various offenses, and many of the names and offenses had been crossed out. S.E. Rude at the office… T.L. Disrespectful in front of K.P… J.O. Unkind to wife… P.B. Discourteous again… S.W. Ignorant as always… L.B. Distrusting asshole… T.M. Dishonest…

He'd notified Skye as soon as he learned it himself, but she hadn't had time to talk. She'd been about to go into a meeting of some kind. So when his phone rang an hour later, he thought she might be calling him back.

Dragging himself out of his immersion in the notebook, he answered. "Detective Willis."

"This is Miranda Dodge. You left me an e-mail about Oliver Burke."

David scooted his chair closer to the desk. "Yes, thanks for calling, Ms. Dodge."

"It's Miranda. I'm sorry I couldn't get back to you earlier. I help out at my daughter's school every Thursday and just got home."

"I understand."

"What can I do to help? Has Oliver gotten himself in trouble again?"

David set aside the notebook. "I suspect he might be responsible for some pretty heinous crimes. What can you tell me about him?"

"Not a lot. We were never really friends."

"When do you remember first becoming aware of him?"

"I guess when you look at it that way, we go back a few years," she said with a little laugh. "My family moved to Sacramento while I was in fifth grade. He was in my class at Schweitzer Elementary."

"Did you like him?"

"Not especially. But I felt sorry for him."

"Why?"

"Everyone picked on him."

Surprised, David tapped his desk with the eraser end of a pencil. Burke came from a supportive, middle-class home, he possessed a higher-than-average intelligence and he was generally considered good-looking. "What was there to tease him about?"

"He was small for his age and sort of uncoordinated. When we'd go out for recess or have P.E., the other boys would fight about which team had to take Oliver. Pretty soon, he quit trying to play with the boys and started hanging out with the girls. Except that didn't work so well, either. They were the only ones who'd accept him, but he sometimes acted like he hated them for it. And, as he got older, some of the kids started accusing him of being gay, refused to change in front of him in the locker room, that kind of stuff."

"How did he react?"

"It enraged him. I mean, beyond what you might expect. At lunch, a boy yelled out that Oliver had tried to touch his butt and Oliver freaked out. It's the only time I ever saw him fight."

David nodded at another detective who called out a greeting as he passed by. "It actually came to blows?"

"Only that once, at least as far as I remember. It was in the eighth grade. Oliver definitely got the worst of it. But I saw his father when he came to the school that day. Here was this slender boy with a rather pretty face, covered in blood, yet Mr. Burke expressed absolutely no concern or alarm. He looked almost…triumphant, as if Oliver had finally done something he approved of."

David wondered if Burke had started keeping lists way back then. "Did the taunts stop after that?"

"Unfortunately not. If anything, they grew worse. Until high school. By then, the kid he'd fought had died in a drowning accident, so he wasn't around to harass him anymore. Besides, Oliver was no longer that small for his age, and he'd managed to find places where he could fit in. Debate team. Academic stuff like that. He was also old enough to pair off with a girl, and did so whenever he could, which stopped most of the slurs on his masculinity."

"He seemed happier?"

"Definitely. Especially after he got a steady girlfriend who was older, a hairstylist or something. Then he walked around acting like he was the coolest guy on campus."

"So when did you catch him peeping at you?"

"After the Homecoming dance when we were seniors."

David typed the details into Microsoft Word. "That was after he hooked up with Jane."

"Jane?"

"His wife. He married the older girl you mentioned."

"I didn't know that. But I find it interesting that he'd bother spying on me if he was still with her."

So did David. It showed that having Jane in his life didn't stop Burke from acting on his less-than-appropriate impulses. "Did you ever hear of him bothering other girls—peeping, stalking, that sort of thing?"

"No, but I'm almost positive he was the one who sent

me anonymous love letters. I can't imagine how he got the combination to my locker, but that was where he'd put them."

"What makes you think Oliver was behind the letters?"

"The way he'd stare at me. Especially right after I received one. It was as if he enjoyed my mortified reaction."

"What'd the letters say?"

"Some were really explicit. Gross, particularly to a seventeen-year-old girl. And they always included suggestions of violence and these little drawings along the edges."

David eyed the picture of a knife dripping with blood in the notebook. "What kind of drawings?"

"Various pictures of boys and girls, hands, faces, wedding rings, eyes, sexual organs. It changed, except for the naked breasts and the knife. Those were always there."

A rush of adrenaline propelled David to his feet. "Tell me you still have one of those letters."

"No. I'm sorry. They weren't something I wanted to keep. I told my parents about them, and they had me turn them over to the principal."

If David could connect those letters to Burke, along with this notebook, he'd be able to prove Burke had entertained fantasies involving knives and women well before his attack on Skye and the murders along the river…. "Did the principal ever question Oliver?"

"He once called us both into his office. Oliver showed him that the handwriting didn't match and claimed he'd have no way of knowing the combination to my locker. Mr. Easton let him go."

"Did you receive any more letters from him after that?"

"No. But it was only another week or so before I caught Oliver peeping at me through my bedroom window."

David guessed this was where Oliver's cravings had begun to escalate. "Did it make him angry that you told your parents?"

"Not that he revealed. He made up some elaborate lie about how he'd just been trying to get my attention, to see if I'd come out and talk to him."

"What happened after that?"

"Nothing. We moved across town and I finished my senior year in Roseville."

That move might've saved Miranda's life. Or the move she made afterward, the one that took her away from Sacramento and the young man who was sexually obsessed with her. "When did you leave the area entirely?"

"After I graduated from high school. I headed to New York to start my modeling career."

"Is that where you live now?"

"No, I'm in Jersey. More house for the money."

"Has Burke tried to contact you since you left Sacramento?"

"He sent me a card once, after the spread in *Playboy*."

"How'd he get your address?"

"He contacted my mother and dropped enough names of kids I'd gone to school with that she believed we were old friends."

"She didn't remember the stalking incident?"

"No, it was so far from her mind at that point that she didn't clue in. Even if she had, she probably would've discounted the past, figuring it'd been what so many people claimed it was—typical teenage sexual experimentation and curiosity. Especially when he introduced himself as *Dr.* Burke."

"What'd the card say?"

"He told me he was an 'affluent' dentist now and that if I ever came back to town he'd whiten my teeth for free. He also said I could stay in his guest house."

"Did you respond?"

"No. I didn't want him to start bothering me again. It wasn't just the peeping incident. I still believe Oliver was the one who wrote all those scary letters."

David read over his notes. "Is there anything else that sticks out in your mind about Oliver Burke?"

There was a pause. "Not really. But he always gave me the creeps. There's something odd about him, no matter how successful he became. That's why I wasn't surprised by the attempted rape conviction."

Moving his mouse out of the way, David pulled the notebook toward him. There were several repetitions of Miranda's initials, which indicated she was on Burke's mind in a recurring fashion even after she left. *M.D. Didn't respond… M.D. Thinks she's too good… M.D. The informant.* If those initials belonged to another woman, it'd be one hell of a coincidence. And David didn't believe in coincidences. "Thank you for your time, Ms. Dodge," he said. "You've been very helpful."

"Those heinous crimes you mentioned," she said. "Are we talking about other rape cases?"

"I'm talking about rape—and murder."

Silence. Then she said, "But he's still in prison, right?"

David instinctively checked his watch, which he'd been doing more frequently as it drew closer to the end of the day. It was nearly five. "He gets out tomorrow morning."

She gasped. "You don't think he'd ever look me up again, do you?"

M.D. Doesn't realize... M.D. Someday. "I hope not. But you might want to take down your Web site."

"What?"

"If he Googles you, those pictures and the accessibility offered by that e-mail button will only whet his appetite for more contact."

"But my husband and I are...having some problems," she admitted. "I-I'm pretty sure we'll be separating, and I make my living off that Web site."

David rubbed his forehead. What could he say? He knew it'd be wiser to remove the temptation, but she had to be able to pay her bills. "I don't like it," he said. "But if you can't take it down entirely, at least remove the more risqué pictures. Then keep your eyes open. And call me immediately if you hear from him."

"I will," she said.

She sounded nervous, but the subsequent click told him she was gone.

Noah Burke was older than his brother, but he was also bigger and better-looking. Although he had Oliver's fine sandy hair and blue eyes, his jaw and forehead were more pronounced, more masculine. As far as Skye was concerned, Jane had traded up. Except that Noah wasn't really available for a relationship. And the affair could easily trigger a murderous rage in the little pervert she'd married.

"What are *you* doing here?" Noah asked.

The only other people in the room, a secretary and a subcontractor—judging by the conversation—glanced up from the invoice they were discussing.

Obviously, Oliver's brother recognized her, from TV or the trial or both. His eyes held suspicion, but he hadn't raised his voice.

"I need a few minutes of your time," she told him.

His eyes swept over her as if he was considering whether or not to throw her out. "We have no business together."

Skye threw back her shoulders. "I have to at least *try* to make you understand."

The awkward silence on the part of the other two people seemed to convince Noah that this meeting might be better handled without an audience. Pursing his lips, he gave a little shrug. "Come on back to my office."

Surprisingly, he held open the swinging door that allowed her to pass through the reception area. Then he waved her ahead of him into a luxurious room with a large window, a tall mahogany door, wainscoting, crown molding and a hardwood floor.

"Nice office," she said.

"Thank you." He motioned to a chair. "Would you like to sit down?"

Skye had appeared at Noah's place of business prepared to dislike him. He was cheating on his wife and children and, unwittingly or not, he was putting the object of his desire in harm's way. But she had to admit he was polite, although he had no reason to be. In his view, she'd falsely accused his brother of a serious crime.

She remembered him sitting in the courtroom,

trying to comfort Jane and his mother after the verdict had been read. Later, his face could've been chiseled in stone when they nearly bumped into each other on the way out of the building. "I hope you're happy," he'd muttered.

"What brings you here?" he asked now, taking his seat behind a large desk.

She sat rigidly, wishing she were somewhere else. His skepticism and doubt weren't easy to deal with. "Like I said, I need you to understand something."

His expression revealed little of his thoughts. "I'm listening."

"I wasn't lying."

"About…"

"Any of it."

His gaze fell to his desktop, and he slowly straightened his calendar, pencil holder, clock. "It's irrelevant," he said at length. "Oliver's served his time. It's over."

She slid to the edge of her seat, trying to catch his eye. "I'm afraid it's not over. He's getting out tomorrow. Unless he's changed a great deal, which I highly doubt, he'll attack someone else. It's just a matter of time."

"Stop it!" he snapped. "You're crazy or paranoid or both."

"I'm neither! He held a knife to my throat while he groped my breasts, okay? He ripped off my pajamas!"

A pained expression appeared on Noah's even features. "Look. You…you seem to believe what you're saying. And I'd be lying if I didn't admit that I've occasionally wondered. But it doesn't make sense. You're talking about my little brother. I grew up with him. He was the gentlest kid on the block, so gentle that my friends used to ask me where my little *sister* was. That little 'sister' is who you're calling a rapist."

It was one thing to endure the ordeal she'd endured, another to have others think she was maliciously inventing a story that could destroy a man's life. Sometimes Skye thought the lingering doubt was worse than the actual attack because it never seemed to end. "Why would I lie about that?" she asked.

"Because you were high or…or momentarily out of touch with reality or half-asleep. I don't know, but you're remembering it wrong. You've got to be."

She jumped to her feet. "I'm *not* remembering it wrong. That's something I'll never forget, something I have to live with every day!"

He stood, too. "But you've certainly turned it to your advantage, haven't you? That charity is paying your bills. Jane's the one who's really suffered. She's got nothing."

"Except you, right?"

He gaped at her. "What'd you say?"

"You heard me," she said. "And if your brother finds out, I won't have to convince you the little son of a bitch is dangerous. You'll learn it for yourself. Or Jane will." Grabbing her purse, she started to march out of the office.

"Ms. Kellerman."

The panic in his voice made her pause. Turning, she found him watching her with an ashen face. "If you tell anyone… I mean, I don't want to hurt my wife or my brother. I never intended to…*we* never intended… It just—" at a loss, he shrugged "—happened."

He hung his head as if the weight of the world rested on his shoulders, and Skye surprised herself by feeling sympathy for him. "I don't want to see anyone hurt, either," she said softly. "That's why I'm here."

He eyed her dubiously. "You won't tell?"

"Only Detective Willis, and that's because I'm hoping he can protect her."

"Oliver would never hurt Jane."

"Believe what you want," she said. "Just don't bet your life on it."

"*My* life? He wouldn't hurt me, either," he argued. "Even if he tried, I'm bigger and stronger than he is."

"Strength isn't all that matters. Oliver is cunning." She thought of David's call, which she'd received just before she walked into the construction office. That book of Oliver's was a record of every offense, petty or otherwise, he'd suffered to that point. "And he never forgets a slight."

11

Skye sat alone in the crowded restaurant, examining the animated faces of the strangers around her. They were laughing, talking, gesticulating, eating—*living*. That wasn't what she did anymore. Since Burke's attack, she hovered along the perimeter of life. Usually she was better at going through the motions than she was today. But no one else in the restaurant knew that a killer was about to be released—a killer who looked every bit as trustworthy and good-natured as the guy next door.

With a grimace, she took another sip of the French onion soup she'd ordered from the cafeteria-style restaurant. It was her last supper, she thought wryly, the last meal she'd have knowing Burke couldn't hurt her—at least not with his own hands. And she'd decided to eat it alone.

She could've invited Jasmine and Sheridan to join her. Then she wouldn't have had to feel quite so separate from other people. But she was too preoccupied to be good company tonight. And she was afraid the conversation would lead to an argument about her snooping into Burke's life. When they'd checked with her an hour ago, she'd told them she was going home to bed, and they'd eagerly encouraged her to do so. She needed the rest, but David had recently called to tell her that the notebook she'd retrieved from the Griffins had Oliver's fingerprints all over it, and that alone made any attempt at sleep futile.

Hard as she fought the paranoia that had ruled her immediately after the assault, it was taking over again, creeping into her life like a persistent vine. She could beat it back and beat it back, but it always found some crevice in which to grow.

Closing her eyes, she tried to avoid the anxiety attack that suddenly threatened. There was no reason for it. This was the slow, quiet part of her day, the first time she'd actually sat down for a meal instead of eating while working at the computer or driving her car. But it was also the night before Burke's release.

Breathe deeply. Imagine you're sleeping on a deserted beach, with the sun radiating heat and brightness overhead and the waves lapping the shore a few feet away. You're safe and relaxed. You are content, comfortable, warm. Your mother is with you, smiling at you.

Because she refused to resort to medication, the psychologist she'd visited for almost a year after the attack had taught her how to use her mind to overcome her body's autonomic reaction. It didn't always work, but tonight she thought she'd regained control—until she opened her eyes and saw a man staring at her from across the room. He was wearing a pair of jeans and a long leather coat, and he was sitting alone. With his goatee and holes in his earlobes big enough for a pencil to fit through, it was difficult to tell how old he was, but she guessed around twenty-five.

She met his gaze. If he was staring without realizing it, she knew courtesy would dictate he look away. But he didn't. He gave her an enigmatic smile and kept staring, which put her on edge and evoked the usual question: Was he another Burke? A psychopath who thrived on violence, abuse, power?

Her heart pounded as she brought her herbal tea to her lips. The beach. She was on the beach. The sun was warm. There was sand.

She glanced up again. He was still there, making no secret of his interest. And that smile. It was as if he understood how uncomfortable he was making her and enjoyed it.

Scowling at him, she felt in her purse for her gun. There it was. Forget the beach and the sun and everything else. She had a weapon, and she'd use it if she had to.

When she pulled her purse closer to her body, he returned his attention to his meal and she decided it was time to go. Despite the gun, she'd lost the ground she'd made up with her "mind over matter" technique and was beginning to perspire.

Grabbing her tray, she dumped her food into the wastebasket and headed for the door, but he moved to intercept her.

"Excuse me."

Did this man have a knife hidden in his long coat? It was possible. He had his hands in his pockets....

She knew it was unlikely. Not every odd or rude person was a killer. But panic didn't respond to common sense or statistics, especially when she'd already been that one in a thousand.

Tempted to pretend she didn't notice that he'd addressed her, she raised her hands to push open the door and brush past him. But then she hesitated. Was she over-reacting? Letting the past dictate the present? Maybe he thought he knew her from somewhere or recognized her from news clips on TV.

Determined not to run before there was sufficient cause, she forced herself to stop. "Yes?"

"I couldn't help noticing you sitting over there by yourself and...well, I think you're a very attractive woman."

So that was it? She couldn't help being irritated that he'd scared her for no good reason. "Thank you."

He shuffled his feet, obviously trying to appear self-conscious, but it didn't really put her at ease. "This isn't the most original line in the world, but I'm new to the area and would like some companionship, if you're not seeing someone. Is there any chance you might go to a movie with me?"

"Now?"

"Unless you have other plans."

He was certainly direct. But he was handsome enough that part of her said she should be flattered. Another part said she should even consider going out with him. It wasn't as if she had much hope of a relationship with David. How many times had she, Sheridan and Jasmine talked about the unfortunate way they'd let their lives become defined by their work? This was an opportunity to change that, to start seeing someone new. Even if he was a little younger...

"Not tonight, thanks."

"You have plans?"

No, she just preferred to isolate herself. Much as she

longed for human contact, she felt safer going back to the office, where she could take care of some of the work that was piling up. There were letters to answer, calls to make, notes of gratitude to write, fund-raisers to plan, help and support to solicit.

"I have things to do."

"I see." He grinned in an attempt to be endearing. "And there's no way I can talk you out of it?"

If she was going to heal, truly heal, she had to make some effort to overcome her resistance to meeting strangers and taking chances. She repeated that sentiment to other victims all the time. But still... She'd never recommend driving off with a man who'd barely introduced himself. Maybe some women did that and lived to tell about it, but her trust had been destroyed. She couldn't take the risk.

"No."

"I'm sorry. I'm being too forward. But could I give you my number, at least? Then you could call me if you ever feel like grabbing a bite or going to a movie."

That minimized the risk, didn't it? If she decided to call him, she could do a background check first. "Sure."

She expected him to hand her a card, but he turned back to one of the tables and jotted something on a slip of paper he'd pulled from his pocket.

"Have a good day," he said as he gave it to her. Then he walked away, and she hurried to her car. Only once she'd driven a few blocks did she bother to open the note. And then she had to pull over so she didn't cause an accident.

She'd been curious to know his name. But the note didn't contain a name or a number.

We'll be together soon. Love—O.B.

Nearly sideswiping a van that was coming from the opposite direction, Skye wheeled around and drove directly back to the restaurant. Her body was clammy, her hands cold, but she could think of only one thing—she had to figure out the identity of the man who'd passed her that note and discover his connection to Oliver Burke.

He wasn't the person who'd called her. She would've recognized the voice. Or maybe not. She'd been too shaken by this man's pointed interest, too absorbed with controlling her own reactions….

Shit! Dashing a hand across her upper lip, which was beaded with sweat, she double-parked, hopped out and ran inside. But he was gone. She searched every face, the bathrooms, studied all the men in the parking lot. She even asked the people who'd been eating near her if they'd seen a man fitting his description.

Some had seen him. But no one knew who he was, where he'd come from or where he'd gone.

With Oliver Burke getting out in the morning, David couldn't sleep. He kept flipping through cable channels on TV, wondering what Skye was doing, what she was thinking. She had to be terrified. Especially after some of the fingerprints on that notebook, lifted through a chemical process using ninhydrin, proved beyond a doubt that it had, indeed, belonged to Oliver.

Fortunately, she'd taken the news well. She'd expected it. But that didn't mean it didn't bother her—or him. The dates in that journal of offenses went way back, beginning years before Oliver had even purchased the house in that gated community. Did he plan some sort of revenge for everyone he'd listed? Why else would he keep track of every insult or slight, and cross out some but not others?

David was willing to bet that most of the people in that book weren't even aware they'd angered Burke. Or they didn't care. Oliver was probably so insignificant to them that they'd bumped into him somewhere and gone on their way, scarcely acknowledging him at all, while he, offended by their lack of notice, plotted and planned his revenge.

David wished he could connect more of those initials to actual people so he could test that theory. He doubted Oliver had tried to *kill* all the people on his list. It was too long for that. There would've been bodies turning up everywhere. And he already knew that Miranda Dodge was alive and well.

Maybe Meredith Connelly was his first. Her initials weren't the last ones listed, but she was close to the bottom. There was no L.F. for Linda Farello or P.P. for Patty Poindexter, both of whom had been murdered after Meredith.

Tossing his remote on the coffee table, David got up and went into his office. The "offense" beside the initials M.C. was "couldn't even remember my name."

How was such a small slight important enough for Oliver to record? How could anyone hold a grudge about something so inconsequential?

Maybe he'd met Meredith at Pepe's, the restaurant where she worked as a waitress. If she was dealing with the public, she might be friendly, even warm, in her manner but it wasn't personal. Oliver didn't seem to understand the difference and adjust his expectations accordingly. It was possible he'd gone there to eat, had Meredith as his waitress, liked what he saw and left her a big tip and his card. Then, when she didn't remember him the next time he came in, he'd been insulted and begun following her around, watching her—and eventually raping and murdering her.

David thought that scenario was plausible, but he didn't know how he'd ever prove it. He'd checked Oliver's credit card records to see if he'd ever paid for a meal at Pepe's that way. Nothing. He'd spoken to Meredith's coworkers, too. None of them remembered Burke coming in on a regular basis or having any contact with Meredith. But that wasn't surprising. Oliver had one of those faces that could blend into a crowd. He certainly didn't look threatening.

The phone rang. Dropping the printed list back onto his desk, David sank into his chair as he answered. "Hello?"

"Daddy?"

Jeremy. "Hi, bud. What's up?"

"If Mr. Green Grocer has thirty-six cucumbers on sale for $1.39 each, how much would it cost to buy five of them?"

David smiled. Math homework. "First you have to decide how to set up the problem."

"Just tell me the answer," he said, his voice impatient.

He always tried to get out of doing the story problems. "Sorry. You have to solve it yourself, but I'll help you figure out how."

"Da-ad, I want to be done so I can watch the rest of my movie."

Movie? David checked his watch. It was after nine o'clock. "Isn't it a little late for you to be up?"

"No. Mom hasn't told me to go to bed yet."

"Where is she?"

"In her room."

"Asleep?"

"Talking on her cell phone."

"To whom?"

"Someone named after the sky. Isn't that funny?"

David didn't think so. "What's she saying?"

"I can't hear. When I went in, she made me leave and close the door."

"Did Skye call her?" he asked. But he knew better. Skye didn't have any reason to contact Lynnette. Besides, she didn't have Lynnette's number, and it wasn't published anywhere.

"I don't know," Jeremy said.

"Never mind. Let's get that problem done." David said, but his mind was on Skye the whole time. And when he hung up, he tried to reach her himself.

Skye stood in her office with the lights off, peering through the blinds. Except for her car, the parking lot was empty. She had the doors locked, and her gun on the bookshelf close at hand, but she still felt uneasy, spooked by the fact that a total stranger, a man somehow connected to Oliver Burke, had tried to get her into his car. He must've been following her. How else would he have known she'd be at that restaurant?

Was he out there?

She didn't think so, but it was difficult to tell. David's wife had called, distracting her. For those few minutes he could've walked through the front door and she wouldn't have noticed.

Is something going on between you and my husband?

Taken completely off guard, Skye hadn't known how

to answer. She'd finally come up with, *Your husband? Last I heard, you were divorced.*

We're still trying to make it work. We don't need you getting involved and destroying that. There's a child to consider.

Why had she answered the phone? She wasn't trying to destroy anyone, least of all David's son.

The office phone rang, causing her to glance over her shoulder. But this time Skye didn't even move close enough to check the caller ID. She didn't want to speak to anyone. Tonight, the whole world felt hostile.

Damn you, Oliver Burke. Damn you to hell. Without him, her life would've been completely different. Before that night, she'd been a happy, confident, carefree young woman. She'd had no fear of anyone. But Oliver had left more scars than the one on her face.

She fingered the raised bump that followed the arc of her cheekbone. If it weren't for Oliver and what he'd done, she probably would've been married by now, started a family...

Her cell phone chimed in her purse. Evidently, whoever had just called the office was looking specifically for her. But she couldn't bring herself to move away from the window.

When the chiming stopped, the office phone started again.

"Go away," she muttered. Then, more exhausted than she could ever remember being, she forced her legs to carry her over to the couch, where she lay down below the portraits of the killers that faced her every day.

"Why do you do what you do?" she asked them, ignoring the persistent ringing.

A lack of caring? A lack of empathy? That was what the professionals said. Skye suspected there was more than that, but she wasn't sure exactly what. No one was. She only knew that Burke had changed her life irrevocably.

Finally, whoever was calling gave up, and she was able to close her eyes. The warmth provided by her coat felt like a protective cocoon. If only she could sleep for a few hours…

But it wasn't twenty minutes later that she heard someone at the door.

Trying to get in.

The interior of The Last Stand was dark, which made David uneasy because Skye's Volvo was in the lot. If she wasn't here, where was she? She wasn't answering the office phone, her cell phone or her home phone, even though Sheridan and Jasmine had both told him she'd gone to the delta house to get some rest.

Standing in the harsh glare of a motion-activated floodlight, David continued to pound his fist against the door, hoping to draw her out from some inner sanctum, a break room, conference room or kitchen. After the frightening call she'd received earlier in the week, he didn't like not being able to get hold of her. But his knocking brought no response.

"Skye, it's David," he shouted. "Are you in there?"

Silence.

"Skye?"

She wasn't around. But she couldn't have gone far. It wasn't all that long ago that Lynnette had been talking to her on the phone.

His pulse raced as he turned around and stared at the busy street. She wouldn't have walked anywhere. She knew better than that. Or maybe not. The way she could handle a gun made her feel safe.

He gazed at the fast-food restaurant across the street. There wasn't anyone in the place. It was closed, except for the drive-through.

He was about to drive to the delta house—to see if she'd gotten a ride with someone else—when a light finally snapped on.

Closing his eyes for a second, he told himself to calm down. She was fine. He could see her coming toward him, but she looked more like the shocked, disillusioned woman he'd met in the hospital than she had in three years.

When the lock clicked, he swung the door open before she could even touch the handle. "Are you okay?"

She didn't answer right away. "What are you doing here?"

"I came to check on you."

"I'm fine," she said, but he could tell that wasn't true. She was having a bad night—and he wasn't sure how much of her misery could be attributed to Lynnette, which meant it came indirectly from him.

"Something's wrong," he said.

She reached into her pocket and handed him a piece of paper.

When he'd read it, he understood. "Who gave you this?"

"A man at a restaurant."

He wanted more details. But not here. "Come on," he said, still holding the door.

She blinked in surprise. "Where're we going?"

"To my place." He knew it was crazy to take her

home, especially now that Lynnette was suspicious of their relationship. But Skye was so busy trying to help every victim in Sacramento she wasn't taking proper care of herself. And with Burke getting out…

The dark smudges beneath her eyes testified to the fact that she was exhausted. "When's the last time you had a good night's sleep?" he asked.

She shrugged. "You know how it is. Places to go, people to see."

He wanted to run his hand over her cheek, cup her chin and promise to make everything all right. But he knew he'd kiss her if he did—and his decision to do the right thing by Lynnette stopped him.

"Let me stand guard tonight, okay?" he said softly.

Her eyes connected with his, and although he could sense how weary she was, she straightened her spine. "You don't need to worry about me. I can handle this."

"I know you can." Taking her hand, he rubbed the fine bones above her fingers. It wasn't much, but it was all he could allow himself. "This way, maybe I'll be able to get some sleep myself."

A smile curved her lips. "Okay. I'll do it for you."

He chuckled as he led her outside. "Thanks for the favor."

Fresh from a hot shower, Skye sat at David's kitchen table, wearing a T-shirt, a pair of boxers and his robe. He still had the note she'd given him earlier and seemed engrossed by it. She sipped the glass of wine he'd poured to help her relax—and it was obviously working because she was now distracted by the contours of his body, apparent beneath his Gold's Gym T-shirt and worn jeans. Unfortunately, she was even distracted by the clothing he'd lent *her*. The T-shirt and boxers were right out of the laundry, so they smelled of soap, but the robe hadn't been washed in a while. She could tell because it smelled just like *him*.

"Who could this guy be?" He frowned as he pushed the paper into the center of the table.

She pulled the collar of the robe higher, practically up to her nose. She was still tired, but she was hungry, too—hungry for physical intimacy, reassurance, the positive things in life. She'd dealt with the devastating results of violent crime on an up-close-and-personal basis for too long. She needed to compensate, and she knew exactly how she wanted to do that.

But David had been very careful not to touch her since he'd shown her into his apartment.

"I'm thinking he's a friend of Oliver's." She let go of the robe's collar for a moment to take another sip of wine. "Or maybe someone he paid to scare me."

"Describe him again."

"He was about five-eleven, 190 lbs. Dark, shoulder-length hair, brown eyes, an olive complexion, a giant piercing in each earlobe and a goatee."

"Any additional scars? Tattoos?"

"No. Other than the holes in his ears, he could change his looks easily enough. All he'd have to do is shave off the goatee, bleach and cut his hair and put on a pair of glasses. At that point, he could probably walk right past me and I wouldn't recognize him—unless I happened to focus on his earlobes."

David rubbed at the condensation on the table from his glass of water and turned the paper over. The man had written on the back of a fast-food receipt. "It's not like this tells us much, either."

"I wonder how long he's been following me. If he knows where I live." The fear of that had stopped her from going home, even though she hadn't felt like working anymore.

"It's not like Burke to collaborate. He might appear friendly on the surface, but on a deeper level he's very antisocial."

"He strikes me as a loner, too," she agreed. "Only a loner would make that list. It's such a juvenile way to react to people." She shook her head. "He's a dentist, an educated man, for crying out loud."

"Just because he's advanced intellectually doesn't mean he isn't retarded emotionally."

"What do you think screwed him up?"

He raised one shoulder. "Tough to say. It might have to do with his upbringing."

"But he has a good family."

"In most respects, I suppose."

She liked the sound of David's voice, his large hands loose around his glass. "Have you found something I don't know about?"

"Nothing earth-shattering. A guard at the prison told me he saves every letter from his father, but throws away all the others. And there've been a couple of other statements by various people in Oliver's life that make me wonder if there wasn't some problem between him and his father when he was growing up. Jealousy of his brother. Feelings of inadequacy. Confusion over his sexual identity. Something."

"I wish his mother would open up and talk honestly about what he was like as a child."

"She's too deep in denial for that. She has a son who's a serial rapist and murderer, yet she insists he was a perfect boy and had a perfect family."

"Noah seemed to turn out okay," she said.

He arched an eyebrow. "You've met Noah?"

She braced herself for more of David's disapproval. "I spoke with him today. At his office."

"Do I want to hear this?"

"Probably not. But you can't do your job with only half the facts. This isn't directly related to those three murder cases, but it's peripherally connected."

"Why'd you go see him?"

"Why do you think? I had to warn him what could happen if Oliver found out about the affair."

"Warn *him?*" Obviously frustrated, David stood up and shoved a hand through his hair, making it stick up in front. "You realize that means the person who approached you at the restaurant could've been Noah's hired man and not Oliver's, don't you? Now he's aware that you know he's having an affair with his brother's wife. And I'll bet he's told Jane that you know, which makes *two* people—besides Oliver, of course—who'd love to see your lips sealed forever."

"At least they're all members of the same family," she quipped, watching him pace.

He gave her a dirty look and didn't answer.

"What did you expect me to do? Ignore the risks Jane and Noah are running? They believe Oliver's like everyone else, David. And I knew that if Jane ever wound up dead, I'd feel responsible because I saw it coming and did nothing to prevent it."

He stopped pacing long enough to face her. "What

about your own safety, Skye?" he asked, sliding his thumbs into the pockets of his jeans.

She stared at the wine in her glass. "That's another issue entirely."

"No, it's not!" He crossed the room and bent down to stare into her eyes again. "You scare the hell out of me."

She studied him, felt the chemistry between them despite his frustration. "In more ways than one, right?"

He'd obviously noticed the changed inflection in her voice because his eyes fell to her mouth. "You're a temptation," he admitted.

A temptation he was determined to resist. And, after speaking to Lynnette, Skye was equally committed to avoiding any deeper involvement. She didn't need the complications of falling in love with a man who wouldn't allow himself to love her back.

She scooted her chair away from him, putting more distance between them. "Yeah, well, you don't have to worry about that anymore."

He stayed where he was, leaning on the table. "Why not?"

"Because I'm no longer interested."

Straightening, he folded his arms and watched her from beneath half-closed eyelids. The sexual tension between them called her a liar, but she was hoping he didn't feel that tension quite as strongly as she did. "You've met someone else?"

She held up her glass in a toast. "Not yet. But I haven't been very open to the idea. Until now."

"Until now," he repeated. "Now you're looking for someone?"

She downed the rest of her wine. "Why not? I deserve a man who wants what I have to offer."

His scowl darkened as he drew close again and lowered his voice. "Sounds like you're interested in a serious relationship."

"I am." She ran a finger around the rim of her glass because she knew what her eyes would reveal if she looked up at him, especially now that he was only inches away. "Maybe even marriage."

"What provoked this decision?"

She risked a quick glance at his face. "You did." Even while she was speaking to his ex-wife, she'd been harboring a glimmer of hope and defiance. It wasn't until she was sitting at David's kitchen table, wanting to touch him so badly her arms ached, that she realized how stupid she was to nurture any feelings for him.

"*I* did?" he repeated.

"Of course." She stopped trying to hide her emotions and gazed up at him. "I'm in love with you, David. I want to make love with you—but you have nothing to give me."

His expression grew tormented. "You think I'm not dying to carry you into my bedroom right now?"

"You can't. At least not without feeling terrible about it. And what kind of relationship would that allow us?"

He didn't answer, didn't move, but his muscles bunched as if he was fighting the impulse to do just that.

"So…" She took a deep breath. "It's time to put an end to the waiting. I'm ready to have a man in my life, which means I'm going to have to look elsewhere. I've closed myself off from the possibility for too long already." She thought of the fund-raiser and how much she'd been anticipating it. Now it seemed silly to go with David. What would one night change? Nothing. He'd still have Lynnette and Jeremy and all his old reservations. Sheridan's neighbor had irritated her for crying in his beer over his ex-wife and refusing to let go, yet she was doing the same thing with a man who'd never promised her *anything,* never mind a commitment. Work was her drug of choice instead of alcohol, but that was the only difference. "As a matter of fact, I don't need you to take me to the Hyatt Saturday night."

Sinking into his seat, he looked at her warily. "Why not?"

"Someone else will be going in your place."

His jaw tightened. "Oh, yeah? Who's that?"

Skye scrambled to think of someone—and resorted to the only guy she knew who'd be available and willing on such short notice: Sheridan's neighbor. "His name is Charlie Fox. He's a nice guy." She had no romantic interest in Charlie whatsoever, but he was suddenly preferable to David. Being with David would make her crave a night of hot, steamy sex and a million tomorrows; being with Charlie would make her glad she was going home alone.

"Charlie," he echoed as if it was the stupidest name on earth.

She nodded. "He's a nice guy."

"You said that already."

They stared at each other in a silent standoff. Then his eyes moved over her with an intensity that left gooseflesh in its wake. He wanted her as badly as she wanted him. But Skye refused to take that into consideration, refused to allow it to change her mind. That was what had kept her hanging on for so long already. She needed to cut away everything Burke had brought into her life that made it difficult to go on—which included her infatuation with the detective who'd investigated her case.

"Lynnette must've made quite an impression."

Skye frowned. "You know she called me?"

One muscular shoulder lifted in a shrug, but the motion didn't strike her as careless. "Jeremy mentioned that she was on the phone with someone named after the sky." He gave her a grin that contradicted the hollowness in his eyes. "Had to be you."

"Is that why you came to the office?"

"Partly." He rubbed his lip. "What'd she say?"

"What I knew. That you both want to make your relationship work."

"And what'd you tell her?"

"That I don't want to stand in the way." She swallowed around the lump rising in her throat. "And that's true."

His face looked set in stone, but she knew she was doing the right thing. Putting herself out of reach made it easier on him and would ultimately make it easier on her, too.

"She had sex with someone else this week," he said.

There was no strong emotion in his bald statement, so Skye wasn't sure how to respond. She wasn't even sure why he'd decided to share such private information. "I'm sorry if it bothered you."

"It didn't."

His tone suggested that surprised him. But, considering his commitment to Lynnette, his indifference wasn't exactly a good thing. "Then I'm sorry about that, too."

She could barely hear him when he answered, "You and me both."

Silence settled over them again, but it was a deafening silence, one filled with everything they weren't saying. After a few minutes, he opened his mouth as if he intended to put words to some of the emotions that hung there in the room. But then he closed it and kept turning his glass around and around on the table.

"We'd better get to bed," Skye said at last.

Briefly pressing his fingers to his eyes, David breathed a deep sigh. "Right. You can have the big bed. I'll take Jeremy's room."

12

David stood by the bed, watching Skye move restlessly in her sleep. Maybe she was only dreaming, but she wasn't at peace, and that bothered him. He wanted to hold her, comfort her, make sure she knew he'd do whatever he could to protect her, no matter the cost.

But he understood where such comfort would lead. He also realized Lynnette wouldn't easily forgive him. She'd know that any encounter between him and Skye would not be the mechanical, empty experience she'd shared with another man this past week.

Unfortunately, that didn't stop him from wanting to make love to Skye.

Transfixed, he stared at the tangled blond hair strewn across his pillow. He longed to run his fingers through that silky mass, press his lips to the hollow of her throat where he could feel her steady heartbeat. She was in *his* bed, *his* apartment, and she'd already admitted she wanted to be with him.

He imagined gently waking her, then slipping into the warmth of the bed and stripping the clothes from her body. The mere thought made his pulse race. But it was more than desire that had brought him to her bedside.

She'd been through so much. He wanted to love her as she deserved to be loved.

If only they could have this night. But morning would come, and with it his responsibilities to Jeremy and Lynnette. He couldn't have Skye *and* his family, couldn't do justice to both. He should've sent her to Jasmine's or Sheridan's tonight instead of just calling to tell them she was okay.

Rubbing his face, he glanced at the pictures on his dresser. In one, his son balanced on his shoulders, wearing a Kings jersey and hat. In another, Lynnette cradled Jeremy as a newborn. David had been happily married then, or fairly so. Some of the cracks in his relationship with Lynnette had already appeared, but he'd still been idealistic enough to believe they'd celebrate their fiftieth wedding anniversary someday. Just like his own parents would in another decade.

Instead, he and Lynnette had divorced, reconciled and separated again, all because he'd become too immersed in his work—and because he'd met Skye. That alone had diminished his ability to overlook what needed to be overlooked with Lynnette. From the moment he'd first seen Skye, there'd been a spark. He couldn't explain the intensity of the attraction, but he'd been fighting for his integrity ever since. Even more so, now that Lynnette was sick.

Keeping that picture of Jeremy firmly in his mind, David returned to the other room, where he was supposed to be sleeping. At least Skye was safe from harm. For tonight. Knowing about that recent phone call and the guy in the restaurant, he could take some pleasure in having her close, couldn't he?

But he wasn't so happy to have Skye in his apartment when he woke the following morning.

"David? Are you in there?"

Someone was knocking on the apartment door. Yawning, Skye opened her eyes and blinked at the ceiling. David's ceiling. The knowledge of where she was sent a thrill of excitement through her, despite last night's resolution to forget him and move on.

Rolling over, she buried her head in his pillow and breathed deeply, trying to take in the essence of the man she loved. But when the voice at the door spoke again, Skye realized it wasn't a friend or neighbor.

"David? It's Mom."

Sitting up so fast her head swam, Skye looked at the clock. It was only seven-thirty. Probably much earlier than David expected visitors, especially family. Or he would've warned her. Especially after they'd talked about Lynnette having called her last night!

The creak of footsteps indicated that David was crossing the floor. He didn't seem to be in a rush—and she could certainly understand why. But he didn't tell her to stay out of sight, either. He didn't say anything.

Then she heard the door open and his mother's voice, much louder now, rose to her ears. "Don't you have to work today? You're usually up by now."

"I had a late night."

"Hi, Daddy!" A third voice chimed in, and Skye cringed anew.

David's son. There'd been plenty of times she'd wanted to meet the person who was more important to him than anyone else. But now wasn't one of them. She knew how her presence would be interpreted.

"What brings you to town so early, Mom?" he asked after greeting Jeremy.

"Actually, we got in after ten last night. I thought you'd already be asleep and I knew Jeremy's bed wouldn't be big enough for your father and me, so we stayed with Lynnette."

"Where's Dad?"

"Getting some breakfast. He has an appointment with a real-estate agent to visit some investment properties. I'm not interested in looking at rentals all day, so I thought I'd take Jeremy to school and drive up to Auburn to see my old friend, Virna Washington. She moved there a year ago, you know."

"And where's Lynnette?"

There was a slight pause. "She wasn't feeling well this morning. She might try to go to work later."

David didn't question why his ex-wife might not be feeling well. "I'm glad you stopped by," he said.

Skye felt no such sentiment. Her eyes darted to the bathroom, where she hoped to hide until Mrs. Willis and Jeremy left. Kicking back the covers, she climbed out of bed, careful to move slowly and quietly. But it made no difference in the end. Halfway across the floor, she found herself facing a young boy with dark hair and wide green eyes, just like his father's.

"Jeremy!" David snapped. But it was too late. David's son stood in the doorway, staring at her as if he'd never seen a woman before.

"Who are you?" he breathed.

"Just—" she cleared her throat "—a friend of your father's."

"Is there someone else here?" His mother had heard the exchange.

Skye's stomach muscles tensed as Mrs. Willis appeared behind Jeremy and gaped at her in astonishment. "You have a…a woman in your bedroom?" she said, turning to her son.

David had pulled on a pair of sweatpants, but he wasn't wearing a shirt. He shot Skye an apologetic glance. "Mom, this is Skye Kellerman. Skye, this is my mother, Georgine Willis."

Running a self-conscious hand through her tangled hair, Skye managed what she hoped was a polite smile. "Nice to meet you."

"She's wearing your underwear!" Jeremy exclaimed, which saved Georgine from having to call forth the words that seemed to be stuck in her throat but did little to change the horrified expression on her face.

David ran two fingers over his left eyebrow, as if he had a headache. "I lent them to her because she needed something to sleep in."

This wasn't good. Skye knew word of it would travel back to Lynnette at lightning speed. But she had no idea how to improve the situation—other than to get out of the apartment as soon as possible. "Sorry to rush off, but I—I need to get to work. I didn't mean to sleep so late."

"Looks like you didn't sleep any better than my son," Mrs. Willis said dryly.

Skye didn't know how to respond, so she didn't. Scooping up her clothes, which she'd piled on a chair next to the bed, she hurried to the bathroom, pausing only long enough for a quick wave before closing the door.

Fortunately, when she opened it again, they weren't standing there anymore. They'd gone to the kitchen. She could hear David offering his mother a cup of coffee.

"Is she your girlfriend, Dad?" Jeremy asked.

Skye braced herself for the answer, which was exactly what she'd expected it to be. "No, she's just someone I know from work, someone who needed a safe place to stay last night."

Safe? With the memory of his mother's disapproval firmly etched in Skye's brain, and David's own voice playing in her head—*She's just someone I know from work*—it felt anything but safe.

Tossing his clothes on the bed, she started down the hall. Normally, she would've cleaned up after herself. But she wasn't about to stay an extra second in David's apartment.

He was taking some cereal from the cupboard when she stepped into the kitchen. As the sound of her movements drew all eyes, her fingernails curled into her palms.

"Would you like something to eat before you go?" David asked.

"No, thank you." Swallowing against a dry mouth, she tucked her hair behind her ears, suddenly conscious that she hadn't even combed it.

His expression was unreadable, but he had to be as mortified as she was. "I'll call you later."

"No, it's okay." Staring into that room, with the three of them staring right back, she felt like an interloper.

"But we need to make arrangements for the fund-raiser."

"No...uh...I'm covered for that, remember? But thanks. I appreciate your putting me up for the night."

Stubbornly refusing to let the smile slip from her face, she nodded at Georgine and Jeremy. "Nice to meet you," she muttered again. Then she dashed through the entry and let herself out.

It was Friday. He'd made it.

Leaning up as far as the limited space between his bed and the ceiling would allow, Oliver stared through the bars of his cell at the two guards conversing on the catwalk across from him. He'd spent a restless night, with the minutes dragging by like days, but morning had arrived at last. And he was still alive.

Because he hadn't given Vic an opportunity. He'd skipped his art class the night before and pleaded illness to avoid his final day of fixing teeth. He'd also refused his trip to the yard—time usually spent in the library anyway—and gone without meals. Now he was famished, and exhausted from all the tossing and turning, but he was going home. Nothing else mattered.

Kicking off the blanket, which was too thin to keep him warm in the drafty, cavernous building, anyway, he climbed off his bunk. "This is it," he told T.J., who was barely beginning to stir. "Jane will be here to get me in a few hours."

"You're a lucky man," T.J. muttered.

It wasn't luck. He used his head, unlike the others in here, who thought brawn was all that counted. Men worried about who had the biggest muscles or the biggest penis. They never cared who had the biggest intellect.

Shows how stupid they really are.... "Vic figured he

had me. But I'm the one walking out of here. I'll be home tonight, making love to my wife."

"Oh, yeah? Who's been making love to her while you were in here?" T.J. asked, then laughed at his own joke.

Oliver was sitting on the stainless-steel toilet, which had no actual seat. He had to relieve himself—badly—but now his body wouldn't cooperate. "Jane isn't like that. Jane's been waiting for me."

"The way you've been waiting for her?" T.J. hooted even louder. "I hope she's been more careful about what she's put in her mouth than you have."

T.J.'s words made visions of what he'd done flash through his mind, only now he was seeing his actions in a whole new light—through the eyes of someone living on the outside. He knew what others would think of the favors he'd granted. What his father would think: that he was a weakling, a homosexual, a loser.

"It's not the same," he said, trying to convince himself. "It—it's different in here."

"What happens in San Quentin stays in San Quentin, eh?" T.J. got up and shoved Oliver off the toilet. "You keep telling yourself that, okay, little buddy?" he said as he peed. "But I know how much you enjoyed it. What about all the 'playing doctor' that went on in your dental office? You examined more than teeth up there, huh?"

"Shut up!" Oliver longed to retaliate. He was tired of being pushed around. But he restrained himself and started cleaning up the mess T.J. had made around the toilet, as usual. He'd write about this later, take care of it when he could, he told himself as he sat down again.

"What's your daddy gonna think about his dentist boy now? Are you gonna tell him how many guys you fucked in here? That no one gives better head? That's something to hang your hat on right there. I won't be the only one who'll miss you."

The singsong quality of T.J.'s taunts carried Oliver back to elementary school. *I bet you play with dolls....* He knew not to respond. He'd learned at a young age that the torment grew worse if he did. But he was too rattled this morning, too hungry and desperate and eager for his imminent departure to maintain any emotional distance. "My dad thinks a lot of me. He always has. He knows I'm no fag."

"If you ask me, you like guys a lot more than you like women."

"Shut up!"

"Is that what you write about in that little journal of yours? Are you keeping track of how many times you sucked my cock?" he asked and knocked the small stack of Oliver's belongings, which Oliver had piled neatly on his shelf, to the floor.

Oliver stared at his father's letters, which were strewn at his feet. Such chaos made him anxious, upset. He *wasn't* a fag. His father understood that. "He knows I shouldn't even be in here, that I'm innocent."

"Skye Kellerman knows you're innocent, too, right?" He laughed.

The sarcasm dripping from those words caused Oliver to tighten his jaw as well as his colon. His father's letters were all over the grimy floor. He was already constipated. How could he relax and use the toilet with his belongings in such a state?

Don't listen. Ignore him. I'll get the letters. Soon. They'll be fine. Count to ten—

T.J. interrupted. "Open your eyes when I'm talking to you."

Oliver kept his eyes firmly closed and continued to mumble to himself. Until T.J. kicked him. "Hey, you. She'd laugh if she could see what's become of *Dr.* Burke in here. I should send her a picture of you sitting there, trying to take a shit and being too uptight to do it." He rubbed his hands. "Or better yet, I should send her a detailed description of you giving me your best deep throat last night. Moaning and groaning as if—"

"Shut up!" Oliver stood at the same time he tried to pull up his pants, but he was in such a hurry that he nearly fell, which only made T.J. laugh louder. "You promised you—you wouldn't tell anyone about that!"

"No wonder Skye would rather stab you than spread her legs. Look at your sorry little pecker!"

One minute, Oliver seemed to be thinking coherently, reminding himself to keep cool. The next he was slugging T.J. with every ounce of strength he possessed. "You bastard! I hate you!"

T.J. wasn't laughing anymore, but he seemed strangely calm. His fist slammed into Oliver's chin, whirling him around. But before the pain could fully register, something pierced Oliver's back. The forward thrust sent him tumbling over the toilet.

"That's from Vic," T.J. told him, and suddenly Oliver understood. T.J. had provoked him on purpose. He'd needed this to get his adrenaline flowing, make it easier to do Vic's dirty work.

It was one of the worst betrayals Oliver had ever suffered—because he hadn't seen it coming. He'd played it smart, had never crossed T.J. How could T.J. turn on him for Vic? He'd given T.J. anything he'd ever asked for.

T.J.'s eyes glittered. "You pathetic piece of shit. I should do society a favor and finish the job."

Oliver put up his hands to protect himself. T.J. had time. The guards were hollering and pounding down the walkway, but one more thrust would only take seconds. It could be over, for good, before they ever arrived.

Instead, T.J. spat, nearly hitting Oliver in the face, and withdrew to the far corner. "But what has society ever done for me?" he grumbled.

"You…you did…" Oliver gulped for breath. He was pretty sure T.J. had punctured his lung. "…this for…for Vic?" As far as Oliver knew, T.J. didn't even like Vic.

"He promised to make it worth my while. But I didn't do it for him. I did it for *her*."

Oliver couldn't have heard him properly. He was getting so dizzy. "Who?"

"Skye Kellerman."

Two guards were at the cage door, giving the signal for the electronic release that would open it.

Closing his eyes, Oliver concentrated on breathing. "You don't…even know…Skye."

"I know you did what she said you did. And, unlike you, I believe in treating a woman right." Then the guards were in. One guard cuffed T.J. and dragged him out while the other called for medical help.

Oliver listened to the noise, watching the hurried activity from between his lashes. There were germs crawling all over him and his belongings. He could feel them multiplying and spreading…. But the blood that puddled beneath him wasn't so bad. It was the first time since winter set in that he'd been warm in this godforsaken place.

"What was that all about?"

David's mother had taken Jeremy to school and returned immediately, scarcely giving David time to shower, shave and dress for the day before she cornered him in the kitchen.

"What was *what* all about?" he replied, trying to act as if the encounter with Skye was no big deal.

She stood behind him as he buttered his toast, too agitated to sit down. "That woman you had here." She lowered her voice. "Are you involved with her? Lynnette told me months ago that she thought you were seeing someone else, but I wouldn't believe her. And what about *Jeremy?* Can you imagine how he must've felt to have a woman who wasn't his mother get out of your bed?"

"You're overreacting," he said.

"Lynnette has MS, David. Do you know how difficult that is to deal with? She needs to be able to count on us. She needs to be able to count on *you.*"

There was nothing to say; he couldn't deny it.

"No wonder Lynnette's so withdrawn. You promised her that you'd love her and no one else—"

"I know," he interrupted. God, did he know. He'd meant it at the time. But he also knew that if it wasn't for Lynnette's illness, he probably would've broken that promise and gotten together with Skye three years ago.

"So how can you expect to repair your marriage when you're entertaining another woman? Is that what broke up your family in the first place? *Have you been cheating on Lynnette?"*

If her voice had been sharp, he could've reacted in anger. But she wasn't yelling, she was pleading. And that did more to awaken his conscience than any amount of yelling could ever do.

"No. Last night was...nothing," he lied. "Skye's a victim from one of my cases, that's all."

He carried his breakfast to the table, hoping to put a few feet between them, but his mother followed and perched on a chair that she pulled even closer. "You don't bring other victims home with you."

"Someone threatened her, and she was scared, okay? I invited her to stay here, hoping she'd be able to get some rest."

His mother folded her arms, her expression clearly skeptical. "You're telling me you didn't sleep with her."

"I didn't sleep with her," he said, but he felt guilty as he said it because whether or not he'd actually had sex with Skye seemed like such a technicality. The desire was there, stronger than anything he'd ever experienced. Sheer willpower was the only thing that had stopped him.

"The way she ran out of here..." His mother's voice softened, but she still seemed doubtful, confused. "It *felt* as if there's something between you."

Taking a bite of toast, David talked around it. "Jeremy barged into the bedroom and woke her up, and then you followed him in. You weren't expecting to see her. She wasn't expecting to see you. It was an awkward situation."

"So I'm assuming the worst and I shouldn't be?"

Dammit! Why'd she have to press him so hard? "I'm

doing the best I can, Mom," he said, his frustration finally boiling over. "Just stay out of it."

He knew he'd revealed too much when her tone grew wary. "You mean—"

He raised his hands, toast and all. "I don't want to talk about it anymore. The man who tried to slit her throat is being released from prison today, okay? I believe he's responsible for three *murders.* I've got to get to work."

"David…"

He could tell she was about to issue another warning. *Who'll take care of Lynnette? Think of what this will do to Jeremy.… There's no guarantee that a new relationship will work any better than the one you already have.… You've got an obligation to your first wife. You're simply trading one set of problems for another.…*

But she didn't say any of it. She reeled in her apparent concern and said something that hit him even harder. "Never mind. I know you'll do the right thing. You're a good man."

You're a good man. Those words echoed through David's head all day long—every time he thought of Skye and regretted not taking advantage of the opportunity presented to him last night.

He'd expected to hear from Lynnette about the debacle of his mother's visit. But his ex hadn't called. His mother must've kept the incident at his apartment to herself. Which meant he had until three-thirty—another hour— before Jeremy got home and blurted out the details of the whole encounter to Lynnette. *I met the lady named after the sky, and she was wearing Daddy's underwear!*

"Hey, what's wrong with you today?"

David glanced away from his computer to respond to Tiny, who leaned into his cubicle.

"Nothing. Why?"

"You haven't been to lunch with us for a week."

"I'm just busy, trying to catch a break on those murders along the river. We need one. Fast."

"Maybe not as fast as you think."

Confused, David studied his friend. "What does that mean? You know Burke gets out today."

"He's already been released. But he's not on his way home. He's in the hospital."

David felt his eyebrows shoot up. "What happened?"

"His cellmate stabbed him."

"You're kidding."

"No."

"Is he going to pull through?"

"He'll pull through, but he'll have to heal before he's capable of attacking anyone." Tiny handed him a slip of paper. "This is the address of the hospital where they sent him."

David studied Tiny's hen-scratch printing. The hospital was in the Bay Area, not far from the prison itself. "When will he be allowed to go home?"

"Warden said the doctors plan to keep him for two nights. After that, if all is well, he can finish recuperating wherever he wants."

David pictured Burke as he'd seen him last week—confident to the point of cocky. "Why'd his cellmate stab him?"

"No one knows for sure."

"When you nark on someone in prison, I guess you gotta expect retribution."

"Exactly." Tiny jingled his keys. "I know I haven't been much help this week," he said. "I've had too many other cases. But I've got some time today." He jerked his head toward the door. "Wanna drive down to the prison with me? Talk to a few of the inmates who knew Burke and see what they have to say about him? Maybe peek in on Oliver himself?"

"I can't," David said. "It's my turn to take Jeremy for the weekend, and I promised Lynnette I'd pick him up from her place before dinner."

"No problem. I'll check in with you later then, let you know how it goes."

Relieved that Tiny was taking over and giving him the short break he needed in order to spend some time with his son, David turned off his computer and gathered the files he planned to take home. He was just putting Oliver Burke's notebook on top of the stack when a fragment of what Miranda Dodge had said came back to him.

By then, the kid he'd fought had died in a drowning accident, so he wasn't around to harass him anymore....

The story of Burke's fight in eighth grade had been part of a general history, not something that immediately stood out. But it was another example of someone who'd wronged Oliver meeting up with an unpleasant fate, wasn't it? What if that kid's initials happened to be on Oliver's list? Some of the early entries didn't have exact dates, just years, but a few went all the way back to what would've been Oliver's high school days. It was possible.

Picking up the phone, David called the number Miranda had given him.

A female voice answered. "Hello?"

"Miranda?"

"No." There was a soft giggle and a low whisper as whoever had answered the phone spoke to someone else. "This guy thinks I'm my mom."

David couldn't help smiling. The "hello" had sounded adult enough, but he could now tell that this girl was far too young. "Is your mom home?"

"Yes. Just a minute." There was a clunk as she dropped the phone. A minute later, Miranda came on the line.

"Hello?"

"Miranda, this is Detective Willis."

"I hope you're calling to tell me they've decided to keep Burke in prison."

"I'm afraid not. But it'll be a while before he's fully functional."

"What do you mean?"

"Someone stabbed him this morning. He's got some healing to do."

Her voice lowered. "I wish I could say that makes me feel sorry for him."

David could understand why it wouldn't. He doubted Burke would get much sympathy from Skye, either. "I have a quick question for you."

"What's that?"

"I was hoping you could give me the name of the boy who got into that fight with Oliver in the eighth grade."

"Eugene Zufelt. Why?"

David didn't answer right away. He was too busy checking the initials at the top of Oliver's list. About ten lines down, he paused. Sure enough, there was an E.Z.

with *bully* written next to it. Both the initials and the infraction had been crossed out.

A tingle told David he was on to something. "You said he drowned. Do you remember the circumstances surrounding his death?"

"I know his parents were vacationing in Hawaii at the time. And his older brother, who was staying with him, was out with friends. When the brother came home, he found Eugene floating in the pool."

"What was he wearing?"

"Nothing. He was nude."

David tapped his fingers on the desk. "Did they ever discover what happened?"

"He'd been drinking."

"With friends?"

"Alone."

"That seems a little odd for such a young teen. What was he, fourteen? Fifteen?"

"Fifteen, I think. But he was a perennial troublemaker. And there were signs of his having gotten into his parents' liquor cabinet. They figured he got drunk, wasn't thinking straight, dived into the pool and hit his head. It was one of those freak accidents."

Maybe. Maybe not. "Did you go to the funeral?" he asked.

"Of course. They dismissed school early. Everyone went."

"Even Burke?"

"No. At least, I didn't see him."

Despite her negative response, David was willing to bet Burke had been somewhere close by. That would be his moment to celebrate having paid Eugene back—

with interest. "Do you have any idea how to reach Eugene's parents?"

"They might be in the phone book." She hesitated. "You don't think Oliver had anything to do with Eugene's death, do you?"

"Probably not. But it's worth asking a few questions." Besides, he'd done all he could on the cold cases he'd been struggling with for three years. He needed a new angle, and looking further into Burke's past might provide it.

"That would be so awful."

He agreed and disconnected, then called Tiny on his cell.

"What's up?" Tiny said.

"When you see Burke, ask him how well he knew a boy named Eugene Zufelt."

"Why would I want to do that?"

"I'm curious about his reaction. See if he attended the funeral, too."

"You gonna explain this to me?"

"Later." David checked his watch and grabbed his jacket. Jeremy was just getting out of school. "I've gotta go." If he hurried, maybe he could pick up his son before Jeremy walked the half block home from school and mentioned Skye to Lynnette.

13

"So how'd it go last night?" Jasmine asked, poking her head into Skye's office.

Skye pretended to be more engrossed in the letter she was writing than she really was. "Fine."

"That's it? That's all you've got to say?"

She scowled. After leaving David's apartment this morning, she'd gone home, showered and returned to the office, but she hadn't bothered with makeup. She wondered if she looked as sleep-deprived and grumpy as she felt. "What do you want me to say?"

Jasmine sauntered in. Half East Indian, she had the darkest complexion of the three of them—beautiful golden skin—and unusual blue, almond-shaped eyes. At only five-four and less than 100 pounds, she was also the shortest and slimmest. She could eat anything and never gain a pound. "You know what I want you to say. Did you sleep with him?"

Sheridan had already asked her the same thing. "No," she answered curtly.

"No?"

Jasmine sounded almost as disappointed as Skye was, but Skye didn't want to hear it and certainly didn't want to discuss it. She tried to reread the line she'd just written to the chief of police, once again asking him to support one of their events. But it was impossible to concentrate. "He's going back to her, like I said," she muttered when Jasmine didn't leave.

"He said that?"

"More or less." For a second, she considered telling Jasmine about the call she'd received from Lynnette. Lynnette's words still churned inside her because they suggested she'd actively pursued someone else's man. But Skye hadn't come near David when he was married. During those times, they didn't even speak, except perfunctorily over the phone and only regarding Burke. But why complain about Lynnette? It didn't matter. Skye was putting her feelings for David behind her. Much to Sheridan's chagrin, she'd already asked Charlie to be her escort to the fund-raiser tomorrow night. And he'd agreed.

"Something's wrong with that detective," Jasmine said, dropping onto Skye's couch.

"When David commits, he commits."

"Does that mean you're finished with him?"

The letter. Keep working on the letter. Otherwise, Jasmine will see that it's killing you to answer this question. "Of course. Why would I go on being stupid?"

"Loving someone isn't stupid. I'd actually *like* to fall in love."

This succeeded in pulling Skye away from her computer. "Even with a man who doesn't love you back?"

"Even with a man who doesn't love me back. Then maybe I could feel something besides the emptiness I feel now." Sighing, she leaned back and gazed up at the pictures above her head. "This is creepy, Skye," she said, her tone suddenly far less wistful. "You know that, don't you?"

Skye had started typing again. *We would be delighted to honor you for what you've already done for the community and...* "What's creepy?"

"That there are pictures of psychopaths hanging on your wall. Doesn't it bother you to have them staring down at you?"

Skye studied the pictures. "Sometimes. A lot of times," she admitted. "But they motivate me. They're the reason I show up here each day, despite knowing I'll never get rich, never be completely safe, never be able to forget what I've seen and heard."

Jasmine stood and clapped her hands once. "Aren't we a barrel of laughs today."

As long as they were talking about such serious subjects... "Any word on the man who killed that little girl in Fort Bragg?" Skye asked.

Her face pale, Jasmine moved toward the door. "No."

"They'll find him," Skye said, feeling guilty for being so wrapped up in her own problems.

Jasmine paused and turned toward her. "He works at the lumber mill."

Skye froze. "How do you know that?"

"I keep seeing the saws. Every time I close my eyes, there are saws. Loud, deafening, going around and around, slicing through one log after another."

"Have you called the police?"

"Of course."

"Do they believe you?"

"Probably not. But they've promised to take a blood sample from every worker who's willing to be tested."

"They have a DNA profile?"

"Not yet. But they found semen on the body and sent it to a lab."

Skye grimaced at the mental picture that created. It was so distasteful, she needed a moment to reel in her reaction, but then she said, "If the killer works there, he'll simply refuse."

"Then they'll take a closer look at him, and maybe they'll find cause to make it compulsory."

Skye studied her friend's face, mystified and a little frightened, as usual, by her gift. *He works at the lumber mill....* "Can you tell me where the man who's been following me works?" she quipped, only half-joking.

Concern flooded Jasmine's face as she approached the desk. "Someone's been following you?"

"Maybe. Maybe not. Something's going on. I'm not sure what."

Her eyebrows drew together. "Does he drive an old Jaguar?"

Skye's heart skipped a beat. "You're...what? Seeing an old Jaguar in some sort of vision?"

"No." Jasmine laughed at their miscommunication but sobered quickly. "Sheridan said there was an old Jag in front of her house last night. It freaked her out because she'd never seen it in the neighborhood before, and someone sat inside it for hours, watching the building."

"Why didn't she mention it when she came in this morning?"

"She didn't think the incident was associated with you and I'm sure she didn't want to add one more thing to your list of worries, not with Burke getting out today."

"By trying to protect me, you and Sheridan could get me killed, Jasmine."

Skye saw that her friend was wounded by her words. "It's a fine line," Jasmine said after a pause. "At what point are we jumping at our own shadows? Becoming paranoid? Adding undue stress?"

Safe was always better than sorry. But Skye didn't care to argue about it just now. She was more interested in pursuing the information. "Did she get a good look at him?"

"He had a goatee. She could see that much. And metal rings in his ears, the kind that make those really large holes."

Memories of the man she'd met in the restaurant surged through Skye's brain as she got to her feet. "Anything else?"

"He acted as if he *wanted* to be seen."

"Did she get his plate number?"

"She tried. She and her neighbor walked out to take a look, but he'd removed them. He laughed as he waved the back of one plate at her and drove off."

Skye couldn't resist glancing past her friend to the photos on the wall. Was this guy another one of *them?*

No. The note he'd given her had Oliver's initials on it. The Jaguar driver was probably nothing more than an ex-con he'd bribed or hired to help him, someone motivated by financial gain, not bloodlust.

But that didn't make him any less dangerous. Especially if Oliver Burke was pulling his strings.

"Dad, it's your turn."

Picking up his PlayStation controller, David once again tried to focus on the video game he was playing with his son. But his mind was occupied with other things. Lynnette had refused to speak to him when he'd missed Jeremy at school and gone to the house to get him, which probably meant Jeremy had already mentioned seeing Skye at his apartment. He hoped the underwear detail had been omitted, but he couldn't imagine that it had. His parents hadn't brought up the incident when they all met for dinner an hour later, but they'd seemed worried. And he'd received a call from Sheridan a few hours ago. She'd told him some guy had been hanging around her place the night before, acting suspicious.

That concerned him most of all. Particularly when he learned that the man's description fit that of the guy who'd approached Skye at the restaurant.

He'd immediately called down to the station, given them Sheridan and Jasmine's addresses and asked for a couple of uniforms to do periodic drive-bys. Skye lived too far out. He'd had to contact the sheriff's department to get some police assistance there. Fortunately, the deputy he'd spoken with, a man by the name of Meeks, seemed understanding and supportive. He'd promised to look into it and call if he saw any sign of a white Jaguar—or anything else that appeared to be amiss.

David hadn't heard back and was hoping that meant he could relax. But it was early yet. Early enough that he wanted to be out looking himself. Normally, he loved spending time with Jeremy; tonight, however, he was too anxious that those who'd taken over his watch might miss something important.

"You just crashed your car and died—*again!*" Jeremy laughed. "You're doing horrible today!"

Because David was too worried about the real kind

of dying. He'd tried calling Skye to tell her about the stabbing, hoping to give her a short reprieve from the fear she felt at Burke's release, but he'd gotten her answering machine at home, voice mail on her cell and some volunteer at the office who said he didn't know where she'd gone. David was pretty sure he'd heard her in the background. He had the feeling that she was standing right next to that volunteer mouthing "I'm not here," so he hadn't panicked. But he wished she'd call him.

Instead, when the phone rang, he heard Tiny's voice on the line.

Telling Jeremy to switch to a one-player game, he managed to keep his disappointment to himself. "How's Burke?"

"Pale, puny and weak. Pretty much the same, despite the injury."

David laughed. It felt good to let go of a little tension. But this wasn't a laughing matter. The fact that Burke's looks were so deceiving made him even more dangerous. "Did anyone at San Quentin have information that might help us?"

"T.J., the guy who stabbed him, was more than happy to talk."

"What'd he say?"

"That Burke's obsessed with Skye Kellerman. He clipped every newspaper article that mentioned her, talked about her more than his wife and kid, indulged in sexual fantasies that always seemed to revolve around her and had pictures of her taped inside a spiral binder. T.J. said he'd bet fifty bucks Burke kills her before summer."

David's heart plummeted to his knees. "Did you tell

him we're watching very closely to make sure that doesn't happen?"

"More or less."

"And?"

"He said it doesn't matter. Even a full-time body-guard won't be able to save her, according to him. T.J. claims Burke will simply bide his time and wait for the perfect moment."

David thought of Eugene Zufelt. If Oliver had caused the incident that took Eugene's life, he'd turned into a killer a long time ago. And he'd grown bolder and bolder with his attacks, eventually going after women in their own homes—women who didn't even know him well enough to hurt him as so many of his earlier targets had. Was that because he'd focused his hate and anger on a certain group? Young, attractive women who'd rebuffed him or were likely to?

"Did T.J. have anything else to say?"

"He shared an interesting story."

"Which is…"

"The details are sketchy, mostly the rumors you find in any prison, but T.J. said that last year Oliver made a very good friend in prison, a guy by the name of Larry Millwood. Oliver and Larry were close, if you know what I mean."

"Lovers?"

"That's what T.J. implied. But it all came to an abrupt end when Oliver found out that Larry was making fun of him with another guy, whom Larry was also roman-tically involved with."

"And then?"

"Oliver acted like it was no big deal. He has a lot of pride, as you know. But T.J. says he was seething inside.

He'd lie awake for hours, scribbling in his little notebook and drawing pictures."

Pictures again. But David let that pass for now. He was too interested in hearing the rest of the story.

"Shortly afterward, Oliver stole something from a very dangerous man named Enrique, a lifer, and gave it to Larry as a gift," Tiny went on. "When Enrique heard Larry had it in his possession—thanks again to Oliver, apparently—he assumed it was Larry who'd stolen it and killed him in the yard."

David whistled. "That's ruthless."

"That's Oliver. What's more, T.J. said he acted completely indifferent to his lover's death. He gloated as everyone talked about it, then went back to his journal."

"He likes to write." David and Tiny had been going in different directions all week. This was David's first chance to tell him what had been found at Burke's former residence, but Tiny wasn't surprised.

"Makes sense," he responded when David explained. "T.J. said he pored over his journal almost every night, making notes, some of which were in code."

"Did Oliver leave any of that behind?"

"Unfortunately not."

"So what do you think?"

"What I thought before. He's a killer."

"Did you ask him about Eugene Zufelt?" David asked.

"I did. He was pretty drugged up because of the pain, but the question still caused a reaction. He looked at me kind of strange, then smiled and said, 'Yeah, I knew Eugene. Eugene was a friend of mine.'"

"Eugene called him a fag, then beat the shit out of him in eighth grade," David said.

"Some friend."

"Eugene also died in a very strange drowning incident two years later."

"Somehow that doesn't surprise me, either. Not when you'd already asked me to see if Burke attended his funeral."

"Did he?"

"Yes."

"He admitted it?"

"Freely."

"Interesting." Although distracted, David managed a smile and a nod when Jeremy turned around to show him his game score.

"How'd he do it?" Tiny asked.

"I don't know yet. I'd sure like to talk to Eugene's parents, though."

"Will you be able to find them?"

"I've already gone through the phone book with no luck. The only Zufelt listed turned out to be a distant relative who said they moved but he didn't know where."

"That's too bad."

"He's going to see if he can track them down through the family grapevine. If I learn anything, I'll let you know."

"Thanks."

"After what happened to Larry, isn't T.J. scared that Oliver might try to get back at him?" David asked.

"He says he has a lot more friends inside than Larry ever did."

"What if those 'friends' aren't as loyal as he thinks?"

"I mentioned the possibility. He shrugged and said it was still worth it. He's never met a more deceitful, cunning son of a bitch."

David gazed down at his tennis shoes. "And that's one killer talking about another."

"T.J. classifies his crime a little differently than Burke's. He's in for murder, but he didn't attack a woman, said he never would. The man he killed had been beating on his mother."

"And he's a lifer?"

"It was particularly gruesome. He plotted it well in advance and then he covered it up."

"With that background, he probably wasn't the safest cellmate for a rapist to have."

"In San Quentin, everyone's dangerous. T.J. has an anger-management problem, but I don't think he's a psychopath."

Shielding the phone with his hand, David snapped his fingers to get Jeremy's attention. "High score, huh, buddy? Good job!"

Jeremy responded with a broad smile and restarted the game.

"Was Jane around while you were at the hospital?" David asked Tiny.

"Yeah, she was in the room, wringing her hands and staring out the window."

"What'd she have to say?"

"'I can't believe what she's done to me. It just doesn't end.'"

"Who's 'she'?"

"Skye, I guess. Jane wouldn't address me directly. She seemed very upset."

David couldn't help feeling some sympathy for Burke's wife. Her only mistake, at least before the affair with Noah, was marrying the wrong guy. He felt sorry for Burke's family, too. All the publicity surrounding the trial, and Burke's subsequent incarceration, had humiliated them. But they'd rallied around him, stood by him in spite of it.

Problem was, if Oliver was really the calculating killer David thought, they were about to get hurt again. And so was whoever Burke chose as his next victim….

"Thanks for doing all that," he said. "Jeremy's waiting so I'd better go."

"Just tell me one thing."

"Sure."

"What's going on between you and Lynnette these days?"

"Same old, same old. Why?"

"She called me a couple hours ago."

David's hand tightened on the receiver. "What for?"

"She asked me if you're sleeping with Skye Kellerman."

It took David a moment to absorb that. But part of him said he should've expected it. "What'd you tell her?"

His friend blew out an audible sigh. "The truth."

"Which is…"

"That I don't know."

Jeremy crashed his simulated race car, but instead of starting the game over, he tossed his controller aside. "Daddy, can we go out for ice cream?"

Once again splitting his attention between his telephone conversation and his son, David raised a hand. "Just a sec, okay?"

"Are you?" Tiny pressed.

"Not yet," David said and hung up.

"Dad?" Jeremy looked up at him hopefully. "Can we get a strawberry shake?"

Maybe he couldn't forget Skye, but he could deliver on ice cream. "Why not?" he said.

Enjoying the hot water and the scent she'd added to make her bath a little more luxurious, Skye sank deeper into the tub, careful not to get the headset attached to her iPod wet. She'd been functioning on a strictly practical level for so long that this felt like an indulgence—maybe even a waste of time—but it took her mind off the fact that it was Friday night and Burke was probably home by now. So did thinking about the dress she'd bought at a small boutique off Fair Oaks Boulevard. Made of a delicate sea-green fabric in a classic halter-top style, it molded to her body, then flared out slightly at the ankles, but it had no plunging neckline or thigh-high slit to make her feel self-conscious. It was simple and elegant, which was just what she'd been looking for. Of course, she wasn't nearly as excited about attending the fund-raiser now that she'd be going with Charlie Fox instead of David, but something about lying in David's bed without him last night had made her long to improve her desirability. She'd let herself become too consumed by the past, too cautious and scared.

It was time to make another concerted effort to resist the changes Burke had caused in her. Sometimes, she didn't even realize she was backsliding. But she realized it now and was officially searching for love and companionship. When she got out of the tub, she planned to forgo the weight training and aerobic exercise that normally ended her day in favor of searching the Internet for new ways to do her hair and makeup. Maybe she'd even check out an Internet dating service. One had to be careful about meeting men online, but it was the easiest way to begin. Initially, she'd feel safer shielded by an e-mail address. If she ever met anyone in cyberspace she wanted to know better, she'd do a complete background check first. Then she'd arrange lunch in a public place.

Despite how hard she'd fought it, the fact that she was finally broadening her horizons came as a relief. Skye didn't know how she'd survived being so isolated and alone for the past three years—and found it ironic that she was planning to break out of her shell on the very day of Burke's release. His impact on her life had been so all-encompassing it was as if he'd established a whole new reckoning of time. Anything that happened before the attack was B.B.—Before Burke; anything that happened afterward was A.B.—After Burke.

All carefree dating and romantic relationships had definitely happened B.B. But Burke was free to start over now. She should be, too.

Turning the tap back on to bring the temperature of the water up a few more degrees, she leaned her head on the rim of the tub and listened to Chris Daughtry's new song.

What jewelry should she wear with her new dress? she wondered, watching steam fill the bathroom. But before she could consider the possibilities, she heard something, felt a strange vibration, that made her tense and sit up.

She'd locked all points of entry into the house. She knew that because she'd checked them twice. She'd also set the alarm, which hadn't sounded. So why was she suddenly feeling as if she was no longer alone?

Turning off the water, she pulled the headphones from

her ears. Besides the tinny sound of distant music, there wasn't any noise. But she was fairly sure she could smell cigarette smoke.

Was it her imagination—the old panic coming back? She didn't *think* so….

"Jasmine? Sheridan?" she called.

They were the only people who had a key to her house. She'd given them each one in case she ever locked herself out.

But Jasmine and Sheridan didn't smoke.

They didn't answer, either.

Standing, she switched off her iPod and listened intently. The wind was blowing outside, whistling through the eaves, but she couldn't hear anything else. Except her own heart…

Stepping onto the bath mat, she grabbed a towel and wrapped it tightly around her. She normally kept a gun close at hand. She had one in her nightstand, her purse *and* the hall closet. But not in the bathroom. Here she was cornered, especially since the only window was a narrow rectangle above her head. Even if she could figure out how to break the thick glass, she had no way of boosting herself through.

Closing her eyes, she breathed deeply through her nose, trying to determine if she was really smelling cigarette smoke.

Yes—she was sure of it. Smoke. Or *someone* who smoked. And it was as real as the *plink, plink* of water that suddenly dripped from the faucet.

Skye's fingers tightened on her towel. None of her friends were smokers. Jasmine used smoked as a teenager, back when she was hitchhiking across the country to escape the small town where she'd been raised. But that was years ago.

Hoping to reach the bedroom and the gun she had there, Skye edged closer to the door. The floor creaked beneath her feet, stretching her nerves taut, but she forced herself to keep moving. *Think. Act.* She wasn't as vulnerable as she used to be. All the training she'd had—and tried to pass on to others—had to make a difference.

I'm prepared for this, she told herself. *I've been expecting it.* But her body didn't want to cooperate. She was shaking so violently, it was a struggle just to keep from cowering in a corner.

Not again, her mind screamed. *I can't do it.* But she knew she could if she had to. She'd done it before. Besides, she'd wanted Burke to make his move soon, right? To spare her the agony of waiting and wondering?

Maybe she was getting that wish….

Opening the door a crack, she eyed the hallway. She couldn't see anyone, but she heard the slight rustle of movement. Where? In the kitchen? She sensed whoever it was creeping through the house, slowly, methodically. But he was so damn quiet. And how had he disabled her alarm? Probably quite easily. All he had to do was snip a wire. She lived too far out for monitoring.

Slipping into the hallway, she hurried to her bedroom, where she recovered her gun from the nightstand.

14

Skye didn't want to be caught in a towel. Being naked made her feel vulnerable, even when she was holding a gun. So she set the weapon on her dresser and put on a pair of sweats and a T-shirt. There was no time for shoes. Or a call to the police. It would all be over before they could reach her, anyway. Trying to remain calm, which wasn't easy, she poked her head back into the hallway.

Silence. She wasn't sure anymore that she'd ever smelled smoke. It was tempting to believe she'd imagined everything. Until she crept down the hall to the front entry and saw the cigarette butt discarded by the coat rack. The front door stood ajar, letting the wind rush through.

How'd he unlock the door? She'd used the dead bolt. But she was too frightened to work out the logistics. There was no question now. She'd been right all along. She had a visitor.

The wind was intermittently stirring the drapes and the papers on the table, and she had no idea if that was what she'd heard earlier or not. He could be anywhere....

With her back to the wall, Skye peered cautiously

around the corner, into the living room. She had to find
him before he found her. But she wasn't expecting him
to be behind her. From the corner of her eye, she saw a
flash of movement as someone stepped out of the
bathroom she'd vacated only minutes before. Then there
was a deafening blast and a bullet whizzed past her head.
She had a fraction of a second. No chance to aim. Crouch-
ing and turning at the same time, she fired just as he
squeezed off a second round.

His bullet missed and buried itself in the wall behind
her. Skye's didn't. It pierced the intruder's chest. After
that, he didn't even last long enough to gasp and gurgle
like gunshot victims on TV. His jaw dropped briefly, he
glanced down at the wound and he crumpled.

Judging by the hole and the blood, Skye was pretty
sure she'd hit him in the heart.

Shaking more badly than before, she stared down at
the face of the man who'd approached her in the restaurant. Without any animation, without any *life,* his
skin looked waxy, strange. If not for the holes in his
earlobes and that goatee, she might've thought he was
someone else.

She tapped his leg with her foot, hoping he'd groan
or move or something. She actually prayed he would.
She wanted him to be incapacitated but not *dead;* he had
to tell her who he was and why he'd invaded her house.

But he didn't move.

Swallowing hard, she set her gun on the hall table,
crouched next to him and pressed two fingers to his neck.
Those fingers were so cold that contact with his skin
seemed to burn. But that warmth was deceiving. She

couldn't find a pulse. Her restaurant suitor had died almost immediately. There wasn't much blood. His heart had probably stopped beating as soon as the bullet entered his chest.

"Oh God," she whispered. As much as she'd wanted to eliminate the threat Oliver posed, it wasn't easy to kill a person. She couldn't possibly feel good about it. Especially when that person wasn't Oliver Burke. She knew the kind of memory this would become, knew she'd collected too many harrowing memories already.

Creeping away from that lifeless body, she tried to stand, but her legs wouldn't support her. Rocking back into a sitting position, she gasped for breath and rubbed her eyes, hoping that when she opened them again she'd see something different.

But the corpse was still there—growing colder by the second.

Skye was growing colder, too. The freezing wind coming through her open door didn't help. Too bad she didn't have the strength to get up and close it. She was too shaken, too overcome with the emotions she'd experienced four years ago, when she'd awakened to find Oliver looming over her bed. That sense of violation—and the lack of security and peace of mind—immediately returned to swallow her.

It had happened again….

She covered her mouth, fighting the urge to vomit. He would've killed her if she hadn't killed him. The bullet holes in the wall testified to the seriousness of his intent. But she still couldn't cope with the shock of it.

Taking a deep breath, she slid even farther from the body. She didn't want to see it, didn't want to acknowledge what she'd done. It was so *permanent.* She'd taken a life....

She needed to calm down, get a grip. She'd *survived* again. That was what mattered. She'd always known that future threat, future violence, was a strong possibility. She'd trained for it—and that training had done exactly what it was supposed to do. It'd saved her life. And this time, the man who'd broken into her house wasn't capable of causing her any future harm.

"You asked for it," she hissed. "You had no right to be here."

Slowly, her strength returned and her thoughts became more coherent. Maybe this man couldn't tell her who he was, but he might have some ID.

Reluctantly reversing her direction, Skye averted her gaze from his unseeing eyes as she searched the pockets of his jeans.

He didn't have a wallet. He had two pieces of paper folded into squares, which turned out to be computer-generated maps giving detailed directions to her house and someone else's.

Holding the second map up to the light, Skye easily recognized it, too. Directions to Sheridan's condo.

Fresh fear blasted through her. What if this man had visited Sheridan's house again? And what if—

Suddenly strong enough to move mountains if she had to, she launched herself to her feet and ran for the kitchen. Grabbing the phone attached to the wall, she started to dial. Then it dawned on her that there wasn't any dial tone. The phone was out of service or, more likely, the line had been cut. Of course. She'd known he must have disabled the alarm system.

Frantic, she dug through her purse, which was sitting on the kitchen table, just where she'd left it. Obviously, her intruder hadn't broken in to rob her. "Come on, come on, come on," she chanted. If Sheridan was hurt—or worse…

Tears blurred her vision as her fingers closed around her cell phone, but there was too much adrenaline flowing through her system to make it easy to dial. She had to start over three times before she punched in all the right numbers.

"Hello?"

Skye sank into a chair at the kitchen table, weeping when her friend answered on the first ring. Sheridan was alive—and she sounded fine.

"Hello?" Sheridan said again.

Skye was too choked up to answer.

"Skye?"

Wiping her wet cheeks, she finally managed to speak. "It—it's me," she whispered.

"What's wrong?" A spurt of anxiety filled Sheridan's voice. "Are you hurt?"

"No. I—I think I'm okay."

"What do you mean, 'think'? What's going on?"

Skye glanced over her shoulder. She could see the tennis shoes on the feet of the corpse lying in her hallway and shuddered. "That m-man who was w-watching your house? The—the one in the old J-Jag?"

"Yeah?"

Her teeth were chattering so hard she could barely talk. "He's d-dead."

"How do you know?" Sheridan asked.

Skye started to laugh. She had no idea why. But she couldn't stop. "Because I just k-killed him."

* * *

After leaving the ice cream parlor, David headed for the delta. He wanted to drive by Skye's house, see for himself that everything seemed okay. He hated leaving her safety up to strangers, no matter how well-intentioned they seemed to be.

And he was definitely glad he'd had that impulse when he received a call from Deputy Meeks. "I've spotted a white Jag near the residence you asked me to watch," the deputy said with little preamble.

David looked in his rearview mirror at Jeremy, who was finishing his strawberry shake. This wasn't the kind of news he felt capable of handling with his son in the car. But it wasn't as if he had time to take him back to Lynnette. "Where?" he asked.

"It's parked next to a levee less than a mile from Skye Kellerman's house. I'm there now. It's locked up tight."

"Did you run the plate?"

"Came up stolen."

Son of a bitch. Fervently wishing he had somewhere safe to leave Jeremy, David punched the gas. He didn't want his son anywhere near a possible crime scene, but he was already halfway there, and Skye's life could hang in the balance. "Get over to her house. Now."

"I'm on my way."

David hit the End button, then tried to call Skye, to warn her. The phone rang without answer. When he tried her cell phone, it was the same.

"Wow, we're going fast!" Obviously impressed, Jeremy was trying to loosen his seat belt to see the speedometer.

David used his rearview mirror again. "Leave your belt alone and sit still," he said, but even at eighty miles an hour it seemed to take forever to reach Skye's house, especially with Jeremy chattering the whole way.

"What's wrong?...Where are we going?...Are you after some bad guys, Dad?" And his favorite question, "How fast are we going?"

When David got there, he saw that three cars from the sheriff's department had beat him—and prayed to God they'd made it in time.

Coming to an abrupt stop, he rammed the gearshift into Park and jumped out. "Stay here," he barked to Jeremy. Locking the car behind him, he ran to the entrance.

The front door stood open. Inside, he could see several uniforms crowding the living room and entrance hall. They were deputies, and they were talking about a body.

David froze at the threshold, his blood running cold. He'd never forgive himself if he'd let Oliver get to Skye, despite everything. The man had been stabbed less than fifteen hours ago. He was in the fucking hospital. She should've been safe tonight.

"Has someone called the coroner?" one of the deputies asked.

"I did, as soon as I realized what we had here." That voice belonged to Meeks. David recognized it immediately. "Sheriff's on his way, too. Wants to handle this one himself."

David tried to go inside, to see what had happened, but he was immobilized by fear of what he might find. *Skye...* His chest constricted until he could feel every beat of his own heart.

"I'm glad he wants to handle this mess," the first deputy responded. "The press will be all over it. She was attacked once before, remember? What was it...three, four years ago? By that dentist?"

So Skye *had* been attacked again. David rubbed his chest, finding it even more difficult to breathe.

"Daddy? What's wrong?" Jeremy called from the car. He'd removed his seat belt, opened the door and stuck his head out.

"Nothing," David said. "Get back inside and keep the doors locked until I come back!" He hadn't meant to sound so impatient, but the adrenaline flooding through him made it hard to control his voice.

A pouting expression appeared on his son's face, but the door shut as a deputy came to the stoop, drawn by the noise. "Who're you?" he asked, scowling in confusion.

Numbly, David felt in his pocket for his badge. "Detective Willis. Sacramento PD."

Older and broader than his counterparts, the deputy glanced at it, then hooked his thumbs in his heavy black belt. "Aren't you a little out of your jurisdiction, Detective?"

"This is part of a case I worked a while back. A case I'm still working." *I should've kept her with me. I should've protected her.*

"Hey, he's okay." Meeks walked up behind his fellow officer. "He's the one who told me to keep an eye on the place."

The first deputy's skepticism cleared. "I see."

David took as much of a breath as his aching chest would allow. "What happened?"

"We have a body in the hallway."

The lump rising in David's throat threatened to choke him. "Did you catch the guy?" Because if they didn't,

David certainly would. He'd go to the ends of the earth, if necessary.

"The *guy?* It was a woman who shot him."

David blinked. Had he heard correctly? "Ms. Kellerman's okay?" He knew his face must be giving away the personal nature of his concern for Skye, but he couldn't hide his emotions tonight.

Meeks grinned and squeezed his shoulder. "She's a little shaken, but I think she'll be fine." He motioned with one hand. "She's in the living room. We're waiting to question her until the sheriff arrives."

The relief that swept over David left him weak. "Who's the man she shot?"

Meeks shook his head. "We have no idea."

"David?" It was Skye, calling him from inside the house. He was feeling much better, but the tension, exhaustion and fear in her voice still made his heart ache. What had she been through tonight? He hoped it wasn't as bad as before.

"I'm here."

Asking Meeks to keep an eye on his son for a minute, David ducked inside to find Skye perched uncomfortably on the edge of her own couch. She had a mug in her hand—most likely that green tea she'd mentioned when he was here the last time—but she wasn't drinking it. She looked pale, hollow-eyed.

"You okay?"

Wordlessly, she set the mug aside and reached for him, and he pulled her into his arms. "I've got you," he murmured against her silky hair.

Her body convulsed on a sob, and he kissed the top of her head. He knew others were watching, but he didn't care. He'd nearly lost her…. "Don't cry. Everything will be okay."

"He came in through the back bedroom." She spoke into his coat, through her tears. "I don't know how he got the bars off. He must've done it before I got home."

"I'll take a look at it."

"Then he waited for me to go inside and lock up before he cut the alarm and phone lines." She sniffed. "Otherwise, I would've been alerted at the front door when the alarm signal didn't go off and might've been able to make it back to my car."

"So you were in the hallway when he confronted you?"

"I was in the tub when I first realized he was here. He came in through the window and opened the front door so he could get out fast."

"Who is he?"

"I don't know. He—he has to be a friend of Oliver Burke's, though, doesn't he?"

That note had been signed O.B. But maybe that had been intended to mislead. With all the publicity surrounding Oliver's attack, anyone who wanted to scare Skye could've written those initials. "If Oliver's behind this, he must've arranged it while he was in prison. Maybe weeks or even months ago," David said. "He hasn't been home yet. He was stabbed by his cellmate and went straight from prison to the hospital."

"He did?" She drew back, looking up at him with troubled eyes.

"My partner just visited him. He's still there."

"But he has to have set it up."

It was possible. David believed Oliver Burke was

sneaky, that he planned his revenge against those on his list well in advance. Only a crafty kid could drown a fellow student and get away with it, and then have the nerve to show up for the funeral.

"Sheriff's here," someone said and David let go of Skye. Now that he could think straight, he remembered why it was important to be circumspect. Married or divorced, he'd been in a committed relationship for years. He didn't want to embarrass the department, or Lynnette and Jeremy, any more than he already had.

"Sit down and try to relax," he told her.

"Are you leaving?" She sounded fatalistic, as if she expected him to. And of course she would. He'd never been there for her, always had to go back to the life he'd chosen. He felt obliged to do so even now. He couldn't leave his son in the car indefinitely. And he couldn't bring him in. He didn't want Jeremy subjected to the sight of a man who'd been shot to death.

"I've got Jeremy in the car."

"Right." She sniffed and lifted her chin, her eyes bleak. He nearly told her about Lynnette's illness then. He wanted to, but he also knew it wouldn't be fair to Lynnette to divulge to anyone, especially Skye, that duty bound him far more than love.

"I'll call you."

She didn't respond. She stood, her spine stiff, as the sheriff approached.

"Ms. Kellerman, I'm Sheriff Bailey. I hope you won't mind if I ask you a few questions about what happened here tonight."

An older gentleman with white, wavy hair and a trim physique that belied his true age, which had to be

around sixty, the sheriff acted respectful and nonthreat-
ening. Nonetheless, David wished he could be present
for the questioning.

"No, of course not," she said, but her eyes lingered on
David, and he felt as if he was abandoning her to drown
in a sea of old memories and renewed fears.

"Detective Willis? Your kid's getting antsy out here.
He wants to know where you are."

Pulling his gaze away from Skye, David forced
himself to face Deputy Meeks. "I'm coming."

There was nothing inside the Jaguar to put a name to
the man she'd shot. Skye heard one of the deputies—
Deputy Meeks—say that to the sheriff sometime after the
coroner arrived at her house, pronounced the obvious
cause of death and removed the body from her hallway.
But Skye hoped the intruder's identity wouldn't remain
a mystery for long. She wanted to face this threat head-
on. Instead she felt as though she was shadow-boxing.
Yes, she'd killed the man who'd climbed through her
window, but she didn't even know who he was. There
was no reason for him to come after her, unless someone
else had hired him to do it. And that meant she hadn't
eliminated the real threat at all.

After he'd finished questioning her, the sheriff took a
full set of fingerprints from the deceased, which he planned
to run through AFIS. If her intruder had any kind of police
record, they should get a hit almost instantly. And, judging
by how smoothly the goatee-wearing criminal operated,
Skye was fairly certain he hadn't just taken to a life of
crime. She was sure they'd come up with something.

How he'd managed to get her address, Skye had no

idea. But the ease with which he'd found her was terrifying.

Would Burke hire someone else to come after her? If he could do that while he was in prison, what might he be able to arrange now?

It was a question Skye didn't want to address at the moment. She was exhausted, mentally and physically. But sleep wasn't in her immediate future. It was after five in the morning by the time everyone cleared out. By then, she was tired of the buzzing activity and the questions she couldn't answer: Why do you think this man would want to harm you? But you just told us the dentist who attacked you has been in prison for the past three years. How could he be behind this?

She chafed beneath the guarded glances of one particular deputy, who seemed to suspect her of using more force than necessary. But the indifference of the rest wasn't much better. They didn't care enough to wonder. They came and went as if this was more of the same old routine, while she was dying inside.

Sheridan was the only person she wished would stay. Her friend had arrived shortly after David left and had sat through much of the interview with the sheriff. Sheridan had also taken it upon herself to clean up the blood in the hallway, as well as the splatter on the wall, so Skye wouldn't be faced with that stomach-turning task. Skye was grateful for the support, but then Sheridan had to hurry off to make an early-morning appointment with an eighty-year-old woman whom she feared was being abused by her temperamental son.

Skye knew Jasmine would've come, too, if she'd been around. But as soon as she'd returned home from the office yesterday, she'd received a call from the Fort Bragg police and headed back to the coast. They'd singled out a suspect in the slaying of the little girl. Jasmine wanted to speak to him as soon as possible, to get a feel for whether or not he was also responsible for kidnapping another girl, who'd gone missing from a small town about an hour south of Ft. Bragg three years ago.

That left Skye alone and feeling bereft.

Picking up her cell phone, she called Marin Memorial Hospital. She'd heard the sheriff use that name while talking to the officials at San Quentin.

How badly hurt was Oliver Burke? Was he seriously injured? Or were his wounds superficial? If he'd already been released, she wanted to know.

The phone rang three times before a professional-sounding female voice answered. "Marin Memorial."

"Yes. Um…" Skye swallowed hard, unsure of how she might feel if Burke actually came on the line. "Oliver Burke's room, please."

"I'm sorry, but we don't disturb patients this early, ma'am. You'll need to call back after seven."

"B-but I just heard what-what happened," she stammered. "He'll b-be okay, won't he?"

Her nerves made her sound worried, and the woman softened. "I'm not sure. I just handle the phones here at the main desk. But…" There was a brief pause. "It's 6:40. I guess I could ring the nurse's station on his floor and ask them to check if he's awake. Do you have the room number?"

"I'm afraid not."

"Then give me a minute to locate him."

"No problem," she said, and the woman put her on hold.

Skye wiped her damp palms on her jeans while she waited. Then, without another word to warn her that the call was going through, the phone began to ring and a different woman picked up. "Nurses' station."

"Oliver Burke's room, please."

"May I ask who's calling?"

Skye drew a deep breath. "His mother."

"If you'll hold, I'll see if anyone's awake."

Skye expected to hear from the nurse again, but she didn't. Instead, the phone rang again and someone whispered, "Mom?"

It was Jane. Skye recognized her voice from the other night. Burke was at the hospital, probably being doted on by his wife. And Skye was standing alone in her house after shooting the man he'd sent to kill her. "Jane?" She kept her voice low and breathy and, she hoped, unidentifiable.

"Yes?"

"How's Oliver?"

"He—he's going to be fine. *Who is this?*"

"Just someone who knows the kind of man he really is," she said and disconnected.

Tears streamed down Skye's face—for no particular reason. She was alive. She kept reminding herself that she should feel relieved. But Burke was alive, too. He was recuperating in a hospital room for now, but as long as he was still out there, somewhere, she knew this wasn't over.

15

The ringing of the phone and his wife's quiet voice woke Oliver after a night of drug-induced sleep. Opening his eyes, he glanced around the colorless hospital room, noted the IV trailing to the shunt in his arm, the dotted yellow line on the monitor beeping steadily as it showed his heart rate, and finally Jane, who was standing with her back to him at the window, as she had much of yesterday.

This had hardly been the joyous homecoming they'd anticipated.

"Hey," he said, his voice cracking.

Jane turned but didn't approach the bed. "How'd you sleep?"

He winced because the simple act of clearing his throat brought pain. It radiated from his wound down the left side of his body. "Better than you, apparently."

She offered him a feeble smile. "They didn't give *me* any morphine."

"I'll ask for some Valium, if you want."

Her smile became more of a grimace. "I don't think it would help with what's really bothering me."

He knew what was bothering her. It bothered him, too.

They'd lost far too much, and the suffering had gone on for far too long. "We'll reclaim our lives. This is just a temporary setback."

She nodded but hardly seemed convinced. She was different than Oliver had expected. She seemed more like a stranger than his wife, and it wasn't hard to tell that the years he'd spent in prison had been hard on her. She used to be a bright, bubbly woman, quick to smile. Now she was subdued, withdrawn. New lines around her eyes and mouth made her look older, too, even a little hard-bitten. She'd gained a few pounds. And now she smoked.

Smoking was a distasteful habit. Oliver hated it. His parents hated it, too, especially his father. Concerned about Kate's exposure to secondhand smoke, Maurice had mentioned Jane's new vice in one of his letters, and Oliver had asked her to quit by the time he was released. But he could tell that hadn't happened. She must've gone out for a cigarette a few minutes before he woke because he could smell the residual stench as if she'd lit up right in the room.

"Who just called?" he asked.

A certain wariness entered her eyes, which were smudged with mascara from when she'd been crying yesterday. "Wrong number," she mumbled.

"In a hospital?"

"The caller was looking for another patient." She returned her attention to whatever she'd been looking at beyond the window. "The floor nurse patched it through by accident."

"Oh." He let his gaze wander over her backside, hoping to feel some kind of lust. He wanted to prove to himself that he hadn't changed sexual orientation while he was in prison. It'd be disappointing and embarrassing if he couldn't get it up for his own wife. But he felt nothing.

It's the pain. And the medication. No man would feel like having sex right now, regardless of how long he'd been in prison.

But he should want to *touch* her, shouldn't he? He shouldn't be thinking that the added weight made her look sloppy. She'd been up all night, watching over him. Where was his gratitude?

"Is Mom bringing Kate today?" he asked.

"They'll be here during visiting hours."

His parents had stopped by yesterday, too. Oliver seemed to possess a hazy memory of his mother smoothing the hair off his forehead, but with all the medication they'd given him, he wasn't positive that had actually occurred. In fact, he wasn't sure of anything after T.J. stabbed him. He didn't even remember the ambulance that had brought him to the hospital.

"I've got to go." Jane began gathering up her purse, coat and novel from the cart that otherwise served as his meal tray.

Surprised by this announcement, Oliver shifted carefully in the bed. "Where?"

"To work. I asked for the day off, but they couldn't give it to me. We're too busy on weekends."

"It's still early."

"I have to get home and shower, then check on Kate. I'd like to see her for a few minutes before I go in."

She saw Kate every day. She hadn't seen *him* for years. "Doesn't your boss know I'm in the hospital?"

With a sigh, Jane ran a hand through her hair, which

she'd begun to dye to hide the gray. He could tell because it was so much darker than her natural color. "They know. They just don't care."

"That's pretty insensitive, don't you think? I wouldn't go in if I were you."

"If I don't show up, they'll fire me."

"Let them fire you! That's ridiculous!"

"Oliver, *someone's* got to support us until you're well enough to work."

The irritation in her voice annoyed him. She'd never used that tone with him before. He'd thought she was feeling sorry for *him,* but this suggested she was feeling more sorry for herself. "My parents will help us," he said.

"Your parents are living on a fixed income. And they spent their entire savings, even their retirement money, on your defense. They can't help us indefinitely. Who knows how long it'll take you to heal, how many months before you find work? Who even knows what that work will be?"

"They used me to fix teeth in prison. It's not as if I had the chance to learn a new trade!" he snapped.

The furrows between her eyebrows deepened, and Oliver realized he was seeing the expression that had formed all the lines on her face.

"You say that as if…" She waved impatiently.

"As if what?"

"As if the government owes it to every prisoner to re-educate him. Prisons aren't built to *serve* people who break the law. Prison is supposed to be a punishment, a deterrent to future crime."

"But I didn't do anything wrong to begin with."

"You went home with her, didn't you?"

The bitterness in her voice shocked him. "Who are you?" he asked at length. "I don't know you anymore!"

Her eyes narrowed. "So? That's not nearly as frightening as the fact that I might not know *you!*"

He glanced away because he didn't like the ugliness in her face. "So, after everything I've been through, *you're* going to doubt me? Is that how it's going to be? I haven't suffered enough?"

They glared at each other. Then, deflating like a punctured balloon, Jane covered her face with her hands. "I-I'm sorry. I'm tired and—and worried, that's all. And that detective. He's getting inside my head."

"What detective? Willis?"

"Who else?"

"Has he been harassing you?"

"Not really. He's just so…certain."

A moment earlier, the pain from his knife wound had made it impossible to lie in any position except one. Now Oliver was so preoccupied he could scarcely feel his injury. "You used to be just as certain I was innocent."

"I still am." She smiled, but there was no commitment in her voice, no faith in her eyes.

Suddenly, he *wanted* her to leave, to get out of his sight. When had she gotten so hideous? "Can you find my spiral notebook?"

"It's in the trunk of my car, with your other belongings. But…you're hurt. Do you think you can write?"

"I *have* to write. It helps me sort out my thoughts."

"Yeah. I remember." She shrugged wearily into her coat and placed the strap of her purse over her shoulder. "No problem. Anything else?"

How about a little loyalty? And some gratitude for the

money and social status I provided before Skye managed to bring it all to a grinding halt? "No, thanks." He smiled despite the anger surging through him, which wasn't that difficult. He prided himself on being able to hide what he was really thinking and feeling. He could fool just about anyone, even his parents.

"I'm sorry, Oliver," she said. "I—I know you've been through a lot. Prison must've been terrible."

Eager for more pain medication, he pressed the nurse's call button. "I'm glad to be out." He allowed some of his disappointment to show because he knew it'd heighten her guilt. "You'd think having me home would be a positive thing for you, too."

"It will be. I mean…it *is*. We've got a lot of time to make up for, that's all."

"I understand." He poured enough warmth into those words that she finally nodded.

"Okay, I'll run and get your book."

"Can you turn on the TV before you go?"

"Sure." She changed channels until she found the local news, then bent over the railing of his bed to kiss him in a rather awkward brush of the lips. "I'll bring your notebook in a few minutes."

"Thanks," he said. Then he made a face at her back and turned to the television, hoping it'd entertain him until a nurse arrived.

A short brunette wearing a blue smock responded to his summons shortly after Jane had brought him his notebook, but by then he wasn't feeling much pain. He was preoccupied again. And not with writing.

"Good morn—"

"Shh!" He lifted a hand to indicate absolute silence.

The announcer had just started talking about something Oliver didn't want to miss. A delta woman had shot and killed an intruder last night.

Her picture flashed across the screen before the announcer could give her name but Oliver didn't need to hear another word. He recognized the woman instantly: It was Skye Kellerman.

"How are you feeling today?" the nurse asked when his eyes, if not his thoughts, shifted back to her.

"Better," he said. "I'm ready to go home."

"I don't think I can do this." Jane's voice shook as she held her cell phone with one hand and the steering wheel with the other. She'd left the hospital twenty minutes earlier, was on her way to Sacramento, but she'd had to wait to call Noah until he reached his office. She'd used the plugged-toilet excuse too many times. And everyone in Oliver's family knew she wasn't at home, anyway. "How am I going to get through the next year? Two years, five years…"

"What do you mean?" he asked. "Surviving Oliver's prison term—that was supposed to be the hard part. Now you'll have some support."

"It doesn't matter. This is worse. There's nothing left. I—I don't love him anymore. I don't want to…to be his wife. I—"

"Don't say that," he interrupted. "He just got out yesterday, and he couldn't even go home like we expected. This is a stressful time for everyone."

"No kidding." Even Noah's loyalties were split. She couldn't win. She sobbed, a little hysterically, then noticed that the woman driving the car next to hers was watching, as if a crying woman was some kind of carnival act.

Jane's stomach twisted. Hadn't she already endured more than her fair share of unwanted attention?

"Yes, I'm a freak," she shouted, even though the woman couldn't hear her. "My life is shit because my husband's a fucking murderer!"

"Jane!" Noah yelled. Obviously, he was appalled, but she had no idea whether it was her burst of temper, the obscenity or the slight to his brother that bothered him. She didn't care. She couldn't have him. She couldn't break up his family, add more pain and stress to the lives of those she loved. She wasn't sure she'd be able to steal him, even if she decided to put her own needs ahead of everyone else's. And that called into question Noah's love for her. Something she'd been relying on that might no longer exist. Oliver's release was changing everything.

The gawking driver slowed to get another look at her. So Jane gave her the finger and laughed mirthlessly as the other woman sped away. Jane could almost hear her thinking, "My God, that woman's lost her mind."

Maybe she *had* lost her mind. Maybe, after everything that had happened, she was finally cracking up….

"You don't really believe Oliver's a murderer," Noah was saying, trying to calm her by using his "soothing" voice. "He's as innocent as I am. And this has been tough on him, too."

"So I'm supposed to feel sorry for him?"

"He was asking for trouble when he went home with Skye Kellerman," he conceded. "But he's not what the detective claims."

She wiped her eyes with the back of her hand and dried it on her sweater. "I'm beginning to wonder," she said.

"You're upset, and you've got every reason to be, but don't lose faith, Jane. He's Kate's father."

"I can't help losing faith." Reaching across the seat, she fumbled in the glove compartment for a napkin. "After what you told me about Skye coming to visit you—"

"She has nerve, I'll give her that."

"But she wouldn't have approached you unless she really believes Oliver's dangerous. She doesn't have anything to gain."

He didn't seem to have a good argument to counter that, so he responded with an aside. "She had no business snooping around in the first place. I resent her butting in."

That was a whole other issue. Now her husband's victim, if *victim* was the right word, was watching her every move, prying into her private life. But the fact that Skye had caught Jane with Noah and hadn't done anything about it, other than warn them to be careful, made Jane wonder if Skye could really be the evil bitch she wanted to believe.

Jane *had* to believe Skye was lying in order to trust that Oliver was telling the truth. But now... "She's probably frightened, too," she mumbled, letting herself imagine, for the first time, what Skye had to be feeling— what she must have felt all along—*if* she was being honest about what had happened. Had Oliver really crept into her bedroom *with a knife?* Tried to *rape* her?

That kind of behavior was so far from what her husband was capable of. She'd known him since he was sixteen!

But Willis believed Skye....

"Willis came by last week," she told Noah. "He warned me to keep a close eye on Oliver."

"You don't need to hear that crap," he said, sounding disgusted. "He's just being selfish."

"How?" she demanded. Everyone had a different view, and they were all so confident in their opinions. Except her. She seemed to be the only one bouncing around like a pinball, hating Skye Kellerman one minute, pitying her the next. Missing Oliver one day, fearing him the next. It was all so damned confusing.

"Look at it practically, Jane. Willis is trying to close some old cases. He doesn't want them on his desk anymore. We've talked about this. He can't prove anything. He's tried and tried to pin those murders on Oliver and hasn't been able to. That should tell you something."

Slowing for traffic at the bridge, she scrabbled in her purse for correct change to pay the toll. Normalcy was finally supposed to return—yet her life felt more foreign than before.

After blowing her nose, she wiped away her tears before the toll-taker could stare at her the way that other driver had. She was so tired of feeling conspicuous, different, somehow tainted because of her connection to Oliver. "It tells me that one of them is wrong. But I'm no longer so sure it's Willis."

"Babe, knock it off!" Noah said. "That's my brother you're talking about. I feel bad enough already, for…for what we've done."

"If he killed those women, he did it before we started seeing each other."

"Good morning." The toll-taker put her hand out for the toll, but Jane had been silly to worry about unwanted attention *here*. The woman didn't even glance in her direction. She looked completely bored as she listened to music on the radio in her narrow booth and stared down the line of cars.

"Thank you," came the woman's mechanical response to the money. Then the light turned green, and Jane gave her old Lincoln—Oliver's parents' cast-off—some gas.

"Jane, I just told you he didn't kill anyone," Noah said.

"You don't know that."

"He's my *brother,*" he said miserably. "My *little* brother."

Noah would never believe that Oliver was dangerous, not in the absence of irrefutable evidence. Had she been leaning on the brother of a killer? Someone who couldn't see the truth any more clearly than she could? And how would that affect her future, Kate's future, the future of any other woman Oliver might meet—and, God forbid, want?

A shiver crawled up Jane's spine as she remembered that odd weekend when she and Oliver had been experimenting with sexual-enhancement drugs. That experience suddenly seemed stranger than ever before.

You're convinced my husband is a murderer....

Completely....

Why *did* Oliver shave? Was it possible that he could be hiding more than a few illicit affairs?

The conversation she'd had with Noah, when he'd called to tell her that Skye Kellerman had visited him at work, came back to her.

Skye Kellerman knows about us....

But...that's impossible? How?

The car in front of your house? It was her.

Why was she there?

It's not enough that Oliver's been in prison for three years, I guess. She wants to punish him even more.

After that comment, terror had almost immobilized her. *So she's going to tell him?*

An awkward pause had ensued. *No. At least, she said she wouldn't.*

Why would she keep our secret?

Because she claims he'll kill us both if he finds out.

Initially, they'd scoffed at that. But Jane couldn't explain why Skye would approach Noah unless she believed what she'd said.

Or maybe she was just showing off. It wasn't as if Jane had been very kind or friendly to Skye. Now, she was embarrassed by the harsh things she'd put in some of the letters she'd sent to The Last Stand.

"Are you still there?" Noah asked.

Jane had to pull herself out of her thoughts. "I'm here," she said. But she wasn't the same woman she'd been even yesterday.

The musical ring of her cell phone, a snippet from Sheryl Crow's "Soak Up the Sun," woke Skye at two o'clock in the afternoon. She was still groggy. She'd finally taken a sleeping pill, which hadn't quite worn off. But she knew it was probably Sheridan or Jasmine calling, trying to wake her for the fund-raiser, so she made an effort to rouse herself. She needed to get there early to help out, make sure the event went off without a hitch.

Then she'd spend the evening trying to forget the nightmare of another intruder with one completely unsexy, unappealing Charlie Fox.

"Argh…" She shoved her head under the pillow on the couch where she'd dropped off to sleep. She didn't want to face the day. Neither did she want to face what had happened last night. The memories were already pressing close—the panic, the chaos, the body lying in the hallway. Who was that guy? Who'd sent him? And where had he come from?

The questions were worse than the memories, bad as they were.

Skye was tempted to ignore the phone and slip back into the dark void that had brought her a short reprieve from conscious thought. But the fund-raiser was too important. Jasmine might not make it back from Ft. Bragg in time to attend. Skye couldn't leave it all to Sheridan.

I want to soak up the sun...

Kicking off the blanket, she stumbled through the living room to the kitchen and found her cell phone on the counter.

"Hello?"

"It's me. Did I wake you?"

David. His voice was enough to fill her with yearning. She hated how deeply and effortlessly he affected her. "Yes."

"I tried to wait until later, but...I've been worried. I had to be sure you were okay."

"I'm still breathing." And her intruder wasn't. She supposed that was something. It could easily have been the other way around.

"How are you feeling?"

"I don't know yet. I...I need to get my bearings, figure out who that guy was and why he was after me."

"His name was Lorenzo Bishop, originally from L.A."

"AFIS came through?"

"Immediately. He's got a rap sheet a mile long, been in and out of prison, mostly for petty crimes—assault and battery, possession, spousal abuse."

"Was he ever in San Quentin?"

"No. He started in juvey, after which he did some time in county jail. Then he spent two years at Folsom."

"So how did Burke know him?"

"I'm looking for the connection."

"There has to be one, right? He was here to kill me."

"I'm glad you had that gun. Without it…" He paused. "I don't even want to think what would've happened without it."

She smiled as she rested her forehead against the door lintel. She liked the warmth in his voice, the concern, but her head was still spinning. Maybe she shouldn't have gotten up just yet. "How come you're working? I thought you had Jeremy today."

"I do. I'm piddling around from home, trying to track down some people named Zufelt. Their son crossed Oliver when the boys were in eighth grade and didn't live another two years."

"You think he's a victim?"

"At this point it's just a hunch."

"What's Jeremy doing while you piddle?"

"He's organizing his room."

"I don't want this to take you away from your time with him."

"It's okay."

But wasn't that what David was afraid of—that if he let himself care about her she'd eventually compete with Jeremy for his love and attention? "Isn't the sheriff handling what happened here last night?"

"Deputy Meeks is contacting some of the people who went to high school and college with Burke, asking if anyone recognizes the name Lorenzo Bishop. I'm going to call Jane, and Oliver's parents, see what they have to say. We need to find out if he ever knew this guy. If not, he could be connected to some other case you've been working on at The Last Stand. Or maybe Noah Burke sent him."

"Noah wouldn't send someone to kill me," she argued. "It's a pretty big leap from adulterer to killer."

"I've met other men who've made that leap, Skye, and women, too. Self-preservation is a pretty strong instinct."

She understood that. It was for the sake of self-preservation that she was attempting to get over David and move on with her life.

"Are you still going to the fund-raiser tonight?" he asked.

"Of course."

There was a brief silence. "With that guy—Charlie something?"

"Charlie Fox."

"How well do you know him?"

Was that jealousy in his voice—or just caution? "Why do you ask?"

"Because he's taking my spot. Call him up and cancel. Tell him you have a date."

She couldn't believe how badly she wanted to do exactly what he suggested. But that survival instinct warned her against it. "No. It's your weekend with Jeremy. Stay home and enjoy him."

"I have a sitter lined up, a friend's teenage boy, a kid I trust and Jeremy likes. We're all set."

What did she say now? That she'd dump Charlie?

No, David had had his chance. She was finished with wanting him and getting nothing. "It's too hard, David. Especially now."

There was another silence, this one longer than before. Finally, he said, "What's changed?"

"I guess I just got tired of waiting."

"So you're over me already?"

"Yes," she lied and hung up.

16

Skye had never seen Peter Vaughn, their most reliable volunteer, wearing anything other than a pair of holey jeans and a Black Sabbath T-shirt, but he looked great in a tux, despite the faux Mohawk.

Spotting her the moment he came through the door, he walked over to say hello.

"Wow, I almost didn't recognize you," she teased as he approached.

The shy smile he gave her made her smile, too. "I can hang with the 'in' crowd," he said proudly, and brushed an imaginary speck of dust from his immaculate lapel. "I sold fifty tickets to this thing. I had to come see how it turned out."

At eighteen, he was probably the youngest attendee in the room—and the only one with tattoos all the way up his neck—but Skye was glad he felt such a part of The Last Stand. "You did a great job."

"We're making a difference."

"I hope so." Skye fingered a strand of hair that had fallen down her nape from her up-do. She'd taken thirty minutes to have her nails done before the fund-raiser began, and she used one to shove that derelict curl back into place. She figured she might as well enjoy such a feminine luxury while she had the chance. The new nails would have to come off tomorrow. They made it too difficult to handle a gun.

Briefly, she wondered how many other women in the room had to worry about fake nails getting in the way of shooting someone.

"Hey, you look pretty hot yourself," Peter said, and she belatedly realized he'd been sizing her up for some time.

She let her smile widen. "It's the nails."

"It's the body!" he responded bluntly.

She laughed. "A side benefit of my passion for exercise, I guess."

"Most people think that's the *main* benefit."

"I'm not most people."

"I heard about what happened," he said, growing serious.

He was referring to the shooting at her house last night, of course. Thanks to her affiliation with The Last Stand, and her background, which was already sensational enough, the incident had been splashed all over the news. A local program with an especially zealous reporter had even picked up on the fact that this second attack had occurred on the same day as Burke's release from prison, and had reported his stabbing, too.

It was a violent day for both victims' advocate Skye Kellerman and the man who attempted to rape her at knifepoint four years ago....

Since the guests had begun to arrive, Skye had had to respond to some comment or question about last night from almost every person she met.

I'm so glad you're okay.... That must've been terrify-ing.... Do you know the guy who broke in?... No? Do you think he's affiliated with that dentist who attacked you before?... But Oliver Burke's in the hospital, right?... I saw that on the news.... Since you're okay, I can say this: You couldn't have staged a better publicity stunt. What a turnout!... I bet you raise some serious dough tonight, eh?... Good thing you got him....

In some respects, it didn't feel like such a good thing. Lorenzo Bishop had to be someone's son/grandson/brother. Maybe husband, or, God forbid, father. Skye was doing her best not to consider that aspect, not to think of him as human at all, so she could hold herself together long enough to get through this night. If only she could forget the gory details... But she couldn't have forgotten a second of it, even without all the reminders.

"Peter, you haven't seen anyone unfamiliar hanging around the office, have you?" she asked. Skye had told herself she wouldn't investigate tonight. It wasn't the time or the place. She needed to focus on wining and dining the people who'd paid to be here and could make such a positive impact on what she, Sheridan and Jasmine were trying to build. But she planned to question all the volun-teers as soon as possible and couldn't resist the opportu-nity to ask Peter right now.

He blinked at her. "Unfamiliar?"

"The man who came to my house last night had a map."

"That doesn't mean he was hanging around the office."

"I'm unlisted."

"Doesn't matter. Anyone who owns property or has a utility account can be traced."

He'd already learned a lot at TLS. "I have to start somewhere," she said.

"I wish I could help you, but I haven't seen anything out of the ordinary."

Before Skye could press him for the names of anyone who'd been in the office this past week—it was his job to organize the other volunteers—Sheridan joined them. "You okay?" she asked, touching Skye's elbow.

Skye allowed herself to be drawn into a quick hug. "I'm fine."

Sheridan and Peter hugged, too. "You look great," Sheridan told him. "I feel like a proud mother."

He grimaced at her words. "*Mother?* Come on. I'm almost nineteen. Maybe if I dressed up at the office occasionally, one of you wouldn't mind the age difference between us."

"Why settle for only one?" Skye quipped.

"Good point." He straightened his tie, his tone purposely cocky. "I can handle both of you at the same time. That's the beauty of youth."

Sheridan rolled her eyes. "Where's Charlie?" she asked Skye.

Skye glanced around the room, which was beginning to fill up. "I asked him to meet me here. I wanted to have a good reason to keep him away from the booze tonight. The fact that he'll have to drive himself home is it."

"Smart," Sheridan said with a chuckle. "And practical, since we had to come early to decorate." She angled her head slightly to the right and lowered her voice. "Did you see Senator Denatorre come in?"

"No." Somehow Skye had missed him. But that didn't surprise her. She wasn't exactly at her social best and had mostly stayed in the corner opposite the hors d'oeuvres table where there was less of a crowd. She'd also been searching for Charlie. Since he was here as her guest, he didn't have a ticket. She wanted to make sure he felt comfortable. And, for once, she was eager to hear all about the latest evil machinations of his ex-wife. At least it had nothing to do with her own problems.

"I already greeted the senator," Sheridan went on. "So you don't have to go over right away, but you should probably say hello before we sit down to dinner. He wants to meet you and Jasmine."

"Where is Jas?" Skye asked.

"Still on her way from Ft. Bragg. She'll be here soon."

"I'll say hello to the senator once I've got my *escort* in tow," Skye said pointedly. "Wouldn't want to give him the wrong idea."

"Whatever it takes to impress him."

"Damn, even in the charity realm you gotta suck up to somebody," Peter muttered. But he'd spotted a fellow volunteer and didn't seem to be paying a lot of attention. "Catcha later," he said with a wave and left to join his friend.

"So, where's *your* date?" Skye asked.

"He's here somewhere."

"Who is it?"

"Jonathan."

"Stivers?"

"Do we know another Jonathan?" she asked innocently.

"That's not fair!" Skye complained. "That's like asking one of the volunteers!"

"I didn't say you couldn't ask one of the volunteers."

"I was under the impression we were trying to get *real* dates."

"You consider Charlie a real date?" Sheridan countered.

Charlie had arrived and was making his way over to them so Skye had to be careful not to speak too loudly. "Jonathan's a worse cop-out than Charlie, and you know it," she said under her breath.

Sheridan smiled brightly—for Charlie's benefit. "I don't think so. Sleeping with Jonathan would be like sleeping with my brother, but I'd still go to bed with him before Charlie."

Skye had no chance to respond. Charlie was too close. Sheridan said hello to him and moved on. Skye stayed where she was, making small talk while scanning the room for Jonathan. She wanted to ask if he'd found anything more on the Regan case—she felt terrible about Sean—but she didn't see the private investigator anywhere. He was probably standing out in the hall, talking on his cell phone. A bona fide workaholic, he was always on one phone or another.

"Who are you looking for?" Charlie asked when he had to repeat his question about how her work was going. He hadn't mentioned last night's incident, and hard as it was to believe, Skye was pretty sure he hadn't heard.

"Sheridan's date."

"Who'd she bring?"

"Jonathan Stivers."

"I've heard that name before."

"They're friends. He sometimes works as our private investigator."

"I didn't know she was seeing anyone."

"They're not seeing each other. Not really." Jonathan was an old flame of Sheridan's, which would've made Sheridan's choice of escort much more interesting, except that Skye knew the flicker of romantic interest had guttered out more than two years ago.

"Time to live a more balanced life, huh?" she mumbled sarcastically.

"What'd you say?" Charlie asked.

"Nothing." Taking a deep breath, she threw back her shoulders and slipped her hand into the crook of his arm. It didn't matter whether or not Sheridan had gotten a real date, she told herself. She'd invited Charlie for a reason, and it certainly wasn't to get laid—no matter how long it had been. "We need to go over and say hello to Senator Denatorre."

"We do?"

Skye paused, surprised by his lackluster response. "That's okay, isn't it?"

"I'm a Democrat," he said. "I hate Denatorre."

"Don't worry about it. This is a bipartisan event."

"My ex-wife is a Republican."

Oh, boy...more scarring. "Don't mention your ex-wife to the senator," she said and dragged him over.

The senator and his wife were busy conversing with a small crowd. Skye was standing politely nearby, waiting for a chance to introduce herself, when Bob Gibbons, an aide she'd met at a press conference after the Ubaldi case, noticed her. Taking her elbow, Bob guided her into the circle.

"Senator, this is Skye Kellerman. She's one of the founders of The Last Stand, and possibly their most ardent devotee."

The senator looked as distinguished as a senator should. With dark hair combed back from his forehead, intelligent eyes and perfect teeth, he was a handsome man in his midfifties. "It'd be tough to be any more devoted than her associates," he joked, but he extended his hand. "It's a pleasure to meet you, Ms. Kellerman."

"The pleasure is mine," she responded. Then he introduced her to his wife.

Perfectly trim and stylishly dressed in a black gown with white cuffs and collar, Roxanne Denatorre gripped Skye's hand as soon as her husband released it. "And who's your companion, Ms. Kellerman?" she asked.

Charlie was standing slightly behind Skye, looking like he'd rather be home. "This is my friend and escort for the evening, Charlie Fox."

"Charlie, you're a lucky man to be in the company of such a lovely woman," Mrs. Denatorre said.

Charlie's eyebrows went up as if he hadn't noticed. "Oh…um, yes. Yes, I am." He shook hands with everyone in the group, then slumped back into his depression. But at least he wasn't spouting off about his ex-wife—or Republicans.

"It's wonderful that you could come this evening," Skye said to Senator Denatorre.

"I admire what you're doing, Ms. Kellerman." He studied her a bit more closely. "But I have to say I'm amazed you're here. I wasn't expecting it after your most recent brush with danger."

The fear, the shooting, the dead body rushed through Skye's mind. It was still so fresh. "The loss of a life is always unfortunate," she murmured, struggling to distance herself emotionally.

"Better his life than yours," he responded.

"I can't argue with you there."

"But…"

She blinked. "But what?"

"I sensed a bit of hesitancy in that statement."

This wasn't a good conversation to be having in a social setting, but Skye couldn't resist the invitation to open up. She'd never been one to waste time with meaningless platitudes. If the senator wanted to talk shop, she'd talk shop. She might never get another audience with him. It wasn't as if he attended all their fundraisers—or even returned her calls to his office. "I was just thinking that it'd be easier to deal with what happened if I knew why Mr. Bishop came after me in the first place."

"The police can't tell you?"

"So far, no one can."

His eyes met and held hers. "You're in a dangerous line of work, Ms. Kellerman."

She managed a shrug. "It goes with the territory."

"Does that ever make you want to give up?"

"Randy," his wife admonished quietly, but he merely patted the hand that clasped his arm and waited for Skye's response.

"No," she told him. "It makes me more determined."

"Some folks fear you as much as they admire you," he said. "They view you as a maverick, a vigilante."

Mrs. Denatorre didn't object again. That tap the senator had given her hand had begged a little leeway, and she was granting it. Besides that, she was obviously curious to hear Skye's answer. So was the rest of the group, judging by the way they watched her.

"You must be talking about the chief of police," she said, deciding to be straightforward despite her audience. The senator was the one who'd brought this up.

"Chief Jordan isn't your biggest supporter."

"Not because he's afraid I'll turn into some sort of vigilante, if that's what he told you," she scoffed. "He doesn't like the scrutiny I bring to his force."

"He's not the only one."

"I don't care if the whole force doesn't like it. Shining a spotlight on crime is bound to make certain folks uncomfortable, even some who aren't criminals. But Sacramento needs to look at what's going on before we can take steps to improve things."

Mrs. Denatorre smiled as if pleased with her answer, but the senator wasn't finished with her yet. "There's a lot of personal sacrifice involved in being the advocate you are," he pointed out. "Last night probably wouldn't have happened if you were in another line of work."

The eyes of the group once again shifted to her, but Skye steeled herself against the added attention. "We don't know whether last night was a consequence of my work or an attempt at revenge by the man I helped send to prison for putting a knife to my throat. And even if it *was* a result of my efforts at The Last Stand, that doesn't mean I asked for it. If you're going to take that line of reasoning, what provoked Burke's original attack? I was twenty-six years old and an account executive for Wear Well Carpet—hardly what most people would consider a risky job—unless you're severely allergic to carpet glue."

His eyes twinkled as he clapped softly. "Impressive."

"See what I mean?" His assistant jumped in, wearing a proud smile.

"I do, Bill. You're right. She's formidable." The senator rubbed his chin thoughtfully. "Getting involved with her—with The Last Stand—could turn out to be a political hot potato, but I think I'm a pretty good judge of character. And I like that she's willing to stick her neck out for her ideals." He reached inside his suit coat and withdrew a business card. "Call me this week, Ms. Kellerman," he said, handing it to her. "I'll ask the mayor to join us for lunch and we'll see what we can do to help."

Skye was so shocked it took her a moment to respond. By the time she stammered a thank-you, he and his party had already started toward the tables. Only Mrs. Denatorre glanced back to smile at her.

"I can't believe it!" she breathed to Charlie.

"Believe what?" he asked, completely indifferent.

"We've got him! He's taking me to lunch."

"Of course he is. Republicans are big law-and-order types. Justice, not mercy. That's their motto. My ex-wife is like that," he said and immediately launched into a story about how his ex had promised to forgive him for the mistakes he'd made in their marriage, then left him anyway. But Skye wasn't really listening. She was too excited. She pulled Charlie along as she made a beeline for Sheridan, who was sitting with Jonathan at one of the dinner tables.

Coming up behind them both, she bent to whisper in her friend's ear. "Guess what I just landed?"

Sheridan and Jonathan both twisted to look up at her, and Skye flashed the senator's card. "Lunch. With Denatorre *and* the mayor."

"You're kidding!" Sheridan exclaimed. But if she or Jonathan made any further comment, Skye didn't hear them. She straightened as two people she hadn't expected to see moved into her line of sight. One was a tall black detective she recognized as Tiny.

The other was David.

As soon as he saw Skye, David knew he'd made a mistake in showing up at the fund-raiser. She was wearing a slinky green dress that hugged her body in all the places he dreamed of touching—more than a slight distraction. And with her hair up she looked prettier than ever. He almost grinned; as elegant and feminine as she was, especially in that gown, she could probably bench-press more weight than most men in the room and run farther if not faster.

Tiny nudged him, and David realized he'd stopped moving. "What?" he said, suddenly irritable because he'd spotted the man in the tux at Skye's side—Charlie Fox—and immediately disliked him.

"I thought we were going to find a seat."

"We are," David said, but that meant pulling his gaze away from Skye and her companion so he wouldn't walk into anyone, which wasn't easy.

Tiny chose two seats near the back. When they sat down, the others at their table nodded politely and made introductions. Then the caterers brought out the salads. But it wasn't five minutes later that David decided to relocate. He knew he'd be better off staying where he was, but there was a single seat open at Skye's table, and he intended to fill it.

"Some date you are," Tiny grumbled when David leaned over to tell him what he was going to do.

David lowered his voice so Tiny was the only one who

could hear him. "You don't need me. You'll have your hands full mixing and mingling and looking for anyone who doesn't fit in."

Tiny cocked his head at a challenging angle. "I'm not worried about what'll be filling *my* hands."

David quickly formulated a good excuse for wanting to be closer to Skye—it was easier to keep track of anyone who came into contact with her, easier to monitor everything that was said. But he couldn't fool Tiny so he didn't even try. "If we slip off together, come after me before I do something I might regret."

"Don't depend on me. You know what I think."

Actually, David didn't. Tiny rarely shared his personal thoughts or feelings. "That I'm getting too emotionally involved?"

"That's an outdated opinion."

"What are you talking about?"

"You've been fighting this long enough. You need to decide which you'd regret more—taking what you want or giving it up." Tiny's tone suggested it was that simple. But it wasn't simple at all. Wanting Skye, and succumbing to that want, went against everything he believed in—keeping the promises he'd made to Lynnette, sticking with her through thick and thin, being a good father, maintaining some self-respect.

He stood up. "Like I said, come get me."

Tiny turned up the palms of his hands. "Sorry, buddy, you're on your own."

"What a guy."

"You might thank me later," he said, chuckling.

David didn't respond. Mumbling a "Nice meeting you," to the couple on his left, he crossed the room and stood behind the empty seat at Skye's table. "Mind if I join you?"

A woman to his immediate right smiled broadly. Young, maybe twenty-one or twenty-two, she was obviously with her parents, which made them a threesome and created the open seat. "Of course not."

The man on his other side pushed out the chair. "Sit down," he said. The others added similar sentiments, but Skye said nothing. Giving him a mutinous frown, she turned to her companion, Charlie Fox, who—according to the quick background check David had run—had one divorce on record, two children, no arrests or convictions and no speeding tickets.

"So what do you do?" It was the woman on his right again, who was slightly overweight but fairly pretty nonetheless.

"I'm a detective with the Sacramento Police Department," he replied.

She clapped enthusiastically. "Oh! You're not here to investigate the shooting last night, are you?"

Skye was sitting directly across from him. She immediately pasted on a smile for the benefit of the others, but David sensed the weariness and fragility behind it. "No." He was here under the excuse that he needed to be sure she was safe. If Oliver had sent Lorenzo to kill her, he could send someone else. But the truth was that he couldn't make himself stay away. It bothered him that Skye was turning her back on what they felt for each other—and yet he approved. One of them had to do *something*. They couldn't go on hovering in this agonizing limbo.

"What shooting?" Charlie Fox stopped eating and glanced questioningly around the table.

"You haven't heard?" the girl said. "It's been all over the news. And…you're here with Ms. Kellerman, aren't you?"

"Since my wife left me, I don't watch the news or read the papers," he said. "It's too depressing. What happened?"

The girl's father, who was sitting on her other side, leaned close and said, "Have some sensitivity, Jillian." Or something to that effect because she suddenly grew uncertain. "Um…I'm not sure Ms. Kellerman wants to talk about it," she said belatedly, backing off.

Skye raised her chin. "It's fine," she said, but David knew Skye well enough to realize what this evening was costing her. She hadn't yet come to terms with the life she'd taken, still didn't understand the reason behind Lorenzo's appearance at her house. Yet here she was, once again the focus of public attention and speculation. David hated to see her put in the same vulnerable position she'd been in after Burke's attack. It made him angry and defensive that she'd do this to herself by showing up tonight. She needed time to mourn what had happened, to recover.

But he knew she'd do anything for The Last Stand.

"In those situations you do what you have to do," David said. The finality in his voice was meant to shield Skye from any further questions. But the man sitting next to Skye—Charlie Fox—didn't get it.

"You were involved in a shooting?" he said, gaping at her.

The blood drained from Skye's face. But her brittle smile remained stubbornly in place. "There was an intruder. I—I had to defend myself."

"That means you shot him? He's *dead?*"

Forks stilled around the table as the uncomfortable silence snuffed out all other conversation.

"It wasn't as if… I mean, I—" Skye started. But then her throat worked as if she was struggling to swallow, and she began to blink rapidly.

David could tell she was on the verge of tears. Shoving her chair away from the table, she fled the room without another word.

17

Before the door to the bathroom could sweep shut behind her, David was there. Skye almost told him he couldn't be where he was, that it was the women's restroom, but it really wasn't. It was a small, single family-style bathroom meant for use by either men or women. Skye had chosen it rather than the women's room because she could lock the door and be alone, away from the prying eyes and comments she'd have to endure elsewhere. She needed the privacy, but she wasn't sure why. Charlie Fox had meant no harm. Not really. It was just…all the questions.

Lorenzo Bishop *had* planned to harm her; she'd only defended herself. Then why did she feel so bewildered and hurt?

Covering her face to hide her tears, she dodged David's hand when he tried to pull her into his arms.

"Come here," he said and turned her in spite of her attempts to rebuff him, forcing her to look at him.

She did so defiantly. If he was going to see her tears, he was also going to see the anger and confusion *he* caused. But the expression on his face was so tortured her anger didn't last. With a sob, she threw her arms around his neck and clung to him.

"It's okay," he whispered, kissing her temple and holding her close.

"No, it's not okay," she said. "What's going to happen to us?"

"I don't know," he whispered, cradling her face between his large hands as he gazed down at her. "I can't rid myself of what I feel for you, no matter what I do. The more I try to shut you out of my thoughts, the more you appear in my dreams. I make love to you over and over again and I can never get enough."

Feeling the hard ridge of his erection against her stomach, she stared breathlessly up at him. "No, David. It's too late. I can't take you constantly shoving me away. I have to forget you, move on."

He raised his hand and gently trailed a finger over the swell of her breast. "I can't forget *you.*"

Her body reacted in spite of her desire to remain unaffected. But she was still defiant. "You don't really want me."

"That's where you're wrong," he said. "I've never wanted anything more."

His finger touched the very tip of her breast and stayed there, brushing the nipple ever so lightly.

Several seconds passed as they stared at each other, held by an attraction that was stronger than Skye's ability to resist it. Then, slowly, she reached up and untied the bow that held the top of her dress in place.

As the fabric dropped, she knew by the look on his face that nothing would stop them now.

With a low growl, David cupped the soft flesh of Skye's breasts while using his tongue to explore every inch of her mouth. Then he shifted, because in some dim, scarcely thinking part of his brain he knew he needed to lock the door.

"Making love won't help anything," he muttered, but clicked the dead bolt into place.

"I don't expect it to change anything," she said. "You can walk away afterward, forget about me."

Obviously, she had no idea how much she meant to him. "You think if we have sex we'll be able to move on as if it never happened?"

"Yes," she said confidently.

But David suspected that was her own need talking. Regardless, he was in too deep to back out now. His hands were lifting her skirt….

Somehow, amid the breathless, frenzied groping he managed to pull back long enough to admire her, to take in what he'd been dying to see since he'd first met her in that hospital room. Sympathy and righteous anger had come before desire, but not by much. He'd wanted her from the beginning, hadn't he? Even with his divorce barely behind him, even with a much more idealistic view of his ability to resist the temptation she posed, he'd wanted her.

Staring at the smooth curve of her left breast, his hand shook as he rubbed the tip against his palm. When she gasped and shivered at the contact, he took advantage of her parted lips to kiss her again. "Tell me you're on birth control," he muttered several crazed seconds later.

She froze. "No. I—I haven't made love in years."

The only condoms he possessed were probably still in the nightstand next to the bed he'd shared with Lynnette. But he couldn't stand the disappointment filling her eyes—knew he wouldn't be able to stand his own disappointment if they had to stop now. "I'll pull out," he said.

She didn't verbally agree, but her hands were almost frantic in their attempt to unfasten his pants. And when she touched him, he felt every muscle in his body quiver in response.

It'll be okay, he thought. *I'll pull out. There's nothing to worry about.* But the moment he got her panties down and felt her close around him, so warm and tight, he knew he was asking too much of himself. Although he'd never had problems taking the necessary time, he feared he was going to embarrass himself today. And, sure enough, as she locked her legs around him, he felt his control slip.

He didn't have the staying power he normally did. Not with her. He was about to warn her, but every moment felt so indescribably wonderful he put it off another second and another—until she shuddered and whispered his name, and that was it. He couldn't hold off another second, another fraction of a heartbeat. He finally forced himself to withdraw, but he was pretty sure he hadn't done it soon enough.

"We might be in trouble," he whispered as they both slumped against the wall, trying to catch their breath.

But it wasn't until his heart rate had returned to normal that he fully appreciated what that might mean.

"That was stupid," he muttered.

Skye didn't comment, wouldn't even look at him. Which told him he needed to swallow the disappointment he felt in his own irresponsible actions and shut up.

She didn't need anything else to worry about, not after everything she'd been through already. Besides, what were the chances that this encounter would result in a pregnancy? He knew it happened, but it wasn't all that common, was it?

"You okay?" he asked as they cleaned up.

She nodded but wouldn't really give him her full attention. Instead, she focused on retying the halter part of her dress and using the mirror to fix the strands of hair he'd knocked loose from the clips that held it up.

He reached over to straighten the sad-looking bow at her neck, but she stepped away. "It's fine. Don't worry about it. Don't worry about anything, okay?"

Their eyes finally met in the mirror. "What do you mean by that?" he asked.

She offered him a tremulous smile. "Just what I said. It was…nothing. A moment of weakness, that's all. Don't beat yourself up over it."

"Skye—"

"I have to get back to the fund-raiser." She took a last peek in the mirror, rubbed away some smeared lipstick and hurried out.

David wasn't sure how to interpret her reaction. She probably didn't know what to make of what had just occurred any more than he did. A torrid affair wasn't characteristic of either one of them.

He considered going after her. He knew they should talk. But he needed a few minutes to come to grips with what *he* was feeling—the resulting euphoria, his desire for more of the same and the cold, clawing fear that once might prove damaging enough.

He thought of his son. He'd left Jeremy at home with a babysitter so he could corner Skye in a hotel bathroom. *Way to do exactly what you'd been trying to avoid, you idiot.*

And he'd told himself he'd be safe. That there'd be people here.

Still, he couldn't bring himself to completely regret the encounter. He hadn't experienced anything so emotionally intense since…he couldn't remember another time. He'd always been able to think straight, to act cautiously, no matter what he was doing.

Stepping up to the sink, he splashed some cold water on his face and was drying his hands when he heard a knock at the door.

"Dave? You in there?"

Tiny. *Now* he decided to appear.…

David opened the door and sent his friend an irritated look. "It's a little late for the cavalry, don't you think?"

"I told you not to count on me. Besides, how was I supposed to know where you'd gone?"

"There aren't a lot of options around here."

Tiny grinned knowingly. "I figured my timing might be a little off when I saw Skye come into the ballroom looking so…"

"So what?"

"Rumpled." From Tiny's mischievous grin, David knew he'd just resisted the impulse to state her flustered appearance in a cruder fashion.

"Do I look as 'rumpled'?" David asked, trying to brush the wrinkles from his clothes.

Tiny clapped him on the shoulder and started leading him back to the ballroom. "No, you just look satisfied," he said with a laugh. But Tiny was wrong. David wasn't satisfied. That encounter in the bathroom had only increased his appetite.

"You're quiet tonight," Charlie said to Skye as they danced to the band's rendition of Celine Dion's "All By Myself."

"I'm just tired," she said. And she still had a long night ahead of her. The fund-raiser wasn't even half over. She would've gone home—she'd already achieved that lunch date with the senator, which was as much as she could aspire to in her current frame of mind—but she couldn't face the thought of returning to the delta house alone.

"There're a lot of people here. At five hundred bucks a head, you guys have raised some good money tonight."

It was a struggle to get through the small talk, even when it concerned The Last Stand. But Skye didn't want to concentrate on the lyrics to the song, either. They were especially poignant after her encounter with David and the emptiness she felt in knowing he considered it a mistake.

That was stupid....

Maybe so. But she couldn't keep herself from reliving every moment. She could still smell his cologne on her clothes. And when she closed her eyes, she could feel him inside her....

"Skye?" Charlie said.

Opening her eyes, Skye searched her recent memory for his last comment. He'd been talking about the fund-raiser, the money... "I won't know the exact amount until we close. That's when we're doing the direct drive."

"What's that?"

She could feel David's gaze on her from where he stood at the periphery of the room. He'd been watching her ever since they'd left the bathroom, but he hadn't approached.

Realizing that she owed Charlie more attention than she'd been giving him, she forced herself to smile and put some cheer into her voice. "We're going to have several of our past clients tell their stories. Then we'll ask people to raise their paddles if they're willing to commit $10,000 to help them and others like them."

"*Ten thousand dollars?* You really think people will step up and pledge that amount?"

"I do. The money helps victims *now,* fulfills an immediate need, which is very motivating, especially once you see what some poor souls have suffered."

She was afraid he might make another reference to her own experience with violent crime or the shooting, but he didn't. He must've gotten the hint when she left the table earlier.

"I saw a burn victim when I first got here."

"That's Gina Wilkinson. She's on the program."

"What happened to her?"

"Five years ago, she told her husband she wanted a divorce and was nearly burned alive when he drugged her and set fire to the house that very night. She lost one of her twin boys to the blaze." Skye's voice softened as she thought about Gina. "She's a powerful speaker."

"That's tragic," he said. "But…ten thousand dollars is a lot. What if no one feels they have that much?"

"The bids go down from there. The last call is at the hundred-dollar level."

"Since I didn't pay to get in here, I think I can handle that much, at least." As Charlie turned her to the music, he must've spotted David watching them because he jerked his head in David's direction. "What's up between you and that detective? Are you guys seeing each other or something?"

Skye cleared her throat. "No."

"Well, he won't let you out of his sight. I think he wants to hook up with you."

He already had. She'd never experienced a frenzy like that. She tingled at the memory of it. But she knew allowing herself to want more was crazy. Her life was spinning out of control. Tonight she'd pulled up her dress in a hotel bathroom for a man who planned to remarry his ex-wife. Last night she'd shot and killed an intruder.

What would she do next?

"He's here because he's helping me with a case," she said. She didn't mention that it was her own case.

The song came to an end, and Charlie let go of her. But Skye didn't want to sit down, didn't want to create an opportunity for David to speak to her. It seemed easiest to pass the time in the middle of the dance floor, buffered from deep conversation by the loud music. "Want to keep dancing?"

Charlie hesitated, obviously reluctant, but he acquiesced when she moved closer. "Okay, I guess. If you do," he said, but he'd just slipped his arms around her waist when David put a hand on his shoulder. "Mind if I cut in?"

Charlie shot Skye a meaningful glance and stepped back. "Not at all. I'm ready for a drink."

Then Skye found herself in David's arms, swaying slowly to "I Will Always Love You" by Whitney Houston.

David didn't say anything as they danced. He was holding Skye a little too close for propriety, knew it wouldn't look good if anyone decided to notice, but he couldn't seem to stop himself. All he could think about was her openmouthed kisses, and making her gasp and moan and call out his name the way she had only thirty minutes before. He wanted to rent a room, but that fell under the category of "premeditated," which was even worse than a "hit and run" in the bathroom.

Still, he'd already screwed up and would be paying a heavy price. Why not make the evening worth the repercussions?

He imagined running a shower and letting the water cascade over Skye's breasts as he licked away the drops. He could go out and buy some condoms first, meet her later. Then no one would see them leave together.

But if they were going to rendezvous, they needed to make the arrangements now. His babysitter couldn't stay too late.

"Will you get a room with me?" he murmured.

Skye pulled back a few inches. There was a touch of surprise in her expression and also something else, something he couldn't name. "Tonight?"

"Yes." If he didn't act immediately, guilt would set in. Then he wouldn't be able to indulge the cravings that were driving him mad.

I know you'll make the right decision. You're a good man....

Mentally, he shook his head, trying to rid himself of

that echo. The hunger was too strong, too visceral to keep fighting it. Maybe, if he succumbed and made love to Skye until he was satiated, he'd be able to control his wayward desires and start over, behave more rationally.

"Are you asking what I think you're asking?" Her eyebrows drew together in confusion.

"I didn't get enough. Did you?" He smiled for Sheridan's benefit; she was watching them from a few feet away, where she was dancing with her own date. He turned Skye slightly, away from Sheridan's prying eyes, and whispered in her ear, "I'm dying to make love to you again."

"And you want to get a room here?"

"Unless you'd rather go somewhere else."

She angled her hips to exert more pressure on his groin, and he felt his blood rush south. The smell of her, the feel of her—it was absolutely intoxicating. He couldn't even think of Lynnette when he held Skye in his arms.

"But you'll go back to her, right?" she said. "You're already planning on it."

If he ever wanted to look himself in the eye again, he had to.

When he didn't respond, she stiffened and tried to draw away. "Forget it."

"Wait. I—I don't really have a choice," he finally answered.

The hurt in her eyes wounded him more than any cutting words she could've uttered. "Then I don't have a choice, either, David. I won't take the leftovers. Just…just leave me alone, okay?"

"Wait! That's not how it—"

"Ms. Kellerman?"

Skye had begun to free herself from his grasp, but

David didn't want her to walk out on him before he could say something to make her understand. He hung on, only to be blinded by the flash of a camera.

"I'm Juanita Lowe with *The Sacramento Post*," a short, stout woman announced when they could see again.

David dropped his hands.

Skye looked flustered but quickly composed herself. "You're doing a piece on the fund-raiser?"

"Not on the fund-raiser per se." Ms. Lowe's eyes cut between them. "I'm planning to do a series on The Last Stand."

"That's wonderful." Skye smiled that same fragile smile he'd seen earlier. Damn it, he wished she could understand how torn he felt.

"Many of my past clients are here if you'd like to talk to them," Skye was saying.

"I'd rather start with you, if that's okay. Do you have a few minutes so we could discuss the shooting last night?"

No wonder Ms. Lowe was interested in Skye. She wanted the inside scoop on the latest excitement.

Unable to resist trying to protect her, David said, "Ms. Kellerman isn't in a position to speak about that yet."

Ms. Lowe's shrewd eyes swept over him with predatory interest. Obviously, she didn't appreciate his involvement. "And you're..."

"David Willis."

"Ms. Kellerman's husband?"

He winced. They'd been so caught up in their attraction they hadn't exactly been dancing like casual friends, or even colleagues. This question suggested that the journalist had definitely noticed. "No, just a friend."

"Oh, of course. Ms. Kellerman isn't married." She

smiled slyly. "But your name sounds familiar. Have we met?"

"I don't think so," he said, but it took her only a second to place him.

"You're the detective who originally investigated Ms. Kellerman's case, aren't you? I wrote for the 'On the Spot' section before I moved to the crime beat, but I followed Burke's trial pretty closely. You were mentioned quite often, as I remember."

Too often for David's taste. Sometimes the media worked to his benefit by quickly disseminating information. But they also disseminated the kind of information he'd rather not take public. In his experience, journalists couldn't be trusted. "I could've lived without that," he said.

"It's great that the two of you turned out to be such close...friends, but—" she looked at Skye and assumed a more innocent air "—isn't it up to Ms. Kellerman to tell me whether or not she'd like to speak to me? After all, she's the one who faxed over a press release earlier this week."

"I'd love to stay and chat, but I was just on my way out," Skye said and started for the exit.

David knew Skye wasn't capable of putting on the public persona she needed right now. What they were feeling was far too intense.

"It won't take more than a few minutes," the journalist called after her.

The wan smile that curved Skye's lips as she turned back made David feel guilty about the complication their involvement posed. "I'm sorry, Ms. Lowe," she said, "but I have a terrible headache. If you're still interested in an interview, why don't you give me a call at the office sometime this week?"

Juanita Lowe frowned but nodded toward her camera-man, who snapped another picture as Skye walked away.

Skye didn't so much as glance back or wave. She stopped briefly to say goodbye to Charlie Fox. Then she passed into the hall.

David wanted to go after her. He hated that their con-versation had ended the way it had, interrupted by this journalist. But, as long as Lowe was watching, he was better off keeping his distance. Telling Skye about Lynnette wouldn't change anything; Lynnette would still stand between them.

"How long have you and Ms. Kellerman been seeing each other?" Juanita Lowe asked.

David smiled as blandly as possible. "Now you're interested in doing a story on her private life?"

She shrugged. "You've scared off my quarry. I might have to take what I can get."

"Who on earth would care whether or not we're involved?"

Her eyebrows went up. "Your wife?"

"Fortunately, I'm not married," he bluffed.

"The department?"

Most of the guys at work, including the chief, wouldn't be any happier to see him with Skye than Lynnette would, but he wasn't about to give Lowe any traction. "Sorry. She's a victim from one of my old cases—a case that's been closed for three years. That's hardly a conflict of interest," he said and strode to the exit himself. He hoped he'd disguised his emotions suffi-ciently, that Ms. Lowe would forget about what she'd seen. But the picture on the front page of the paper the following morning told him she'd decided to exact what revenge she could. It showed him with Skye in his arms, both of them wearing an intense expression, certainly nothing one would expect to see on the faces of acquaintances at a charity ball. The caption read: *Detective David Willis of the Sacramento PD and victims' advocate Skye Kellerman dance at last night's fund-raiser, which netted $121,500 to assist victims of violent crime.*

The accompanying article focused on the story of a burn victim who'd been helped by The Last Stand. It didn't mention David, which made Ms. Lowe's annoyance with him all too obvious.

"Thanks a lot," he muttered as he sat at his kitchen table, glaring down at it.

"What's wrong, Daddy?" Jeremy asked, yawning as he came into the room in his pajamas.

David quickly folded the paper, put it aside and got up to rinse out his coffee cup. "Nothing, bud. How'd you sleep?"

"Good."

"What do you say we go out for breakfast?"

"To Carolina's Country Kitchen?" he cried.

"If that's where you'd like to go." It wasn't David's favorite restaurant, but Jeremy was fond of Carolina's biscuits and gravy. And getting out of the apartment was better than sitting around, wanting to call Skye. He'd tried to reach her once, late, after he'd returned home. She hadn't answered, but she'd been on his mind ever since. If he wasn't remembering what took place in the bathroom, he was worrying about the results of acting like an overexcited teenage boy.

He sighed as he grabbed his car keys. With his luck, he'd gotten her pregnant....

18

Skye squinted at the bright sun pouring through her windows. Her first thought was that it was sunny and not foggy, as it had been for weeks. Somehow that seemed significant, uplifting, and indicative of a break from the gloom of the past few days. Her second thought was that she'd made love with David last night. That seemed significant, too, more significant than anything else, but also surreal. Particularly since they'd taken a risk she'd never taken with any other man.

Who would've supposed that after more than three *years* of restraint, she and David would succumb to their attraction so unexpectedly?

She put a hand to her stomach, wondering if she could be carrying his child. She expected pure panic at the possibility. He was so loyal to the son he already had, and to that son's mother, she'd likely be a single parent. Definitely not what she'd hoped for her future. But she wouldn't use any loyalty he might feel toward a new baby to win him over. Either he loved her and wanted her—or he didn't. And if he didn't, it wasn't as if she was a young girl without options. She was nearly thirty years old, had a home and enough experience and skills to make a living. She also *wanted* a baby. She hadn't allowed it to become a major issue, but she'd felt that way for a while.

But would she be able to do the kind of work she did now if she had a child?

Rubbing her eyes, she told herself it was premature to even *try* to answer that question and turned her thoughts in other directions as she hurried to get ready for work. It was Sunday morning, which she typically spent at home, cleaning, reading, surfing the Internet or catching up on paperwork for The Last Stand. But after the shooting, she didn't want to be here at all. The delta house no longer symbolized the peace, comfort and safety of her childhood.

Don't think about the shooting. Skye tried to concentrate on basic activities—such as having a shower, applying makeup and choosing clothes—but it was no use. She kept imagining the breathless excitement of David's hands seeking the most intimate parts of her body—and worrying about the possibility of a baby.

There's no baby. It almost always took more than one encounter. The possibility of conception was remote, anyway, since she was so late in her cycle.

She wouldn't let herself dwell on the very slim chance that she was pregnant, she decided. But when she stopped at the grocery store on her way to the office to buy some apples, she found her gaze trailing after a mother carrying a baby. As she waited at a traffic light after leaving the grocery store, she caught herself staring wistfully at a little girl in the backseat of the car next to hers. And, for the first time in her life, Skye noticed the existence of a children's furniture store on Howe Avenue that had obviously been around for years.

* * *

"What are you staring at?"

Skye roused herself from the trancelike state she'd fallen into during the past few minutes. Jasmine was at her office door. As far as Skye knew, she hadn't shown up at the fund-raiser. But it was possible she'd come late, after Skye had left.

"Nothing, really," she said. "Just taking a break. I've been on the phone all morning, calling our volunteers."

"What have you found out?"

"Felicia Martinez said a man approached her, asking for my address. He told her he had a box to deliver to my house. He said it was a thank-you from someone I'd helped."

"The volunteers don't have your address, do they?"

"It wouldn't be too hard to find around here. I could've used an old box with a shipping label to carry something in, or asked one of them to drop something off—" A sheepish expression came over Jasmine's face, causing Skye to stop midsentence. "What?"

"Actually, now that you mention it, I think your address might be in my Rolodex."

"See? There are ways."

"So did Felicia give him that information?"

"She says not. But she didn't tell me about the encounter before I asked, either. So that's a concern."

"She probably thought it was nothing."

"That's exactly what she thought."

"Did the man have giant piercings in his earlobes? A goatee?"

"No. She described him, but it wasn't anyone I recognized."

"*Someone* handed over your address."

"And I'm sure it was just as innocent. Information provided as a courtesy."

But how did this man, whoever he was, know whom to approach? Was he watching the office?

Skye gazed down at the list she'd been using. She was so grateful to their volunteers; she couldn't believe any of them would purposely betray her. They were a team, working for the same cause. They trusted each other.

And now Burke, or someone else, was using even them against her.

She set the list aside because she hated thinking about the possibilities. "When'd you get back from Ft. Bragg?"

"A few minutes ago."

"You spent the night there?" If so, it didn't look as if she'd gotten much sleep. Skye could see the smudges beneath Jasmine's eyes despite her dark coloring.

"I had to. It was really late by the time I finished dealing with the police."

"How'd that go?"

Her friend's eyes moved to the photographs on Skye's wall, then darted away. Obviously, the faces of those killers created too much of an emotional trigger for her right now. "The police have the right guy," Jasmine said.

"Did he work at the lumber mill?"

"Yes."

"And did he kill the other little girl, too?"

"Whitney Jones? He's denying it, of course. But I'm sure he's the one."

"What makes you think so?"

Jasmine shuddered as if the experience of meeting him had been harrowing. "He's just…twisted. I could sense it from standing in the same room with him. And—" her chest rose as she drew a deep breath "—I'm convinced these two girls aren't his only victims."

"There's *more?*"

"Maybe. The police are putting out the word, asking other departments to go through their records."

Skye studied her friend for several seconds, concerned by the drawn look on her face. "I hope they're grateful for your help, Jas. These kinds of cases always take so much out of you."

"It's not just the case, Skye," she said. "Not this time. I mean, you'd have to be inhuman not to react to such a heart-wrenching situation. The families of these little girls…well, it brings back so many terrible memories. But…"

"What?" Skye prodded. Jasmine usually wasn't so reticent.

"I had a frightening dream last night. I can't tell if it really means anything, but I had to see you."

"A dream?" Skye sometimes teased Jasmine about her psychic abilities, but she believed in them, even if she didn't understand how it all worked. She knew Jasmine had given the police important clues—such as telling the Ft. Bragg police their perp worked at the lumber mill. *She's alive and in some sort of warehouse. There are a lot of loud noises and traffic, a wrecking yard nearby…. She's buried by some train tracks next to a rice paddy…. He held her nose and mouth, then pushed her face in the dirt while he tied her hands behind her back….*

Skye had seen how often these pieces of information panned out. But something told her she'd rather not believe in Jasmine's abilities now. "About what?"

"You."

Feeling edgy, nervous, Skye shook her head. "But… that isn't how it usually works, right? I mean, you've never had a dream about me before. You touch some object that belonged to someone who's missing and you get feelings about where they might be or what might've happened to them."

"This was different." Agitated, Jasmine raked her fingers through her long black hair as she stepped farther into the room. "I'm not sure whether I should be worried. Maybe it was a dream just like everyone else's dreams. But it was so vivid, Skye, so much like…like the visions I've had before. The ones that do come true. I'm afraid to discount it."

After what had occurred on Friday night, Skye was afraid to *hear* it. "What happened in this dream?" she asked, folding her arms to hide the clenching of her hands.

"There was a woman who had short, choppy, bleached-blond hair. She was screaming that she wanted to kill you, that you've ruined her life."

"I don't know anyone with short, choppy, bleached-blond hair."

"No?" Jasmine seemed relieved.

"You didn't get her name, did you?" Skye asked, smiling weakly.

Jasmine was too preoccupied with her concerns to respond to this lame attempt at humor. "I have no idea who she was, but she stank of cigarettes. It was so strong it seemed as if I could still smell the smoke after I woke up."

The scent of cigarette smoke had accompanied Lorenzo's appearance in her house. Had Jasmine somehow gotten a mixed message? And how much of what she saw was real and how much could be attributed to the subconscious meanderings everyone experienced? Sometimes, even Jas couldn't tell.

"We were fighting?"

"I think so. She kept crying and swearing and lashing out. There was a knife and blood. Every once in a while, she'd yell for someone named Kate."

Kate. Skye's heart jumped into her throat. She'd met Jasmine and Sheridan at a support group *after* Burke's trial. They weren't privy to everything that had gone on in that first year after the attack, only what Skye had told them, and their discussions had focused on the trauma caused by the actual violence, not the trial that followed. Sheridan had lived in Sacramento, but not long enough to know Burke or be aware of the trial. And Jasmine had just moved to town when they met. So was it a coincidence that Jasmine had named Oliver's daughter? It had to be, didn't it? Jane had long dark hair. And as far as Skye knew, she didn't smoke.

"It's nothing to worry about," she said. "I don't know anyone who fits that description."

Jasmine's eyes remained troubled. "Be careful, anyway, okay?"

Skye was always careful. That was one of her biggest problems. She was too wary to trust, to reach out to people. Sometimes it felt as if she lived in some kind of snow globe, with everyone else moving around outside it.

"I will," Skye promised. Then she told herself not to take Jasmine's dream too seriously. Kate was a common enough name; it was entirely possible that the Kate in her dream was an adult. Besides, even Jasmine wasn't sure if her dream had any relevance to the real world.

"What do you think triggered this nightmare?" she asked.

Jasmine sank into the chair across from her. "Sheridan had just told me about the shooting at your house. Maybe it was that."

"Probably," Skye agreed. Then she tried to hide the sense of foreboding that had settled over her by launching into a recap of the fund-raiser, how they'd made twenty thousand more than they'd expected and landed a lunch with Senator Denatorre and the mayor.

"That's great!" Jasmine finally smiled. "And did you enjoy Charlie? Did he stay sober?"

"I think so."

"You don't know?"

"I left before the party was over."

"So, romantically speaking, it was pretty much a bust?"

"Pretty much," Skye muttered, averting her gaze. She didn't see any point in telling Jasmine about her rendezvous with David. That was such an intimate exchange, so all-consuming, at least for her, that she'd take the secret to her grave—unless a certain amount of weight gain about six weeks from now revealed that she'd been with *someone*.

David had known the call would come. But Lynnette took longer to contact him than he'd expected. He'd already taken Jeremy out to breakfast and over to the mall to buy him a new pair of basketball shoes before he heard from her.

"You left Jeremy with a babysitter so you could be with Skye Kellerman?" she asked without preamble.

The bitterness in his ex-wife's voice scalded like acid. Here it was: the backlash. He tried to convince himself that the situation was worsened by Juanita Lowe and the picture she'd published in this morning's paper. But it was the pictures in his mind that convicted him.

"It was a fund-raiser, Lynnette." He wanted to say it was no big deal but it seemed too disrespectful of Skye. Last night had been a *very* big deal. When he closed his eyes, he could still hear the desperate way she'd said his name, feel how she'd arched into him....

"A fund-raiser you attended to be with *her,* David. Don't try to deny it."

"Surely you know about the shooting," he said, trying to move the conversation onto safer ground. Lynnette must've heard about Skye's intruder. She seemed to possess antennae that picked up on anything to do with Skye, and news of the shooting had been in all the papers.

"What does that have to do with *you?*" she asked.

"I'm trying to keep her safe."

"By *sleeping* with her?"

He said nothing.

"Did you think Jeremy wouldn't mention that you had a woman over? That she was *in your bed?* I may not have been a saint, David, but neither have I allowed my son to find a strange man in my bed. And I wouldn't make a fool of you by having my picture splashed across the front page of the paper—a picture of me holding someone else, looking like I'm ready to rip his clothes off."

He veered into the video store, hoping to distract Jeremy and prevent him from hearing the conversation. Covering the mouthpiece, he motioned to a Nintendo

Wii. "Hey, bud, look what they've got. Why don't you check it out?"

Jeremy didn't need to be asked twice. He hurried over to the game station, dropped the bag containing his new shoes and started playing. Meanwhile, David stood in the aisle between two rows of video games. "I had no idea Jeremy was coming over Friday morning. My mother brought him by unexpectedly."

"Maybe that wouldn't have happened if you'd been honest with me."

"I've never lied to you, Lynnette."

"You said you want to get back with me."

"I'm struggling with that," he admitted. These days, the thought of getting back with her felt like some sort of prison sentence.

"What does that mean? Are you getting together with *her?*"

"I don't know. I want to spend more time with her. That's all I can tell you."

"So you slept with her!"

David glanced up to see Jeremy's body jerking as he frantically manipulated the controls of the Nintendo Wii. The sight of his son, still so young and vulnerable, pricked his conscience. "I don't want to talk about that."

He heard her quick intake of breath. "You did sleep with her!"

Miserable, he leaned an elbow on the sales rack to his right. He wasn't self-sacrificing enough to do what he had to do. He was letting her down despite all his efforts.

"David?" she prompted.

"Not now, Lynnette."

"I was honest with *you!*"

He hesitated, wondering how to explain, when her voice suddenly softened and the inevitable tears began. "Do you love her?" she asked on a sob.

Shit. How the hell had he made such a mess of his life?

He massaged his forehead, searching for the gentlest words he could find. "Lynnette, I need some time to…to figure out what kind of threat she's facing, if it's connected to Burke, if Burke's going to harm someone else. That has to come before any of this. Afterward, I'll be able to sort out how I feel. There's a lot going on at the moment. Too much."

"I'm not asking about Burke!"

"But like I said, I have to figure that out first. The rest of this—"

"Dad, look! Aren't the graphics cool?"

David managed a weak smile as he waved to acknowledge Jeremy's comment. "—we'll have to work out later, okay?"

"Once again your job comes before me. But I can't just put my life on hold until *you're* ready!"

"This could be a matter of life and death, Lynnette."

"So my feelings don't count. You don't need me anymore. I'm damaged goods, no one you want to be burdened with, especially now that you can screw such a pretty woman *while* you work. How can I compete with that kind of one-stop shopping?" she snapped and hung up.

David smothered a groan as he shut off his phone. It rang again almost immediately, but according to caller ID, it was his mother.

No way in hell he was gonna answer that call right now.

"Dad?"

Silencing the ringer, David shoved the phone into the pocket of his jeans. "What?"

"Will you buy me one of these?"

"No, bud. Not today."

"Pull-eze?"

It was difficult to concentrate long enough to give coherent answers, and impossible to calm the turmoil inside him. "Maybe for your birthday."

"That's a year away! Can't I earn the money myself?" His eyes were hopeful, earnest. "I could wash your car and…and maybe you could pay me to take out the trash and—"

"You already have a PlayStation," he interrupted before Jeremy could think of more ways to lengthen the list. "And you got three new games for Christmas."

"But the PlayStation's always at your place."

"It should be at my place. Your mom's house is in a good neighborhood, not an apartment block like mine. When you're there, I want you out getting exercise and playing with other kids."

"But you keep saying you're gonna move back in and you never do. I don't have the PlayStation for when my friends come over. It would be okay to play it once in a while, wouldn't it?"

David knew his son didn't *need* a second game station. But, considering what was happening to his plans to reunite with Jeremy's mother, he felt he owed the kid *something*.

"Fine," he said and tossed his VISA on the counter.

Jeremy's mouth dropped open at the sudden reversal. "Thanks, Dad! You're the best!" He flung his arms around David's waist and hugged him, but somehow that didn't make David feel any better. He was trying to replace the important things he should be providing for Jeremy—an at-home father, a complete family—with objects.

Exactly the kind of behavior he'd been hoping to avoid....

"I want to see you."

Jane held her breath while she waited for Noah's response. Going behind the building meant she was standing near the smelly Dumpster, but the smoke from her cigarette helped cloak the stench, and she was too preoccupied to be bothered by minor annoyances. Noah had been acting so strange the past week, ever since Oliver had come home from the hospital. It was as if he felt personally responsible for the stabbing. He visited often, generally to bring food or a video to keep his brother entertained while he recuperated, but when he came he hardly even glanced in Jane's direction. The two men talked and laughed, as though they hadn't been apart for three years.

Jane had never felt more alone.

"We can't," Noah said. "You know that."

"Are you saying you don't care about me anymore?"

"I'm saying—" he seemed to struggle for words "—ever since Skye Kellerman showed up here at the office, it's been...different for me somehow."

Skye? Again? "How?" she asked, panicking because she was losing her only support. Life was difficult enough. She couldn't go on without Noah. Not now. She had to get her feet under her first. "She hasn't told anyone. Oliver doesn't know. He doesn't even *suspect*."

"Jane…please understand. I'm not trying to hurt you. I know you've been through too much. It's just that…when she came here and confronted me, I felt like scum, and that's not what I want to be. I—I have a good wife, Jane. It's a miracle Wendy's still with me after how…distant I've been. I don't want to lose my family, not Wendy and the kids or Oliver and my folks."

"So you can…turn off what you feel for me? Just like that?" Her cigarette burned dangerously close to her fingers, but she simply watched the glowing end eat up more of the white paper.

"It's not easy, but I can't see any better way to fix what we've done. Confessing certainly won't improve the situation."

The fact that he'd even mention confessing told Jane he'd contemplated it. She'd always known his guilt would be a problem. But she'd assumed his feelings for her would overcome it. "I'm wearing that little miniskirt you like. And…and I've done something new to my hair. It's blond and short." She made an effort to keep her voice steady, to sound more sexy than needy. "I could stop by the office after everyone's gone. We could do it on your desk, like we did a few weeks ago. You liked that, remember?"

"I remember." But his voice was flat.

"What do you say? We could make it quick so you won't even be late for supper."

At least he hesitated before turning her down. "No. I'm done, Jane. I don't want to cheat or lie anymore. I need to be able to respect myself again."

Jane imagined going home without the bolstering knowledge that Noah still wanted her, and felt desperate.

Helpless. Oliver hadn't recovered sufficiently to make love, but he was getting stronger. Today he'd called to tell her he was going out for a drive. He was even picking up Kate from school instead of having his mother do it. Now that his mobility was increasing, it wouldn't be long before he wanted a sex life.

But she wasn't interested in sleeping with him. He was so moody. There'd always been periods when he was sullen or withdrawn. She'd learned to wait him out, but prison had made his mood swings so much more dramatic. Sometimes he'd barely speak to her. Whenever she asked if he was okay, he'd tell her he needed time alone. Then he'd lock himself in the bedroom with his binder. Or he'd sit in the dark, not doing anything. Other times, he was as friendly and gregarious as ever, even talked about having a barbecue for their old friends so he could see everyone again.

Evidently, he didn't understand that most of their former friends weren't interested in resuming a relationship with a convicted sex offender, that he'd likely be snubbed the way Jane had been. She'd told him, of course. Several times. But he didn't seem to get it. He also didn't realize that they were barely surviving financially. How could they afford to throw a party? And why would they want any of those people, who prided themselves on the size of their homes and the number of cars and boats they owned, to see the dump they lived in now?

"That's it, then?" Jane said. "You don't want to see me again?"

"I want to be an honorable person. You understand, don't you, Jane?"

She understood. She even admired him for it. She just didn't know how she was going to withstand his rejection.

Her cigarette scorched her fingers, and she finally tossed it away. The burn stung, but it was nothing compared to what she was feeling inside.

The phone beeped. She had another call.

"I'll let you go then," he said.

Jane didn't respond. She checked her caller ID. Oliver was trying to get through.

"Jane?" Noah said.

Again, she didn't answer, didn't mention the other call. She hoped he wouldn't hang up. But he ended the conversation anyway. "I'm sorry," he said, then *click*.

Numb, Jane stood in the chill wind, watching the butt of her cigarette smolder on the asphalt. Oliver wanted to talk to her. And he was all she had left.

19

The nights were the hardest. And knowing Oliver had been released from the hospital and was probably gaining strength every day only made them worse. Skye imagined she saw him around every corner. As the working day came to a close, she'd stare out her office window, watching the parking lot as if she'd see him hovering in the shadows, waiting to drag her into the bushes the second she stepped outside.

When she left the office, she usually walked out with Sheridan and Jasmine, or, if they had appointments elsewhere, she'd hurry to the Volvo with her hand in her purse, clasping her gun. It was the same if she was leaving the shooting range or one of her classes. As soon as she slipped into her car, she'd lock the doors and keep an eye on her rearview mirror the whole way home. Then she'd barricade herself inside the house until morning. She'd had the window and the telephone fixed, but the company that had installed the bars was no longer in business, and she decided not to bother finding someone else. Since the incident with Bishop, she felt as if they shut her in more than they shut anyone out. And she didn't really have the money

to deal with it this month, anyway. She hadn't recon-
nected the alarm, either. It wasn't worth the added
expense if it could be disarmed so easily.

She just had to be careful. But all the caution in the
world couldn't make her feel secure. Lorenzo Bishop had
managed to get inside her house although she'd been as
careful as she could be.

David had put together a file of all the details he'd
been able to collect on Bishop—information on his past
crimes; his family, who still lived in L.A. and claimed to
have had no contact with him for nearly three years; the
places he'd worked; the cities where he'd resided; his
chronic drug dependency and trips in and out of rehab.
But she didn't know much more about him than she'd
known ten days ago, when the shooting had occurred. At
least, she didn't know the one thing that really counted.
Had Oliver sent Bishop? Or was it someone else?

She longed to put her doubts to rest. But they were
still guessing, despite the fact that David was working
around the clock to dig up answers.

They'd been in touch several times since the fund-
raiser. They'd talked about her lunch with the mayor and
Senator Denatorre, which had gone even better than
she'd hoped. The mayor had agreed to speak with the
chief of police, to see if they could improve cooperation
between TLS and the department; Denatorre had said
he'd fully support it. Other than that, her conversations
with David always revolved around Burke or Bishop
and were never personal. David rarely had anything
hopeful to report, and he sounded more exhausted with
each passing day.

"What's wrong?" she asked when she answered his

call and he didn't immediately launch into another work-related conversation.

"I can't find any connection between Oliver and Bishop." His voice was filled with frustration. "I've dug through six years of high school yearbooks, interviewed hundreds of people, put the screws to the people closest to Oliver, and…nothing."

"What about his parents?"

"I couldn't get through to them until today. The mother finally picked up and told me she was going to sue the city for harassment if I didn't quit leaving messages on their recorder."

"What did you say?"

"I asked if she'd ever heard the name Lorenzo Bishop."

"How'd she respond?"

"She didn't. She hung up on me."

"And Jane?"

"She broke into tears, saying she doesn't remember the name but that she doesn't know what's up and what's down anymore."

It was only four in the afternoon, but Skye had driven home early because she couldn't face making the trip after dark. She'd needed a reprieve from the gut-gripping fear she felt every night after work, and the bright blue sky and mellow sun of a late-January afternoon had helped.

But now it was growing dark, and the old, clawing fear was stealing up on her again.

"He must not be connected to Oliver," she said.

"He has to be."

"Maybe it's someone else, someone like Kevin

Sheppard. He wasn't happy when I had to turn him away as a volunteer."

"It's not Kevin Sheppard."

"How do you know?"

"Because I checked him out after you mentioned him a few days ago. He moved to Texas and is now living there with his mother. Plus he has no ties to Bishop."

"What about Tamara Lind's husband?"

"Layne? Tamara went back to him before Bishop broke into your house. I don't think he'd bother with revenge and risk going to jail if he had what he wanted in the first place."

Skye hated that Tamara was once again in an unsafe situation. She'd done everything she could to convince her to stay out of harm's way. But Tamara wouldn't listen.

"He hates me, though."

"He blames you for interfering in his marriage," David said, "but Bishop doesn't show up in his life anywhere, either. And he's a hothead, the type to come after you in the heat of the moment, not the kind of guy who'd hire someone else to do it."

She opened the cupboard where she'd put the pregnancy test she'd bought three days earlier. Every evening she told herself she was finally going to put her anxiety over that incident with David to rest.

And every evening she talked herself out of it. She was too afraid of what the results might be, had no idea what she'd do if the test turned out positive.

Would she tell David?

How could she? She didn't see any point in making him more conflicted than he already was. And she definitely didn't want him to support the child out of obligation. No, if she was pregnant, she'd raise the child on her own.

But that would cause all kinds of changes in her life....

"So who else could there be?" she asked when she realized the conversation had fallen into silence.

"Noah."

"I told you, Noah wouldn't do anything like that."

"I checked anyway."

"And?"

"You're right. No connection to Bishop."

Shutting the cupboard with a decisive snap, she moved back into the living room to make sure she'd lowered all the blinds. After Burke and then Bishop, she always felt as if she was being watched. "That doesn't surprise me. What about Jane?"

"She doesn't have the money it'd take to hire someone."

Skye thought of Jasmine's dream and the uncanny and possibly coincidental mention of someone named Kate. Although it was a long shot that Jane would conspire to have her murdered, anger and depression sometimes did strange things to people. "But Bishop was a drug addict. Sometimes those people will do a lot for very little."

"That's true. I did a cursory check and found nothing, but I'll look deeper."

"Thanks."

Their business was over, but neither one said goodbye. Skye closed her eyes, feeling a poignant longing for the kind of intimacy that would add a new dimension to her life.

When David finally spoke, she understood why he

hadn't ended the call. "Skye, about what happened the night of the fund-raiser…"

She tightened her grip on the phone. "I told you, it was nothing. Don't worry about it."

"I *am* worried. I need to know if you're pregnant."

"No," she said quickly and hoped to heaven it was true.

"You know for sure?"

The relief in his voice told her what her answer had to be. "Yes."

"I'm sorry. I never should've put you in that position, especially with everything you're going through."

She went back to the kitchen to stare at the cupboard with the pregnancy test. "It's fine. I've already forgotten about it."

"You have?"

"Of course."

"That makes exactly one of us," he said and hung up.

She let her breath go in a long exhalation as she returned the handset to its cradle. She *wasn't* pregnant, she told herself. She couldn't be. They'd had sex once. No big deal. Sure, they hadn't used protection, but other people got away with it all the time.

She argued with herself for another fifteen minutes but, in the end, she forced herself to retrieve that test and take it into the bathroom. There, she carefully followed the instructions and held her breath as she waited for the results.

It'll be okay…it'll be okay…it'll be okay, she chanted to herself. But when the indicator turned pink, she knew it wouldn't be okay at all.

Careful not to tear the thin newspaper clipping he'd been saving for more than a week, Oliver turned it over and gently pressed a glue stick along the outside edges, then pasted it into his binder as meticulously as all the other pictures he'd collected.

Afterward, he sat back and gazed at Skye in Detective Willis's arms.

That photograph proved he'd been right from the first. Willis wanted Skye. It was obvious from how closely he was holding her, the expression on his face. And, apparently, there was nothing standing in the way. Willis didn't have a wife anymore, just as Oliver had thought. Oliver had checked the county records this morning and confirmed that Willis was divorced.

Oliver studied Skye, wondering if she returned the detective's interest. It was possible. Willis had a good build, was an attractive man. Oliver liked to imagine them sleeping together, but not as much as he liked the idea of making David watch *him*. There were drugs that rendered a person helpless, unable to move a muscle. With enough money, Oliver could get some of those drugs. He had a lead on some roofies already. The Internet was *so* amazing.

Picturing David slumped in a chair, unable to get his body to respond to the commands of his brain while he watched Skye being raped made Oliver rock-hard. More ready than he'd been since he'd come home from the hospital.

"Oliver? You in there?"

It was Jane at the door.

"What perfect timing," he muttered to himself. Then he closed the binder, slid it between the headboard and the wall, stripped off his pants and positioned himself sideways in the chair to make the most of what he had to offer.

"Come in."

She opened the door rather timidly. He'd snapped at her the last time she'd bothered him. But he hadn't meant it. He'd always been good to her in the past. He was just having trouble adjusting.

Her eyes immediately dropped to what he'd exposed, but she didn't smile or move closer as he might've expected after three years. He tried to ignore that.

"Where's Kate?" he asked.

She blinked several times before answering, and when she spoke it took her a moment to find her voice. "Her friend—" she cleared her throat "—her friend Valerie invited her to stay the night."

"So we have some time alone." He gave her his most boyish smile.

"Are you sure you're…feeling strong enough? I—I wouldn't want to…hurt anything."

That was why she was so reluctant. Now he understood. "What do you mean? I've been biking for the past three days," he said. "It won't hurt me. Come here."

When she hesitated, he nearly lost his erection and felt the anger that simmered so close to the surface these days overwhelm him. Didn't she realize how difficult this was for him? That he couldn't even get hard without imagining she was Skye?

Of course not. Jane was too stupid. He used to love being the smart one, seeing that adoration in her eyes when he said something beyond her intelligence or used a word she wasn't familiar with. But it didn't seem so endearing anymore. The moment she came home, he left the house and rode up and down the bike trail on his new bike, just to retain his sanity. At least when he was on the trail he could relive the moment he'd first spotted Meredith, and Amber and Patty. He'd also ridden, several times, past the point where he'd first seen Skye sitting in a lawn chair outside her apartment, remembering how he'd waved and she'd smiled in response....

"You want to make love?" Jane asked.

"Don't you?"

She nodded. "Of course." But when they got into bed and started kissing, he went flaccid and nothing she did made any difference.

"Maybe it'd help if you let me tie you up," he suggested.

"What?"

She sounded appalled, which made him want to scream at her. This wasn't *his* fault. If she hadn't let herself get so flabby and unappealing, maybe he'd be able to do it. "You know, it might be fun if we tried something a little different," he said.

She leaned up on one elbow to peer into his face. "But we haven't made love in the, ah, traditional way for more than three years, what with the trial and everything. You can't be bored with it already."

"So you're as unadventurous now as you were before." He didn't hide his disappointment.

She caught her bottom lip between her teeth. "I'm not unadventurous."

"Then what *are* you willing to do?"

"What do you want me to do?"

"I told you. Let me tie you up."

Propping herself against the headboard, she hugged her bent legs to her chest. "With what?"

"Sheets. That's not too threatening, is it?"

"No-o-o," she said slowly.

He hurried to raid the linen closet. But when he came back, she seemed even less sure about what he had planned.

"Getting tied up doesn't excite me," she said.

"I've been celibate for three and a half years, Jane. Waiting to be with you again. I just want to make this an occasion to remember. Can't we make it different? Special?"

Finally she smiled. "Okay."

"Turn over."

She blinked in surprise. "Why would I turn over?"

"Because I want you to be facedown."

"Then we won't be able to see each other."

And he wouldn't be constantly reminded that she wasn't the one he wanted. "A lot of people do it like this. Come on. I'm not going to hurt you. Have I ever hurt you?"

"No." Her chest lifted as if she'd taken a deep breath. "I know you won't hurt me," she said. Then she stopped frowning and stalling and turned over so he could tie her up.

"That's too tight," she complained once he'd finished.

He didn't loosen her bonds. This was just starting to get exciting. "It won't be any fun if you can get free."

"But the sheets are cutting off my circulation."

"I won't leave you this way for long. Hold still, I want you to wear a blindfold, too."

He got the bandanna he used to clean his reading glasses from his sock drawer and attempted to tie it over her eyes. But she didn't want him to use it. She kept shaking her head, which made it difficult to get the darn thing on.

"Why do we have to add a blindfold?" she asked.

So you won't see the knife I bought today. He didn't have any plans to use it on her, of course. He just wanted to feel it in his hands while he enjoyed himself. "This is only a little game of sex slave, Janey," he said, using her nickname to calm her. "Relax, okay? Couples play it all the time."

"I don't want to be blindfolded," she said again, but she was already tied up so he made her wear it anyway, and that act alone, with her twisting and fighting and begging him to set her free, told him he wasn't going to have any trouble finishing *this*.

"Oliver, stop," she wailed. "I don't like what you're doing."

Which was precisely why *he* liked it so much. He longed to put the knife to her neck, to feel the warmth of her blood. That would shut her up. Remembering the stifled whimpers of past encounters sent a shot of pure testosterone to his groin.

"Come on, Jane," he pleaded. "I've been in prison for three years. Can't you give it to me how I want it at least once?"

She stopped trying to pull free. "It's just that I feel so helpless. I don't like it."

He couldn't force her, or she might complain to his family, which would call into question everything he'd told them about his past. "I know. But you'll do it for me, won't you? Please? I'll let you tie me up after."

She said nothing.

"I'd never hurt you."

"I know," she said again, but once he had her tied and blindfolded and held that knife in his hand, he was afraid he *might.* He was no longer the little guy who was always getting pushed around. He could command respect. Her very *life* was in his hands, a life he could take with one flick of his wrist.

"What's that?" she asked a few minutes later, a hint of terror in her voice. "What's that in your hand?"

He held the blade farther away. "Nothing," he lied. Then he fondled her neck with his free hand, wishing he didn't have to be quite so careful.

Jane waited until Oliver fell asleep, then slipped out of the bedroom. He'd been rough with her, rougher than he'd ever been in the past. And although he'd tried to make up for it by kissing her and hugging her afterward, and thanking her repeatedly for being such a good sport, she felt rattled. Scared. She wasn't sure if prison had caused this change in him, or merely brought something previously hidden closer to the surface, but she had to tell Noah. She was beginning to believe that Skye was right: Oliver was dangerous.

Creeping into the bathroom, she closed the door, then turned on the light and gazed in the mirror. With her new haircut and bleach job, she scarcely recognized herself. But her eyes quickly moved down from her face. Her breasts were red and sore from the way he'd squeezed and pinched them, she had teeth marks on one shoulder and her bottom was sunburn-red from being slapped. He hadn't broken the skin or drawn any blood, but what he'd done certainly wasn't *making love.* There'd been a cruelty involved that was as shocking as it was terrifying. And he'd had some object in his right hand, something he hadn't wanted to reveal to her. He'd kept it from coming into contact with her, but the bottom of something hard and flat had brushed her arm when he finally collapsed at her side.

Jane studied her hands, swollen from being bound. That was another thing. He hadn't cared that he'd tied those sheets too tight, hadn't even followed through on his promise to make the experience a quick one. Just when he seemed ready to finish, he'd hold off and wait a few minutes, trying to drag the session out as long as possible, and he did that over and over again.

Feeling tears prickle the backs of her eyes, she held her breath as she listened for any movement in the bedroom. Nothing. Oliver was probably out for the night. What he'd done to her—she couldn't think of it as what they'd done together—seemed to satisfy him more completely than anything they'd ever done before.

Heartened by Oliver's lack of movement, she grabbed her bathrobe from the hook by the shower, carefully opened the door and crept out to the kitchen. She could smell the onions from the meatloaf she'd made earlier, as well as the mildew that always seemed to permeate the place. She'd thought she'd hit bottom when Oliver was convicted of a crime she didn't believe he'd committed and she'd turned to an affair with his brother for the love and support she needed. But being married to an ex-convict whom she now believed was guilty of attempted rape, at the very least, and possibly murder, was definitely worse. She had to get away from him, get Kate away.

But she had no resources. Thanks to the bike he'd bought, her checking account was already overdrawn and would be until she got paid. Oliver had also insisted

she buy champagne to celebrate his return, and filet
mignon. She'd done it, hoping such a lavish dinner would
help them adjust and recover, but it had been an unnecessary extravagance. When she'd told Oliver she was
overdrawn, he'd shrugged and said the store could wait
to get its money. When she'd added that the bank would
charge them twenty-seven dollars for each bounced
check, he'd given her a dirty look and said, "You don't
think I'm worth twenty-seven dollars?"

Taking the phone from the cluttered counter, where
dinner dishes awaited her—which she'd have to do
before heading to work in the morning—Jane stepped
out onto the porch and dialed Noah's number.

Wendy answered with a sleepy, "Hello?"

"Wendy, it's Jane."

There was a long pause. When Wendy spoke again,
she was much more awake. "What's wrong, Jane? Is
your toilet stopped up again?"

Jane's heart skipped a beat. Wendy suspected. Or
maybe, by now, she knew. It'd be like Noah to tell her.
But Jane couldn't let herself react to the sarcasm that had
tinged her sister-in-law's response. "No, it's about Oliver.
I—I need to talk to Noah, if you don't mind."

"This can't wait until morning?" she asked.

Jane supposed it could. Now that Oliver was asleep,
she wasn't in immediate danger. And she'd get up before
he did in the morning. It was just that she felt so…used
and violated and…and unloved. "I-I'm sorry, Wendy."
She started to cry. She couldn't help it.

"Jane, I know you've been through a lot, but now
that Oliver's back, you have to stop relying on my
husband so much."

"But this is *about* Oliver."

"The adjustment won't be easy. But you can do it. Okay? I'll have Noah call you in the morning. Or, better yet, maybe this is something you can talk over with Betty or Maurice."

Noah had told her. He'd confessed. Wendy had always been sympathetic, and she was being generous now, considering. But Jane felt stripped naked and lashed raw.

"Right. I—I understand. I'll—" she struggled with the lump in her throat "—I'll call them tomorrow."

"Good," she said, and then she was gone.

Jane was tempted to drive over there and throw a rock at the window. She knew Noah wouldn't be able to shut her out quite so easily. He still cared about her. He had to. It wasn't very long ago that they'd been together at his office.

But then she heard a noise behind her. Turning, she saw Oliver staring at her through the front window. The way he looked at her was so chilling that, for a moment, she couldn't move.

Finally, he stopped staring and opened the door. "What are you doing?"

Was it her imagination that he sounded suspicious? "I had to call Wendy," she said. "She—she wants me to cut her hair in the morning, but as I was going to sleep, I realized I've double-booked myself."

"It's after one. Isn't that a little late to be bothering her about a hair appointment?"

"I thought maybe she'd still be awake, watching a movie. I didn't want her to get up early for nothing." Jane was beginning to shake. Her robe was thin, and she wasn't wearing any shoes, but he was blocking her entrance to the house. "I—I did it out here so that I wouldn't disturb you," she added.

He didn't move. "You're not going to make a big deal out of one light bondage session, are you?"

He hadn't completely bought her story. "Of course not."

"Then you liked it?"

She'd hated it with every cell of her body, but she forced a smile. "It wasn't so bad."

"Sex is a give-and-take between husbands and wives. You understand that."

"Of course."

"And what happens in our bedroom stays between us, right, Jane?"

His voice was deceptive in its gentleness. After the past few hours, Jane had learned just how deceptive. "It's no one's business but ours," she concurred.

Then he stepped away from the door and let her in, but he didn't reach out and take her hand, or lead her back to the bedroom with him. Finished with her for the night, he left her standing in the kitchen, staring out into the darkness.

20

"**I**'ve found the connection."

Skye resisted the impulse to cover her stomach with one hand as David stood up to pull out the chair across from him. He'd called her just before noon and asked her to meet him at the California Bar & Bistro on Arden Way for lunch, and she'd agreed because he'd said he had news.

She knew she should be making an announcement of her own. But she'd already decided not to tell him about the baby. She'd known she was pregnant for little more than a day—hadn't yet come to terms with the shock of it herself.

"Don't tell me it's Jane," she said in surprise.

"It's Noah."

The waitress interrupted with a greeting for Skye and a glass of water. Skye managed a rather vacant smile in return, but her attention was on David. *Noah?* "But you said it wasn't Noah."

"I was wrong. Lorenzo once worked for him on a construction site."

"NSL Construction didn't show up in Lorenzo's work history." Skye had read through the information David had already gleaned, several times.

"Actually, he worked for one of Noah's subcontractors for almost a year. Even that didn't show up on his employment record because it was under the table."

"He took cash wages?"

"Exactly."

"How'd you find out?"

"I waited until Noah was out of the office, then dropped in to have a chat with his secretary."

Skye remembered the slight, willowy young woman she'd seen there when she'd stopped by to confront Noah about the affair. "She remembered Lorenzo?"

"No, but she gave me a list of the subs they've used over the past several years. Last week, I mailed each one a copy of Lorenzo's picture, and this morning, one of the workers at C&L Concrete contacted me. When he saw Lorenzo's picture on his boss's desk, it caught his eye. He read the request for information at the bottom and called me to say he'd worked with Lorenzo on a few occasions."

Skye propped her elbows on the table and leaned closer, so the customers around them wouldn't be able to eavesdrop. It was busy even for a Friday. "But how would Noah get to know the temporary worker of one of his subs well enough to hire him to kill me? From everything you've compiled on Lorenzo, they don't seem compatible as friends."

"It's not as big a stretch as you might think. A general may spend several days working on one part of a job while his subs work on another. When you come into contact with someone every day, even for a week, you get pretty familiar."

She shook her head. "I can't see Noah sending Lorenzo to my house."

The waitress came to take their order, so Skye quickly

perused the menu and chose a chicken salad. David opted for a bacon burger.

"I'm not sure how it all came about," David said. "But this gives us the start we've been searching for."

"Maybe Jane could tell us more. She knows Noah as intimately as she does Oliver."

"Jane's not holding up well. I'm afraid she's going to have a nervous breakdown."

"She's doing that badly?"

"I stopped by her work yesterday. She took one look at me and ran for the bathroom. She shut herself in and wouldn't come out."

The depth of her own concern surprised Skye, considering how vehemently Jane hated her. "What about her little girl, Kate?"

"She's fine. She spends a lot of time with Oliver's mother." He drank a sip of his ice water. "I'm thinking of talking to Noah's wife, Wendy. She was pretty tight-lipped throughout the trial, but she seemed to take it all in and process it with some objectivity. Something tells me she's got a good head on her shoulders. She might listen to reason."

"Maybe she'd be more receptive to *me*."

His eyebrows rose. "Are you kidding? You're the devil incarnate, as far as Oliver's family is concerned."

"I know. But I'm not as threatening as a police officer. And of all his family, Wendy was the only one who looked at me with any kindness during the trial."

"You think she believed you?"

"No, I think she believed him—that I attacked him while I was on drugs. But she knew I was telling the story I thought to be the truth."

David scowled. "I wouldn't want Noah to see you talking to her."

"I wouldn't want him to see me, either."

"And he has kids, so you can't go to the house."

She toyed with her silverware, wondering how she was ever going to eat. She was too uneasy about Noah's possible involvement and Jane's desperate state. And then there was the baby, always in the back of her mind. *I'm carrying your baby.* "Where, then?" she asked.

"Her work, I guess."

"Where does she work?" He had razor stubble covering his jaw, as if he hadn't taken the time to shave this morning, and there were fatigue lines around his eyes. Skye couldn't help noticing—and worrying about him.

"She's a substitute teacher."

"That's going to make it pretty hard to track her down."

The waitress brought their food. "I'll see what I can do and give you a call once I've selected a good time and place."

"Okay." Skye reached for the salt at the same moment David did. When their hands brushed, she expected him to draw back immediately. He'd been all business since the fund-raiser, one hundred percent back to his former self. Obviously, he wanted to make sure that what had happened at the Hyatt didn't happen again. But he didn't withdraw. His fingers interlaced with hers and his thumb stroked her palm, a motion that was both erotic and tender.

Skye shivered as sexual awareness skittered through her.

"You are *so* beautiful," he said.

"Weren't you the one who said this kind of thing isn't going to help?" she responded. She tried to pull away, but he wouldn't let go.

"I can't fight it anymore."

Her chest grew tight with anticipation. "What do you mean?"

"I want to spend more time with you."

"What about Lynnette?"

"I've already told her."

She looked at their entwined hands. Would he enjoy the next week or two with her, then go back to his ex-wife? "I don't know, David," she said. There was so much more at stake now. Skye didn't want a brief affair. She wanted to marry him and settle down.

But a long-lasting relationship had to start somewhere, didn't it?

"Is that a no?" he murmured.

"Do you have Jeremy this weekend?"

"Not this weekend, no."

She met his steady but inquiring gaze. "Then why don't you come over for dinner tonight?"

He gave her a sexy smile. "What time?"

"Seven?"

"Okay," he said. But when he released her hand and she started her meal, she could've sworn she glimpsed Lynnette standing outside the door, staring at them through the glass.

"What is it?" David asked, following her gaze. But the woman was gone before Skye could get a good look at her.

"Nothing," she said distantly and finished her food.

Noah didn't call her. Jane waited, thinking he must've heard the phone ring last night, heard his wife talk to her.

He'd probably been lying in bed right next to Wendy. But if he *had* heard, he didn't care. Jane finally became so overwrought she could scarcely work. How could Noah tell Wendy about them? That was such a betrayal, so unfair. Now he got to be the repentant one, the one with an opportunity to apologize and try to make it up to her. And Jane was the slut who'd caused it all, someone to be shunned by both of them.

"What's wrong with you today?" Danielle snapped when Jane dropped her scissors on the floor and had to resterilize them for the third time.

"Nothing," she grumbled. Danielle wouldn't understand. A single mother who'd lost her only living parent last year, she didn't have an easy life. But no one had problems quite like Jane's. Jane had lost her mother long ago, as well as the aunt who'd raised her. She'd never known her father. And that was *before* she married Oliver Burke.

As soon as Jane finished the haircut she'd been working on, Danielle pulled her aside. "You need to calm down or you're going to end up hurting yourself with your own scissors."

It already looked as if she'd hurt herself. She'd been biting her cuticles so badly she had sores on almost every finger. She had to cover them with Band-Aids when she came to work so she didn't scare the customers.

"I-I'm trying." She craved a cigarette even though she'd had one only twenty minutes earlier.

Danielle's expression softened as she gazed at Jane's bandaged fingers. "Look, why don't you take off early? I don't know how you can cut hair with all those on, anyway. I can manage on my own."

Jane couldn't figure out what to make of this kindness. At the shop, it was pretty much a dog-eat-dog world. They were all too mired in their own difficulties, struggling too hard for survival to do many favors for each other.

"You're sure?" she asked. She knew it'd mean that Danielle would have to stay late, that she'd get less time with her son, which was all she cared about, but Danielle nodded and shoved Jane toward her station.

"I'm sure. Get your purse and go," she said gruffly.

Relief and a little bit of hope surged through Jane. It was early enough that, with any luck, she'd be able to catch Noah at his office. He worked until six on Fridays, trying to wrap up the week.

Grabbing her purse and keys, she nearly ran out of the shop, then drove to his office.

When she arrived, she spotted the bumper of his truck from the side alley—it was in back, where he always parked it—and knew this was her chance. *It'll be okay. Don't worry. Calm down.*

Judging by the fact that his secretary's car was gone, Jane assumed Noah was alone. This was a perfect opportunity to tell him about the degradation she'd suffered, the doubts that plagued her more than ever, the fear.

Except that the office was locked and she couldn't get him to come to the door.

"Noah? Noah, it's me!" She knocked. "Please answer."

No response. It was only when she continued pounding, refusing to give up, that he finally appeared. Even then, he cracked the door barely a few inches and stood in the opening, as if to bar her entrance.

"I have to talk to you," she said, breathless from the anxiety that had poured through her all day and the exertion of pounding.

Disapproval etched deep lines in his forehead. "I can't let you in, Jane. I've promised Wendy I won't be alone with you again, and I plan to keep that promise. If you need something, you're going to have to go to your husband."

"You told her," she whispered.

"I had to," he said. "It was the only way to put an end to this, to make sure I wouldn't break down again."

"What about *me?*" Jane wailed.

"It's best for both of us. This way you'll learn to depend on your husband instead of coming to me. I don't want to stand between you. Who gains from that? No one. Both families lose."

"But—but Oliver hurt me last night, Noah. He's not the same. He's...*dangerous.*" Jane knew she was talking too fast, that her agitated state was costing her credibility, but she was desperate for him to believe her.

Noah rolled his eyes. "Stop it. He's having a hard time, like the rest of us. Worse than the rest of us. He has to start all over and he has no idea how he's going to support his family."

"But he did it, Noah. I think he killed those girls and he tried to rape Skye. I believe he'll do it again, given the chance. It's just a matter of time."

He lifted a hand to silence her. "I don't want to hear it. You're acting crazy. He didn't do it, okay? *He didn't do it!*"

She glanced around the empty parking lot. What she had to tell him was too private to air out on the street, but Noah had left her no choice. She knew he wouldn't break Wendy's "no being alone together" rule. "Last night Oliver and I made love for the first time."

Noah grimaced. "I don't want to hear about that, either. Just…live your life and be happy, okay? Make my brother happy, too." He started to go back in, but she clutched the edge of the door and held on.

"Noah, you *have* to listen to me. I don't know who else to turn to. I don't know if I'm going nuts or if he's really dangerous, but it *feels* like he is. Last night, he insisted on tying me up. He wanted me to be facedown. I had to wear a blindfold. He didn't care that I hated it. He—he liked that I was whimpering and begging. It excited him—"

"Did he hurt you?" he interrupted.

"Yes!"

"How?"

She tried to remember. The physical injuries weren't so bad. It was more the way he'd behaved. His total disregard for her comfort. His self-absorption. "He—he squeezed my breasts."

"He squeezed your breasts," he repeated dismissively.

"Really hard," she added.

He bent to look at her more closely. "*That's it?* Most men like to squeeze a woman's breasts!"

"He bit me, too." She pulled down the neck of her sweater to reveal the mark on her shoulder, but the impression hadn't been deep enough to last.

When he saw nothing, Noah shook his head. "You need to see a counselor."

"I swear he bit me. Just not hard enough to draw blood."

"*I've* bitten you before, Jane. And you liked it."

"This was different. This wasn't playful or loving. Love had nothing to do with it. I felt hate. *Extreme* hate."

"Give me a break. Oliver loves you. When we went out to lunch today, he told me you guys had the best sex of your lives last night, that you're everything he's ever wanted in a woman, a real tiger in bed."

That comment left Jane speechless. Oliver knew she'd talked to Wendy last night. He was doing damage control, trying to undermine anything she might say so that Noah and Wendy, and maybe even his parents, would think they already knew what had occurred and decide it wasn't that bad.

Oliver was so clever. He was smart *and* dangerous.

"If you won't listen, I'll have to go to your parents." She wheeled around to do just that, but he caught her arm.

"Don't you dare!" Real anger, the kind she'd never seen from Noah, flickered in his eyes as he spun her back to face him. "My parents have suffered enough, do you hear? Whatever you're going through, you'd better tough it out without burdening them. They've mourned what happened to Oliver all these years. They've nearly bankrupted themselves trying to help you both. And now they're getting old. Don't you dump this in *their* laps."

"But I have to tell them what I think. I need to protect Kate, protect myself."

"From a husband who wants to get in your pants? You let me get in your pants as often as I wanted without any complaints."

She winced at the disgust in his voice. "You wanted to be with me," she challenged.

He threw up his hands. "I did. I admit it. But I don't want it anymore, and you won't let go. Don't you get it? It's over."

She couldn't stifle the sob that rose in her throat. What had she done to deserve this? The whole world had turned against her. "But he—he tied me up even though I begged him not to. He—he squeezed my breasts and— and slapped my ass and bit my shoulder. It was horrible."

At last, she saw a flash of the old Noah in his eyes, the one she'd thought loved her. "He used ropes?" he asked, concern in his voice.

"No, sheets."

Noah didn't wait to hear the rest. He waved her away, repeating the word *sheets* as if he'd never heard anything more ridiculous.

"He tied them really tight," she called after him. "It wasn't normal sex play. You weren't there. You didn't see what he was like."

Pivoting just before the door could close, he caught it and pointed an accusing finger at her. "It's you, Jane. It's not him. You've been cracking up for a while now. You need therapy and probably a good dose of Prozac." Slamming the door shut, he locked it.

Tears slipped down Jane's cheeks as she watched his retreating back through the glass door. She'd scratched that back, massaged it—slept with him, *loved* him.

But Noah wasn't hers to love. He never had been, not really. She was married to the psychopath who was waiting for her to come home and make him dinner.

Knowing he'd be spending the rest of the evening with Skye made it difficult for David to think of anything else. There were so many doubts crowding his brain—and, as always, the nagging guilt over Lynnette and Jeremy. But he didn't see how remarrying Lynnette would work if he didn't really *want* to be with her, despite her illness and the compassion and sympathy he felt about the diagnosis. He couldn't even touch Lynnette, felt absolutely no desire to do so.

On the other hand, he didn't know where he expected his relationship with Skye to go. He was trying not to think that far down the line, because then he had to consider the prospect of giving his son a stepmother, deciding whether or not he wanted other kids, acknowledging that Lynnette would have it far rougher without him, even if he tried to support her as a friend, and figuring out whether or not he could live comfortably with Skye's work putting her in constant danger.

Whenever he confronted all those issues, he felt overwhelmed and wanted to force his life back to its original path, which meant trying to reconcile with Lynnette, and that started the whole confusing cycle over again. So he decided he wouldn't think about the future. He'd take one day at a time—and this day was going to be pretty damn great because, after his last stop, he'd be heading out to the delta to have dinner with Skye. It was nearly six already.

Slowing his police-issue sedan, he read the addresses on the street, trying to figure out which residence belonged to Noah Burke. He'd interviewed Oliver's brother before the trial nearly four years ago, but that interview had taken place at the station.

He frowned as he remembered the twenty minutes he'd spent with Noah, which had been a waste of time. Noah had maintained the family story: Oliver was a joy to be around, he'd never been a troublemaker, he had no dark side and wasn't capable of attempted rape. But David hadn't come to talk about Oliver today.

The four numbers he'd been searching for glinted in brass from a mailbox with an elaborate brick pedestal covered in ivy. Judging by the house, Noah was doing all right for himself. A two-story giant built with New England–style dormers and shutters, it fit perfectly with the other custom homes in the area. The lot alone, which had to be half an acre, was probably worth $500,000. Although Noah and his family weren't on the river, where many of the real mansions were, he'd paid a pretty penny for the property.

Turning into the brick-rimmed drive that formed a half circle with lighted pillars flanking each side, David parked behind a minivan with its doors open. A quick glance told him no one was inside, but as he approached the house he realized why—Noah's wife was just leaving.

"Oh! Excuse me," she exclaimed when she nearly bumped into him on the front stoop. "I didn't hear the bell."

He hadn't had a chance to ring it. He'd been checking the manila file folder he was carrying to make sure he had Bishop's picture. "I didn't mean to startle you. I'm looking for your husband, Noah. Is he around?"

She hadn't recognized him at first. She'd caught herself to avoid a collision and apologized, but her face clouded as she placed him. "You're that detective, the one from Oliver's trial."

"Detective Willis." He held out his hand and she took it, but a trifle reluctantly. "Is your husband at home?" he repeated.

Before she could answer, a boy of about ten darted

through the door and cut around them, bouncing a basketball as he ran for the van.

"Noah just got home from work. He's changing and I'm—"

"On your way out. I can see that. If you'd tell Noah I'd like a minute, I'll wait for him here on the stoop."

She hesitated as if unsure how to react and settled on cautiously polite. "You can have a seat in the living room if you'd prefer."

"That's okay. This is fine."

She lowered her voice and visibly braced herself. "Oliver hasn't done anything else, has he?"

"Else?" David repeated.

When she didn't immediately retract that telling word, he knew she'd become a little disenchanted with her brother-in-law. Or maybe she was tired of the whole situation.

"I'm not here to talk about Oliver." He opened the folder for the second time and handed her the picture inside it. "Have you ever seen this man?"

Her expression remained blank. "No. Who is he?"

"Lorenzo Bishop. He used to work for one of your husband's subcontractors."

The eyes that met his were full of curiosity. "Has he done something wrong?"

"Yes."

"Then, I wish I could help but—" she shrugged and returned the picture "—I've never seen him before in my life."

"Mom! Come on," the kid yelled from the car. "If I'm late, Coach Green will make the whole team run liners."

Wendy Burke's keys jangled as she slid the strap of

her purse onto her shoulder and ducked her head back inside the house. "Noah!" she called. This elicited no response so she raised her voice. "Noah!"

"What is it?"

"Detective Willis is here to see you."

No other sound came from the house, at least nothing audible. David guessed Noah was cursing under his breath. David wasn't a popular figure with this family.

"Did you hear me?" she called. "He has some questions about a man who used to work for you. I have to go or Brian'll be late for basketball practice."

"Go ahead. I'll be right down."

A stiff smile curved her lips. "He shouldn't be long."

David thanked her and watched as she drove off, then studied the street. It was a nice neighborhood—beat the hell out of his utilitarian apartment, that was for sure.

"Why are you here?"

David turned to find Noah standing at the door, wearing a clean pair of jeans, loafers and a sweatshirt. It was obvious from his wet hair that he'd just had a shower.

"I've run across a friend of yours."

"Of mine?" he repeated doubtfully. "You and I don't exactly travel in the same circles."

"Which is what makes it rather…coincidental that I've discovered a link between this man and you, wouldn't you say?" He produced the picture and waited for Noah's reaction—a reaction that seemed as innocuous as his wife's.

"This is Lorenzo something or other," he said.

"Bishop," David supplied.

"That's it. He used to work for one of my subs."

"Do you know where he is now?"

"No. I haven't seen him for years."

"How many years?"

Now that David wasn't questioning him about a family member, Noah appeared eager to help. "Maybe... four? I was building the deck on the McCurdy house while he was pouring the new drive. That has to be at least four years. Why?"

"He's dead."

Suspicion drew Noah's eyebrows together. "You don't think Oliver killed him, do you?"

"No, I don't. I already know it was someone else."

"Who?"

Evidently, Noah hadn't been keeping up with the news. Of course, a lot had happened in the past few weeks. His brother had been released from prison, stabbed, hospitalized and sent home to Jane and Kate, who hadn't seen him for three years. The whole Burke family had probably been too busy dealing with their own private hopes and fears and adjustments to worry about other people.

"Skye Kellerman," he said.

Noah's eyes went wide. "She killed Lorenzo? That's gotta tell you something. It's not my brother who's—"

David broke in before he could go too far down that road. "He cut her telephone line, broke into her house and tried to kill her. That's when she shot him."

Noah shook his head. "You're kidding."

"No."

"What did he have against Skye?"

"I was hoping you could tell me."

"I have no idea."

"You didn't hire him to do it?"

His face reddened with genuine shock and anger. "Are you kidding? Now you think *I'm* a killer?"

"Skye knows about your affair with Jane."

Noah leaned closer and enunciated each word. "So does my wife. I broke it off with Jane. I confessed." He gestured in a helpless motion. "The guilt was too much for me. I'd hate for my brother and parents to find out what I've done, but maybe they should know, too. Maybe that's the only way to really wipe the slate clean."

David was too surprised to come up with a response.

"If you don't believe me, you can ask Wendy. Do you want to come in and call her on her cell?"

David studied him. "No," he said and walked away.

"I'm going to tell them," Noah called after him. "I'm going to tell my whole family."

David turned back before reaching his car. "Don't."

"Why not? I can't carry this secret anymore. It's time to break free of the past, start over."

"You'll put Jane in danger if you do," David warned. But Noah waved him away. "I'm serious."

"My brother's innocent," he said, and then he went in and it was too late to say anything else.

David didn't drive off immediately. He sat in his car, wondering if he should go back to the house and try to convince Noah of the danger Jane might face. He would have, if he'd thought it would do any good. But he knew it wouldn't. He doubted Noah would even answer the door. Noah didn't believe his brother was capable of such savagery, and nothing David said would convince him.

David decided to warn Jane, just in case Noah didn't do her that courtesy. But she was no longer at work, and when he called the house, he got a recorder. Unwilling to leave a message—he didn't want Oliver to hear his voice—he hung up and made a mental note to try her again later.

21

Now that they stood face-to-face, Oliver realized the man he'd hired via the Internet wasn't a man at all. Oliver knew he'd never win any prizes for guessing ages at the state fair, but this kid was barely seventeen if he was a day. He had more pimples than whiskers. His hair, which didn't look as if it had been washed recently, fell to his shoulders, and he had a baby face and braces to go with his baggy jeans and Sex Wax T-shirt.

"Do you have the money?" the boy said. He'd kept Oliver waiting while he spoke on a cell phone. But he'd finished his conversation and was apparently ready to do business.

Now Oliver understood why his Internet "investigator" had wanted to meet in an alley. He had no office. He probably lived with his folks and spent too much time holed up in his room, doing things on the computer they had no idea he could do.

"I've got the money," Oliver responded. He'd had to pawn Jane's wedding ring, which she'd inherited from her grandmother, to get the money he needed, but the ring didn't fit her anymore, anyway. She'd gotten too fat, hadn't even glanced inside her jewelry box in ages. "The question is...do you have what *I'm* looking for?"

"Of course. I told you I'd get it, didn't I?" The kid reached into another pocket and pulled out a piece of paper that had been folded into a tight square. "It's right here."

"Let me see it."

The boy he knew only as *Iseeyou@Internetcraze.com* handed the paper over without hesitation, and Oliver opened it to see an address on Sherman Island. He was familiar enough with the delta, having studied it after that news broadcast he'd seen in the hospital, to know that Sherman Island was one of the delta's myriad small towns. But it could still be a made-up address.

He studied the kid skeptically. "How do I know this isn't fake?"

"Because it's not," *Iseeyou* said with a careless shrug.

"How'd you get it?"

"None of your business. But I can find anyone, anywhere—as long as they've got family, friends, utilities, credit cards, property. You can run but you can't hide." His cocky grin was definitely at odds with his braces, but Oliver didn't care about that. After waiting *months* for Victor to provide this information, and walking away empty-handed, he finally had what he wanted. This two-bit teenage hood-in-the-making was able to get it for him in a matter of three days.

"Nice work," he said, suitably impressed.

"You can thank me with the money." The boy held out his hand when Oliver made no move to pay him.

"You shouldn't have given it to me until I gave you the cash. Now I have no incentive to follow through with my end of the bargain." Without his knife, Oliver knew he couldn't overpower most people, but he felt sure he could teach this teen a lesson—until the kid motioned to either end of the alley and he saw that the boy wasn't alone. Two other teenagers, both of whom looked very much like *Iseeyou,* blocked the openings, each holding a switch-blade.

"You're smarter than you look," he told the kid as he pulled out the money.

"That's the problem with the citizens of this country. They judge people by appearances."

"Comes in handy for you, doesn't it?"

"Sometimes." *Iseeyou@Internetcraze.com* counted the bills, then nodded. "You're free to go. You know how to reach me if you ever want to do business again."

When Oliver didn't leave, the boy stalked off ahead of him to join his associate at the north end of the alley. The third boy disappeared before Oliver could turn to check on him; he was probably going around to meet the other two rather than risk an altercation by coming straight through.

"Damn smart," Oliver muttered, and chuckled as he imagined those kids blowing all five hundred bucks at an arcade. Video games were one hell of a waste of a one-carat diamond, but Oliver had what he needed. That was all that mattered.

The house was dark and closed up tight when Jane arrived, and the truck Noah had lent Oliver was gone. She didn't think anyone was home.

"Oliver?" The last time Jane had spoken to her husband was just after lunch, when he'd promised to pick up Kate from his parents' house at four o'clock. Jane was grateful he was pitching in—the traffic was always so bad when she got off at six. But if he'd gotten Kate, he certainly hadn't brought her home. There was no backpack on the kitchen table, where she usually tossed it, no sign that she'd been here at all.

Had Oliver left Kate at his parents' house? Maybe he'd taken the truck back to Wendy, and Wendy had given him a ride home. In that case, he could be sitting in one of the back bedrooms in the dark. He did that sometimes. Or maybe he'd gone out on his bike....

"Oliver?" she called as she walked from room to room.

It made her uneasy to think of Kate alone with him. Noah didn't believe Oliver was dangerous, but last night had convinced Jane. She was still shaken from it, knew she'd never be able to look at him again without suspicion.

The guest bathroom door was closed. Thinking she'd found him, she stood outside it and knocked. "Oliver?"

There was no response.

Opening it, she discovered that the room was slightly damp, as if he'd recently had a hot shower. Why he hadn't used the shower in *their* bathroom, she didn't know. But, obviously, if he was gone, he hadn't left all that long ago.

She started to move on when a disposable razor sitting on the edge of the sink caught her eye. Entering the small bathroom, she saw a can of shaving cream in the shower, too. It hadn't been there before. The sight of it motivated her to look further and, sure enough, there was a lot of curly dark hair in the drain.

Pubic hair. Oliver had shaved himself.

A lot of men shave. He was a cyclist.

Cyclists shave their arms and legs.

It's popular to do a lot more than that these days.

But Oliver hadn't done it since he'd been home and he'd been biking for almost a week. Why now?

Jane's stomach began to churn. What was he up to? Was he waiting for her in one of the back bedrooms?

The floor creaked as she checked Kate's room. She paused, listening for other noises, but heard only the barking of the neighbor's dog and two teenagers yelling obscenities at each other while they skateboarded in the parking lot of the nearby convenience store.

"Oliver? Are you home?" She pushed open the cracked door of their master bedroom, listening to the hinges squeal as it swung wide.

The bed was neatly made.

Oliver wasn't in it.

She checked the master bath, then hurried back to the kitchen, where she picked up the phone and called her in-laws.

"This is Jane," she said as soon as Betty answered.

"Hi, Jane. Are you running a little late today?"

"Oliver was planning to come by for Kate. Has he shown up yet?"

"Not yet, dear."

The relief that swept through her made her knees weak. She needed to get out of here, she decided, and she needed to take Kate with her. She didn't know what she'd do or where she'd go, but she knew she couldn't stay, couldn't live in constant fear. There had to be shelters and other hiding places for women like her. She'd go online and find one, so they wouldn't spend the

night in the street. Then she'd grab Kate and get as far
away from Sacramento as she could.

"Noah's coming over soon," Betty was saying. "Do
you want me to ask if he'll drop Kate off on his way
home?"

Jane twisted the phone cord nervously around the
fingers of one hand. It pinched, hurting the cuticles
she'd shredded, but she scarcely felt the pain. "No, uh,
I'm planning to surprise her with a little outing, a
mommy/daughter date. Don't…uh…don't let her go
with anyone else, okay? I-I'll be over to get her in
thirty minutes."

"No problem," Betty said. "How was work?"

Jane didn't have time to chitchat. "Good, but Kate and
I will be late for our movie if I don't hurry, so I'll talk to
you in a few minutes." She hoped Noah wouldn't be
there when she arrived. She didn't want to face him,
couldn't stand the contempt in his eyes. He thought she
was crazy, that she'd finally lost it. But it was Oliver who
wasn't right. She was sure of it.

"You bet, dear," Betty said. "See you soon."

Jane tripped on the cord, knocking the phone off the
hook in her haste to get back to the bedroom, but she
didn't bother to pick it up. She didn't dare waste a
second. Dragging a suitcase from under Kate's bed, she
threw some of her daughter's clothes in it, pulled it across
the hall and piled in some of her own.

Then she paused. What if Oliver tracked her down?
Sued her for custody of Kate? That would mean trouble.
She had only her suspicion to back her up. She had to be
able to convince a court of law. Or she could lose Kate.
To him.

Remembering the object Oliver had concealed from her last night while he was having his fun at her expense, she glanced around the room. Where would he have hidden it?

In the dresser? She pulled out one drawer after the other and dumped the clothes on the floor.

Nothing.

Between the mattresses? She tore the bed apart. Again, nothing.

Under the furniture? Getting down on her hands and knees, she put her cheek to the carpet and looked underneath the bed frame, dressers and nightstand.

No.

What was it and where had he put it? She suspected it was a knife. It wasn't until she'd voiced her concerns to Noah that she'd become completely convinced of that, but now she couldn't imagine it was anything else. He'd been reliving his past crimes, using her to fantasize.

Then she remembered the notebook he was always scribbling in. She didn't know if it contained anything that could help her. He was fiercely possessive of it and wouldn't let her read it. She hadn't even tried since he'd been home. It was all in some kind of code, anyway. But she was fairly sure she knew where he kept it.

Reaching a hand between the wall and the headboard, she brought out that notebook and began glancing through the pages. It was mostly in code, all right, one he'd made up on his own, if she had her guess. But there was also a picture of Skye he'd cut out of the paper.

Shoving it in her purse, which she wore across her body to keep her hands free, she charged into the bathroom. She had to find that knife. Then she'd know

beyond the shadow of a doubt that Oliver was everything
Detective Willis said, and she could show that knife to
Noah and the rest of the family, if need be.

After scooping out the hairspray, cosmetics and nail
polish from the cabinet under the sink, she took off her
purse and rolled onto her back to peer up at the
plumbing. Had Oliver taped his weapon up there, where
he'd assume she'd never look? No. Again she came up
empty-handed, as she did when she checked the under-
side of the toilet-bowl lid.

Damn it! Putting her purse back on, she glanced nervously at her watch. She'd have to give up. He'd probably
taken it with him. And she couldn't risk staying in the
house much longer. Oliver could come home any second.
She knew he didn't love her, but she also knew he
wouldn't want to lose her, or Kate. Having a wife and
child ensured that his family remained sympathetic to
him and helped him keep up appearances while he
plotted and planned with his stupid notebooks and coded
words. She was also his meal ticket right now.

Heart racing, she took a final look around. The mess
alone would drive Oliver crazy, she thought with satisfaction, and headed out of the bathroom to get the
suitcase. As terrifying as her actions were, she felt
strangely empowered, free. She was leaving him. She
would never have to suffer his touch again. There had to
be something better for her out there....

She was dragging the heavy suitcase down the hall
when a new thought occurred to her. Although Oliver had
always kept the receipts for everything he purchased and
entered it in QuickBooks, he wouldn't be stupid enough
to save a receipt that showed he'd bought a knife. She

was pretty sure he wasn't allowed to own anything other than simple kitchen knives without violating his parole. So, if she could prove he possessed something on the list of forbidden objects, they'd send him back to prison, wouldn't they? Then she'd be able to keep the house and her job until she could come up with a better solution.

Chances were good that he'd disposed of the receipt immediately, before he even drove home. And if he hadn't, he'd probably thrown it in the trash.

Dropping the heavy suitcase in the middle of the living room floor, she adjusted her purse so it wouldn't get in the way as she rummaged through the inside garbage. When she didn't find what she was looking for, she went out the side door and lifted the lid of the county's refuse can.

A car pulled into the drive before she could dig very far.

Heart pounding, Jane peered through the cracks of the fence. Just as she'd feared, it was Oliver.

David grimaced when caller ID on his cell phone indicated his ex-wife was trying to get hold of him. Her timing, if she wanted to ruin his evening, was almost perfect. He'd just pulled into Skye's driveway and was reaching for the wine he'd bought.

With a frown, he turned the ringer to vibrate and shoved the phone in his pocket. He refused to let her make him feel guilty right now. But when she called back two more times before he could even get out of the damn car, he decided he'd better answer. God forbid, but it was possible that there was some problem with Jeremy.

"What's going on?" he asked, trying to quell his impatience.

"Hey!" Her voice sounded thick, strange.

"What's wrong?"

"Nothing. I'm out having a good time."

He could hear music in the background, but it was distant, as if she was standing outside a building. "Where's Jeremy?"

"At my mother's."

That was odd, too. Lynnette's mother rarely agreed to babysit. She occasionally dropped by on a Sunday afternoon to take Jeremy out for ice cream, but she'd been single for the past ten years, ever since Lynnette's father had left her for a much younger woman, and liked to go ballroom dancing on the weekends. She and Lynnette had never really gotten along.

"How'd you convince her to do that?"

"I told her you were fucking someone else, just like Dad did, and she felt sorry for me."

David bit back the anger that rose at her words. There were more differences than similarities between him and her father. David had never slept with another woman while they were married. And he hadn't left her for someone else.

But it wasn't worth arguing about. Not when she was obviously intoxicated. "Is there a reason for this call?"

"Your car wasn't in the lot at your apartment building."

"I hope to God you're not driving tonight."

"Why would you care?"

"You could kill someone."

She laughed bitterly. "So it's not me you're worried about."

He glanced toward the house, anxious to get off the

phone. "I don't want anything to happen to you, either. You know that."

"Where are you?" she asked.

"Out."

"With *her?*"

David took a deep breath. "Lynnette, have fun tonight, but make sure you have someone drive you home."

"I'm not going to my place. I'm going to find someone to go home with."

"Whatever." He honestly didn't care, but that seemed to be the very thing that pushed her over the edge.

"What'd you say?"

"Do what makes you happy."

"You son of a bitch!"

"Lynnette—"

"I hope Burke *does* kill her!" she said vehemently and the phone went dead.

David looked tired and upset when he came to the door. Skye had no way of knowing what had happened since they'd seen each other at lunch, but she could tell that his afternoon hadn't been good.

"You okay?" she murmured as she stepped back to admit him.

"I've been better." He handed her a bottle of wine, but she didn't take it to the kitchen. She held it, watching him. "What's going on?"

With a sigh, he scraped a hand over his whisker-roughened jaw. "Don't worry about it." He smiled. "I'm not going to let it ruin dinner."

For her. Because whatever was troubling him had already ruined his. And it had to be personal. If it was work-related, he would've told her what was bothering him, even if he didn't want to get specific: Another case came in.... I'm at a dead end with Bishop.... I'm afraid I'll never be able to prove Oliver was behind those murders.... *Something.*

Skye set the wine on the shelf of the hall tree, but she didn't take her eyes off him. "You don't have to be here if you don't want to be, David," she said softly.

"It's not that," he told her.

And yet he obviously felt torn. "Is it Lynnette?"

He raked his fingers through his hair. "Come on, something smells good in here."

She refused to let him tug her into the kitchen. "Quit shutting me out."

"I'm not shutting you out. I'm trying not to burden you with my problems, okay? I can't imagine you want to hear me complain about my ex-wife. Isn't that some kind of standing joke about dating a divorced guy?"

She pulled out of his grasp. "It's not as if I want to dwell on your past relationships, but there's got to be some sort of happy medium. She's part of your life, David, and because of Jeremy she always will be. If we're going to...to be seeing each other, even casually, she'll be part of my life, too, right?"

He pinched the bridge of his nose for a few seconds before dropping his hand. "Is that what you think? That this is casual?"

"I don't know what it is yet, do you?" She was carrying his baby, but she doubted he'd welcome that news. And she knew the existence of a baby didn't nec-essarily change anything between them. There were too many other problems to deal with first.

"I sure as hell know it isn't casual," he said. "I wouldn't be doing what I'm doing just to get in your pants!"

"But don't you understand? That's what you're making this when you won't let me shoulder some of your emotional load. What, you'd rather set me off to the side somewhere and come by only when you'd like to get laid? How deep is that?"

"I'm trying to save the evening. What the hell do you want from me?"

"More than a fun date, that's for sure! You think I can't take the bad with the good? That I'll run at the first hint of the problems you're trying to shelter me from?"

Glaring at her, he muttered a curse. "Fine," he said. "Lynnette's out partying tonight, okay? I wouldn't care about that, except she seems to be unraveling. And if she can't hold herself together, where will that leave my son?"

Lynnette wasn't going to let David go easily. Skye knew that from the conversation they'd had on the phone. "Where is he now?"

"With his grandma."

"Is that a good place?"

"Physically, he's safe. But Lynnette's mother wears her emotional scars like some badge of honor and is always spouting off her theory that men aren't capable of loving anyone, that their emotions are all self-serving and superficial. I don't like what she says to my son, how she makes him feel about the fact that he'll grow up and become something she can't admire. And I can guess what she's saying about me." Now that Skye had him talking, it all came out in an angry torrent. "Maybe I could put up with it and simply try to talk him out of the pseudo-feminist bullshit she fills his head with if she liked little boys any better than men, but she doesn't. She prefers her other grandchild—a girl, of course. She dotes on Amberly. But Jeremy's a different story."

Pivoting, Skye left him standing in the entry so she could turn off the oven, where she was cooking her mother's special rosemary-and-herb chicken and potatoes.

"What are you doing?" he asked, nearly bumping into her when she emerged from the kitchen.

She grabbed the wool coat hanging on the hall tree. "Getting ready to leave."

"What for?"

"Because we're going to pick him up."

"What about dinner?" he asked.

"It can wait till we get back." She turned to face him, knowing this was the moment of truth. "Unless you have some objection to including your son in our evening together."

Skye held her breath as she waited for David to respond. If he wouldn't allow her to associate with his son, their relationship was doomed from the start. How could they ever get close, and stay that way, if he refused to share the things that were most important to him?

"Well?" she said earnestly when he didn't immediately give her an answer.

Cupping her face, he stared down at her for several seconds, his gaze turbulent, intense. Then he kissed her more tenderly than she'd ever been kissed. "Let's go."

Oliver had never looked more docile than he did as he got out of the truck he'd borrowed from Noah and shut the door. Taking a piece of paper out of his pocket, he glanced down at it, smiled, then whistled as he bounded up the walk.

Jane thought of the suitcase lying in the middle of the floor, the overturned drawers, the scattered items in the bathroom and felt panic rise like a hot air balloon in her chest. He'd know she couldn't be far; her car was parked right next to his truck. And she had his notebook. If he caught her with that...

She had to leave *now,* without so much as a change of clothes. She couldn't waste even thirty seconds. By then he'd realize what she was doing.

She heard him call her name, knew he was walking through the house as she had done and was so frightened she almost couldn't get her limbs to move. *Open the gate! Run!*

One hand fumbled in her purse for her keys as she lifted the latch and darted out.

"Jane? What's going on?"

Oliver's voice came from inside the house as she opened her car door and ducked inside. She tried to start the engine, but it merely coughed and sputtered and, after a few revs, died.

"Come on, baby. Not now," she mumbled, cranking the starter again. "Not now."

The noise brought Oliver to the window. Just as the recalcitrant engine fired, she saw the look on his face, and it terrified her. He was a soulless stranger, a man she'd never really known.

He disappeared, presumably headed for the door. Afraid he'd reach her before she could get away, she wrenched the gearshift into Reverse and floored the accelerator. The Lincoln jetted back and crashed into her neighbor's car. The impact caused a whiplash effect, which slammed Jane's mouth against the steering wheel, but she didn't stop, even for a second. In some deep recess of her brain, she knew if Oliver managed to drag her back inside the house she wouldn't come out of it alive.

"Jane! Stop!" he called as she rocketed away.

She heard nothing but the screech of her own brakes as she took the corner at forty miles an hour. An Acura was coming the other way. She had to swerve to avoid a head-on and sideswiped a tree, but she didn't care. She was high on adrenaline, panting for breath and shaking so badly she could hardly drive.

The burning smell of rubber filled her nostrils as she squealed around the next corner, joining the traffic on Sunrise Boulevard. At that point, she couldn't travel very fast. She could only watch her rearview mirror to make sure Oliver wasn't following her.

But he didn't have to follow her. He knew where she was going.

His parents still had Kate.

22

Planning to race after Jane, to chase her down, Oliver yanked the keys from his pocket and jumped into the truck. He didn't know what the heck was going on, but he wasn't about to let her leave him. Had she found the pills he'd purchased from the tattoo parlor? That had to be it. He couldn't imagine anything else that would send her into such a panic. She'd been fine when he'd talked to her at work this afternoon.

He'd find her and bring her home, where he could talk her out of her fears. She'd believe him because she wanted to believe him. She'd believed him up until now, hadn't she? But if she was on her way to get Kate, he'd have his parents to contend with, too....

He was already making up the lie he'd use when he got there—*Those pills are just something I take when I can't sleep.... Jane knows about that, she's had problems sleeping in the past.... It's not easy adjusting to the outside....*—when another thought occurred to him.

He slammed on his brakes. What if Jane wasn't going to his parents' house? What if she was going to the police?

The gears growled as he threw the standard transmission into Reverse. Backing up, he parked in the drive. The truck sat there crookedly, but he didn't care.

The collision moments earlier had brought the neighbor into the street. She was pointing and screaming about the dent Jane had left in her car.

Oliver couldn't deal with that right now. If Jane was going to the police, he didn't have much time. He had to retrieve everything that might incriminate him. But if she had the pills he'd just bought, there wasn't a lot to recover. He had the knife with the eight-inch blade and Skye's address in his pocket. And he'd wiped the memory on his PC, so no one could trace where he'd been on the Internet. All he had to do was grab his notebook.

"Hey, what're you going to do about this?" the neighbor demanded, jogging across the lawn to catch him before he could enter the house.

"Our insurance will cover it, ma'am, no problem," he said politely.

"You have insurance?"

"Of course. What kind of people do you think we are?"

As usual, his pleasant smile and courteous manner worked, and she began to settle down. "The woman who lives here seems nice enough," she said, a little sulkily. "Keeps to herself for the most part. I didn't even know she was married. Are you her husband or something?"

"Yes. We've been married for eleven years. You haven't seen me because I've been in prison for attempted rape."

This caused the neighbor's eyes to widen and her jaw to drop.

"I was reckless enough to use a knife, which sort of compounded the charges," he confided with a grin. "Assault with a deadly weapon and all that."

Blinking rapidly, she backed up. "Oh…well…never mind. I guess we can figure it out later," she said and ran straight home.

"Okay," he called after her. "I'll have Jane stop by when she gets back." *Bitch,* he added under his breath, then stalked into the house.

At the sight of Jane's suitcase lying on the floor, his hands curled into fists. Whatever she was doing, she wouldn't get away with it. She wasn't intelligent enough to outsmart him. He'd lived with her for eleven years, and she'd never suspected him of anything.

Kicking the suitcase aside, he went directly to the coat closet, where he removed the floorboard and checked for the pills.

They were there, exactly where he'd left them.

What did that mean? What had set Jane off?

He didn't know, but he didn't dare take any chances. Shoving the pills in his pocket, he hurried into the bedroom to get his notebook. Jane had torn the bed apart, looking for something. The bathroom was in no better state than the bedroom. Which wasn't fair at all. He'd controlled himself with her last night; it wasn't as if she could claim he'd abused her. And she'd been fine this morning. At least, she'd acted fine.

The mess made him uneasy. What had she been looking for? And what had she found?

He didn't have time to wonder. Returning to the bedroom, he reached behind the headboard, where he'd stashed his notebook.

It wasn't there.

Oliver's blood ran cold. She'd never paid much attention to his notebooks before. He wrote enough regular stuff in them, about job opportunities, investment opportunities, plans for a new house, car or pool, that it shouldn't give her any cause for alarm.

Unless she'd cracked his code.

Surely she hadn't managed that....

But just in case she hadn't already turned it over to the cops, he *had* to get to Kate before she did. Kate might be the only thing for which she'd be willing to trade that notebook. Oliver didn't think that what he'd written would be enough to incriminate him on its own. He hadn't recorded details. But he couldn't take that risk. Even if she hadn't cracked his code—and she probably hadn't—the police had people and computers that could.

Noah was at the Burkes' when Jane arrived. The sight of his truck in the drive made her chest ache with longing. But she steeled herself against the pain. He didn't want her. They couldn't have each other, even if he did.

She had to think about Kate. Only Kate.

Checking the street one last time, she got out of the car. Driving down Sunrise, she hadn't seen any sign of Oliver. It was easier to watch for him once she'd turned onto Zinfandel because there was less traffic, but as far as she could tell, he wasn't following her.

Thank God.

Jogging up to the house, she rang the doorbell. Normally, she would've knocked, then walked inside. But after her recent exchange with Noah, she felt estranged somehow. Without physical proof, she knew Betty and

Maurice wouldn't believe her about Oliver's rough treatment, any more than Noah had. And losing faith had put her in a different camp altogether—the enemy camp.

Betty answered the door. "Is it true?" she said without a greeting.

Jane didn't know how to respond. Red rimmed her mother-in-law's eyes as if she'd been crying, and there were tears in her voice.

"Is—is what true?" Jane stammered. Noah had warned her not to tell his folks what she'd told him. He hadn't driven over here and volunteered the information himself. Or had he?

"Don't play stupid. Not now." Betty's voice cracked. "Have you been sleeping with Noah?"

Jane's heart nearly seized in her chest. "N-no," she said. It was an exclamation of dismay, not a denial of the truth, but Betty didn't interpret it that way.

"That isn't what *they* say." She stepped aside and pointed at the people behind her.

Jane's eyes cut to the living room. Wendy was there with Noah. They sat side by side on the couch, holding hands. Maurice was there, too, in his recliner. Initially, she'd seen only his legs, but now he leaned forward to get a look at her face.

"Why would Noah confess if it isn't true?" he demanded. Gone was the friendly smile he usually reserved for her.

Jane could barely speak above the rushing of blood in her ears. "I—I didn't mean to," she said softly.

"How do you not *mean* to have an affair with someone else's husband?" Wendy wanted to know. Her eyes, usually so kind and forgiving, watched Jane with such disappointment it was almost more than Jane could bear. She loved these people. They'd been her family; she had no one else.

But whatever they'd been to each other was over. She had to worry about Oliver, had to get Kate and go away. "Where's my daughter?" she asked.

"She's in the back, coloring. Do you think I'd want her to hear this?" Betty responded.

Jane licked dry lips. "Will you get her for me, please?"

"Are you kidding?" Betty shook her head. "You don't deserve her. Oliver's been through hell—do you hear me? Hell! And for you to do this to him in addition to everything else he's endured…."

Despite her heartbreak, a spark of anger came to Jane's rescue. "You don't get to decide whether or not I deserve my own daughter."

"Yes, I do. Oliver just called. He said you're leaving him. He said not to let you take Kate, that you must be on something, you're acting so crazy. And Noah agrees with him."

First, Noah had betrayed her to Wendy, then to his parents, and now he was siding with Oliver. It was the lowest blow yet. "Crazy," she repeated in amazement, staring at him.

"You need help." Noah had difficulty meeting her eyes, but that was little comfort in the wake of what he'd done. Now she had no credibility whatsoever. The elder Burkes didn't even want to let her take Kate.

"Kate's my daughter, too. You have no right to keep her from me," Jane said.

Noah spoke up. "You're not stable."

He believed it, she realized. He knew her better than any of them, and yet he fully believed what he'd just said.

"We'll release her to her father," Maurice added.

Jane rounded on her father-in-law, struggling to keep the hysteria from her voice as she started to laugh, but it was impossible. "You think her father's stable? Her father is a murderer!"

"You—you don't know that," Betty stammered.

Jane confronted her mother-in-law with defiance for probably the first time. "Yes, I do."

Betty's face fell, as if part of her feared it was true, but Jane knew Oliver's mother would never stand up against the others in the room. Leaning to one side in order to look past her, Jane addressed Noah. "I'm pretty sure he bought another knife this week. I think he was tempted to use it on me last night. If you don't do something fast, he's going to hurt someone. Do you want to live with *that* on your conscience? If having sex with me made you feel guilty, try that on for size."

Maurice got to his feet, his ruddy face even redder than usual. "You're talking about Kate's *father.*"

"You think I don't know that?" Jane shouted. "That's caused me more pain than you can imagine. But his connection to Kate isn't what's bothering you. It's his connection to *you.* He's your son. If he's a killer, you have to ask yourself, 'Where did I go wrong? How did I miss it?'"

Noah released Wendy's hand and stood, too. "Stop it, Jane! They've been through enough without you making things worse."

"And I haven't been through enough?" she countered. "If you won't give me my daughter, I'll come back with the police."

"I guess you'll have to do that," Maurice said.

"Because I won't let you drive off with Kate, not in your present state of mind. She's Oliver's daughter, too. And, regardless of what you think right now, he's entitled to some consideration. He's paid his debt to society."

Panic fluttered at the edges of Jane's mind. She *had* to get her daughter and get out of here. She was afraid Oliver would show up before she could return with the police and the Burkes would hand Kate over. Without any proof that he'd broken his parole or done anything wrong, she wasn't sure Detective Willis or anyone else could help her. They'd tell her this was a family dispute, that it'd have to be handled in divorce court.

Saying a silent prayer, she nodded stiffly. "Fine. I'll be back." She stalked off.

Trying to make her reaction as believable as possible, she reversed out of the driveway, parked around the block and returned to the house on foot.

From the side window, she could see Noah, Wendy, Betty and Maurice in the living room, talking intently— which meant Kate was still in the back room, being sheltered from the conversation.

Jane could only hope….

Her heart banged against her chest as she slipped through the gate leading into the backyard. Betty and Maurice had a Saint Bernard, but Horse knew her well enough that he didn't bark. He was so big and lazy he probably wouldn't have bothered to get worked up, anyway, even for a stranger. He stood and lumbered over to greet her and, when she'd given him a pat, resumed his nap on the comfortable pad in his doghouse.

"Good dog, Horse," she whispered and made her way to the rear entrance of the house.

Because the Burkes were expecting the police at their front door, not a kidnapping through the back, Jane wasn't surprised to find the door unlocked. Kate often came out to play with the dog or use the swing set, so it was generally open during the day.

Stepping inside, she moved as quietly as possible, quickly arriving at the room the Burkes had converted to an extra bedroom for Kate. She played here, watched Disney movies here, even slept here upon occasion.

Jane was worried about the noise her daughter might make when she entered the room. One squeal could give them away. But Kate was so mesmerized by Cinderella dancing with Prince Charming that when Jane cracked open the door, she didn't look up.

It was Jane who spoke first. "Kate, you must be very quiet, okay?" she whispered. "Mommy's come to get you, but Grandma and Grandpa mustn't know we're leaving."

"Mommy!"

"Shh."

Kate's eyebrows gathered above her glasses. "Why are we whispering?"

"I just told you. We can't let anyone hear us."

"Why not?"

"I'll tell you in the car. Promise me you won't make a sound. If you're very, very quiet, Mommy will buy you an ice cream cone."

Kate started to clap enthusiastically, but Jane stilled her hands. Then she embraced her daughter, nearly overcome with relief to have Kate in her arms.

"Grab your shoes," she said. "You can put them on in the car."

"But it's cold outside."

Jane pressed a finger to her daughter's lips as a reminder. "That's okay. We'll turn on the heater as soon as we're inside. We have to hurry, Kate. Move fast."

Kate must've sensed the gravity of the situation because she grew very somber. "Won't Grandma be mad?"

"No, Grandma will be fine. She's busy, and I don't want to disturb her. We'll call her later, okay?"

Although Kate seemed puzzled by this answer, she didn't argue. She quietly collected her shoes and allowed Jane to take her hand and lead her out. But they hadn't quite reached the back door when Jane heard what she'd been listening for all along: Oliver's voice in the living room.

"What did you say?" Oliver asked. Fear was sending rivulets of sweat down his back, making his starched shirt stick to him. He felt frantic, cornered. How had Jane, of all people, done this to him?

"Jane's been here and gone," his mother said.

The panic swelled. "You didn't let her take Kate…."

"No. Kate's coloring in the back room."

"Good." He sighed in relief and started to cut through the living room, where Noah, Wendy and his father were sitting, watching him anxiously. What had Jane told them? Whatever it was, he'd have to repair the damage. But not now. He didn't have time.

His mother caught his arm before he'd taken five steps. "Jane claims she's bringing the police."

All the more reason to hurry. "We're having some marital problems," he explained. "But don't worry. We'll work it out."

"We hope so," his father said.

His mother's eyes darted to Noah, then she cleared her throat. "There's something we need to tell you." Sympathy softened her expression as she drew him toward the couch, toward the others.

Oliver attempted to extricate himself. "If she's bringing the cops, I'd better get Kate and go. Who knows what that Detective Willis will do? There's no need to have Kate involved in some tug-of-war. Especially since things'll be fine once Jane cools down."

"We've got a few minutes," his mother said. "Jane just left. And this…this is important, too. It might explain some of Jane's behavior, help you understand what's really happening. I think we should get it all out here and now, then put it behind us."

The stunned silence he'd encountered since his arrival finally seeped through Oliver's preoccupation, convincing him he had to deal with the damage Jane had caused right now. Quickly. "Listen, I don't know what Jane told you, but you can bet it's not true. I've always treated her like a queen. We're in the middle of an argument, that's all."

"Sit down, Oliver," his father said.

His father's somber demeanor made Oliver even more nervous. He did as he was told, but only because he was always polite to his parents. "What is it?" He glanced from one face to the next. Everyone looked ashen, especially Noah, who was hanging his head and staring at the carpet.

When no one spoke, Oliver appealed to his mother. "Mom?"

She nodded in Noah's direction. Noah straightened and met Oliver's eyes. "I—I don't know how to say this,

Oliver." Tears filled his eyes, began to drip down his cheeks.

"What is it?" Oliver said again. "Has someone died?"

"No. Thank the Lord it isn't that," his mother murmured, but Oliver could barely hear her because Noah was talking again.

"Jane and I had an affair," he mumbled. "While you were in prison."

At first, Oliver was convinced he'd misunderstood. Surely, his brother didn't say what he'd thought he said. Wendy was sitting right there; his parents were in the room. *"What?"*

"I'm sorry," Noah said. "I'm so sorry." Wendy placed a comforting hand on her husband's thigh as the tears were coming faster now.

Oliver swallowed hard, his brother's confession spinning around and around in his head. *Jane and I had an affair....* "You slept with my wife?" he said. "All those cold nights when I was lying awake in San Quentin, pining for Jane, she was fucking you?"

They all glanced awkwardly at each other, obviously uncomfortable with his language. He didn't typically use obscenities. It was too low-class, and Oliver aspired to something higher. But that was what it boiled down to, wasn't it? Noah and Jane had been going at it like animals.

And that was probably why she was leaving him now. Oliver had blamed so much on Skye. In a roundabout way, Skye *was* responsible, even for this, because he would never have gone to prison without her testimony. But she hadn't forced Noah to usurp *his* position in Jane's bed.

If he couldn't trust his own brother, who could he trust?

"I—I had to come clean, Oliver," Noah was saying, "to tell Wendy and you and everyone else. I couldn't stand the constant lies, couldn't look myself in the eye anymore. I don't understand how it happened in the first place. But now the spell is broken. I—I won't ever make a mistake like that again. And I hope that, someday, you'll be able to forgive me."

Forgive him? Oliver almost laughed aloud. What kind of man screwed his brother's wife, then went to him to say, "Oops, sorry." And Jane—how could Jane deceive him all that time?

He remembered the last call he'd placed from prison, when Noah had been at his house. Jane had said Noah was there to fix the plumbing. Now he knew the only plumbing his brother had been working on was hers.

The images that passed through his mind made him sick. He'd been wrong about Jane. She was no better than all the other women in his life, women like Miranda Dodge, Patty Poindexter, Skye Kellerman. They thought they were too good, that if they held out long enough someone better would come by.

"You're the reason she's leaving me," he said.

Noah's gaze dropped to the carpet. "I—I tried to break if off with her. She just…didn't want to let it die. But I know she'll come around. She's confused, like the rest of us. Maybe we can get some counseling, do something to heal after everything we've been through. I'm willing to do whatever's necessary."

"He's sorry," Betty reiterated. "He didn't mean for this to happen."

"We have to do what we can to hold our family

together," Wendy said. "I'm doing my best to forgive him, to save our relationship. I'm hoping, after you've had a chance to think about it, that you'll be able to do the same with Jane."

"You're letting him back in your bed after what he's done?" Oliver asked.

Wendy flushed. "He made a mistake, Oliver. They both did. It was a difficult situation. He was going over there all the time to help out, he felt sorry for Jane, and she was so lonely. Please, try to understand."

"I don't want to understand," he said. "I was in prison when he stole my wife."

Noah visibly blanched. "I feel terrible."

Witnessing his humiliation, Oliver felt almost triumphant. He'd always been second-best to Noah—second-best in his father's affections, second-best in his mother's admiration, second-best in the esteem of others. Noah had been tall and handsome and far more athletic than Oliver. He'd been much more successful with the girls. But that was just the point. Noah had all that—and still he'd taken Jane, Oliver's one prize.

What kind of brother did that?

A dead one, he decided. "Get Kate," he said dully.

Betty wrung her hands. "Oliver, I—I don't know if you should take Kate tonight. This is all so fresh and painful, and—and you're upset. I wouldn't want her to hear about any of this. Let's spare her what we can, okay?"

"Get my daughter before Jane returns with the police."

"Oliver—"

Standing, he avoided her clutching hands and strode

quickly down the hallway. "Kate? Kate, your dad's here. Let's go."

There was no answer. The others trailed after him, arguing, apologizing, cajoling and trying to convince him he should leave Kate behind for the night. But he ignored them. Reaching the door to his daughter's room, he swung it wide—only to find it empty.

23

"Grandma wasn't very nice tonight," Jeremy said.

David glanced in his rearview mirror. It was after midnight, but his son seemed wide-awake as they drove home from Skye's. "She's not very happy with me right now, I'm afraid."

"She said you're a scum-sucking pig, like all men."

David wanted to say something about what a nasty old crone she was, but he held his tongue. "People sometimes say things they don't mean when they're upset," he said and thought that was pretty generous, coming from a scum-sucking pig.

"Is that why Mommy said you're worse than Grandpa? That you're gonna run off and leave us and you don't even care that she's going to die?"

"She's not going to die." He hoped. "And I'd never leave you, you know that. Your mother and her mother are just confused."

Silence reigned for a few minutes, then Jeremy spoke again. "I heard Mom tell Grandma that Skye wants to spread her legs for you."

This angered David more than anything else. Lynnette should be more careful about what she said in front of their son. "What's that supposed to mean?" he asked, playing dumb.

Jeremy wrinkled his nose. "That's what I was going to ask you."

"Your mom shouldn't talk about Skye since she's never even met her."

"I know! Skye's nice. I like her."

"I do, too." *A lot.* Tonight hadn't been anything like he'd expected, but it had been exactly what he and Jeremy had needed. The three of them had shared a quiet dinner, watched the movie *Cars,* which they'd picked up at the video store, and then had dessert. They'd been planning to have a bowl of ice cream, but Jeremy had told Skye she'd missed his eighth birthday last month, so she'd insisted on baking him a cake to go with the ice cream. He'd loved the attention, and he'd deserved it. David had been preoccupied with work lately. And Lynnette was so consumed with her health problems and meeting her own emotional needs, David didn't see how she could be very sensitive to Jeremy's. What she'd said to her mother right in front of him was a case in point.

"Did you like the movie?" David changed the subject, hoping the talk he needed to have with his son could wait until morning.

"Yeah."

David and Skye had purposely not touched each other in Jeremy's presence, which had left David a little unsatisfied, but he hoped the friendly way they'd behaved had been reassuring to his son.

"So are we going to see Skye again?" Jeremy asked.

David gripped the steering wheel tighter, almost

afraid to ask the question that immediately came to his lips. "Would you like to?"

His son paused. "Does it mean you won't be moving home?"

Evidently, they were going to have to have The Talk tonight. David considered pulling over, so he could give Jeremy his full attention, but he was afraid the dramatic impact of that would only frighten him, so he kept driving.

"Jeremy, I won't be moving home—but Skye's not the reason."

He looked bewildered, then sad. "What is?"

"You know how you and Josh Palmer used to be really good friends in second grade?"

"Yeah."

"But you don't really hang out together anymore."

"Yeah."

"You told me it's because you like to do different things now."

"We do. I play soccer at recess, and he plays tetherball."

"But you still like him."

"Sure."

"That's how I feel about your mother. We used to enjoy the same things. But as the years passed, we started to change and pretty soon we had different interests and weren't as good at being together."

"But she says you're gonna let her d-die alone."

"I'll do as much for her as I can. I promise."

Jeremy said nothing.

"Do you understand?" David asked.

"I guess." He stared at his feet. "You're going to stay divorced, right?"

The full realization of his failure made David wince. But he knew he had to face the truth. Doing anything else would merely put off the inevitable. "That's right. But it'll be that way whether I continue to see Skye or not, so don't blame her." David wished there was an easier way to break the news, but he couldn't think of one. "I'm sorry, buddy. Your mom and I tried to make it work for a long time, mostly because we both care so much about you."

"That won't change, will it?" Jeremy's gaze finally lifted from his sneakers.

David pulled to the side of the road and twisted in his seat to look back at him. *Now* he wanted to make a dramatic impact. "No matter what."

Skye was more frightened tonight than ever before, and for once it had nothing to do with preserving life and limb. She was pretty sure someone other than Burke had sent Lorenzo, someone who was very much aware of her and where she lived, but she had difficulty believing it was Noah.

In any case, she was too absorbed to work on the puzzle tonight. The list of possibilities seemed far too long, the clues too few. At this moment she was facing what felt like a bigger threat. After spending four years obsessed with improving the security of her home, using a P.O. box instead of her street address, lifting weights and exercising like a fiend, learning to shoot until she could hit a can at fifty yards, she'd become good at recognizing danger and working from a defensive position. But the one thing she hadn't relearned since Burke was how to do the opposite—trust, open up, let herself love and be loved. Wanting a relationship with David was like recognizing a potential threat and going in unarmed anyway, which went contrary to every self-protective instinct she possessed.

But if she didn't take a chance on what she was feeling, she might miss the one *really* great thing to happen to her in a long time.

She just wished it wasn't so hard, that the situation wasn't so complicated. David had told her that Lynnette had been diagnosed with Multiple Sclerosis. Considering her health, he felt guilty about moving on, and she felt guilty being part of the reason. No wonder Lynnette was so desperate to keep him. And then there was the baby. What if David found out about the pregnancy too soon? They wouldn't have an opportunity to explore whether or not they had a relationship independent of that.

She had about four months before she began to show. Would it be enough?

For the first time in a long while, she wanted to talk to Jennifer or Brenna. Since telling Jennifer about Burke's release, she'd given them both a couple of obligatory follow-up calls. She'd also spoken briefly with Joe. But she'd been careful to keep things polite and impersonal. Now she wanted to connect, to know how they managed to love despite the fear of losing, which was something she, Sheridan and Jasmine no longer seemed capable of doing. They'd started The Last Stand to help themselves heal by making a difference in the lives of others. But, in a way, it had done just the opposite. The horrors they dealt with on a daily basis kept their wounds open and bleeding. As passionate as Skye felt about what she was doing, she realized that now. Those pictures on the wall in her office were a reminder of the chasm between her and her lost innocence.

Was it time to forget? To lay down her weapons and just *live?*

David had issues; she had issues; Lynnette had issues. Maybe they'd be able to work them out, maybe they wouldn't. But she wanted to try. She loved David enough to try.

She hoped he felt the same.

Picking up the phone, she dialed Jennifer's number although it was after midnight.

"Hello?" Surprisingly, her sister answered on the first ring, sounding wide-awake.

"It's me."

"Are you okay?" Immediate panic and concern.

"I'm fine. Relax."

Jennifer took an audible breath. "Did you find out who sent that Lorenzo guy?"

"No. But I didn't call to talk about that."

There was a brief silence. "What's up, then?"

Skye smiled and touched her stomach, wondering what it would feel like as the pregnancy progressed. "I think I'm in love."

"With the detective you told me about?"

"Yeah."

"That's good, isn't it?"

"Except that I'm more scared of this than anything else."

Jennifer laughed softly. "You two are getting closer?"

"He brought his son over tonight, Jen. It's the first time he's ever let me spend an evening with Jeremy, and it was…"

"What?"

She smiled to herself. "Wonderful."

"So you like this boy?"

Skye closed her eyes as she remembered the grin on Jeremy's face when she lit the candles on his cake. "I do. He's darling."

"Do you think you could *love* him?"

"I'm sure I could."

"So what's the problem?"

"What if I let go and fall headlong into this and…and it doesn't work out?" What if the guilt took over, and he went back to Lynnette?

"You'll get hurt, like the rest of us when we're rejected. Then you'll pick yourself up, dust yourself off and move on. Heartbreak is part of life, Skye. Protect yourself against that, and you're not really living."

She'd known that all along, of course. She'd told herself the same thing before she'd called Jennifer. But she'd needed to hear someone else confirm it. "So I shouldn't call him up and tell him I don't want to see him anymore?"

"No!" Laughter filled her stepsister's voice. "You should get some sleep and see what tomorrow brings."

"Right. Sleep," Skye repeated, and for the first night since Burke, she didn't check her doors and windows repeatedly before climbing into bed.

It was time to live like a normal person, even if that meant trusting something as changeable and fickle as love.

The ringing of the phone sounded ominous even in her sleep. Reluctant to stir, Skye tried to block it out—

until she realized it might be Sheridan or Jasmine. If one of them was calling this late, it'd be important.

Rolling over, she nearly knocked the phone off the nightstand in her half-awake attempt to answer. "Hello?"

"Skye, it's David."

She rubbed a hand over her face, trying to shake off her lethargy. "Is anything wrong?"

"Nothing for you to worry about. It's just work. I got a call. Someone stumbled across a body in an empty lot, and I gotta get over there. Any chance you could spend the rest of the night here so someone will be with Jeremy?" His voice fell, and his next words revealed a certain amount of embarrassment. "I'm sorry to ask you this, but I can't reach Lynnette. I don't know if she's still out drinking, or if she went home with someone or—"

"No problem. I'll throw on some clothes and leave right away."

"So you're naked?" he said.

She laughed at how easily he'd been distracted. "Not quite."

"It's still a great mental picture."

"See you when I get there," she said, smiling.

The next time Skye awakened, it was to the sound of cartoons in David's living room. Was David back? She wasn't sure, but Jeremy was most definitely awake.

Covering a yawn, she sat up and took a moment to orient herself. Then she got up, ran a comb through her hair and brushed her teeth before she went out to explain why she'd once again been sleeping in David's bed. She didn't want to startle Jeremy when he came searching for his father.

But Jeremy didn't seem surprised to see her. "Did I wake you up?" he asked, slightly chagrinned.

"No," she lied, deciding it was pointless to make him feel bad just for turning on the TV.

"Good. My dad said I wasn't supposed to wake you up."

She perched on the arm of the couch. "You've talked to him already this morning?"

"Yeah, he's at work. He said you should call him when you get up."

She couldn't believe she'd missed the ringing of the phone, couldn't remember a time she'd slept so deeply in the past four years. "He must be tired after being up all night."

"Being a policeman isn't easy," Jeremy said, and Skye had to smile at how grown-up he sounded.

Leaving him to his cartoons for a few minutes, she went into the kitchen to call David.

"Hey, how'd you sleep?" he asked, his voice instantly warming.

"Really well." She loved being in his home, smelling a hint of him in the bedsheets. She didn't love lying to him about the pregnancy, but she figured they were going through enough difficult transitions right now. Opening herself up to love and loss was one thing; committing relationship suicide from the get-go was another. "Where are you?"

"Still at the crime scene."

"What happened last night?"

He didn't answer right away.

"David?"

"Maybe you should sit down."

She gripped the phone a little tighter. "Why would I need to sit down?"

"You know the victim, Skye."

"I do?" She took a deep, shaky breath. "Who is it?"

"Sean Regan."

She slumped into a chair. Poor Sean. She was supposed to make a difference. But not this time… "Are you sure?"

"He was wearing a Medic Alert bracelet," David was saying. "He was a diabetic."

"I didn't know that."

David said nothing, allowing her a moment to grieve.

"Who found him?" she asked.

"A man named John Roberti. The body was in a creek behind a vacant lot at a Quick Shop."

"How was he killed?"

"The corpse was too decomposed to tell. Someone stuffed it into a canister and rolled it into the water. It looked like it had been there a while. If this was summer, there wouldn't have been anything left besides bones and…"

He let the sentence dangle, but she knew what he meant. Bones and liquefied flesh.

She pressed a hand over her mouth to control the sudden nausea. This was what had happened to the man she'd met at her office before Christmas. "Is there any evidence that might lead you to his killer?"

"We'll try to lift prints from the drum, of course. But it's rained too much to get any shoe or tire impressions. The body might tell us more once a pathologist has a chance to look at what's left."

"It was his wife," she said as she had from the beginning. "And maybe his wife's boyfriend."

"We'll get whoever it is, Skye." He'd tried to inject some energy into his voice, making it more reassuring, but Skye doubted he was feeling optimistic. He sounded weary, beleaguered.

"Jonathan Stivers can help. He's put together all kinds of circumstantial evidence against Mrs. Regan."

"That's what Mike Fitzer said. He'll be taking over from here on out. Once we identified the body, I realized this wouldn't be my case."

"But will Mike work with Jonathan?"

"He will now. He doesn't want an unsolved homicide on his desk. Besides that, he knows he's got me looking over his shoulder."

"When can you come home?"

"I'm on my way."

A knock at the door made Skye sit up straighter. "Someone's here."

"Oh God. Don't tell me Lynnette's there to get Jeremy. I'm coming as soon as I can," he said. But Skye knew it wouldn't be soon enough to avoid a confrontation with his ex-wife. Jeremy had already jumped up to answer the door. Before Skye could hang up, David's ex-wife was standing in the apartment, glaring at her.

"I'm sorry, but David's not here right now," she said, feeling more self-conscious than ever before in her life. She knew what MS could do; she had a good friend who'd ended up in a wheelchair in less than ten years.

Lynnette's eyes narrowed as they combed over her spaghetti-strap T-shirt and pajama bottoms. "Who do you think you are?"

It was one of those rhetorical questions designed to start an argument. Or maybe a fight.

Raising a placating hand, Skye stepped back. "Listen, this isn't the time or the place. I'm only here to babysit."

"Are you telling me you're not sleeping with my husband?"

"He's your *ex*-husband." Skye glanced meaningfully at Jeremy. "Anyway, your son is here."

"That's right. He's *my* son. And I don't want you having anything to do with him."

"He doesn't need any added grief," she said quietly. But Lynnette didn't seem to have the emotional wherewithal to care about that. Judging by the stilettos, miniskirt and low-cut blouse, she'd had a long night and hadn't been home yet.

"You're the whore who's causing him grief." She frowned at Jeremy, who was watching them both with wide eyes. "Get your stuff. We're leaving."

Obviously embarrassed by his mother's rude behavior, Jeremy collected his overnight bag, then bent his head as he shuffled past Skye. He was almost out the door when he turned back. "Don't feel bad, Skye," he said under his breath. "My mother doesn't hate you. Or she wouldn't have taken your picture."

Although he'd spoken low and fast, Lynnette had obviously heard him. "I've never taken any pictures of you. He doesn't know what he's talking about," she said, but the furtive look that entered her eyes chilled Skye to the bone.

"I'm not lying." Goaded into a louder response now that his mother had called his truthfulness into question, Jeremy spoke clearly. "You had her picture on your phone—"

"Shut up!"

"And you gave it to that man with the big holes in his ears, remember? There was a picture of Skye in a car and coming out of—"

Grabbing his hand, Lynnette jerked so hard he gaped at her in surprise.

Skye was tempted to pull Jeremy back into the apartment and close the door. She hesitated to let this woman take him, even if she was his mother. But she didn't want to put Jeremy in the difficult position of being torn between them. "Lorenzo Bishop," she muttered.

"I don't know anyone by that name," Lynnette said and hurried away, dragging Jeremy behind her.

Lynnette's car wasn't in the parking lot when David arrived. But he took the stairs two at a time anyway, hoping the transfer of his son from one woman to the other had gone smoothly.

He found Skye alone, sitting at the kitchen table, staring off into space.

"What is it?" he asked, concerned by the dazed expression on her face.

She raised her eyes. "It was your ex-wife who sent Lorenzo Bishop." She sounded incredulous, so incredulous he didn't know whether to take her seriously.

"You're kidding, right?" He knew Lynnette could be difficult, that she hadn't been herself lately. Ricocheting between hate and clinginess, bitterness and neediness, she'd been extra-hard to tolerate. But there was no way she'd try to have someone *killed*. Maybe he dealt with that kind of stuff at work, but it always happened to *other* people.

"I'm not joking," she said.

Her steady gaze finally convinced him she believed

her own words, but he still couldn't accept it. "Skye, Lynnette's jealous of you. There's no doubt about that. She hates you because you've been a constant distraction to me. When we were supposed to be putting our marriage back together, I was thinking about you. I'm sure she realizes that, and blames you more than she—"

"She gave pictures of me to Lorenzo, David," Skye interrupted. "I don't know where she met him, but from the sound of it, the pictures were candid shots she took while she was following me. Jeremy said there was one of me in my car and was about to mention others, when she shut him up."

David shoved a hand through his hair as he searched for another explanation. It was a lot to take in after such a rough night. "That can't be right. You must be mistaken about Lorenzo. Maybe she wasn't the one watching you. Maybe she hired someone else to see if we were secretly meeting, and after what happened you naturally thought—"

"No. Jeremy specifically said she gave the pictures to a guy with *big* holes in his ears."

The bad feeling in the pit of David's stomach was getting worse. There weren't a lot of guys who had that kind of piercing. "Did you confront her?"

"When I said Bishop's name, the blood rushed out of her face, and she wouldn't look at me anymore. She'd been downright hostile just a second before, ready to fight, but at that point she grabbed Jeremy and ran out of here."

David wanted to continue denying that Lynnette was capable of any such thing. But love triangles created strong emotions, which sometimes led to unconscionable actions. He'd seen it too many times. Was he caught up in the same kind of thing that had caused that woman astronaut to drive across the country to kill her rival? No one had expected that from her, either.

"We tied Bishop to Noah," he said.

Skye shook her head. "That was a loose connection at best, certainly nothing incriminating."

He couldn't argue. She was right. And Lynnette had known about Oliver Burke getting out of prison. She was also privy to information about the original case, at least all the stuff he could talk about. No one would better understand how that threatening call and a note signed "O.B." would send David scrambling to pin it on Oliver. Lynnette had been setting him up to believe it was Oliver so that when Skye died, he'd automatically take the investigation in that direction. It was smart.

And evil…

"Does she have access to your contact records?" Skye asked.

Of course. He'd lived with Lynnette on and off over the past three years. She could easily have gotten Skye's telephone number and address from his phone. He charged it on the nightstand when he slept. She could've gone through it while he was in the shower, eating, on the home phone. The opportunities would've been endless….

Slumping into a chair, he kneaded his forehead with one hand. Lynnette's complicity made too much sense to disbelieve it. But he was praying, for Jeremy's sake, that there was another explanation.

He didn't want to go after his ex-wife for attempted murder. But if she'd done what Skye thought she had, he'd have no choice.

When Jane opened her eyes, she was relieved to see that Kate was still sleeping. The run-down motel room smelled of mold and who knew what else—considering the women hanging around when they'd arrived last night, Jane didn't even want to contemplate the origin of those smells—but at least the place provided a roof over their heads while she tried to figure out what to do next. She'd managed to slip out of her in-laws' place with Kate before anyone realized it, but now that she was facing a new day, she was beginning to doubt the perceptions and panic that had led her here.

She'd gone to Safeway and used her credit card to purchase a few necessities, then she'd stopped at the bank and gotten a six-hundred-dollar cash advance, which put her at her limit.

Six hundred dollars wouldn't get her very far. And she was beginning to wonder about the fairness of her actions. Now Oliver would have *no* money. She wasn't sure he deserved any. She'd been the one to earn it. But he'd earned all their money before, and she'd been perfectly happy to spend it. If, by chance, she was wrong, if he was as innocent as he claimed, she'd just left him without wife, daughter or money, which would make it that much more difficult for him to get back on his feet.

Was she being too hard on him? There were moments it certainly felt that way. Especially when she focused on her own shortcomings. She'd cheated on him, after all. With his own brother. Maybe she was trying to shrug off her own guilt by imagining something much worse in him. Confused and hurt as she was by what Noah had done, she supposed that was plausible.

She had no proof that Oliver was a murderer. She'd found nothing incriminating when she'd searched the house. Sure, she had his notebook. But she'd known about it long before she'd decided to run. Oliver had always kept a journal, and he'd always written in the same code he was using for this one. As a very private person, he liked knowing no one would be able to read his words, but that didn't mean he was guilty of what Detective Willis believed. He was very sensitive. Writing things down helped him deal with his emotions. And it wasn't even all that weird that he'd keep a picture of Skye Kellerman. They both hated her, didn't they? They were both furious about her ability to spin the situation to her advantage.

Had she misjudged Oliver? Noah seemed to think so.

Jane had to cover her mouth to stifle a sob at the thought of how Noah had treated her. He should've told her what he intended to do. Instead, he'd made a terrible, hurtful mess of everything.

But she wasn't handling things so well, either. Perhaps he was doing the best he could, just like her. She *was* acting a little crazy. She'd been in an emotional tailspin ever since she'd learned that Oliver was getting out of prison.

Could she trust her own head? Her own emotions?

Oliver had acted oddly, distant, when they'd made love, but he hadn't been brutal or violent. Not exactly. Of course, she told herself, being with him would feel strange after three years. Maybe she'd bailed out before giving their post-prison marriage a chance. They used to have something special, a good relationship, a strong family, the American Dream. He wanted to rebuild all that. Didn't she?

She studied the water damage that stained one corner of the ceiling. Or did she prefer *this?*

"Before Skye, everything was fine," she murmured. After Skye, there'd been nothing but grief. That meant it was Skye and not Oliver, right?

Noah thought so. So did Betty and Maurice. And those were the people she'd always been able to trust. Even now their words echoed in her mind: *You're acting crazy.... He's innocent....*

The back-and-forth argument was giving her a headache. She wanted to get up and pace, but she didn't move for fear she'd wake Kate and have her daughter's questions to answer in addition to her own. She had no idea what they were going to do, where they should go, whom they could trust.

She had to do something, though. They couldn't stay here forever. It was already close to eleven. Checkout was at noon.

Moving as quietly as possible, she crept out of bed, pulled her address book from her purse and scanned the contents. She must know someone who could put her up for a few days while she figured out what to do. Didn't she?

No, she realized with a depressed slump of her shoulders, not really. Most of the people listed in that book were friends from before. Jane wasn't even sure why she still had their contact information. To prove she'd once had ties with the rich and influential? Probably, because the only person she felt safe enough to call was someone she'd met last year, someone who didn't have any more resources than she did. Danielle.

But Danielle wouldn't be home. She'd be on her way to work. It was Saturday. Jane was supposed to work today, too. If she didn't go in, she'd lose her job....

"Mommy?"

Jane's breath caught at the hopeful sound of Kate's voice. "Yes?"

"I don't like this place," she said. "Can we go home?"

Jane didn't like it, either. But she was more frightened by the fact that their situation could get a lot worse.

"Let—let me see." Her cell was out of power and she'd left the charger behind, so she lifted the receiver of the motel phone, inhaled deeply and called their house. Maybe Oliver would answer and tell her to come home, that everything would be okay. She *wanted* to believe that, needed desperately to believe it....

Nervously twisting her fingers in the old-fashioned phone cord, she waited through the first, second and third rings.

The answering machine came on. "This is Jane and Kate. We're not available at the moment..."

She hadn't added Oliver to the message yet. Was that evidence of a subconscious rejection? Was she the one causing their problems by being doubtful and skeptical and unaccepting because she'd rather have Noah?

"Oliver?" she said. "If you're there, pick up. I-I'm sorry. I got confused, I guess. I feel terrible. Please, pick up."

Nothing. Where was he? She didn't think he was riding his bike. More likely, he was sleeping after being out all night, searching for them.

The image of him driving frantically all over town made her want to groan aloud. "Oliver?"

Still no answer. Finally, she hung up and turned to her daughter.

"I'm hungry," Kate said.

Taking in her child's impish face and long sandy-blond hair the exact color of her father's, Jane forced a smile. "We'll get some breakfast on the way home."

David stood at the door to the house where he'd once lived, staring down at his ex-wife, who looked like hell. Dressed in her old robe, she still hadn't removed the makeup she'd been wearing last night. Her hair was mussed, her mascara smeared. She hadn't appealed to him in a long time, but she'd never been more unappealing than now. He was pretty certain that was because of what he suspected.

After Skye had left his place a few minutes earlier, he'd told himself to go to work and do the research before accusing his ex-wife of attempted murder. There was always the chance he wouldn't find any connection between her and Bishop. Then he'd be able to convince himself it was someone else, someone like Burke.

But the more he thought about the situation and the timing, the more convinced he became that Lynnette had been behind Lorenzo's visit. He didn't know how she'd met Bishop and orchestrated the whole thing—but he knew why. And he felt partially responsible.

"Tell me you didn't do it," he said, pulling her outside and closing the door so Jeremy wouldn't overhear.

She laughed uneasily, but she didn't get angry, as she would've done if she was innocent. "I don't know what you're talking about."

David clenched his jaw. "Yes, you do."

"Listen, I'm tired. We'll have to talk later." She turned to go back inside, but he caught her arm.

"Lynnette, what happened to you?"

"What happened to *me?*" she asked, her words suddenly venomous. "*You* happened to me."

He studied the hard glitter in her eyes, trying to apportion the blame, to assume his share. He'd felt it a moment before. But he *wasn't* responsible. Not for this. "I had nothing to do with it," he told her.

"Without *her,* you would've come back to me," she said. "Without *her,* you never would've left the second time. We'd still be a *family,* just like you promised."

"When we were together, you were as unhappy as I was," he said. "It's *our* fault we couldn't make our marriage work, not Skye's."

"That's not true," she argued. "We would've been fine without her."

"So you followed her around taking pictures? You tried to get rid of her?" Even now, the possibility was too fantastic to believe.

But Lynnette didn't deny it, as he wanted her to. "She should've been dead already," she whispered vehemently. Tears spilled over her lashes, making fresh tracks in her mascara. "If it wasn't for those scissors, Burke would've killed her four years ago."

Speechless, sickened, David couldn't move. This was the mother of his child....

Starting to cry in earnest, she reached out to him. But the thought of touching her made David's skin crawl. She expected him to commiserate with her about the fact that Skye was still alive? "How can you expect me to feel sorry for you?" he asked. "You stalked a woman and then you tried to have her killed!" *The woman I love....*

Her lips twisted in a snarl. "I didn't do anything. It was you. I had to follow her. I had to see. You were cheating on me the whole time, weren't you?"

"You know that's not true," he said simply.

The door opened and Jeremy poked his head out. "Daddy?" He glanced up at Lynnette. "Why's Mommy crying?"

David thought his heart would break as he looked into his son's worried face. "Because she did something bad, Jeremy. And she knows it'll mean she has to go away for a while."

"No!" Lynnette's eyes flared wide. "You wouldn't! David, it's *me*. I—I didn't mean to do it. I was...*desperate*. It was my disease. It makes me crazy sometimes. You know how hard it is to deal with. I can't face what it's doing to do to me!"

David considered the pictures Jeremy had seen on her phone. "It was too well planned to blame on your illness, Lynn. Where'd you meet Bishop?"

"He came into the clinic to have his blood drawn. He—he's the one who talked me into it. I was just telling him about you and what you were doing to me, and he said he could fix it."

"Don't tell me he's the one you—" he adjusted his words for Jeremy's sake "—visited that night you didn't come home after your class."

She flushed red, telling David that was exactly who she'd been with. "You probably didn't even have to pay him after that," he said in disgust.

"It started as a joke," she said. "I swear. We just wanted to scare her. We thought that call was funny."

"Funny," he repeated, the word like acid on his tongue.

"Things got out of control, I admit. But…but Bishop didn't end up hurting her, so…so it doesn't matter. She's fine. Let it go."

In a way, David wished he could. But a man had been killed as a result of Lynnette's actions. *Skye* could've been killed. "You need to confess and get some help. If you cooperate, it'll go easier on you," he said gently. Who would've thought he'd be having this conversation with his ex-wife? "I'll do everything I can."

Her mouth sagged open. "You mean it," she whispered. "You're going to turn me in, knowing I'm sick, knowing I couldn't help it."

"You could've helped it." Kneeling, he pulled Jeremy into his arms and gave his son a tight squeeze. "Don't worry about anything," he told him. "You'll live with me until your mom can come home, okay? Everyone'll be fine."

Jeremy's eyes moved uncertainly between them. "How long will Mommy be gone?"

"I don't know yet."

"Then you'll have it all, won't you!" Lynnette shouted. "You'll have my son and the whore you've wanted all along!" Darting back into the house, she slammed and locked the door.

David frowned as he stood there. He had a key, but he wasn't about to chase Lynnette and force her into his car in front of Jeremy. He refused to put his son through that kind of trauma.

He needed to take Jeremy away and have someone

from the station get over here, in case she tried to harm herself.

Taking his phone from his pocket, he called Tiny.

Jane needed a cigarette. She'd smoked her last around 4:00 a.m. as she sat staring out the filthy motel window. She should've bought a pack at the grocery store last night or on her way home, but she hadn't dared spend the five bucks. Now she had nicotine withdrawal to cope with—as well as the anxiety of returning to a house she'd ransacked looking for proof that her husband was a killer.

"Stay in the car," she told Kate as she parked in the driveway. Because the truck was there, she assumed Oliver was home, and she didn't want her daughter to witness their first encounter. She had no idea how her husband might react. She'd never seen him really angry—he usually became sullen and withdrew until he'd worked through whatever it was—but they'd never been this estranged.

Kate's hand was already on the door handle. "Why? I want to change my clothes and brush my teeth. It's Saturday. I get to play with Lara."

Lara was the girl down the street.

In the rearview mirror, Jane spotted the damage she'd done to her neighbor's car and felt even more foolish. What had she been thinking yesterday? She'd just… freaked out. All because she didn't enjoy her first sexual encounter with Oliver since prison. But now she was at least halfway convinced it was her own fault for being so unreceptive to him.

"I just need to talk to Daddy for a minute. Then I'll come and get you."

Kate pouted, but she let go of the handle and slumped back against the seat. "Hurry up, Mommy."

"I will." Swallowing hard, Jane got out. She was hoping the neighbor whose car she'd hit wouldn't spot her until she'd talked to Oliver; when no one came rushing across the street, she felt slightly heartened.

Taking a deep breath, she approached the door.

It was locked.

Removing the house key from her purse, she let herself in. Then she stood staring at the mess. It was worse than the way she'd left it. Oliver had dumped everything out of their suitcase and strewn their clothes all over the living room. Their family picture was broken and lying on the floor. Someone had smashed the kitchen window, leaving glass glittering on the linoleum. A dining chair lay turned on its side.

Obviously, he'd reacted violently to what had happened last night.

Feeling even guiltier, Jane made her way silently toward the bedroom. He must care about her if leaving him had upset him this much. Surely, she could rekindle the feelings she'd once had so they could start anew. Even if Noah or his parents had told Oliver about the affair, she'd apologize the way Oliver had once apologized to her—after the incident with Skye. They'd put it all behind them. She wouldn't be able to see Noah for a long time. She knew that what he'd done would hurt for years. But she had Kate to think about. And the future. She had to begin moving in a positive direction.

The door was closed. Expecting to find Oliver asleep, she turned the handle and swung the door wide.

Oliver was in bed. He had the blinds drawn and the blankets pulled up over his head.

Stepping closer, Jane murmured his name. "Oliver? Oliver, it's me. I'm sorry." When he didn't move, she raised her voice. "Oliver?"

Again, there was no response, so she pulled back the covers—and felt her stomach lurch. It wasn't her husband in the bed. It was Noah.

And he was dead.

24

Oliver watched Jane through the crack in the closet door. The handle of the knife was growing sticky and unpleasant as Noah's blood began to dry. He didn't like the sensation. He longed to wash up and scrub his nails, but he couldn't move. Couldn't reveal himself to Jane—yet. He'd never killed in the light of day before, had never had this much time. Except for thinking about how this would affect his parents and Wendy, the whole thing had been far too easy and…rather anticlimactic.

Until he'd heard Jane's keys in the front door.

Would she fawn over her lover? Cry?

Closing one eye, he leaned a little closer to the opening. There she was, chalk-white, ready to faint.

Oliver couldn't help smiling as he contemplated the surprise he had waiting for her….

Jane didn't know what to do, whom to call. She was breaking into a cold sweat, hyperventilating.

Backing away from the bed, she closed her eyes and turned her face to the wall, but the image was imprinted on her brain. *Noah…* He must have confessed to Oliver, and Oliver had done *this*.

But how?

Creeping back to the bed, she used her forefinger and thumb like pincers to peel away the covers she'd dropped a moment before. She didn't want to encounter Noah's blood. She was afraid it'd still feel warm. This couldn't have happened long ago. It looked, even *smelled,* fresh.

Noah was lying on his side, facing her. How Oliver had gotten him into the bed was a mystery, since Noah was so much larger, but his position wasn't natural. Oliver must've lured him to the bedroom and stabbed him when he wasn't expecting it. Leaning forward, Jane could see the holes in Noah's back, evidence of fifteen or twenty vicious thrusts. As if Oliver had always hated his brother…

She stood there shaking for several seconds, then told herself to find the knife. She knew from the trial that the weapon was important. But she couldn't look. She was beginning to retch. At first it was just dry heaves, but soon the bile rising in her throat emptied onto the carpet.

Oliver had murdered Noah. The same way he'd murdered the women along the American River. Detective Willis had told her about those women. They'd been raped before they were murdered, and they'd had their throats cut instead of being stabbed in the back. But they, too, were dead by Oliver's hand.

The violence—the *truth*—made her ill.

"Mom? What happened in here?"

Kate's voice drifted to her from the front room. She'd gotten out of the car, discovered the mess.

Staggering to the wall, where she paused to brace herself, Jane gulped in some air and fought down her body's convulsive reaction. She didn't want her daughter to see what had occurred in the bedroom, didn't want Kate to know just how brutal her father could be.

"St-stay right where you are, Kate." Her wispy voice betrayed the weakness she felt in every muscle, every joint, but she made herself leave the room and start down the hall. "I'm coming."

"Where's Daddy? Is Daddy okay?"

"He's...fine." Jane stumbled as she reached the end of the hall and had to pause again for breath. A rubbery sensation made her legs difficult to control, even though her mind was screaming at her body to take immediate action. She couldn't even think straight. A jumbled mix of memories and fragments paraded through her mind: Noah telling her he loved her, Oliver's phone calls from prison, her standing in Oliver's room at the hospital, talking with Detective Willis at the salon, watching Skye on television calling for tougher laws against violent offenders, seeing blood in the bed she'd shared with the man who was now dead *and* the man who'd killed him...

"Mommy?" Kate hurried toward her. "Are you sick?"

"I'm okay." She managed a tremulous smile, grateful for the slight support her daughter gave her when Kate slipped those skinny arms around her waist.

"Where's Daddy?"

"He's gone." Or at least the man they knew was gone. Maybe he'd never existed to begin with; maybe he'd been just a reflection of what they'd wanted him to be. The real Oliver Burke hid inside the friendly, mild-mannered shell that had fooled almost everyone, that had fooled *her* for years.

Kate looked confused. "But his truck's here."

"He must've taken Noah's car." The mention of Noah's name conjured up the image Jane had just seen in the bedroom and threatened to make her retch again. Swallowing hard, she squeezed her eyes shut and kissed her daughter's forehead, focusing on the fact that Kate was alive and well. "We have to go." *Before your father comes back....*

"But we just got home! I want to play with Lara!"

The confusion and fear in Kate's eyes helped Jane pull herself together. She knew she hadn't been the best mother in the world. Since Kate was two, she'd been consumed by her own misery and the constant struggle to get through each day. But she was going to shield Kate from this if she could.

"Your uncle Noah's had an accident. We have to get some help."

"Let her go to Lara's. I think she'll have a much better time over there, don't you?"

Oliver. The hair on the back of Jane's neck stood up as she sensed her husband behind her. Releasing Kate, she stiffened and stepped back a little to put some space between him and their daughter. She was terrified she'd feel the point of the blade he'd used on Noah, but she was even more terrified he'd try to use that knife on Kate. Kate mustn't catch so much as a glimpse of it. No one was sacred to him. Jane understood that now.

"Daddy, you're here?" Kate tilted her head back and smiled up at him, and the sight twisted Jane's heart. *Please, God, not her. Maybe I deserve it, but she doesn't.*

"Of course I'm here, baby." He put a hand on Jane's waist to hold her where she was. Jane was pretty sure his other hand held the knife. "Everything's fine," he told her. "I'll get the help Uncle Noah needs and Mom can start cleaning up, okay? You run along and play."

Kate seemed to realize something was off. "Where's Uncle Noah's car?"

"I picked him up. I'll be taking him home later."

A flicker of confusion entered Kate's gray eyes, but Jane spoke before her daughter could ask to see her uncle. "Go on now. If you don't, it'll be too late. And when you're done, call your grandma to pick you up."

"Won't you be home?"

"I've gotta work," she lied.

Presented with the opportunity she'd been angling for since she woke up, Kate hesitated only another moment. Then her round face broke into a smile, and she skipped out of the house. "Bye!" she called just before the door slammed.

"Goodbye," Jane whispered. Then Oliver's arm slid around her waist and he pulled her against him.

"You're getting old and fat, you know that, Jane?" he breathed into her ear. "Old and fat has never been very appealing."

She closed her eyes. What did it matter if she was old and fat? It was over. She'd married a man who'd destroyed her from the inside out—and now he was going to finish the job.

"And you stink," he added. "I hate the smell of cigarettes."

She ignored the spiteful jab. "Why?" she whispered.

"Why am I going to kill you?"

"Why did you marry me in the first place?" It certainly wasn't because he'd loved her. She didn't think

Oliver had been capable of love even back then. The only person he'd ever cared about was himself.

"After finding out what you've been doing with Noah behind my back, I've been wondering that myself," he said. "He's waiting for you right now, you know. In the bedroom. He wants to fool around, only this time I'm going to watch. No more making me the stooge. No more lies. Let's see how badly you want him now, huh, Jane? Let's see him get it up for you."

Jane shuddered at the thought of returning to that grisly scene. "Oliver, no," she whimpered. "You won't get away with this. You know that, don't you? Detective Willis will come after you. He'll send you back to prison."

"Don't worry, Jane. I've got a plan. I've always got a plan."

"It doesn't matter."

"Yes, it does. If you fail to plan, you plan to fail." He lifted a hand to squeeze her breast—*hard,* the way he had when he'd tied her up. "I'll be gone before Detective Willis even knows you're dead. And Kate will be with me."

He had blood on his hands. Jane's blood.

Oliver used the brush he kept under the bathroom sink to scrub his knuckles and fingertips, but they wouldn't come clean. Every time he turned off the water and reached for a towel, he'd spot more red under this nail or that, on his neck, on his arms.

He checked the mirror. See? It was in his hair. When he stabbed her, blood had sprayed all over him.

He shuddered, wanting it off as soon as possible.

Jane's death had been ugly, not quick and efficient like the others. Not thrilling, like when he'd punished that bully who'd harassed him in school. She'd fought like a she-devil, had even almost overpowered him at one point. He hadn't expected that.

Shaking from the residual panic, he remembered the power of her grip as she'd grabbed his hand and nearly turned the knife on him. Before that, she'd been crying out for Willis and Skye, as if they cared about her, as if they'd save her. Then, suddenly, a hard gleam had come into her eyes and she'd said, "This is for Kate." And she'd cut him before he could get everything under control again.

He hated the mess. But he deserved this. He hadn't planned it out well enough, the way he should have. He hadn't expected her to walk in on him when she did.

He'd botched it, and now he was upset and couldn't seem to settle down. He'd have to write about this, figure out how he could do better.

That was what he'd do. It'd be okay. He'd have time to fix everything.

But the cut on his chest kept him agitated. It oozed so much blood he no longer knew which was Jane's and which was his. And it hurt. He felt dizzy, nauseous— probably because he wasn't as strong as he normally was. He hadn't fully recovered from what T.J. had done to him.

I'm going to kill you! You've ruined my life! Jane's words echoed in his ears. She'd hated him, would've followed through with that threat if she could. The depth of her intent had surprised him because she was the one woman he'd thought would always love him, always stand by him.

Had she been pretending the whole time? Like the others who smiled politely when he approached but snickered with their friends once he turned away?

He wasn't sure. Everything seemed distorted. He couldn't separate fantasy from reality anymore, wasn't even convinced he'd killed her. He wouldn't do that, would he? He wouldn't kill Janey. Then he'd have no one to take care of Kate. Then he wouldn't be able to regain what he'd lost.

He'd made a mistake. Or maybe it was only a bad dream. He'd dreamed that he'd killed Noah, too. He'd asked his brother to go for a drive, brought him home and coaxed him into the bedroom by claiming he'd found the diamond earrings Noah had given Wendy for Christmas in Jane's jewelry box. Then he'd stabbed him in the back. Noah had never seen it coming. He'd groaned and twisted to see Oliver's face before he collapsed. And that was it.

It had angered Oliver that it'd been so easy. That his big brother, who'd always been strong and confident, sure of himself and everyone else, could die in a matter of seconds. So he'd stabbed him again and again, trying to achieve some satisfaction.

Jane had been much more formidable. That was how he knew it was all a dream. Jane was supposed to be the weak one.

He squinted at some droplets on the floor. Where was all this blood coming from?

He had to change his clothes again. He'd changed twice already, but he couldn't get clean. He'd look and there'd be nothing. Then he'd look again, and there'd be blood!

Maybe he should take another shower....

"Mommy?"

Oliver froze. Kate was home.

"Mommy?" she called from the front door. "Lara's mom has to get her hair done. Can Lara stay with us so we can play some more?"

Oliver waited for Jane to answer. *Answer, damn it! Tell her Lara can stay. We don't mind. We're friendly neighbors, the type of people anyone can trust.*

But Jane said nothing. She just lay there on the bed next to Noah, letting Lara and Lara's mom think the worst.

"Mommy?"

Kate was coming down the hall. He had to do something, or Jane would get him in trouble.

"Daddy?"

Finally, Oliver moved to intercept his daughter before she could come any closer. But when he stepped out of the room, he saw that she wasn't moving anymore. She was standing very still, staring up at a red swipe along the wall.

Jane had made such a mess. She'd never been as neat as he was. His mother had always said he was neat as a pin.

"Are you hurt?" she asked when she saw him, bewildered.

"My wound's bleeding again." He shrugged off the blood smear that had made her eyes go round. "Nothing to worry about."

"Oh." She sighed in relief but still looked concerned. "Do you need a Band-Aid?"

"I just got one."

She smiled brightly. "Good. Where's Mommy?"

"Taking a nap."

"Oh." She shoved her glasses higher on the bridge of her little nose. "Can Lara stay here with us for a while?"

He wanted to say yes. He believed in being a good neighbor. But there was all the blood. And that was a problem. "Not today, honey."

"Why not?"

Because he had to clean up the mess, get rid of Noah and Jane. "We're leaving, too."

"Where're we going?"

"You're going to Grandma's. I have some things to do."

"But I'm hungry. Mommy would only buy me one doughnut this morning."

"We'll get you a burger on the way."

When she didn't answer, he was afraid she'd beg him to let her stay. But she took one more look at the blood on the wall and went back out to give her friend his answer.

"I need money if I'm going to buy lunch," he said aloud, reminding himself, keeping himself on track.

He went back to the bedroom to retrieve his wallet. And that was when it hit him. This morning had been no dream. Jane and Noah were really dead. And he'd killed them. He'd dragged their bodies to the bed. The knife was still lying on the floor.

Picking it up, Oliver cleaned it off very carefully. His brother and his wife were gone. But it wasn't his fault. He never would've done this if they hadn't betrayed him. And they never would've betrayed him if it wasn't for Skye. Skye was to blame for everything. She appeared in his journal more than anyone else, didn't she? It was her, always her....

Taking the piece of paper with her address from the

pants he'd already put in the hamper, he folded it meticulously and slipped it into his wallet. She'd forced him to kill the only people who'd stuck by him. How evil and destructive was that? She deserved to die. He'd known it all along.

So why was she still alive?

Too bad the knife he'd originally used was at the bottom of the American River. Having it now would've provided such satisfaction, such poetic justice.

It was time to pay her back—for everything.

Skye was at the office when David finally called. She'd been attempting to work—she'd spoken to Jonathan about the discovery of Sean's body and he'd assured her there'd be no problem proving it was Tasha and her boyfriend—but she'd been nervously awaiting word from David ever since she'd left his apartment.

"So what's going on?" she asked.

"I'm taking Jeremy to San José. I think he should be with his grandparents for a few days while we...sort everything out."

With Jeremy in the car, David couldn't really talk. Skye felt his reluctance to say anything too revealing. But what he'd told her was enough. If he was taking Jeremy someplace safe, away from Lynnette, what Skye had suspected was true.

Considering the implications, it wasn't going to be an easy few days. "Did she confess?"

"More or less."

Regardless of what David felt about his ex-wife, he had to be heartbroken for Jeremy. "I'm so sorry," she said.

"I know." His voice lowered meaningfully. "That's part of the reason I love you."

Skye caught her breath. Those words had fallen so suddenly, so surprisingly. But he'd meant them. She could tell. "Even during all this?"

"Before, during and after. She must've known it even before I did."

"She wanted me gone."

"She can't do anything now. Tiny—Detective Wyman—" he corrected, "has her in custody."

"You mean he already arrested her?"

"Yes. And he's staying with her, helping her through the process."

Leaning back, Skye rested her head on her chair. "What can I do?"

"Just keep yourself safe until I get back."

"I'll be fine. Don't worry about anything." She thought of the baby and, for the first time, felt a wild, reckless urge to tell him. Somehow it felt right, maybe because it offered hope amid the confusion and sadness.

"David?"

"What?"

Her fingernails curved into her palms. "Remember when you asked me if I was sure I wasn't pregnant?"

"Y-e-s?" he said, drawling the word.

She was in too far to back out, but the fear that he wouldn't be happy about the baby suddenly reasserted itself. "I wasn't really sure. I—I hadn't actually taken a test."

"So what are you saying?" he asked, his voice cautiously neutral. "That there's still a possibility?"

Pressing a hand to her chest to slow the hammering of her heart, she took a deep breath. "Um…more than a possibility."

Silence.

"David?"

"I'm here."

"I didn't tell you because I didn't want you to feel obligated. I just… I'm excited," she admitted. "I *want* this baby even if you don't. I'm willing to raise it on my own."

"Where does that leave me?"

"Wherever you want to be. It doesn't change anything."

No response. She bit her lip until it hurt, regretting the fact that she'd told him. "Are you upset?"

"No…I… It's a surprise, that's all. But I'm not unhappy. As far as I'm concerned, it was just a matter of time, anyway."

"Is it too soon?"

He laughed. "It's too soon. But it'll be okay. There's one problem, though."

She swallowed hard. "What's that?"

"I'd want any—" he lowered his voice "—you-know-what of mine to bear my name."

She knew what he was getting at and couldn't help smiling. "That means *I'd* have to bear your name, too."

"Exactly. Am I going to get any complaints in that department?"

Were they really talking about *marriage?* After denying what they'd felt for so long? "I don't know. I wouldn't want you to make that kind of commitment just because of the baby."

"Obviously, you don't understand how I feel about you."

That's part of the reason I love you…. "What about Jeremy?"

"It'll mean a lot of changes."

"I know. I feel bad about that."

"Fortunately, I think this'll be a good distraction for him. Nothing wrong with having a couple of extra people to love."

He was saying all the right things. She could only hope he truly meant them. "When are you going to tell him?"

"We'll do it together, in a month or two. Once we've all had a chance to know each other better and everything else has been…resolved."

Skye couldn't believe it. She'd gone from trusting no one to being willing to take the biggest leap of her life. Which proved she *did* trust someone. She trusted *him*.

The only thing that gave her pause was her job. She glanced around her office, heard Sheridan talking on the phone in her own office and realized she loved The Last Stand, too. She felt she needed to continue her work, at least in some capacity, but she was pretty sure David wouldn't like the risks involved. In any case, they had enough to deal with at the moment. They could discuss it later.

"I'll come to your place when I finish everything I've got to do," he said.

"Can you stay the night?"

"What do you think?"

She felt her grin widen. "I'll leave the light on."

"Skye…"

"Yes?"

"We'll get through this together."

"That's what I needed to hear. Tell Jeremy I hope he has a wonderful time at his grandma's."

"I will."

Skye was still smiling when she hung up. Now that she'd told David, the baby felt more real. Putting her work aside for the day even though it was only 2:00 p.m., she switched over to the Internet and started shopping for nursery furniture.

She was marrying, having a baby—finally putting Burke behind her. Her happiness at that thought made her feel like a new person.

Standing up, she circled her desk and took down all the pictures on her wall.

25

"Where's Jane?"

Oliver summoned a sad expression as he handed his mother the overnight bag he'd packed for Kate. He shook his head, silently asking his mother not to mention Jane again until they could talk without Kate being present.

"Why don't you run out and feed Horse?" she suggested, putting an encouraging hand on Kate's back. "He gets lonely without you."

Kate ran through the house. Oliver could hear her little feet tapping down the hallway, but he waited until the back door slammed before he spoke.

"Jane's gone," he said as if it was the hardest message he'd ever had to convey.

The eyebrows his mother painted on with a makeup pencil every day arched high on her forehead. "Gone where? I thought, well, when you called to say you were bringing Kate, I'd been hoping maybe you and Jane were able to patch things up."

"I tried. Lord knows I tried." He took perverse pleasure in the fact that he could lie so well. His father generally seemed less prepared to believe him than his mother, but his father wasn't there. He just had to sell this one to his mom, and she'd take care of his dad. "By the time Jane came home last night, I'd had a chance to think about everything and calm down. I realized I didn't want to lose her, so I begged her to give me a second chance. I promised to forgive her and Noah. The situation's been hard on all of us, you know? But she wasn't interested in hearing me out. And this morning I realized why."

"Why?" his mother breathed expectantly.

"She had plans to leave again. Only this time she ran off with Noah."

His mother staggered back. "*What?* No! What about Wendy? And the kids?"

Oliver managed a few tears. "He and Jane are too wrapped up in each other to care about anyone else. Like…like their families." He let go of a dramatic sigh and dashed his hand across his cheek, as if impatient with his weakness.

His mother's lip quivered as tears filled her eyes, too. "How could Noah do this to us? To his wife? Poor Wendy. She was so understanding about the whole thing, so ready to stand by him."

Oliver stared at the ground. "I guess he couldn't appreciate how great she really is."

"How will we tell the children?" his mother asked, wringing her hands.

The door slammed again, signaling Kate's return, and Oliver fell silent as his daughter came skipping down the hall carrying the dog's dish. "I'm going to give him a lot," she announced.

His mother turned away so Kate couldn't see the

distress on her face, but Oliver smiled and nodded. "You do that, honey."

They waited until she was gone again, then his mother dried her cheeks and pulled him into an embrace. "I'm sorry, Oliver. You've been through too much. This isn't fair. And…and I never would've expected it from Noah, I'll tell you that."

"Me, neither," he said. "I guess he wasn't the person we thought he was."

This statement caused more tears, but his mother didn't contradict him. "Does Wendy know?"

"She's got to be wondering. We got together last night, then he had me drop him off at Starbucks. He said he needed some time alone, but I doubt he ever went home because I think he called Jane from there. The last Wendy probably heard was when he left with me about an hour after we found Kate gone."

"Poor Wendy."

"And I haven't told Kate, of course. Maybe I should've, but…I thought I'd wait in case…in case Jane comes back to me." He pretended to choke up again, which elicited another fierce, sympathetic hug from his mother.

"They both know better than this! It's not like Noah to…to break our hearts."

It was difficult not to grimace at her words. Noah was no saint. What he'd done with Jane proved that. As surreal as the morning had been, Oliver was thinking clearly again. He knew he had to play it smart, do a better job from here on out or he'd be spending the rest of his life in the prison he'd just left, or one like it. "I trusted Jane, too." Sniffing, he blinked rapidly, as if fighting tears. "It's a shock."

"Of course it is."

"What's a shock?" His father had just come out of the bathroom, where he spent at least fifteen minutes every time he went in.

"I'll tell you later," his mother said, visibly struggling to bear up under the news.

"I appreciate you two taking Kate," Oliver said. "My injury's really giving me trouble this morning. I think I've been doing too much. And last night was pretty brutal."

"Of course it was." His mother cupped his cheek. "You go home and get into bed until you feel better. Kate can spend the next few days with us. We love the little thing. And she enjoys being here. We'll take care of her."

His father stood watching the exchange, waiting to hear what was going on. The expression on his face said he knew it wasn't good.

"I'll call tomorrow and check in."

"Don't worry about anything here," she said and kissed his cheek.

"What is it?" Oliver heard his father ask, but Oliver was already walking to his car and didn't look back as his mother began to explain. He had to hurry. He'd driven by The Last Stand on the way to his parents' house, had spotted the cars in the lot. Fortunately, Skye was at work, as usual. But he didn't know how long she'd be there, and he had a lot to do.

"Are you sure it was Lynnette?" Wearing jeans, a lightweight sweater and his signature Hush Puppies, David's father stood a foot or so away from David, who was leaning on his own car.

"I'm sure."

"I know she's going through a hard time, but I never would've guessed she'd be capable of such a thing," he marveled, shaking his head.

"I've *lived* with her and I didn't suspect," David said.

"Could it be her illness?"

"I guess it made her feel more desperate, which contributed. But she knew what she was doing."

"What's going to happen?"

"She'll go to prison. Conspiracy to commit murder is a felony." David crossed his legs, stared at the ground.

"Will they look after her there?"

"Of course."

His dad whistled as he scratched his neck. "Your mother's not going to like this."

His mother was inside with Jeremy, buying them a few minutes alone, so they could talk. His father would give her all the details once David was gone and Jeremy was preoccupied with something else. "It happens," he said. "I just never dreamed it'd happen to me. And I wish…I wish I could've loved her like she wanted me to."

"At this point, I'm damn glad you don't love her, or this would be even harder on you."

"It's going to hurt Jeremy."

His dad reached out to squeeze his shoulder. "Jeremy will be fine. He's got you, hasn't he? And he's got us."

He'd also have Skye. "I've met someone else," David said.

His dad gave him a lopsided grin as he dropped his hand. "Let me guess—the woman who was wearing your boxers the other day?"

David laughed. "That's the one."

"Your mother mentioned her."

"I figured she would."

"Do you love her?"

"I've loved her for a long time."

"Then hang on to that," his father said. "It just might pull you through."

"I'd better go. With traffic, it's a four-hour drive." David embraced his father, then got back in the car.

"We'll take care of Jeremy," his father said when David had rolled down the window. "Don't worry about him."

"Dad?"

"What?"

David almost told him about the baby. The more he thought about having another child, a brother or sister for Jeremy, the more excited he became. But, for now, it was a secret he decided to keep, something he would share only with Skye. "Thanks."

"That's what we're here for—the tough times." His father waved as David backed out of the drive and, despite everything, David found himself smiling as he headed for the freeway. But he wasn't smiling for long. He was just getting on 680 when his cell phone rang.

"Detective Willis," he said as he answered.

"It's Miranda Dodge."

He would've recognized her voice even if she hadn't identified herself. "How are you?"

"Not so good."

"What's wrong?"

"I just received an e-mail from Oliver Burke."

David turned down the radio. "He signed it?"

"Yes."

"What'd he say?"

"I'll read it to you." There was some shuffling, then she started. "'A detective visited me in the hospital a few weeks ago, asking about Eugene Zufelt. Are you the one who told him about Eugene? You're always trying to get me in trouble, you know that? You told your parents I was spying on you when I was only watching what you wanted to show me in the first place (you know it's true). You told the principal on me for writing those notes, which I *didn't* write. And now you're talking to the police, trying to make them curious about an accident.

"'What's going on? It's almost as if you're obsessed with me. It's been years! But I can't forget you, either. Maybe we should get together and fan the old spark into a flame.

"'Let me know what works for you. If you're married, we can get a hotel room.

"'Love always, Oliver.'"

David didn't want Miranda or anyone else to get hurt. But he couldn't help feeling a small measure of relief that Oliver seemed to be fixated on someone other than Skye for the moment. He could get the police involved on Miranda's behalf, make sure they looked after her, just in case Oliver was heading that way. Then he could take care of the mess Lynnette had made of her life without having to worry too much about Skye while he was doing it.

"Is he completely delusional?" Miranda demanded.

"He twists reality into what he wants it to be, then lashes out when other people won't conform and he's confronted with how they really feel. I'll make a few calls and see what I can do to get you some protection." David hung up, then contacted directory assistance for the number of the police department where Miranda lived. But halfway through the conversation, he began to feel uneasy. It was strange that Burke had been that overt. It was just *too* clueless for such a smart man. As David thought about it, it seemed increasingly unlikely.

Had Burke sent that e-mail because he was after Miranda? Or was it merely a decoy?

Oliver could hear the jingle of Skye's keys as she came through the front door. Unfortunately, he could also hear her voice. She was on the phone.

Pressing his back to the wall of her bedroom, he decided to bide his time. He'd been ready for a couple of hours, but there was no need to rush her. Giving himself away too soon would only send her running from the house, screaming into her cell for help. Then whoever she was talking to would contact the police. And what was the point of that? He'd already broken the one back window, where Bishop or someone else had taken off the wrought-iron bars. If Skye had walked around the place, she might've spotted the glass, but she'd come through the front door—just as he'd expected.

She was probably too caught up in her phone conversation, or she didn't like the idea of walking outside in the dark.

He'd chosen a good night. The fog was thick and the crickets loud.

The bolt clicked, then the chain slid into place. See? he told himself. She thought she was perfectly safe. And that made his plan even more titillating. He'd take the whole night, use every device he could find to inflict pain, make her beg like no one else. She'd apologize to him for Noah and Jane. He had only to wait for the perfect moment....

"I was afraid to take the test. But then I decided I had to know."

He listened harder, wondering what she was talking about.

"I almost fainted when it turned out positive, Sher.... Sometime in October. I haven't been to a doctor, but I know when I got pregnant...."

Pregnant. The word seemed to ring through the whole house, along with the pleasure in her voice.

Evidently, Skye had been busy. She'd been sleeping with someone. And, after that picture in the paper, Oliver could guess the father of her child. But he didn't have to guess. The next instant, she was talking about David, how he'd responded when she'd told him, how excited she was to think they might have a future together.

How wrong she was about that....

Oliver envisioned the power he'd soon wield against her hopes and dreams. He'd destroy them all, destroy her. She'd be helpless, forced to look to him for every breath. How long had he waited for this? Four years. Ever since she'd denied him the first time. Only it would be better than he'd imagined. He'd be taking what belonged to Detective Willis. And he'd leave the man with nothing.

If she suffered enough, maybe he could cross Willis off his list, too. It would be worse for a man like Willis to live with his failure, to know that he'd lost the woman he loved *and* his baby.

Oliver's grip tightened eagerly on the knife. His revenge couldn't have worked out more perfectly.

"Jeremy's so cute. I feel bad about what he'll have to go through because of his mother," Skye was saying.

Oliver didn't know what that meant. He didn't care. When the hall light went on, he tried to see her through the crack of the door and caught a glimpse of her taking off her coat. She was *so* beautiful. Far more beautiful than Jane had ever been.

But Skye wouldn't be beautiful for long. This time he'd leave more than a few scars.

Skye smiled as she hung up. On her way home, she'd told Jasmine and Sheridan about the baby. They'd talked about the shower they wanted to throw and what she and David might name their child.

There was so much to think about, so much to prepare for. And it was all exhilarating! Oliver Burke hadn't ruined her life. She'd recovered, even from what he'd done. And she'd continue to recover as she and David got married and she became a mother.

She started toward her bedroom, planning to grab her robe and take a long bath. But then she realized she hadn't gone through the stack of mail she'd picked up from her post office box in town. She'd been too involved in her various conversations, with David, who kept calling to check on her, with her sisters and friends, telling them about the baby.

Going back to the kitchen counter, she quickly riffled through the mail. Most of it was junk. But there were a couple of letters from past clients, which made her feel even better. One was from a woman who'd left an abusive situation and had since remarried. She was happy now. The other was from the victim of a hit-and-run. Jonathan had managed to track down the driver and that driver was being prosecuted.

But then she came to a letter that had no return address. Surprised and more than a little curious, she slid out a piece of copy paper on which she found only one computer-generated sentence.

Today I sold your address to a man who insisted on remaining anonymous.

Was this connected to Bishop? Had Lynnette gotten the address of the delta house from someone other than David? It was possible. Skye nearly tossed the paper in the wastebasket—until she noticed the date. This note had been written only yesterday, well after Bishop was dead.

Feeling a chill prickle up her spine, she turned slowly, suddenly afraid she'd missed something important. The front door had been locked; the house looked and smelled the same. But she wasn't about to stay here by herself if there was even a remote possibility that Oliver Burke had her address. Obviously, someone was searching for it. Even if it wasn't him, she probably wasn't safe.

Pulling her keys and her gun from her purse, she started for the front door. She'd go to Sheridan's or Jasmine's until David could get back. But her fingers were shaking so badly she had trouble removing the chain. By the time she'd also unbolted the door, she heard the tread in the hall. Someone was in her house.

Oliver wasn't sure what had tipped Skye off and sent her running, but he wasn't about to let her get out and reach her car. He'd waited too long for this.

He pounded down the hall—and caught her just as she was opening the door. As she pulled it toward her, she had one hand on the edge. And that was where she made her mistake. Although she tried to draw back at the last second, it was too late. Flinging himself against the door, Oliver forced it closed, catching her hand in the process.

When she cried out, he knew he'd regained the advantage he'd lost when she tried to flee. She wasn't going to shoot him like she shot Bishop. Not when she couldn't even use her hand.

Just to be sure, he slammed his shoulder against the door again, and felt her fall to her knees. Then he yanked open the door to release her and slammed it shut again with his foot as he pushed her to the floor.

"You think you can get away from me?" he yelled. "You think I'm going to let you do what you've done to me and then watch you walk away?"

She stared at him, her eyes glazed with fright and pain. "What have I done *to you?*" she breathed, her voice filled with as much hostility as his own.

"You cost me *everything!* You cost me almost four years of my life! Do you *know* what prison is like? Do you?"

When he knelt, pressing his knee down on her crushed hand, she cried out again. "That's what it's like, Ms. Kellerman. I was screaming, too, only on the inside. And now there's Jane. I could never forgive you Jane."

"Did she…leave you…like she should have…long ago?" she panted.

He wanted to recover the excitement of what he was doing. But all he felt was rage. "You're responsible for her and Noah! You're responsible for everything!"

"No," she whimpered. "I had nothing to do with Jane."

"She wouldn't have turned to him if she'd still had me. She would've loved me like she did before." Oliver was surprised to find he was crying, genuinely crying, not putting on an act like he had for his mother. Had losing Jane really hurt him that much? "She was the one woman who always believed in me," he said, his voice falling to a whisper. "She was the only one."

"Where is she, Oliver?"

"She's gone."

"Where?" Sweat was beading on Skye's face, beginning to run into her hair. She looked pale from the pain, as if she might pass out. But her eyes remained focused and lucid. "Did you kill her? Did you kill her like you killed those other women?"

He didn't want to answer. He didn't owe Skye anything. He'd planned to rape her, to take his time and make it as painful as possible. But he didn't want that anymore. He doubted he could even get hard. He was too upset. All he could think about was Jane's blood on his hands and his inability to wash it off. It was back now. He couldn't see it, but he knew it was there. Maybe when he went home and took off his shirt, he'd find the spatter all over his chest again, along with blood from the wound she'd caused….

He needed to end this and leave. But he'd dropped his knife in his rush to stop Skye from escaping. He tried to drag her the few feet he had to move in order to reclaim it, but she understood his intent, and the panic that had immobilized her evaporated. Whatever pain she endured, she managed to ignore as she began to kick and fight as she'd fought four years ago.

"You won't win!" she kept screaming. "You won't win."

"I won with Noah," he said, grabbing a handful of her hair. "I won with Jane. What are you next to them?"

"Whatever I have to be," she said, and then the nails of her left hand found his cheek.

Skye knew she was fighting for her life, but that alone wasn't what gave her the strength she needed. It was the knowledge that she fought for her unborn baby, too, for David and the life they could have together if she came out of this alive. She wouldn't let senseless violence cost her any more than it already had. She'd dedicated her life to stopping it, and she would stop this.

Ignoring the pain radiating up her arm from her injured hand, pain so acute it made her nauseous, she used the momentary advantage she'd gained with her nails to kick Oliver in the stomach and then the groin.

He let go of her hair and doubled up. But he didn't stay that way long enough for her to get back on her feet. Her only option was to come up with a weapon. Her purse wasn't far. She could crawl over to it. But even if she could retrieve her gun, she couldn't fire it. Without her dominant hand, she doubted she'd even be able to turn the muzzle in the right direction as quickly as necessary. Which left the knife.

God forbid…

In a split-second decision, she moved as if she was going to lunge for her purse, and he bought it. He grabbed the purse before she could reach it, but she rolled in the other direction and scooped up the knife. The last thing she saw was the surprise on Oliver's face when he realized she'd tricked him. He fumbled with her purse, but he didn't even get it open before she sank his own knife as deep in his chest as she could.

Four years after the first incident, Skye had stabbed Oliver Burke again. Only this time she'd hit something vital. She could tell by how quickly the strength fled his limbs. He gasped and slumped on top of her, but she pushed him off and managed to scramble away.

She immediately started searching her purse for her gun. But when her mind caught up with the adrenaline flowing through her body, she dropped it. She didn't need a gun. Oliver wasn't moving.

"Help me!" he whispered, but his expression was almost sardonic, as if he was tempting her to refuse him, to reveal that she could be as inhumane as he.

Skye was shaking so badly, she wasn't sure she could move even if she wanted to. The pain that her body had momentarily blocked out was returning. She felt sick, light-headed. But something he'd said earlier worried her.

"Where's Jane?" she asked. "Tell me where she is and I'll stop the bleeding, call the paramedics."

"No...you wouldn't." He tried to shake his head. "Not...for me."

"I'd do it for anyone," she said. "That's how we're different. But you have to tell me what you've done with Jane."

"Janey..." He flinched as if his wife's nickname brought him more pain. "She's..." He gasped, fighting for a few more seconds. "She's in bed with...with Noah... where she belongs." Then he gave Skye a bittersweet smile, as if he'd just told the funniest joke in the world, and was gone for good.

* * *

David received Skye's call as he reached the outskirts of Sacramento.

"I'm almost there," he said. "I'll check on Lynnette and be right over."

"Don't go to the delta house."

He felt his eyebrows go up. "Why not?"

"I'm at the hospital."

That feeling he'd had earlier, the one that had prompted him to call her so many times, returned. "What's wrong?" he said urgently.

"Oliver Burke's dead."

"How do you know?"

"He came after me."

Instinctively, he gave the car more gas, wishing he could get to her sooner. He'd sent a deputy from the sheriff's office to stay with her. Had the deputy not made it in time? "What happened?"

"He was waitin' for me when I got home. I had to stab him. I couldn't use my right han'."

Her words were starting to slur, and he wondered if she was on some medication.

"He slammed it in the door when I was tryin' to get 'way," she continued. "I—I smashed sev'ral bones in my han'. They're goin' to operate."

David clenched his jaw. "Didn't Deputy Meeks come?"

"He came…after."

"Did you tell the doctor you're pregnant, Skye? Before they gave you whatever they gave you?"

"'Course."

"That's good. And…do you think…" He was afraid

to ask about the baby for fear of what the answer might be.

"Babe's gonna be fine. I'm 'cited 'bout the babe."

He sighed in relief. She was hanging on to that thought, and so was he. He knew she was struggling to stay conscious. But then she said something that shocked him.

"Jane's in crit'cal condition."

"Jane *Burke?*"

"By…time they got to her, she'd—she nearly…bled to death. I don't know…how she held on…so long. Stabbed…in the neck, missed jugular by…a fraction."

It was more and more difficult to understand her. "What are you talking about, Skye? Oliver tried to kill Jane?"

"'Fore me. Found out 'bout Noah."

"Is Noah okay?"

"Noah's dead."

That came through clearly enough. But was it true, or was Skye beginning to imagine things because of the meds? "Skye, what hospital are you in?"

She didn't answer. The phone changed hands and someone else came on the line. "Detective Willis?"

"Yes?"

"This is Wanda Neely. I'm a nurse here at Mercy American River. As you can probably tell, Ms. Kellerman can't talk anymore. It's time to take her in for surgery."

"Tell her I'll be there when she gets out," he said. "Tell her I'll be waiting for her."

He could hear the smile in the nurse's voice when she responded. "I'll tell her."

"Do it now, while she's still conscious enough to understand."

"I will. Don't worry, Detective. She'll be fine. She's one strong lady."

David tried to swallow the lump suddenly clogging his throat. "Thank God," he murmured and hung up.

Epilogue

Skye stood at the door of the hospital room, waiting for some acknowledgment from the woman lying in the bed. She hadn't come to upset Jane. She just wanted to be sure the woman who'd been Oliver's wife was okay. Jane had lost so much—her faith in the man she'd once loved, the life of the man she now loved, the father of her daughter. Skye understood what those kinds of losses were like, how lonely it could be when you felt so different from everyone else.

Movement in the bed told Skye that Jane had seen her. Their eyes met for several seconds, then Jane waved. "Come in."

Since her right hand was in a cast, Skye carried the flowers she'd brought in her left. She set them on the small, rolling table as she looked around, relieved to see that hers weren't the only ones. Jane had been in the hospital for over two weeks, but there was still a giant bouquet on the side table, and a simpler one on the windowsill.

"Those are from Oliver's parents," Jane explained when Skye's eyes focused on them.

"That's nice." She paused. "How are they taking the news?"

"Hard. Like any parents would. They've lost both their boys. But—" her voice faltered "—but at least they're not blaming me for what Oliver did. They know they were wrong about him all along." Her voice dropped. "We all were."

"I'm glad they're being supportive."

"These are from Kate." Tears glistened in Jane's eyes as she held up a picture her daughter had drawn of an assortment of flowers, most of which resembled tulips.

"Those are the loveliest flowers here," Skye said.

"I agree." She stared at the picture for a few more seconds.

"And what about the flowers in that vase?" Skye motioned to the windowsill.

"Those are from my friend Danielle. I work with her."

Skye nodded. "They're keeping you on at the salon, then?"

"Yeah."

"That's good."

Jane set her daughter's picture aside. "I owe you an apology."

Skye raised her hand. "No, you don't. I didn't come here for that. I just wanted to see how you're doing."

"I'm going to be okay, but only because of you. I blamed you for everything, and it was Oliver. I can't tell you how I wish I'd seen the truth and moved on. I was…weak and stupid." She grimaced. "Nothing like you."

"Sometimes we see what we want to see, Jane. I'm guilty of that, too."

"But you tried to tell me. So did Detective Willis. I'm…sorry." She reached out, and Skye took her hand.

"Don't even think about it."

Jane smiled through the tears that slipped down her cheeks. Then she sniffed and adjusted the bed to sit up a little higher. "I hear you and the detective are getting married."

"Who told you?"

"He did. He comes by every couple of days to check on me. He's very excited. About the wedding and the baby."

Skye felt a warmth that had everything to do with complete contentment. "So am I."

"When's the big day?"

"In two weeks."

"I hope you'll be happy."

"Thank you."

"Will you be staying on at The Last Stand?"

"I'm pretty sure I've got my husband-to-be used to the idea," she said with a laugh. "But it hasn't been easy."

"Because of the baby."

"Because of the baby." She nodded. "I'll be doing classes and fund-raising but no more case work. Not until our children are older."

"I'm glad you'll still be around. I might take some of the classes you offer. I'm thinking they could help me heal."

Skye set her purse on the foot of the bed and used her left hand to retrieve her business card. "That's probably a good idea. You can call this number to get the schedule. If you need a ride or anything, let me know and I'll pick you up or arrange for someone else to do it."

Jane accepted the card. "You're so nice. You and Detective Willis are perfect for each other."

"We're in love," Skye said simply.

* * * * *